Model Student

Model Student

A Tale of Co-eds and Cover Girls

Robin Hazelwood

THREE RIVERS PRESS
NEW YORK

Copyright © 2006 by Robin Hazelwood

Published in the United States by Three Rivers Press, an imprint of the Crown Publishing Group, a division of Random House, Inc., New York.
www.crownpublishing.com

Three Rivers Press and the Tugboat design are registered trademarks of Random House, Inc.

Originally published in hardcover in the United States by Crown Publishers, an imprint of the Crown Publishing Group, a division of Random House, Inc., New York, in 2006.

Library of Congress Cataloging-in-Publication Data
Hazelwood, Robin.
    Model student : a tale of co-eds and cover girls / Robin Hazelwood.
    1. Women college students—Fiction.   2. Models (Persons)—Fiction.   New York
(N.Y.)—Fiction.   I. title.
PS3608.A9885M63 2006
813'.6—dc22
                                              2005025366

ISBN 978-0-307-33719-1

Printed in the United States of America

Design by Namik Minter

10 9 8 7 6 5 4 3 2 1

First Paperback Edition

For my parents

Model Student

Prologue

The tale of how famous models get their start is always the same. It begins with a gangly, ugly duckling whom no one will take to the dance. Then one day, while engaged in some wholesome activity—selling ice cream, horseback riding, delivering muffins to senior citizens—a prince of a talent scout spots her, a fairy godmother waves her wand to conjure the right shade of lipstick, and poof! Cinderella's on the cover of *Vogue*.

This is total crap.

First of all, models are born pretty. We just are. Sure, everyone goes through some sort of awkward phase, but let's get real here. The problems we face—being too skinny or taller than most of the boys in our class—are the problems of a lottery winner. Boo hoo. No, not one of us walked into a cornfield as the homely geek and stepped out as the homecoming queen. Life doesn't work that way, and I don't know why we ever pretend that it does. After all, did Einstein ever sigh, lean forward, and earnestly confess he was once the dumbest guy in the class?

Second of all, it takes work. *A lot* of work. If there are such things as princes and fairy godmothers, they're not killing time as talent scouts and agents. And trust me: Every, and I mean *every*, model spends marathon time in the makeup chair, gets styled to within an inch of her life, and *still* ends up with a slew of test shots that can best be summed up as cutting-room carpet.

Then again, maybe I feel this way because my own beginning hasn't exactly been what you'd call magical. I got my start in Milwaukee, not on the runways of Milan. I learned everything—wrong, as it turned out—in a two-bit modeling school, not from Irving Penn. I made my debut in a newspaper flyer in acrylic, not in September *Vogue* in Versace.

Humble beginnings? To be sure. But don't worry, we're not spending much time there; we're starting with a good part: my first big break. Yet before we begin, a disclaimer of sorts: This isn't a how-to guide for model wannabes. If you're looking to learn how to contour your cheekbones or achieve the perfect blowout, you'd better look elsewhere, 'cause we're not really covering that sort of stuff here. If, on the other hand, you want to know what it's like to be a model—not a real Super (like Naomi or Linda or Christy) or even a faux Super (like any of The Donald's girlfriends), but a plain Jane, run-of-the-mill six-figure earner, then buckle that belt and get ready, because I'm Emily Woods, I'm seventeen, and I'm going to tell you what it's really like.

Chicago, 1988

Chapter 1

Northern Lights

Frauke, the studio manager, adjusts her glasses, moving them lower on her nose. Wordlessly, she extends her hand.

I cross the foyer. The soles of my tennis shoes squidge against the marble. I give her my modeling portfolio. My heart pounds.

"Chicago Inc," she murmurs, scanning the cover.

"It's-a-new-agency-Louis-is-my-booker," I say in a rush.

Silence. The pages start to turn: one, two. When Frauke gets to page three, a three-quarter of me peeking through the strings of my tennis racquet, the first of my two "sporty" test shots, her eyes rotate.

"You're how old?"

The pages of my portfolio continue to turn. I watch myself go by, unseen.

"Seventeen. I'll be eighteen soon. In a month. July 5th actually."

Oops. Louis told me to stop doing this. "Models should never call attention to the aging process," he has said. Then again, Louis also told me to stop being such a motormouth. "Do you think of Marilyn Monroe as chatty?" he asked me once. "I think of Marilyn Monroe as dead,"

I replied. "Exactly," he retorted. "Icons don't talk." I get it: Shut up. But I can't help it; I'm nervous. I've been nervous ever since I got within twenty feet of this place, my fifth and final stop according to my list of appointments:

Conrad Fuhrmann (photographer)
25 W. Burton Pl. (xDearborn)
Ask 2C: Frauke (studio manager)

It looked harmless enough on paper, I thought. What did I know? I arrived at 25 West Burton Place to discover not a grungy fourth-floor walk-up, an "industrial space" filled with loose wires, dust bunnies, and futon seating, as per usual, but a large town house, a mansion, really, smack in the middle of Chicago's swanky Gold Coast District. Cream-colored and modern with a gravel driveway and sculptured trees, it looked like it belonged in Paris. Not that I've ever been. It looked like what I imagine Paris looking like. It looked imposing.

The inside is imposing, too. Or maybe it's Frauke. With glittering, ebony eyes, and glossy black hair, she sits in the all-white marble foyer looking more than a little like a spider in her web.

Wham. My portfolio cover slams shut. With sudden and surprising crispness, Frauke rises up and leans forward, her red nails gripping the desk's edge, her eyes skittering up my Adrienne Vittadini ensemble (a carefully chosen navy-and-white-striped skirt with matching sweater) and across my chin, nose, cheekbones—every inch of flesh—until they lock with mine.

"Follow me," she says.

I catch up with Frauke's dark form just as it enters a room. My eyes adjust: small study. Two suede couches. Dozens of glossy books. A smattering of silver frames with beautiful people in them.

"Conrad, this is Emily."

And a man. Conrad Fuhrmann lifts his glasses from the V in his cashmere sweater and hooks them around his temples. "Hello."

I swallow. "Hi."

Rising, he clasps his hands together like a dance instructor. "Turn around."

I twirl.

He laughs. "Not so fast. Again. So I can see you."

I spin around slowly, feeling very revolving cake, until I'm facing the couch again, facing Conrad and Frauke, who's now seated beside him. Physically, he's the antithesis of her: small, almost petite, with cornflower blue eyes and delicate features. Surprisingly, I find myself relaxing in his presence.

"How old are you?"

"Almost eighteen," Frauke answers crisply, as if my own might have been different.

When Conrad sits down again, his body tips forward—a question mark of keen interest.

And then it begins.

"Do you exercise?

"Do you dance?

"Do you eat?

". . . A lot?

"How often do you drink:

"—Milk?

"—Soda?

"—Alcohol?

"How many hours of sleep do you get a night?

"How tall are you?

"How tall are your parents?

"How much have you grown in the last year?

"How much do you weigh?

"Do you wear contacts?

"Do you use sunscreen?

"How would you describe your hair?

"Please state your morning and evening skin-care routine, beginning with your cleanser."

And on and on. It's like one of those nightmares where, suddenly, it's finals and you're being grilled by a panel of experts on a topic you haven't studied, only this test's for models, so it's not that hard.

Finally, we've exhausted the Health and Beauty category. Conrad gets the distracted look of someone doing complex numerical calculations in his head.

"So . . . almost eighteen. You've graduated, correct?"

"Yes."

"Are you going to college?"

"Uh-huh."

"Where?"

Not here, too. This is the question plaguing every single one of my classmates this summer, the question asked by every parent, every relative—everyone, that is, except people in the fashion business.

"Columbia University."

Conrad's back on his feet again, stepping toward me. "What about Northwestern?"

What about it? "Umm, it's a good school," I say. *Did he go there?* "But I want to be in New York."

Conrad eyes me steadily for one beat. Then another. "We'll see," he says.

See what? As far as I know the admissions process is over, thank God. But we don't discuss this further; instead Conrad takes me by the hand and guides me into the photography studio, which is vast and white, of course, and nice. Very nice. Against one wall, thick art books and scores of spindly magazines are interspersed with sculptures. A sweep of calla lilies rises out of a crystal vase next to a sleek leather sofa, one of a pair. A lacquered coffee table gleams. Chrome equipment glints in the bright light.

As I look around—really take it in—my stomach roils. From one thought in particular: This guy is major, really *really* major, in a totally different league from anyone I've ever worked with.

And that's before I see the photograph. Hanging right in front of me, only a couple of feet from where we've stopped, is a small black and white, that I stare at and gasp. Because, there, wearing nothing more than a few ounces of Lycra and a sultry smile, is the one and only Cindy Crawford—America's superest of supermodels. Only I've never seen her like this; with her short spiky hair and big soft cheeks, she looks about seventeen. My age.

Wow. I knew Cindy was from Illinois but . . . I turn to Conrad. He's still smiling, his blue eyes still soft and glowing. Slowly, he extends his hand toward my face. "Let's see: if we moved this . . ." A fingertip lightly touches a mole near my hairline before sliding down my cheek ". . . we'd have her." Then taps the location of the famous Cindy sweet spot.

No way. In Wisconsin, where I'm from, it's always been Brooke. We don't really look that much alike except for the eyebrows, but that doesn't stop people from accosting me, convinced I really am Miss-Nothing-But-Her-Calvins, though why the famous star would be wandering around the Midwest in a Balsam High sweatshirt was a mystery to me, unless it was a very earnest attempt at going deep undercover. Still, it's a compliment and who doesn't love compliments? Yet it's nothing like being compared to Cindy—and by someone who's actually photographed her! *This is huge.* I grin from ear to ear, even though it's not exactly ladylike. I can't help it.

And that's it, or a minute later it is. I say good-bye, walk along the gravel driveway, and through the iron gate, which purrs shut behind me. It's raining and a bit brisk, so I shove my hands in my pockets before trudging down the wet, gray avenue, turning at the red light for one last look. In contrast to the dull brick buildings surrounding it, the town house twinkles captivatingly, almost magically, like one of those shiny stones you find on the beach, the ones that look sprinkled with gold. The inside was like that, too. I think of the bright gleam of the foyer, the cozy glow of the library, the clean luminescence of the photo studio—light emanated from every corner of that place, and the world outside seems flatter, duller in its wake.

I have to work there, I think as I continue on. *I just have to.*

I guess I feel this way because so far my career hasn't been exactly what you'd call stellar. How could it be when it started with cheese? Not cheesy photos. Cheddar cheese. *Foam* Cheddar cheese.

You see, my father is the Woods in Woods and Wacowski, a small Milwaukee-based advertising agency. While the firm creates plenty of standard slogans, what they're famous for are bovine double entendres. You know: "Moove on Over," "Cream the Competition," "For a Good Cowse," that sort of thing—the kind of taglines that are perennially popular in the state that declares itself *America's Dairyland* right on its license plate.

Last fall, as part of his pitch to the state tourism board, Dad came up with a hat—*quite* a hat. It's called the Cheesehead and maybe you've seen it? If not, picture a wedge of yellow foam—the cheese—glued to the brim of a baseball hat, then picture someone actually deciding this is a good way to be seen in public, preferably drunk at a Packer game. Bad, right? Well, you should have seen the prototypes. I certainly did; it was either Swiss or Brick that capped off my modeling debut one cold winter day when Dad offered me $72 bucks—the amount in his wallet—to wear them for two rolls of film for his client.

Dale, the agency photographer, shot the two rolls, then asked if he could shoot one more, without the cheese. "You have good bone structure," he said, after he'd instructed me to loosen my fists, turn slightly profile, and look at the lens. "And a killer smile."

I beamed.

After we finished, Dale said something else. He was on his knees, packing away a reflector, when he rocked back on his heels. "I think you could be a model, Emily, I really do," he said, before offering to pass my photo along to a local agency.

I think you could be a model. Those were his exact words. I acted surprised, blasé even, but truthfully? I was thrilled.

And I was ready. As anyone who has visited my room in the last five years can attest, I love fashion. I can't get enough of it. I subscribe to most beauty magazines; the rest I pick up at the newsstand. This is no exaggeration: if the cover features a smiling beauty next to the words "Ten Terrific Tips!," "Looks You'll Love!," or if the issue's simply hefty, it's mine. Every time I bring one home, I follow the same routine. I carry it up to my bedroom (flat so as not to bend the pages and face up with nothing on top so as not to scratch the cover), then I plunk down on my rug and slowly thumb the pages. When I find just the right photo, of Famke maybe, or Rachel, or Elle—I know all their names—I take an X-Acto knife (scissors are too messy and tearing it? *Please*), care-ful-ly slice the picture out, and hold it up to the wall. Usually, it takes several tries to find just the right place. When I do, I tape it up, flop down on the rug, and stare up at my new addition. At her. Her teeth are white, her eyes are gleaming. She's usually running or leaping—inside, outside, it doesn't matter, just as long as she looks like she's going somewhere. Some place that I want to be. Some place else. And lying there, looking up, I know, I just know, that if I could hop up there and go along with her—no, *become* her—then my life would be perfect.

Given all this, I guess it's not a surprise that one week later, when the Tami Scott School of Modeling called to ask if I wanted to enroll in a modeling course, my reply was an enthusiastic "Yes!" I jotted down the details, hung up, and immediately called Christina, my best friend since the third grade who's always right about everything. She told me to go for it.

There was only one obstacle.

"You want to do *what*?" my mother said. I had walked downstairs and joined her in the kitchen. She had just checked the loaf of bread baking in the oven and the room was still warm.

"I want to take a modeling course," I repeated, this time from the fridge. I was looking for the pitcher of iced tea.

I found the pitcher, got a tumbler, some ice, poured the tea, and returned the pitcher. Mom still hadn't replied.

"What?" I said. But I knew. One look at Mom's hemp drawstring pants, her crocheted halter, her beaded necklaces, one look at her Birkenstocks, her waist-long hair, her unmadeup face, one look and *any*one would know: My mom's a "social activist," as she likes to put it, which you are welcome to interpret as "aging hippie." Dad is, too. How my parents got that way, we'll get to soon enough. For now, suffice it to say that the next thing out of her mouth wasn't a total shocker.

"Over my dead body."

"Thanks for being so supportive," I shot back. "Really."

Mom looked pained, but it wasn't from what I had said. "When I refused to let you play with Barbie, I never dreamt you'd try to *become* one!" she spat.

This merited an eye roll. "Mom, *please*. Everyone knows Barbies aren't real. Models are."

"Not the ones I've seen," she rebutted. She was scraping dough off the chopping block. Long thin curls shot to the floor.

Hmm. Personally, I couldn't imagine a time when my mother had ever even seen a model. She never set foot into my room, and they weren't exactly stripping down in *Mother Jones* and *Ms*. But I let this go, which turned out not to matter much; she had a lot more to say.

"What about your schoolwork?"

"The course is every Saturday. It's only two hours long."

"I'm sure it isn't free."

"It's a thousand dollars."

"It's a *what*?"

"Mom, I'll pay you back out of my earnings."

"*What* earnings?"

Our bout lasted several rounds. It took us past the loom in the dining room and onto the sunporch, where Mom watered her plants—mostly jade—in their wide assortment of macramé holders and fondled her wind chimes before heading back into the kitchen to dump the extra water into the mustard-colored sink and examine the spelt barley loaf. Right about the time the crust turned brown and hard, she softened.

"Okay," she said, pulling on her oven mitts, which are normal looking because *I* gave them to her. "If this is what you want to do, Emily, do it and do it well."

Yes! I pumped my fist into the air and then hugged her.

I was happy at that moment—I had won. My happiness didn't last. After all, what is it that ad says, *Be a Model or Just Look Like One*? On the morning of the first day of class I decided that maybe I didn't want to know what category I fell into, that maybe it was better to go through life thinking I could have been a model than to be told in no uncertain terms that I couldn't.

Maybe. But I went anyway. And when I entered the Tami Scott School of Modeling and took a good look around, I realized I needn't have worried. There was only one thing missing from its office corridors and that was the word *no*. It was the safest of safety schools. Women in dire need of orthodontics, women not merely pudgy but blubbery, women over forty, women under five feet two inches—women who were not only not tens, but didn't add up to tens when you included the gals on either side of them—had evidently breezed through the admissions process, assured that the $1,000 ten-week "Professionals" course was just the ticket to a life in front of the camera.

The Tami Scott School of Modeling was a scam.

I had just concluded this when our instructor clapped her hands. She was a former Miss Wisconsin, we soon learned, none other than Tami Scott herself, or really TAMI!, for she spoke with the perky hysteria of someone who has spent quality time jumping out of cakes.

TAMI! kicked things off by showing us her most prestigious job: a deli poster in which she holds a Greek gyro enticingly toward the lens. Then, it was on to a video: *Advanced Makeup Application, Vol 5: Let Your Eye (Shadow) Do the Talking*. And after that, we formed a circle and, one by one, stated our reasons for attending.

"My boyfriend thinks I look just like Cheryl Tiegs," began Winnie, a thirty-four-year-old RN.

Roxy went next. "My husband wants to be married to a model."

"Mine, too!" said Marla. Once she'd high-fived Roxy, Marla pulled out a comb and started fluffing her feathered bangs. "He thinks I look just like Stefanie Powers."

As luck would have it, they weren't the only ones. Christie Brinkley, Kelly LeBrock, Jaclyn Smith—who knew that all these separated-at-birth women could be gathered in one room? In Milwaukee?

Soon everyone was staring at me, including TAMI!, who was beaming so brightly I swore I saw her eyeteeth twinkle.

"And you, Emily? Why are you here?"

It was a good question. I looked around at the women in our circle. None of them even remotely resembled their alleged doppelgängers. I mean, Winnie was Chinese, and Roxy was twenty pounds shy of a deuce. Who were they kidding?

Maybe I was kidding myself.

"You look just like Brooke Shields!" Roxy said.

"So. True." Winnie enthused.

Marla high-fived me. Smack! went our palms. I flicked my hair back and flashed my own smile. *Exactly.*

The course taught us how to apply makeup, style our hair, and walk down a runway. It was wrong about all of it, I'd later learn, but I didn't know it then. All I knew then was that it wasn't what I expected—where's the glamour, TAMI!? The designer dresses? The scenic locations? And don't tell me Kenosha. When "graduation" came, we celebrated with champagne spritzers and celery sticks dipped in fat-free French dressing. Several women cried and had to reapply their makeup. I was not among them. I felt relief. The course was a mistake, but it was over. But then, one week later, the agency division called. Did I want to shoot newspaper ads for Kohl's Department Store? The pay would be $90 an hour, three-hour minimum.

I did.

Other jobs followed. But they were wrong, too. Laser tag packaging? Rubber glove labels? A Kermit the frog Halloween costume? What girl was going to put those on her walls? No one. I was going nowhere. And so, one day, when a Chicago-based makeup artist suggested I call Louis, the cofounder of a brand-new agency called Chicago Inc, he didn't need to say it twice.

That happened a month ago. I've been modeling for nine. And suddenly, this afternoon—right now—everything's changed. I walk into Chicago Inc and I'm immediately ensconced in black cashmere. "Emily Woods, he booked you!" Louis cries, pressing me deeper into his chest. "Conrad Fuhrmann has booked you!"

I shriek, squeeze, and shriek some more, until Louis lets go and tells me about the booking, starting with what kind of job it is. This is because in modeling there are three types of print work—advertising, catalog, editorial—and they're all quite different.

Let's start with advertising, which pays the best. This is because of exclusivity, the notion that once a model becomes associated with a particular brand she's shunned by all competitors. (In other words, even if you have a body of steel and boobs that look fantastic under a sports bra, you can't be the Nike and the Reebok sport bra girl at the same time, sorry.) Of course, to get this kind of exclusivity, advertisers have to pay for the privilege and pay they do, just not very often.

More often you book catalog. Catalog is the lifeblood, or more appropriately, the little black dress of the business, the monetary mainstay for all but the tippy-top models. It doesn't pay as much (catalog in a smaller market like Chicago earns you $150 an hour, whereas advertising rates can run from a few thousand to a cool million), but it adds up. If I work eight hours, I get a bonus and make $1,250. If I work overtime (before nine, after five, or on weekends) or shoot lingerie, the pay is time and a half, or $225 an hour. Not bad for Sears.

Last but not least, there's editorial, which in fashion has nothing to do with newspaper print and everything to do with magazine pictures, though the two do have one thing in common: low pay. Seriously, one day of *Vogue* pays $135—*$135, that's it!* That said, no one turns down *Vogue* because *Vogue* goes in your portfolio, and your portfolio (or book, as we call it) is what advertisers and catalogers look through to decide what model to hire (or book, as we say), which they do by calling your agent (or booker, as we call them—note the theme here). The more *Vogue* (or *Mademoiselle,* or whatever) in your book, the stronger it is, and the stronger it is, the more money you make. It's a tight little circle.

It turns out my job is catalog, a holiday catalog (in fashion, things typically shoot one to two seasons ahead so it's *always* Christmas in July) that Conrad's shooting for an upscale southern department store called Whitman's. I've never heard of Whitman's—who cares? I'm working with Conrad Furhmann. Conrad Fuhrmann, "the legendary beauty photographer," as Louis calls him. Conrad Fuhrmann, the shutterbug king of Chicago. Conrad Fuhrmann, the MAN WHO MADE CINDY CRAWFORD A STAR!

Chapter 2

Well, Hello Dolly!

The intercom at Conrad Fuhrmann's town house peeps out from a layer of creeping fig. I press the button.

"Good morning, Emily. Come straight to the dressing room," a voice bleats. Bzzt.

I pass through the foyer and enter the hallway. The last time I was here, I was running to catch Frauke. Now, I'm alone and I see: photos, *lots* of photos. Famous faces stare from every frame, as if challenging newcomers to take their place. "Catch me if you can," Paulina Porizkova taunts, her chin slightly cocked, her blue eyes accentuated by an azure sea lying calm and flat behind her, as if willed into tranquility by the power of her presence. "Looook at meeee," Stephanie Seymour purrs, clad in a leopard one-piece and curved in a feral crouch, her ass jutting toward the lens like she's protecting prey from prying eyes. "No! Meeee," Estelle Lefebure insists as she arches her back against a column, her curves coated in silk. Others are here, too: Joan Severance, Kim Alexis, Kelly Emberg, Lauren Hutton—face after face after face, all famous, all perfect. It's the supermodel hall of fame.

Ugh. With each step, the pit in my stomach yawns wider. I turn the corner, grateful for the relative security of the dressing room, merely to be hit with another famous set of eyes. Only this time, they blink.

I'm staring at Ayana.

My brain takes forever to process the real, breathing image until long after I've been examined and summarily dismissed.

"H—iiii," I finally stammer.

Ayana simply studies herself in the mirror. I do, too. How can I not? She's my first supermodel, and, why, they're scarcer than an endangered species! Especially Ayana. Everyone knows *her* story: A Masai warrior princess discovered herding goats in a remote part of a Tanzanian crater, Ayana—her name means Beautiful Flower—freaked out when she was snapped by the *National Geographic* photographer because she'd never seen a camera before. That changed. From Tanzania, it was a straight shot to Studio 54, campaigns, covers, stardom . . . and, years later, Conrad's. In person she looks frailer and more delicate—because of her skin, I guess, which is mottled, the two tones beautiful but distinctly different, like a leaf in the early fall.

Ayana removes a heavy gold lighter and matching cigarette case from her Louis Vuitton handbag. I rack my brain for an icebreaker:

How was your flight?

Come to the Windy City often?

So . . . you smoke?

"Jesus Christ! *Shit!*"

A man stumbles in the dressing room, breathless, paunchy, and carrying an impossible number of bags and cases. He winces, drops his load, studies his thumb. And then he spots Ayana.

"Ciao, bella!" he shrieks.

"Vincent darling!" she shrieks.

They kiss each other several times on each cheek and begin yammering away in Italian.

Hello and . . . *ciao.* I decide to be ignored elsewhere, specifically the corner. And it's a good thing I'm out of the way. Over the course of the next ten minutes, three more people enter the room: Maurice, Conrad's in-house clothing stylist; Theresa, a whip-thin, patrician blonde whom I also recognize from the walls of my room (though the loud Texan drawl comes as a bit of a shock); and Laura, the hairstylist, pint-sized but packing a large brush and a big personality, evident from the moment she flies through the door with giant headphones and the declaration "I'm walking on sunshine—wooah!"

Turns out Vincent is the makeup artist, flown in from New York. For me. "I'm here to tutor you, kid, and believe me, it won't be easy," he says while unpacking an endless array of tubes and bottles. "They loovve the paint here."

Hang on . . . "*Tutor* me? You mean, I'm supposed to do my *own* makeup?" I say. I'm shocked. I heard this used to happen, but I mean really, it's the eighties now, there's a makeup artist on every shoot, even in Milwaukee.

Vincent nods. "This place is old school."

Vincent's comment immediately elicits a loud chorus of affirmations. I want to know more, but before I can ask anything else, Ayana grabs the spotlight.

"Conrad *so* reminds me of this one photographer I work with in Milan . . ."

And they're off. Not only are they all veterans of Conradland, it seems, but they've also worked with one another in studios and fashion houses on every continent, giving them much to discuss. As the conversation speeds round the world, snippets float my way:

"Really. I refuse to fly them anymore. I'm sorry: That is *not* first."

"It wasn't one of his best; I looked down and thought Anna was going to vomit."

"The tartare there is like butter."

"I asked the A.D. for water and he—and I'm *totally* serious— pointed to the tap."

"I told them not a penny under twenty. I mean, Poland? Come on."

Wow. Vomit . . . butter . . . Poland. It's all so . . . glamorous. I sit in the makeup chair soaking up the scene: Ayana transforming herself from gorgeous to extragorgeous with the help of some thick foundation, Laura singing "Father Figure" as she wraps Theresa's locks around a succession of large Velcro rollers, Vincent grabbing a pair of tweezers and lifting them toward my face.

Oh no. No way. I duck down and cup my arms around my legs, crashposition style. Louis is always poking and prodding me but he never touches my brows. *Never.* "That's the only part evolution got right," he said once. Why mess with success? Besides—and this is more to the point—it *kills*.

". . . I *tried* to tell Paulina that musicians are for *fucking* not *dating; obviously* she didn't listen . . ."

I hear Vincent sigh. The blunt end of the tweezers drills into my shoulder like a tiny jackhammer. "Look, kid, I'm just going to clean you up a little," he says. "You're looking very wild." Poke. "Very early eighties."

Early eighties? I don't think so. Then again, back in the early eighties I was into things like E.T. and Ms. Pac-Man, and if I had a monobrow, the subject never came up at the arcade. I tighten my ball.

Another sigh. "Ayana!"

". . . So I said to the man from Hermès, forget the Birkin—who's *she* anyway? Make the Ayana!"

"Exactly! And the Kelly . . . what'd *she* ever do?"

"Ayana!"

"Well, she was a princess."

"Like that's hard!"

"Ayana!"

"What?" Ayana says flatly.

"Tell . . ." Vincent upgrades to a whack. "Tell—I'm sorry, what's your name again?"

Jesus. If he's going to inflict pain . . . I turn my cheek so it rests on my thigh. "Emily. Emily Woo—"

"Tell Emily how I do brows." *Whack.* "'Cause look at her! She's terrified!"

Okay, now I feel stupid. I rise halfway up and look at the supermodel, who's staring at my contorted body, her own two arches furrowed in perfect bewilderment.

"He's good," Ayana says before turning back to the mirror, Theresa, and Hermès.

Fine. I sit up and study my brows in the mirror. Obviously, Vincent knows much more about fashion, about what I should look like than I do, or even Louis does—I mean, he's from New York. "Go ahead," I say.

My eyes clamp shut, my fingers curl over my kneecaps. Just as I feel the first pluck, Ayana speaks.

"Of course, I never let him do me, darling; only Raphael touches mine."

My head jerks back. Theresa laughs hysterically. "Bitch!" she yells out, though not angrily.

"What?" Ayana's eyes widen. Her hand flutters up to her chest, which she touches lightly, as if testifying in fashion court. "It's the truth! Not that he won't do an adequate job," she adds. She stares into the mirror. Our eyes meet, reflection to reflection. "The improvement will still be—how shall I put this?—*significant.*"

Oh.

Vincent pats my shoulder. "Ignore her—she's just a hostile old hag," he says, sticking his tongue out for emphasis.

"Bitch!" Theresa cries.

"Hag!" Vincent yells.

"Fuck you all! You're just jealous, you old has-beens!" Ayana retorts.

"It seems to me you live your life like a candle in the wind . . ." Laura belts out.

Suddenly, I wish that I was someplace else, someplace where I know the rules. Like calculus class.

"Like 'em?" Vincent asks, several minutes of stinging pain later. "You look much more grown-up. No more *Pretty Baby.*"

I open my eyes. No more Brooke is right. My brows are half their previous width, surrounded by red blotches. Like them? Who can tell? It looks like I've stuck my head in a beehive.

I'm still studying them when Theresa totters out of the bathroom, a zippered case in hand, and drops it into her purse.

I smile sympathetically. She's on the rag. That makes two of us. Ayana, however, scowls.

"You're joking . . . *now?*"

"No time like the present!" Theresa spins around several times, whirls to a stop, and points at my brow, Bond Girl style. "Ooh, much better!"

Though puzzled, I smile again, grateful for the vote of confidence. Theresa's dressed in the first shot of the day: a cream leather jacket, its puffy sleeves inlaid with gold detailing, and a matching cream and gold miniskirt. Her platinum bob is teased high enough so that it rises several inches off her scalp, framing her heart-shaped face like a golden halo. But it's her eyes that really have it—two aquamarines, a sweep of frosting rising glitteringly above them like icing on a tiered cake.

Theresa's not camera-ready: Her lips aren't done yet, her nose is a little red, especially around the nostrils, but even so, I've never seen anyone so beautiful. Really. "You look so pretty," I gush.

"*Pretty?*" Theresa snorts. "You're joking, right? This thing is hideous—*hideous!*"

Ayana cackles. I feel my face flame. Theresa eyes me curiously. "Where you from, anyway?"

"Milwaukee."

"Oh, Minnesota. I figured."

It's time for makeup. I've arrived on-set per instructions "clean/clean," meaning no products on my face, nothing in my hair. Vincent puts my hair in a quick ponytail, then swabs my face with toner and moisturizer. Only after he's felt the canvas to ensure it's been evenly primed, does he begin . . . on my eyes.

"Aha, your first lesson, kid," Vincent says, registering my surprise. "Eyes before base—you'll see why in a second."

Make that twenty minutes. I watch, first fascinated, then increasingly horrified, as Vincent's brush dips again and again into a pot of steel-gray eye shadow, my lids darkening to the point that I look like I've been on the losing end of a catfight, a look that's only accentuated by the black shadow he dots along my upper and lower lashes and extends from the corner. This accomplished, he wipes a lotion-soaked Q-tip under my eye and holds it out. "Look."

"It's dark," I say.

"Dark? *Filthy!* Just imagine that blended into your undereye concealer—circle city!" Vincent cries, shuddering slightly, presumably at the thought of millions of women walking around with excess baggage.

I find a scrap of paper and grab a pen from my backpack—I'll never be able to duplicate this look if I can't remember it—and start writing: *Step one: eyes. (20 minutes) Begin with steel gray in crease.*

Ayana, made up and waiting for her first shot, flips through a magazine. "I can't believe she got this campaign," she murmurs.

". . . No fucking way!" Theresa lunges forward, an awkward move given that her arms are working their way out of the outfit of earlier. "Wayne booked *her*? Over *me*? Whhyyy?"

Apply with a blunt, rounded brush. Apply a darker shade to lash line with a shorter bristled brush

"Who, Rachel? Oh come on, she's the flavor of the month," the supermodel sniffs, her fingertip flicking the face of the Amazonian blonde I have papered all over my room. "Besides . . ." Ayana's lips curl. "I hear she hits for the other team."

Buy brushes and brush holder at art supply store — much cheaper! (sable or other fur — never synthetic)

Theresa gasps. "Nooo!"

"Yes—including with someone we know!"

Use black shadow along lash line but only a small amount under eyes — 2 much and they'll look 2 small in photos.

"Who?"

And a cream-colored shadow to highlight the brow bone.

"Cleo."

"CLEO'S GAY?"

"No! It was with her husband too. Carlo. A ménage."

"Nooo!"

"And then Carlo and Rachel had a ménage with someone who was *not* Cleo."

"So that's why they're getting divorced!"

Step two: base. 30—40 min. at least. (Vincent: "Half the time on your face should be spent on your base.")

"Steph's doing well," Ayana says as she rises to change into her first shot: a leather and faux leopard bomber jacket complete with fringe and matching pants.

Start with a heavy concealer — not too pale! Dot on red areas and under eyes.

Theresa snorts. "Oh *please*. Sleep with the head of Elite and that's what happens."

Apply liquid foundation — Shu Uemura, Shiseido, Dior good for photos. Use damp sponge. Blend well. Impt: set with loose powder.

"Oh god, Casablancas? No! That's been over since she was sixteen at the *most*!"

For touch-ups, try to blot moisture with tissue instead of adding more powder. 2 much powder = cakeface.

"John is *such* a slime. If I wasn't doing so well there, I *swear* I'd leave in protest."

Step three: lips.

"Ayana?" Maurice pokes his head into the dressing room, one hand waving a roller brush. "Good lord, get those chaps on! We need to shoot this a-sap, then two doubles and then . . ." He eyes me doubtfully, then Vincent. "Emily will be ready for a single by then, won't she?"

"Yes, yes, of course!"

Once Maurice walks off, Vincent smacks his palms—"Okay, kid, the rest of your tutorial will have to happen after lunch because we're all business now!"—and tugs Laura's headphones away from her ears. "Hurry!"

Everyone starts rushing. I take notes where I can. Laura dampens my hair with a plant mister filled with water, then combs through some gel. After partially drying my hair using a paddle-shaped brush, she sections it onto Velcro rollers, then finishes the drying process by putting me under a gold bonnet attached to the nozzle of the dryer. After this happens (not during—my face is the temperature of a cast-iron skillet on an open flame), my lashes get curled *(buy curler)*, covered in two coats of thick black mascara *(Maybelline Great Lash is both cheap and good)* and combed *(buy metal comb)*. My cheeks are defined *(blush on temple and "apple" of cheek — the part that juts out. Contour beneath in lt. brown)*. Laura removes the rollers, partially teases my hair, and brushes it. Maurice gives me off-white stockings ("*the* color for pastels"), a padded bra ("thought you could use some assistance"), and a pale pink suede sheath and matching suede pumps ("*so very you!*"). Vincent lines my lips, custom-blends a lipstick, and—

"Oh, hang on!" Maurice unzips me. "We must . . ." Pulls open a drawer, selects one of at least a dozen pairs of bust pads. "We must . . ." Drops his hand into my bra, adds the pad, and adjusts my boob. "We must . . ." And repeats on the other side. "Increase our bust! There!" He zips me back up. "Look at you! So sexy!"

I'm recovering from the very cold hand plunging down my bra so it takes me a minute to absorb the comment. *Sexy?*

"Back in a flash." He trots off to tend to the suede baseball hat double now shooting on-set.

Sexy? I'm alone. I turn toward the wall of mirrors, taking myself in. I've felt pretty often, beautiful sometimes, but *sexy?* Never. Can you, if you've never done it? Correction: Can you, if you've done it twice: once in the back of Kevin Vituvio's Villager wagon that was parked—for reasons that are no longer clear—in the parking lot at the Milwaukee County Zoo, and once in a totally different scenario (Matt, not Kevin, couch, not car) that was equally forgettable, forgettable because I never came, never was even remotely close to coming, and isn't coming what makes sex sexy?

And yet . . . the girl looking back at me isn't the one I know, she isn't me, she's someone else: Not-Emily. I twirl around. Not-Emily is older. *Twirl.* Not-Emily is pretty. *Twirl.* Not-Emily is . . . I swish my hair. Ninety minutes of styling and it's still straight, only now it has volume and shine. *Twirl.* I blow a kiss out of my glossy, deep berry lips. *Twirl.* I wink. I grin. *Twirl.* Not-Emily is sexy. Definitely.

I'm about to give it another go round when something stops me in my suede shoes. Something's different.

It's quiet.

Oh God. Until this moment, I hadn't realized how soothing the distant pop of the strobe, the click of each frame, and Conrad's murmurings of encouragement were. They meant that things were happening elsewhere, things I wasn't expected to do. But now it's quiet, and that means it's my turn.

On cue, Maurice appears in the doorway. "You're up."

I swallow.

Theresa ducks under his arm: "Go get 'em! Go get 'em! GO GET 'EM!" Followed by Ayana.

"Don't break a leg in those sky-high heels."

Maurice guides me out the dressing room door, across the hall, and into the studio. *Oh God.* My heart flutters into high gear. *I'm not ready.* Directly in front of me is the set, a clear Lucite platform floating on a white paper sea in a space so much larger and whiter than I remembered, I have an Alice-in-Wonderland moment, accompanied by a wave of nausea.

"Aha. Here's our new lovely lady," Conrad says. "Everyone, this is Emily."

The bright lights of the set make it hard to see. I sense a few arms raised in greeting. I wave.

"Okay, let's get her up there!"

A figure breaks away from the hazy herd.

"Watch the paper!" Conrad chides, leaning over one of the legs of the tripod and gazing, eagle-eyed, for any tears in his pristine backdrop.

"Paper's fine," the figure says—actually a guy, a very cute guy— now inches away and staring at me.

"It's Emily, right?"

Right. I nod, taking him in. His eyes are a soft, well-worn green, almost gray, the color of my favorite sweater. Perfect. All I need is another reason to be nervous right now.

As the guy drops a step on the ground, he flashes a warm grin. "I'm Mike. Let's get you on-set."

Mike. He's older: about twenty, I guess. A man. He extends his hand. I'm about to put mine in his when I realize it's clammy. I wipe it on my dress.

"*Em-i-ly!*" Maurice screeches.

I look down. At the wet mark my palm has left. *Whoops.*

Maurice runs off the set, tut-tutting.

"Good job," Mike smirks, hand still outstretched.

"Any day now!" Conrad prompts.

I grab Mike's hand. One good pull and I'm sailing onto the platform.

"Find your mark," Conrad instructs.

In the middle of the Lucite is a masking tape X. I step on it and look out.

There it is, tall, black, and fifteen feet in front of me: the camera. Usually, it seems harmless, even benign. Not today. Today, it looks black and menacing, like a giant insect waiting for its prey. Waiting for me. I throw my head back and inhale, my hands on my hips, the way I see my brother, Tommy, do before a football game, calming his nerves so he can tune out the fans, the opponents, and simply focus on one thing: scoring a touchdown. But what is my goal here? Pose well? Look pretty? The truth is, getting here had been my goal, and now, well, now I just don't want to screw up. *Don't screw up,* a voice echoes. *Don't screw up.* I take another breath, drop my chin, and stare, once more, at the camera. It sits waiting, as they all are, for me to make something happen.

Don't screw up.

"Reading!" Conrad calls.

"120/60!" Mike cries.

Conrad adjusts the lens. His head surfaces above the camera. "Okay," he says soothingly as if cornering something soft and scared, "I'm going to take two Polaroids now as a final status check, Emily, all right?"

I nod.

"Okay, here's one . . ."

I'm actually relieved to be treated like the eight-year-old posing for her school portrait that I've somehow morphed into, my months of modeling experience right out the window.

The camera clicks twice.

"Okay, relax a second."

I unclench my jaw and stare at my fingernails, which is easier than looking at the camera, or for that matter, at Mike, who, once again, is approaching.

"Nervous?"

I force some air into my lungs. "Yup."

"Well, don't be." Mike leans toward me. I catch a whiff of something woodsy. "First of all, you look really cute," he whispers.

Cute? My insides turn even mushier.

". . . And, second, don't worry: The guy's a total control freak. He'll tell you exactly—and I mean exactly—what to do."

"He will?"

Mike nods. "Down to your fingertips. It's actually pretty crazy."

It doesn't sound crazy, it sounds perfect. I feel my insides unknotting and, for the first time since I've been on-set, I can breathe somewhat normally again. *I will be fine.* A grin spreads slowly across my face, this one the real deal.

It doesn't last.

Conrad is speeding toward the set, his fingers gripping the edge of the freshly developed Polaroid. "What happened here?" he barks. An accusing finger points at me.

"I see it! I'm going to dry her right after I accessorize her!" Maurice says, gesturing with a lizard clutch.

"No, not that! I need a ladder!"

A minute later the photographer is on my level and staring at my face, his blue eyes cool and critical instead of warm and welcoming. He taps my brow. "What happened here?"

Uh-oh. I shift from one pump to the other. "Vincent just cleaned me up a little."

"A *little?*" Conrad's head gives a slight shake as if tossing aside my inane comment. " Maurice, get Vincent *now!*"

The stylist opens his mouth, closes it, and then runs toward the dressing room, his arms still brimming with pastel purses in all shapes, sizes, and skins. "Vin-ce-nttt," he yells, the gold straps jangling in his wake.

I can't believe this. *Is Conrad really this upset? Over eyebrows?* I stare at the photographer, searching for some sign, any sign, that this is all a joke, some crazy melodrama to keep the makeup artist on his toes. But if this is the case, I can't see it, only his eyes flicking continually between still life and real life.

"Here I am," Vincent says, his expression saying *anywhere but.* "What's the problem?"

"That's what I want to know." Conrad's index finger taps my brow again. "What is that?"

Color rises in Vincent's cheeks. "They were looking really dated, so I just . . ."

"You just what?"

"I just fixed them, that's what." The makeup artist's voice rises, too, though he sounds more panicked than angry. "They had no shape."

Maurice plugs in the extension cord.

"Emily! Face forward!" Conrad growls.

I snap to attention.

"I know they had no shape here," he continues. "But I liked them *here* and *here.*"

Vincent climbs a couple steps up the ladder, snaking his right arm around the photographer's legs to grab the rungs. "But don't you think they look better up here?" he says, countergesturing with his instrument of choice, the blunt end of the lipstick brush.

Conrad's own brows furrow in concentration.

Maurice climbs onto the bottom rung and revs up the hair dryer. A warm blast hits my belly.

"I mean, it was like the Wild West up there," Vincent insists.

The Wild West? I'd rub my eyes except they'd probably kill me; I'm staring at three men, one large and disheveled, two small and tidy, all perched on a ladder in the sort of wide-eyed pose normally reserved for either bad Christmas cards or Purina Cat Chow calendars. And I'm the birdie—attention that would be exciting, I suppose, if it weren't focused on facial hair and stains.

The index finger is back. "But it's too thin here."

"There?" the pencil counters. "But balances out *here,* don't you think? *Here,* too? And *here?*"

"JUST GET YOUR KIT!"

The kit is procured. Under strict guidance, Vincent plucks two more hairs, then lightly fills in the midsection of my left brow.

"Much better!" Conrad declares before climbing down. "Okay, Vincent, a little powder please. Maurice, fix the waistline a bit. We're going straight to film."

I can't see how two hairs and a smudge of pencil adds up to much of anything. Still I'm relieved the Cuban Brow Crisis is settled. Besides, there's an upside: Now I feel more restless than nervous, eager to get the shot over with so I can take off these damn pumps and pee.

Back by his lens, Conrad once again dons his kind and gentle smile. "Now we're going to play 'Simon Says,'" he informs me. He places his right heel near his left toe and tilts his hips.

I copy him.

"Jut it out more."

I rotate my pelvis and jut my right hip forward.

"Good. Now hand on hip."

I put my left hand on my hip. It feels funny.

"No, other one."

It still feels funny.

"Lean back."

"More."

"Less."

"Chin down."

"Perfect. Just like that for the first few."

And so it begins. Mike's right; for the rest of the shot, no, for the rest of the day, Conrad tells me exactly what to do. No detail is too small, from the arc of my fingers to the position of my heels, and the more uncomfortable and unnatural a pose is, the more he likes it.

Which is exactly how I feel here: uncomfortable and unnatural.

At lunch, Ayana regales the table with stories, such as the time she landed in Paris and her thirteen Louis Vuitton bags didn't. She gives the punch line: "But by the time I left, you better believe there wasn't a single logo bag left in any arrondissement!" Everyone laughs. Uproariously. I swirl the dill sauce around the poached salmon, trying to calculate how many bags the contents of my entire closet, including a rather hefty T-shirt collection, would fill.

When I ask for seconds on the string beans, Maurice says, "My, my, aren't we hungry today," and everyone stares at my plate, including Ayana, who then smirks. I notice then that her plate, though piled with food, remains virtually untouched, while Theresa isn't even at the table.

After the meal, we have touch-ups before we resume shooting, which means a continuation of the tutorial. I sit in the makeup chair. Just as a giggly Theresa returns from the bathroom with her little pouch, Vincent starts rummaging through one of his own.

"Shit!"

"What?"

"My spice lip pencil!"

I stare at the fistful of pencils that all look spicy but on closer inspection are *Naked, Nude, Lip pencil no. 1,* and countless others, all with names that imply you aren't wearing anything. "Anyway," he says, still rummaging, "write down 'Spice from MAC.' It's the exact color of your lips—the only pencil you'll need."

Spice lip pencil—Mack (Only one I need)

"MAC is only sold in London," Ayana says.

"Oh, that's right," Vincent says. "Never mind."

Suddenly, I want this pencil.

"Won't she need burgundy, too?" Theresa hollers.

"Yes, yes, you'll need a good burgundy, too—oh my God, what *are* you doing?"

Theresa is literally bouncing off the walls. With all the mirrors around us, it seems as if she's approaching from every angle. "Here have some . . . of this . . . and this!" she starts yelling, her hand dipping into the pockets of her robe to remove jelly beans, gummi bears, and Jolly Ranchers—soon strewn all over the room as if she's busted open a piñata. On one particularly zestful throw, her arm brushes her lips, smearing lipstick down her chin. After a green jelly bean plinks off Vincent's head and into his glass of Perrier, he grabs his toner, some cotton balls, and corrals the model for an emergency makeover.

Laura corrals me. "Here doll, let me reset your hair."

I slide into her chair. She belts out Stevie Winwood, I get back to the business at hand.

Burgundy lip pencil.

"Vincent, what brand of burgundy?"

"Hold still!" Vincent barks at Theresa. "Let me think," he says to me.

In front of me is a pile of magazines, the detritus of Theresa and Ayana's gossip session of earlier. On a *Vogue* cover, Cindy Crawford sports sparkly earrings and dark crimson lips. "This color?" I flip the pages to find the credit. No pencil is listed, just the lipstick: Iced Roses. Still . . . I close the magazine to examine the color. "Maybe a tube of this would be useful, you think?"

Theresa sniggers. "I don't think so, kid," Vincent says. "Theresa, I said *hold still*!"

"Why not?"

Ayana shakes her head, which given the length of the neck involved, makes it all the more insulting. "Those credits are fake, darling," she says finally. "A gift to the advertisers."

I eye her doubtfully.

"She's right." The red now removed, Vincent grabs Theresa's base off the counter and starts spackling over the bare skin. "It's all about money, kid, and twelve covers equals twelve happy cosmetic companies."

"Besides," Ayana snatches the *Vogue* from my hands and scans the credits. "I know Kevyn Aucoin and, trust me, Kevyn would rather use Crayolas than Clarion cosmetics."

Oh. Now that I look, I see that Cindy's lips really don't look anything like Iced Roses. Then again, roses come in every shade—how the hell was I supposed to know? "That's really wrong," I say, thinking of all those trips to the mall to replicate a cover girl smile. No wonder they were fruitless. I toss the magazine back on the counter. "It's false advertising."

Ayana's brow arches. "Yes, it's amazing what some of us *pretend* to be." My breath catches. My eyes water, threatening to mess up my touch-up. I know I should come up with some line about the irony of hearing this from a former goatherder, but I'm too shocked and scared and out of my element to even open my mouth.

Instead, what I do is watch Vincent get to work on Theresa's lips. First he sharpens a light red pencil. Then, after carefully enlarging her top lip, beginning in the middle of the bow, he sorts through a series of days-of-the-week vitamin cases now filled to the brim with that other essential nutrient, lipstick. When he finds the red series, he swirls Tuesday, Friday, and a dab of Saturday on the top of his hand.

"Hey," I yell over the dryer Laura's flicked on, gesturing to the plastic case. "How'd you get the lipstick in there?"

"Microwave!" Vincent yells back. "Just cut the lipsticks out of the tube and melt 'em—but only for a few seconds."

"Otherwise they'll explode!" Theresa yells, seeing this as an opportunity to throw more candy. Ayana picks a pink gummi bear off the counter and pops it in her mouth. Vincent, however, is less sanguine. "Okay, look. I am doing your lips now, Theresa—YOUR LIPS—so I really need you to HOLD STILL!"

Theresa deflates like a popped beach ball. "Awww, Vince—"

"ZIP IT!"

It's obviously not a good time to ask questions, so I continue to watch. I watch Vincent take the lipstick brush and paint right to the edge of the line so that the pencil mark all but disappears. I watch him fill the center of Theresa's pucker in with a slightly lighter red, making the lips look that much larger and poutier. I watch him examine and adjust and examine and adjust and—finally—blot with a tissue and lightly dust loose powder through it. "Voilà! Perfection!" he says at last.

Theresa beams at her reflection. "Beautiful! Thanks, doll!"

. . . And then I watch the smacks. First, Theresa's lips leaving an exuberant print on Vincent's cheek, then Vincent's hand slamming into her face.

Laura drops the dryer. I drop the *Vogue*. Ayana gasps.

"You just ruined twenty minutes of work!" Vincent hollers.

Theresa looks like a fallen baby who doesn't know whether to laugh or cry.

"Christ, no tears! NO TEARS!" he continues. "You'll ruin your eyes!"

"Here." Ayana steps forward with a tissue. "Blot again and they'll be fine."

The model's eyes shine. Things could go either way.

Maurice appears. "*People!* What is going on here? How come no one's ready?"

Ayana rises to her full height and steps forward. "I'm ready," she says. "What do you want me to wear?"

Part of Conrad's instruction was for me to watch the other girls, so in between my shots, I slip into a robe, sink onto one of the white couches, and catch a performance. Each model has her own distinct style. Ayana approaches the set wearily, as if she still can't quite believe she's even in the Midwest, let alone doing catalog. Once she turns and faces the lens, however, she transforms completely, truly seeming to stretch and lengthen until she's an elegant line against the stark white wall, moving and swaying with grace and precision—a jonquil responding to a breeze.

Theresa takes a different approach. Literally. Tightly bound in a black leather bustier, matching pencil skirt, and sky-high stilettos (apparently Santa's little helpers are going through a leather phase), she nonetheless manages to catapult onto the platform in one easy leap, and then never stops moving. Or making noise; every smile's accompanied by a squeal, squeak, or guffaw.

"Excellent, Theresa, excellent!" Conrad yells as Theresa twists into another perfect pose and beams. He directs these girls, too, I notice, though it's different: "Up a touch!," "Down a notch!," "You're creeping!" he cries; there's a shorthand that they know and I don't, a shorthand that gets seamlessly incorporated into their repertoire of moves.

I'm watching Theresa when I sidle up to Laura, herself slightly breathless from frequent interventions on behalf of the model's whiplashed locks. "God, she really seems to have bounced back," I murmur.

Laura shrugs. "Cocaine has a way of lifting your spirits."

Five minutes to five, I sink onto a stool. We've finished all of the sched-uled shots: fifteen (which I later learn is a lot; Conrad's fast). I was in six of them: three singles, two doubles, one triple, and I'm spent. It isn't physical exhaustion—though there is some of that, the poses are harder than I expected—so much as mental. I've spent the day in high alert: watching, listening, keeping out of the way. And the day isn't over. "Go to Neiman's and buy Vincent's list," Frauke instructs me. "Then go home, scrub half your face, and practice until you get it right."

Once I've changed, I take my voucher book (multicopy receipts verifying the number of hours worked) over to Frauke's vacant desk and start filling one out.

A cold hand hits the small of my back. "What are you doing?"

Yipes. I leap up. "Just filling out my voucher."

Frauke frowns. "Excuse me?"

Did I mumble? I clear my throat. "I'm just filling out my voucher . . ." I pick up the form and hold it out slightly, ". . . for today?"

Everything on the woman's face sharpens. "Didn't Louis tell you? Today's fee went to Vincent so he could teach you." Her chin juts even further. "After all, we flew him in from New York."

I stare down at the form, letting the words sink in. I know I'm new, but even in Milwaukee, a city where Laverne would be regarded as a fashion maven, I make $720 a day. How can they pay me nothing?

The cold hand is back, this time under my shirt hem. "And lose this puppy fat."

It was there, all of it, on that first day: drugs, dieting, sexual tension, the preoccupation with the smallest of flaws. And bad things happened, too: I got poked and pinched; someone else got slapped. But it all burns away. Completely. No, what stays with me on the long drive up Inter-state 94 are two images: Ayana and Theresa moving against the white, white wall. So graceful. So beautiful.

"I can do that," I whisper to the road ahead. "I can and I will."

Chapter 3

Cheese Curd

"Shh! Shh!"
Mom walks along the dock in measured steps, the flickering candles imbuing the occasion with a certain solemnity despite the lopsided cake in hand. When she reaches the edge of the picnic table she pauses, casts her eyes about for fellow choristers, parts her lips, and begins to sing.

She's a Yankee Doodle Dandy
A Yankee Doodle, do or die . . .
A real live niece of our uncle Bob
Born on the Fifth of July . . .

I smile down at my place mat before looking back up at Mom, Dad, Tommy, and Christina. The gang's all here, celebrating this day the way we have for the past ten years, ever since my parents tired of city life and moved us from Milwaukee to Balsam Lake, Wisconsin, thus adding four more to the tally of 8,307 people living ten minutes from Oconomowoc, thirty-five minutes from Milwaukee, and two hours from Chicago.

Yankee Doodle came to the lake

To celebrate Em's birthday
She is our Yankee Doodle Girl!
"Make a wish, Em!" Dad yells, the way he always does, as if I'm still rusty on this aspect of the routine. I take a deep breath and blow. The candles flicker and fade. A spray of beeswax plops gently into the frosting like berries in the snow.

"Thatta girl!"

Dad takes a swig from his beer bottle before breaking into:
She was just seventeen, you know what I mean . . .
No way.
And the way she looked was way beyond compare . . .
I don't believe it.

Dad stands in the middle of the dock, weaving back and forth like a sailor, the drunken part well under way. The motley part, too. His long gray hair flows from a balding crown. His jeans are faded and patched with a variety of Mom's old quilting fabrics. On his feet are a pair of OP flip-flops, their tread as worn as two spent tires. All told, the look is somewhere between Grizzly Adams and the second coming of Cheech.

"Um, Dad?" I say as soon as I'm able. "I'm *eighteen*."

"Really?" The weaving slows to more of a lurch. "Already?"

"Yes, really." I shake my head. *Really.* "You sang that last year, remember?"

Dad grins. "No wonder I'm so good at it." He rubs his palms. "Alrighty then, what's a good song for eighteen?"

No one can think of any.

"I know." Tommy's eyes gleam. "How about 'Devil Inside'?"

"Hey!" I snap. "No being mean to the birthday girl!"

Tommy starts humming. I thump his chest.

"Here, T—" Mom quickly drops a huge slab of cake onto a plate and thrusts it in front of my brother. "That oughta hold you for a while."

"Doubt it," I mutter, "there's a lot of him to hold." This is true. It seems like every time I look at my older brother, he's bigger, broader, his blue eyes floating above an ever-expanding body. And yet, no matter how much beef, ice cream, and beer he consumes, it always comes out as bigger pecs, stronger thighs, and chiseled abs, thanks to his hours on the field. Because, you see, growing up, Tommy threw the baseball at Little League games, the pigskin at the high school games, the Frisbee in the vacant lot, the boomerang over the lake—he threw and he threw and he threw until he had thrown his way onto the University of Wisconsin football team as the second-string quarterback. And now he can eat whatever he wants. It's totally unfair.

A glob of frosting lands on the edge of the serving plate. Mom nicks it with her knuckle and tests it. "Mm! I found this Guatemalan carob and it's just so *nutty*! Delicious with the sweet potato! Christina? A slice?"

"Sure." Christina eyes me, her hand covering a smile. The two of us have been tight since the moment I arrived at Balsam Elementary. I was drawn to Christina's intrepid nature, as exhibited by unusual feats often prompted by a dare. *Christina jumped in the lake in January! Christina ate an entire jar of hot sauce!* Befriending me may just be another example of this—and more than she bargained for; despite repeated exposure, my friend has never gotten completely used to my parents' quirks.

And, looking around, I'd say there are more than a few on display tonight: the handwoven place mats in purple and orange; the hand-thrown plates the shape and color of puddles; the serving dishes containing remnants of our entrée, a meatless protein rendered as Southern Fried "Chicken," one of several dishes in Mom's culinary repertoire that comes with its own set of quotes; the sporks; the unmowed lawn complete with extralarge herb garden; the canoe with a "People Power" bumper sticker slapped inside its bow; the house, which is not only an A-frame but solar powered, too.

Like I told you, the Woodses are hippies.

My parents met in 1962 at the University of Wisconsin when they were both freshmen, both involved in Students for a Democratic Society, a leftist, activist group. At a rally in support of striking auto mechanics, they developed a friendship. At the "Women Say 'Yes' to Men Who Say 'No'" rally, the friendship segued into a crush. But it was at the weeklong student sit-in where they finally fell madly, deeply in love.

After graduation, Mom and Dad decided to "stop protesting the bad and start doing the good," in her words, which translated into the Peace Corps, in Niger. Two years helping the new African nation take hold and they returned to Wisconsin, married, and had Tommy. It was 1969. When Dad's salary from "Beat to a Beat," performance poetry at the local jazz club, proved insufficient for three, he set off in search of something else and landed in advertising. Mom, meanwhile, worked full-time in the women's shelter she founded until 1970, when I came along, whereupon she switched to part-time.

That was all awhile ago, the seventies. Why my parents are still stuck there I haven't a clue. What I do know is that people often tell me it must be "interesting" to grow up in a house like this, "different." Maybe you think this, too. This is because you're not a kid. Kids saw the orange Saab peppered with ERA/NAACP/AFL–CIO/"MAKE BABIES NOT BOMBS" stickers, the llama-hair ponchos and macramé belts that Tommy and I got for Christmas. They watched us pull containers of tofu-mushroom scramble out of brown paper bags and wash it down with sun tea. They came to our birthday parties and plucked beeswax candles from the latest version of Mom's carob sweet potato cake. And after seeing and doing these things, they didn't have to be in advance placement classes to conclude that there was something "different" all right: us. We were freaks. In no time flat, Mark Holtzer, the coolest guy at Balsam Junior High, dubbed Tommy "Wheat Germ." I became "Cheese Curd."

There was nothing hip about being hippies.

But Tommy and I were resilient. We adapted. We insisted on getting dropped off a block from our destination. We stopped wearing our Christmas presents. We ditched the brown bags in favor of lunch boxes that we paid for out of our allowances and campaigned for peanut butter, store-bought bread, and milk. We stopped having birthday parties.

It wasn't enough. We were still Wheat Germ and Cheese Curd, and we were still miserable. For years. So we did the logical thing, the only thing we could. Tommy joined the football team and I became a model. Modeling didn't make me popular—that would have required a miracle—but it neutralized things. I became okay, accepted; I fit in.

"Malcolm X, off the table! Martin Luther, I see you under there. No begging!"

Mom shoos our black cats away and straightens. Her knife slices through the cake. "And last but not least: extralarge for the birthday girl."

"Thanks."

I take a small bite of the slice plunked in front of me. "Puppy fat, puppy fat," I hear Frauke say. I lower my hand. Mom turns; while she doesn't know about the Frauke comment, she's noticed I've been dieting lately. She doesn't like it. "Five feet ten inches and 130 pounds is thin enough," she informed me last week after I made the mistake of telling her my weight. Now, she watches, eagle-eyed. I take another bite.

Puppy fat.

Then again, look at her. The woman is wearing a shapeless sack of a dress, one of several she owns in uplifting colors ranging from mud to dung. My spork clatters against the pottery.

Christina frowns. "You okay?"

"Yeah . . . it was great . . . thanks."

Ignoring Mom's glare, I push back from the table. I don't want to be different ever again. I want to be beautiful. I want to be a star. Not eating—well, it seems like a small sacrifice.

The brow powwow inspires Team Conrad to put all matters relating to my appearance into their very capable hands. The first step is Charles Ifergen for highlights with Mindy. Both the Gold Coast salon and stylist have an illustrious pedigree ("Best in Chicago," *Vogue*, June, 1987). It doesn't matter; Frauke calls so many times during the session to "check in" that Mindy has a meltdown and it takes all of my inconsiderable powers of persuasion just to get the silver foil to stop clickity-clacking in her hands. Surprisingly, the color turns out okay—my long dark mane is less chestnut, more sun-kissed—but it comes at a price: $150 to be exact, including the brow tint. After that, it's over to Windy City Nail for a manicure and pedicure (nails squareish but with a rounded corner and slicked with Ballet Slipper because it's a little more than clear but not so much that it will clash with an outfit): $40. Per *week*. And after that, it's back to Charles Ifergen to get the hair removed on my arms, legs, bikini, upper lip, and forehead (yes, my forehead): $120. When added to the bill from Neiman Marcus for Vincent's entire list of "essentials"—$400—and my car trips back and forth in Mom's old VW bug, I've spent close to $1,000 for Fuhrmann Studio.

On the plus side, I'm working. A lot. Not just at Conrad's but all around Chicago: newspaper ads for Marshall Field's, Christmas books for

Sears. I even shoot some advertising—a print ad for Head & Shoulders featuring me combing my hair in front of a locker with the caption "You Never Get a Second Chance to Make a First Impression." Personally, I would have preferred to have been dangling Harry Winston sparklers or shilling four-figure Bill Blass ball gowns for my wage, but I do the job. The pay is $5,000; I'm not *that* flaky.

Besides, with money like this I can buy the designer goods myself. Not Harry Winston—not yet—but other things are suddenly in reach. The next time I go to Neiman Marcus, I open a charge account and use it to buy my first designer outfit—a Ralph Lauren wool sweater and pants—followed by my second—a Byblos dress in black velvet.

When I took that class at Tami Scott, I thought modeling would be a summer job, a good way to help out with Columbia's higher tuition ("Out of state? Out of your pocket" was Dad's catchy way of putting it). Of course I dreamt of more, but it was one thing to dream it, another to see it coming true. Yet it seems to be. The pictures I shot in the beginning of the summer have started to come out and suddenly it feels like I'm everywhere: full-page ads in the *Chicago Tribune*, life-size photos in store windows, and stacks of fall catalogs on the dining room table, the last mainly because my parents' friends—the ones who consume—send us copies, accompanied by Post-its with perky phrases and extra exclamation points like *What a looker!!* or *You must be so proud!!!*

"We *are* proud!" Dad says, though really, Mom eyes my transformation with more than a modicum of skepticism. In fact, it's Tommy who seems the most impressed, specifically about the blondes. "You worked with *her*?" he says again and again, eyes bulging, "but she's such a babe!"

I take the pictures up to my room, belly down next to Malcolm X, and study them. Sometimes I like the shots, but usually I don't look as good as I felt when I was shooting, if that makes any sense. See, staring into the lens, it's easy to pretend that I look just like the girls around me. Confident. Glamorous. Sexy. *Vogue*-worthy. But in the photos, my cheeks look puffier, my face squarer, my eyes smaller, and I'm not what I imagined. Not yet.

But I know I can get there.

Sports? I'm terrible. Music? I'm completely tone-deaf. School? Okay, I'm good at school, hence the acceptance to Columbia, but not without tremendous effort. Modeling, however, I can do. And the more I do it, the higher I go. And the higher I go, the higher I want to get.

Something's started now that can't be stopped. I'm on a rocket ship, spinning away from Earth toward an unknown destination. Every appointment I go on, every booking I get, fuels me further. *"You're Conrad's new girl,"* they whisper admiringly. *"You know who his last one was, don't you?"*

Yes, I do. And at night, when I'm lying in my room, I find her face on the wall and whisper, "Look out, Cindy, here I come."

Chapter 4

The Big Bust Out

"He's just a capital-P prick!" Laura yells.

"Who's a prick, darling?"

Ayana struts into the dressing room at Conrad's, a pair of black wraparound sunglasses glued to her face, which is looking remarkably sweat-free in the late-July heat. *God no.* I've worked with the supermodel a couple more times since the first day and she still treats me like something stuck to her heel.

"Hi," I mutter softly.

Ayana seems to glance my way briefly—it's hard to tell with the glasses—before turning to the mirror to adjust her T-shirt. Once satisfied that the STAR☆FUCKER is sandwiched perfectly between each nipple, she looks inquiringly at Laura, now muttering under her breath as she pulls a foot-long canister of hair spray from a nylon bag.

"Laur? Who's a prick?"

The model's brown eyes float over to a spray of roses on the counter, all red save for one bud of pink. "Oh, no, not *that* prick! When are you going to understand? Photographers are for *fucking*, not dating."

Laura puts on her headphones.

Perfect. Ayana and I start doing our makeup, united solely by the fact that we'd both rather be alone, the room silent except for the occasional utterance from Laura:

"Hey now, I'm gonna take a new sensation . . ."

"Dirty Diana-nah! . . ."

And from Ayana.

"Oh God, I have *such* a headache!"

"Paris needs me. I simply *must* call."

"What *shall* I do about Lorenzo?"

With the last, I finally take the bait. "Who's Lorenzo?"

Ayana raises her brows, contemplating her eye shadow. "A friend," she exhales, along with a stream of cigarette smoke.

Right.

A petite Japanese girl weighted down by several clamps, two rolls of masking tape, and three pairs of shoes staggers into the dressing room.

Ayana turns. "And you are?"

"Yuki," she says, somehow managing to bow slightly. "Maurice. Assistant."

I met Yuki yesterday. She's from Tokyo, here because we're shooting a "look book" for the U.S. boutiques of Kohana, a Japanese designer of lingerie, sleepwear, and loungewear. Yuki's job is to press the clothing and help us get dressed so that Maurice can spend his time on the set pinning and accessorizing.

Ayana exhales again. "Yukky, be a dear and go get Miguel to make me a skinny cappuccino, at once."

Yuki blinks.

"C'mon, chop chop!"

A beat of stunned silence and Yuki drops her load and departs for the kitchen. A minute later and Maurice sails in, a needle pinched in his fingers. "Yuki?" he calls. He frowns at the pile. "Yu-kiii!" At us. "Good lord, why hasn't she changed you?" Jams the needle into a roll of tape and marches toward the closet.

"Actually, Yuki's getting cappuccino," I explain.

"Oh, a coffee break, how nice for her. Here, Emily, you're in the purple sweat suit. Ayana's in the red robe."

Now this I could have predicted. Colors have rules attached to them, rules as codified as if they were written in some regulation book for stylists. Blondes wear pastels, every shade of white from ecru to winter, khaki, and red, unless a black girl is there, then she gets the red, along with kelly green, orange, hot pink, royal blue, and bright yellow—black girls *own* bright yellow. As for redheads, there are so few of them, I don't really know—other than that they look good in colors I don't. We brunettes get hunter green, burgundy, purple, and chocolate brown. Everyone gets black, the people's color, and navy.

Now of course there are exceptions that have to do with the color of the trim and so on, and any good makeup artist will tell you that if you adjust the lips and the blush you can make almost any color work on any girl, but generally speaking, this is the formula, one that art directors stick to so closely it determines model bookings. What, we're shooting hot pink and chocolate brown turtlenecks on page four and kelly green and purple twin sets on page five? Better book a black girl and a brunette. Oh wait, there's a petal pink top in the triple on page six? Better add a blonde for a half day. In catalog, you're never competing for booking against your opposite, only your twin.

That is, unless you're working with Ayana.

Ayana takes one look at the closet and tosses her head. "I can't possibly wear *that*."

Maurice frowns. "Why not?"

"It's red. I don't *do* red."

Oh please. Maurice will not fall for this one. The STAR ☆ FUCKER T-shirt is red.

"You look fantastic in red," Maurice says.

Ha. Ha. Ha.

"Oh, I know I do. What I mean is I can't do red *today*. Red requires *so much energy* and I just don't have it *today*. I have a migraine." Ayana pauses to study her headache face. "And just looking at that robe makes me feel nauseous."

The robe makes me nauseous, too. Maybe that's because it's quilted, polyester, and ugly.

"Oh, my pet, not to worry; you and Emily will switch," Maurice says. "YUKI!" he yells.

Jesus. I catch a glimpse of a smirk before Ayana takes a final drag and flicks her cigarette on the floor.

"YUKI! Where is she! YUU-KKKI!"

Yuki flies into the room.

"There you are! Now, Yuki, you listen to me. You're in the United States now—THE USA! We work hard here! I can't have you running to take coffee breaks whenever the mood strikes you—you got that?"

Yuki squeaks.

I clear my throat. "Actually she—"

"Migraine!" Ayana gasps. "I need caffeine!"

". . . Or if you're going to insist on taking a break, at least get a coffee for poor Ayana while you're at it. I mean, Christ, woman, think of others!"

With her low pigtails, Mickey Mouse T-shirt, and terrorized expression, Yuki doesn't exactly come across as a grown woman at all, let alone a particularly selfish one; she does, however, happen to be the lowest on the totem pole. After emitting another squeak, she runs off.

"Grab some straight pins while you're at it!" Maurice hollers. "And the small clamps!"

For someone with a throbbing headache, Ayana has sprung into her sweat suit with the speed of a track star. Maurice gets right to work on it. The man is in high styling mode today. A pair of scissors dangles from a cord around his neck. A canvas pack is tied around his waist, the loops and pockets normally reserved for painters' tools brimming with boxes of pins (mostly straight, some safety), tape (double stick, regular, masking, and duct), lint rollers, glue, and spools of thread.

Maurice will use all of it. In print photography, anything that *can* be done to make clothing look good *will* be done. Pins, clamps, and tape give dresses, jackets, and blouses nipped-in waists. Boxy skirts in dowdy lengths are rolled once, twice, even three times (the excess fabric is hidden under a shirtband or belt) then pinned into a more flattering shape. Dresses in skimpy-weight fabrics get lined, pants in light colors get all visible pockets snipped out. Hemlines get lengthened. Pant legs get reshaped.

"Good lord, who would ever put *these* shoulder pads in *this* sweat suit?" Maurice mutters, digging for a seam ripper.

Cheap shoulder pads are replaced with smoother, more natural-looking foam ones. Gaping pockets are taped. Droopy collars are stiffened. There's a reason why models don't order clothing from a catalog: We *know*.

"There!" Maurice steps away from the tracksuit, already looking sleeker thanks to a row of pins up the back. "I'll finish you off on-set. Now, Emily." He steps behind me, his head bobbing over each shoulder as he assesses my outfit. I've already made my own assessment: I look like a giant red bell.

Maurice grabs a clamp from the pile supplied by Yuki—metal with orange rubber tips, the same kind used by the photo assistants—and pinches two inches of fabric between my shoulder blades. "Voilà! Okay, let's get to the set pronto."

Hang on. I'm still looking very . . . bell. "Wait . . . that's all?"

"I'm sorry, Emily, but women who wear this style of bathrobe want to see a generous fit," Maurice explains. "In fact . . ." He drops behind me. I hear fabric splitting. A cool breeze hits my back. "The flowier the better." His head resurfaces. "There! Now come along: Conrad's waiting!"

Supposedly, the six Kohana executives strewn across the studio couches have flown in from Tokyo to oversee the creative direction for the look book. As far as I can tell, they weighed the option of spending five days sitting in their tiny offices against five days of gourmet meals (a sushi chef is on the premises) and an excellent view (models in silk, satin, and lace) and it was no contest.

Conrad gives us our starting position. "Ayana, you're in profile on the right, torso to me. Emily, I need you dead-on for every frame so we don't lose the width of the robe."

Perfect. A bell and its clapper.

Ayana turns profile, Maurice kneels behind her and runs a series of straight pins along the off-camera seam of each pant leg. The model will only hold this position for a few frames; when it's time for her to move, Maurice will just come back and relocate the pins. On photo shoots, it's not the poses themselves that eat up time so much as the styling that goes along with them.

"Yuki! Accessories!"

Yuki speeds to the set with a Lucite tray that, upon closer inspection, I realize is actually a tackle box, the lures du jour alluring indeed: flashes of gold in many shades, shapes, and sizes.

"Here . . ." The stylist's fingers hover, then dive, resurfacing with a pair of earrings that are quickly deposited into my outstretched palm.

"You're kidding," I murmur, lifting them. The earrings are the size and weight of door knockers.

"Women who don this style of bathrobe often don it as daywear," Maurice informs me. After handing Ayana a pair of tiny, demure studs— "Sporty!"—he reaches down and unhooks a large kilt pin from his belt loop.

"Married?" Ayana grunts. "For *this*?"

"Of course, darling." Approximately a half dozen faux gold bands are looped on a kilt pin. Maurice removes two of them and slips them on our respective fingers. "This is sleepwear. No rings and Whitman's will get letters."

So I'm selling to big women who think it's okay to spend the entire day in a red polyester bathrobe bought off the back of a teenager just so long as they dress it up with a pound of gold, but think the outfit is too risqué to be sold by a single person. Interesting. "So being unmarried is a bigger crime than being too lazy to dress properly?" I ask.

"Something like that," Maurice replies.

Ayana guffaws, then turns to me. "Good one."

I stand tall through the rest of the shot.

A couple of hours later, the two of us are back on-set in matching silk pj's and about to go to film when

"*Eieeee! Eieeeee!*"

A strange squeal rips through the studio, part girl, part Shamu. We turn our heads. A blur of sandy blonde curls cascades down the steps, heading straight toward the photographer.

"Con-raddeeee!"

Oh God. Everyone knows Conrad hates excessive physical contact. Cringing in anticipation of what will surely be an awkward moment, I glance at my new best friend, who's now looking equally bemused herself. But Conrad's arms rise up and out, his face melting into an ear-to-ear grin. "My gorgeous darling!"

My gorgeous darling? . . . Who is this chick?

After a generous bear hug, we find out. "Girls?" Conrad cries. "I'd like you to meet Jessica."

Jessica raises her hand, her fingers unfurling like a child's, her soft, pillowy lips parting into a smile. "Hi-yeee!"

"Hi," I respond. Ayana gives her usual grunt. Only this time, I can't blame her: the hair, the lips, the button blue eyes, the Bambi lashes, the white eyelet shirt unbuttoned to where her bustline achieves maximum heft, the skintight jeans: Jessica's a babe. The ad executives plant their hands on their kneecaps and lean forward. Mike—tan, chiseled Mike, Mike my summer crush—and Conrad's other assistants gaze in admiration. I turn green. Why does *she* have to be here? Isn't three a crowd?

After the shot, Ayana walks off to call Paris, I to change.

"Hiyee again."

Jessica's standing in the middle of the dressing room, topless and smiling, her long hair cascading over her shoulders and tickling the top of her bare breasts. Like Eve. Or a slightly taller My Little Pony. "I'm Jessica," she breathes.

Yeah. Got that. "Emily."

Jessica hugs me, thus sharing the love just as she did with Conrad a few minutes ago, before resuming her strip, humming Def Leppard as she does, first softly, then a bit louder as her fingers slowly work their way down the buttons of her white denim jeans. When she reaches the critical point—the arched back, thrust-ass position so well chronicled in movies featuring repairmen with nine-inch tools—I retreat to the study, the tiny sitting room where I met Conrad during my first visit. In the afternoon, I'm there once again, holding a tattered paperback of *Jane Eyre,* a classic I've decided I should read.

"Perfect, that's perfect! Now turn those gorgeous gams profile!"

"Excellent!" Click.

"Excellent!" Click.

"Just! Like! That!" Click. Click.

Sorry, Charlotte. I toss the book and cross the hall to the studio doorway. Jessica's finally made it to the set. She's wearing a lacy bra and panty in the sheerest ivory. Her ass rests—barely—against a Lucite stool, one leg perched on the bottom rung, the other arching down to the platform beneath her. It must kill: all her weight, such as it is, on two toes and one arm that, though shielded from the lens, I know has to be shaking. Still, she bares it gamely, her face never deviating from the perfect this-is-prime-time-not-*Penthouse* lingerie look: eyes off-camera, lips slightly parted—a wistful Penelope just waiting for her ship to come in.

"That was great!" Conrad yells. "Now two more rolls without the stool!"

". . . Let's lose that stool!"

". . . Mike?"

Mike finally manages to pry his eyes off Jessica's tits long enough to get the stool, which puts him considerably ahead of the Japanese executives, who appear in danger of melting into a puddle.

Laura pauses beside me. "Guess in the land of the stick figure, the C cup is queen, huh?"

"I guess." I murmur. Earlier, I was jealous. Not now. Jessica's practically naked out there. Everyone's ogling her, objectifying her. It's disgusting. I'll never do lingerie. Never.

Fortunately, the only outfit I have to worry about is part of a silk robe triple. Everyone's well behaved (though Ayana can't resist saying "Too bad it isn't a deeper blue" when Jessica walks out). We finish the shot and I'm done for the day. We're all done. Frauke comes in to sign vouchers. Waiting my turn, I adjust my new skirt: Betsey Johnson, cotton and Lycra with a clingy fit.

Frauke scrawls her signature, then looks up. "Girls with big hips shouldn't wear floral prints."

Oh. I feel the gravitational pull of several pairs of eyes on my lower half. My heart pounds in my ears. My face burns. I rush out the door. *Big hips. Big hips.*

Footsteps ring out. "Emily!"

It's Laura. "It's okay, I'm fine," I say without looking back. *Big hips?*

"Emily!" She jogs next to me. "Here! You forgot this."

Laura's holding my voucher book. "Thanks," I say, grabbing it. I've lost three pounds since my birthday. I'm now five feet ten, 127. But I guess that's not thin enough.

The hairdresser is still with me. "Better check it," she pants. "I think there's a mistake."

I stop walking, then open the voucher book to the first page. "It looks fine."

"Really?"

I snap it shut. "Yup."

Laura refuses to budge. "Wait, are you saying you got paid fifty dollars for today?"

I nod numbly. *Big hips.* "Every day—well, here, anyway."

"But *why?*"

"Frauke says I'm still in training."

Laura laughs, a long, shrill peal. The words pour out. "Training? What does that even mean, *training?* Conrad poses everyone. And you're in just as many shots as everyone else. And look at the budget! Look at our lunch! Emily, you're being taken ADVANTAGE OF!"

In the seconds that pass, I picture the fresh fish carted through the halls this morning on mounds of shaved ice, fish that I thought was too gross to even contemplate eating. "But why?" I say finally. My voice is hoarse. "Why would they do that?"

"Because they can."

Laura has not said this. Ayana has. I spin around to find her leaning against the wall with the calm air of someone who's been lingering awhile.

"That's right," Laura says. "You're young, Emily. People will try to take advantage of you."

"Okay, sure, *people,*" I say, my head darting back and forth as it spins inside. "But *Conrad?*" My hand swirls to encompass the suede, the silver, the marble.

"*Oh please,*" Ayana says. "How do you think he got all this?"

Oh God. My eyes dampen.

Laura touches my cheek. Her hand feels cool. "Emily, listen to what I'm about to say, because it's important. A model's career is like a dancer's or a professional athlete's; it's hard to get started and it doesn't last long. You'd be lucky to do this ten, twelve years tops, which means you've got to be tough. You've got to fight for what you earn—and I'm not talking about what you earn this summer, or this year. I mean *all* of it—every penny." She blinks. "So, no, Emily, fifty dollars does not cut it. Not here, not anywhere. Do you understand?"

I nod, then step back to wipe off the tears. Ayana approaches . . . to hug me? Flash me another smile?

"Become a bitch," she advises, strutting out.

The next morning I'm on a mission. I move through the office of Chicago Inc so quickly that the wall of composites (the modeling equivalent of business cards: two-sided with photos, measurements, and agency contact information) blurs into a random assortment of legs, breasts, and other body parts. By the time I settle into one of the low-slung black and chrome chairs in Louis's office, I'm panting slightly. Panting but excited. Usually I'm here for what my agent euphemistically refers to as "tête-à-têtes" on any one of his four favorite topics: diet, dress, deportment, and demeanor ("the four D's of divadom" he likes to say, often). Today, however, I'm introducing a fifth topic: deficiency, as in his.

"Conrad's ripping me off and you're doing nothing about it."

"Well, good morning to you, too," Louis says.

I glower.

Louis pats his hair. Naturally a brunet, he's bleached himself to ash blond, resulting in a texture consistent with spun sugar. "Cookie, I told you already. You have to be patient. Your rate with Conrad will go up in time! In the meantime, sit back and reap the benefits: work! A lot of work!"

True, I've gotten steadily busier over the course of the summer; my catalog rate—that is, my rate with *other* clients—has increased from $1,250 to $1,500, and, despite my numerous shopping expeditions, I've earned enough to cover my freshman tuition.

Tough.

"Not 'in time'; now. I insist. I want my rate with Conrad raised *now.*"

"To what?" Louis asks nervously.

"My rate—for catalog, that is. Advertising TBD, but higher. Much."

Louis swallows. His eyes are watering. "I'm not sure Frauke will go for that."

Suddenly I can feel my Inner Bitch tentatively wagging her tail. "Okay, Louis, if you don't want to make the call, you don't have to," I say airily. "I'll just get someone at Elite to do it."

"Elite?" Louis looks like I've poked him with a cattle prod. "You're thinking of switching to Elite?"

"Yup."

"Emily, I'll call Frauke, I promise!"

I smile. This feels great. But now that I've said it, maybe it wouldn't hurt to meet with Elite and hear what they have to say . . .

"But, Emily, remember, if you switch to Elite in Chicago, you're committing to their representation around the world. That's how they work."

Worldwide representation. I pause. About a month ago, Louis sat me down to discuss this very topic.

"Emily, we need to get you an agent," he'd told me.

"I thought I already had one."

"I'm your mother agent," he replied.

"Hubbard, Goose, or the one who lives in a shoe?"

Louis heaved a patient sigh. "Emily, it means your first agent. First but not only," he explained. "I'm not the right person to take you national. You need someone who knows the magazine editors, the advertising executives, the photographers' reps, the agents in Paris and Milan . . ."

"So? Elite has an international network," I tell him now. "That sounds like all the more reason to go with them." I lean forward to pick up my backpack. What started as a bargaining chip is sounding like a better and better idea—I'll go to talk to them right now.

Louis pats his hair again. He's smiling now and surprisingly calm. "That they have," he says. "But they don't have the hottest agent in the country. That man just called me. And *he* wants to represent *you*."

"The hottest agent?" I freeze. "Who's that?"

Chapter 5

Getting Skinned

I get off the airplane and make my way toward baggage claim, where Marc Gold is supposedly waiting. LAX isn't what I expected, in fact, it looks suspiciously like the airport I just left in Milwaukee: all round hubs and curved columns, more Jetsons than jet-setter. Where's the neon? The movie stars?

I'm on the moving walkway, passing a rainbow-colored mosaic, when two things occur to me. One: I have no idea what Marc looks like. On the phone he sounded young, but he's the head of NOW! Models, so he's got to be at least thirty. Two: I have no idea what I look like; I don't think I've even seen a mirror since sometime over the Rockies. As I'm swept from mint to pea, I picture another shade of green: the lettuce from the in-flight salad that, for all I know, is lodged between my two front teeth. I need a bathroom. Pronto. When the walkway ends, I stumble forward, carry-on in hand, trying to separate myself from the other harried passengers who are rushing the door like so many salmon.

"Emily!"

Shit. I've been spotted. As for Marc, I don't know why I worried: his black silk shirt, black pants, and black loafers sans socks make him a tanner, thinner, shinier version of Louis. In fact, he might as well be holding up an arrival sign that says AGENT.

"Gorgeous, baby, just gorgeous!" Marc cries between kisses on each cheek. As he takes my bag he deftly snakes his free hand under the waistline of my jeans until it connects with my bare skin.

Make that a tanner, thinner, *straighter* version of Louis.

En route to his car, I use the opportunity to disentangle. Marc runs his now free hand through his black cropped hair, massaging his scalp as he studies me through thick-templed sunglasses. "Your book doesn't do you justice," he tells me. "You're much more beautiful in person."

I smile, relieved he's saying so many nice things, though obviously, given that I'm a model, it would be just fine if my book *did* do me justice. In fact, that's why I'm here.

As Louis explained to me in his office two days ago, Marc Gold had phoned him one week earlier. "Who is this Emily Woods?" he'd asked. "Aside from my next star?" Evidently, he'd seen my Head & Shoulders advertisement and tracked me down. When I heard his name, I gasped; I'd heard it before. In the last few weeks much of the dressing room gossip has centered around Layla Roddis, the model who pulled off this fall's fashion heist by booking not only the season's hottest ad campaign—Guess?—but also its most important cover—September *Vogue.* Or really, the talk has been about Layla Roddis and the man who made it happen: Marc Gold, the founder and president of NOW! Models of Hollywood, California.

"He's a great agent," Louis told me. "You should meet him."

"But he's in LA," I replied, though already my heart raced. *A star. My next star.*

"LA . . . New York, who cares?" Louis countered. "This is a modern age, cookie: Between the car phone and the fax machine, your next agent could be in the UP of Michigan and it wouldn't matter, so long as he has the connections. And this one obviously does: I mean, look at Layla."

I nodded hungrily. Look? I had already. And I was sold.

Now, I'm sitting right next to the man himself. Marc's on his car phone, working the connections exactly as advertised, the receiver cradled on his shoulder, the cord doing loop-the-loops as he scans the road from left to right, searching for cracks in what seems like a solid block of traffic.

"No!" We're in a convertible Mercedes, black of course. As he floors it and swishes into the emergency lane my hair billows behind me. "Absolutely *not*! I don't want Layla doing fur. No way!"

"Wait, seriously?" Marc spots an opening. We careen into another lane. "Where's it running?"

We're at a red light. The second it turns green, Marc floors it. The guy's a bundle of energy, in constant motion, wired . . . which makes me wonder if he's on coke . . . which makes me wonder if driving counts as operating heavy machinery.

"One day. Fifty grand. Holland only and no endangered species, okay? Be sure of that, Rudy, or she'll flip. She's vegetarian or into animal rights or some feel-good bullshit."

"So, Columbia, huh?"

Huh? "Yeah."

"Cool. Cool."

I smile, then realize he's talking to Rudy again.

The boulevard widens and, suddenly, we're shooting down a concrete chasm. An urban tableau unfurls beneath us, vast and sprawling, looking not so much city as landscape, with field after field of streetlights punctuated by small skyscraper forests and undulating hills beyond. It's stunning but confusing and I can't get my mind around it. Where's the center of it all?

"Fine, mink's fine. Like chicken, really . . ."

And then it's gone. We've dropped into it.

"You ever been?"

Marc squeezes my thigh. Oh—this is to me. "What, to LA? No . . ."

I've never been here before but *Valley Girl, The Sure Thing,* and countless other films make me feel as if I have, though what we're passing now—low seedy buildings encasing tattoo parlors, off-track betting, and girls, girls, girls—isn't exactly the palm tree, pool party, beach barbecue I envisioned. Still, it's different here. Nice. The palette is soft and sun-faded, the signs large and colorful, the script grand and loopy. California, Land of Confidence.

Marc snorts loudly. "There is NO WAY, I repeat, NO WAY!"

I glance at him, startled.

"Sheared beaver," he yelps. Two girls going by on Rollerblades look at him, then at me, then back at him, and crack up.

Marc starts playing tour guide, pointing out things as we approach: Hollywood Hills, Beverly Hills, Nutria.

"What the hell's that?"

I look around, puzzled: Isn't this it? But, no, it's back to Rudy.

"No rodents!" he yells. "Sunset. Melrose. Links . . ."

I turn to see the golf course.

". . . I don't suppose those are farmed?"

Things continue in this vein for a while: my keyed-up driver frantically maneuvering through traffic while holding two conversations, one involving furry animals. The only way I have a clue Marc's speaking to me is when he grabs my leg, which causes me to jerk spasmodically, which causes him to massage it to relieve my "tension." It's an interesting ride and the reason I will, forever after, associate Los Angeles with pelts.

A few minutes more and the fur stops flying; we've pulled up to a restaurant. "Keep it close," Marc says to a valet, handing off a bill that I can't see but must be big, for the man nods empathetically and says, "Of course, Mr. Gold."

Of course, Mr. Gold. I smile: I'm with *him.* "What's this place?"

"It's a restaurant. Chaya."

Food. Thank God. All day I've been too nervous to do more than pick at things; I'm starving.

"You ever been here?"

"I've never been to LA," I remind him.

"Oh . . . of course. Right." Marc steps onto the curb. After helping me up, his hand finds its now-familiar resting place on my bare skin. "This place is great. Quite a scene."

We pass through the open door.

"Hello, Mr. Gold."

"Good evening, Mr. Gold."

"Yeah, hi."

"In fact, babe . . ." Marc peels off his sunglasses. His copper-colored eyes glow against his tanned skin. He touches my cheek. My *northern* cheek. "The ladies' room is right there. You might wanna use it." The hand does a double pat, the second one close to a push. "You're in LA now, you never know what's right around the bend."

I turn pink—*I must look like a disaster*—and head straight for the bathroom. True, thanks to the convertible, my hair is knotted and a bit fluffier than usual; other than that I look the same: no massive pimple, none of the feared green in teeth, so I'm slightly mystified until two ladies emerge from the stalls. The one in the plunging pink halter top immediately coats her lips with gloss as thick as honey, while the one adjusting her baby blue tube top—lower—is tossing her platinum hair around like she's auditioning for Pantene.

California, the Land of Confidence. I pull off my Ralph Lauren sweater, tuck in my tank top, and apply a thick layer of lipstick and two coats of mascara. When Halter Girl douses herself with Opium, I make sure to get caught in the mist. When they exit, I stare at my reflection. "Like me," I mouth. "Sign me." I'm not talking to myself but to Marc. At his suggestion I'm here for two days, three nights; if he doesn't like me, it's going to be a long trip.

Chaya has a high ceiling, several revolving fans, and lots of potted plants. I find Marc under a banana leaf, the electric breeze causing it to dance and weave as if jostled by a tropical storm. Right as I sit down, the waiter plucks my menu. "I come here all the time, I ordered for you," Marc explains. His fingers tear apart a soft roll and plunge it into a dish of olive oil. "So, tell me, what are your goals?"

My immediate goal is to sneak one of those rolls for myself, but beyond that . . . I don't know, get an agent? Graduate from co—

"Do you want to be rich or famous?"

This is the sort of question Tommy might pose late one night after one too many. I laugh.

Marc tears and soaks another chunk. "I'm serious. Wealth or fame, you pick."

As Marc chews, he looks me dead in the eye. He's serious. "Wealth," I say finally.

"Easy." He swallows. "You're a proven moneymaker and that's in Chicago, a nothing market. Between here and New York you can pull in four, five hundred no problem."

Hang on . . . "Thousand?"

He nods.

"As in, *five hundred thousand dollars?*"

"Yeah. Does that work?"

"Yeah, Marc, that works."

I giggle, suddenly giddy: *I can be rich at eighteen, who knew? Five hundred thousand dollars!* I feel like shouting from the tabletop; I settle for smiling at the other diners, my head already swelling. *Are you making that much? You? . . . What about you?* As my eyes hit a table of attractive women, I see they're all staring back, including the hair swisher, who twinkles her fingers at Marc.

"Models?" I ask. "Actresses?"

"Whatever." Marc answers the twinkle with a gesture that's part wave, part brush-off. "There are a lot of wannabes in this town. But not you, babe." he adds quickly. "You're the real deal."

"Here you go!" The waiter places a goat cheese and caramelized onion pizza in front of Marc. I'm the recipient of a green salad. Appetizer size.

Lettuce?

"Can I get you anything else?"

A meal?

"No, we're good," Marc says.

The waiter leaves. *I'm getting five hundred thousand dollars,* I remind myself. I raise my fork. "Whoops. He forgot the dressing."

"Use the lemon." Marc jabs a fork into my greens and piles a considerable portion of them on top of his oozing, bubbling pizza. "Now, Emily, if you had said famous, that would be harder—harder, but still possible. Develop your career the right way and you'll pull in two, three times that amount. For years. Better yet, get into acting—like Layla's starting to—and you could make millions."

My throat makes a gurgling noise. I throw my hands up. "Okay: famous—I want to be famous."

Marc raises his scotch. "Then you will," he toasts. "Just you wait."

Grinning, I tuck into my lettuce. When Marc leaves to make an "urgent" call, I look back at the table of women. *Wannabes.* I'm the real deal. I swish my hair. *Famous. I'm going to be famous.*

After our plates are cleared, the waiter returns with menus. "So, do we feel like being naughty tonight?" He leans forward with a conspiratorial wink. "Because the Death by Chocolate is a great way to go."

"Nope. She's fasting." Marc says briskly.

"I'm *fasting*?"

The waiter beats it.

"Well . . . not completely. Greens, water, maybe a piece of tuna or two—and lots of lemon juice."

Close enough.

"You need to slim down," Marc informs me.

Pause. I've lost five more pounds since the "Big Hips" comment, bringing the tally to 122 pounds, but from the way Marc is staring at me now, I might as well be a Cabbage Patch Kid. "Five pounds at *least*," he continues. The head of NOW! Models signals for the check, then figures since his finger is pointed anyway he might as well jab it into my thigh. "And firm up. In fact—hey, I've got a great idea—when you get to the hotel, why don't you hit the stationary bike for forty, fifty minutes?"

I can think of several reasons. "Bike . . . tonight?" I sputter.

"Yeah, good point." Marc pulls out a wad of cash out of his money clip, drops it on the table, and stands. "First thing in the morning is much better for your metabolism—better schedule a wake-up call for six-thirty instead." He extends his hand. "But don't worry babe, I'll take care of that; I'm your agent, that's what I'm here for."

I walk out of Chaya hungry and crabby. When Marc, back in tour guide mode, says "I've got one more thing to show you," I fight the urge to kick him. But then the car starts to climb up—up, up, up a canyon, into the hills. With each twist and turn the headlights catch something: a well-manicured hedge, a burst of bright blossoms, a thick, clinging vine. My breath catches. Once, in the dead of winter, my sixth-grade science class took a trip to see the Milwaukee Domes: three greenhouses under glass. All of them were warm and exotic, of course, but the best by far was tropical. I'd never seen anything so lush, so green, so perfect. It was magical, a miniature paradise that couldn't possibly survive in the bigger landscape we spent so much of our time bundling ourselves against. Or so I thought. But here it is, all around me. Right here. Different flora perhaps but the same effect. And this is when I realize: This is it—this is where the glamour is, not in gleaming high-rises, but in the fecundity, the abundance, the powerful engine purring beneath us.

"Look, babe, the Hollywood sign!"

The lights. The stars. I tip my head back, breathe in the night air, and reach my hand up and out, as if to touch the beauty of it all. This is it. This is Hollywood.

And I'm going to be famous.

I wake up the next morning to a made-to-order day: sunny, clear, not too hot. I put in forty-five minutes pedaling to nowhere on the bike and sip my lemon water, then turn my room service menu facedown. My stomach grumbles but I don't care: *I'm going to be famous.*

Marc picks me up promptly at 9:00. As we drive, we pass a billboard featuring a blonde with endless amounts of hair and breasts the size of watermelons, the word *Angeline* skirting her right nipple.

"What's Angeline?" I ask. I've never heard of this product.

"She is."

"*She's* Angeline?"

"Yup." Marc flicks his turn signal.

"What's she selling?"

"Herself."

"Don't tell me—she's a prostitute," I say. I try to sound with it, though honestly, I didn't know you could just hang out a shingle for that one.

"No, she's not a prostitute, she's an entertainer; it's self-promotion," Marc clarifies. He's wearing a version of yesterday's outfit but the shirt is short-sleeved, and as he cradles the phone against his neck to dial, his gold watch glints in the California sunshine.

"I don't get it."

Sigh. "Angeline wants to be a star, she buys a billboard. Easy."

Easy for him. I sigh, too, imagining Milwaukee's expressway papered with images of me in a bikini with the sole aim of promoting my product: moi. I'd die—provided Mom didn't kill me first. As it is, she's not thrilled with me. "But Mom, I've never been to California; shouldn't

I broaden my horizons?" I cajoled during the inevitable argument that preceded this trip. "Your horizons or your purse?" Mom shot back. She eventually capitulated, primarily because she has a soft spot for the birthplace of Jerry Brown.

But on the horizon now is not Jerry but Marc, or rather, Marc's agency, a low, green building with NOW! MODELS—MARC GOLD INC. painted across the front in humongous black letters, ensuring that even the aged and infirm know who's running the show. Inside, the place is jumping. I've never seen so many bookers before. Near the garage-door-style entrance, a half dozen or so are sprinkled around two large round tables, each with a pit in its center containing a sunken lazy Susan on which rests a circular file holder holding the charts of every girl at the agency. As the bookers work the phones, the wheels are in motion.

"So you need a blonde? What kind . . . classic?"

"—You liked Cynthia? 'Cause I can give you a first on Wednesday and a second on Thursday. "

"—Exotic?"

"—A half day with Christie is $2,000. Do you want to reserve the time?"

The bookers are cooking up options. Here's how they work. In theory, the first client to reserve a model's time gets the first option, meaning that client has first dibs on the model for that day, the second client to call gets second dibs, and so on. In practice, however, some clients are given a second, third, or fourth option—aka *dream on*—no matter when they call. If Kmart calls to reserve time on you, well, um, great but your agent might give them a second or third in case something better comes along. If nothing does—by 3:00 P.M., say, the day before the shoot—then and only then will your agent call Kmart back and give them a first, so they can confirm the time and thus seal the deal.

"—Yes, you have a first on Tessa, are you confirming now?"

But before you throw a pity party for Kmart, remember: They're doing it, too. Clients usually option several girls for one job—in case they can't get the one they want, or they need a blonde, not a brunette, or a hot new girl walks into their office that day and they simply have to have her at once. Then they blow off the also-rans at the eleventh hour—too late for the girls to secure another gig.

"—So confirm Carrie and release Svetlana for this afternoon?"

The result is that you never know what you're doing until the last minute, which is both exciting and annoying.

"I have a new girl who's really special. Her name is Emily."

I listen as a booker named Jared talks me up to a mystery client, bandying about terms like "chestnut brown," "fresh-faced," "athletic build," and "classic beauty." I sound like a horse. Still, it's good that they're talking me up so soon. Obviously, it's just a matter of time before they sign me. *I'm going to be famous.*

Marc ushers me into his office, where, for the rest of the morning, we sort through my book, or I should say, empty it.

"What the hell is this?"

Marc holds up a misty portrait of me in curls and strapless Laura Ashley, staring contentedly at a blade of grass, before tossing it on the concrete floor with the other rejects—mostly photos I've shot over the last year with Chicago photographers, photos that in the agent-model shorthand, Louis and I have reduced to single monikers, like "Rooftop," "Amish," and, the latest casualty, "Country Maiden."

These photos are tests. "Tests" is shorthand for test photographs, professional-style pictures that are shot for personal use, usually for one's portfolio. Testing happens for a variety of reasons. A photographer wants to try out a new style of lighting. A makeup artist wants to show he can do 1940s glamour. A new model needs photographs for her book. "If a model has to *pay* someone to take *her* photo, she's in the wrong business," Louis pointed out once, so test pictures usually don't cost me anything except a share of the film cost and the price of printing. Still, they can be a waste of time. The photographers who want to test are often newbies themselves, or the makeup artist is, or the stylist, or all of the above and, as they say, the camera doesn't lie: an odd collar, a stray hair, a wrong shade of lipstick, and the shot has to go. Judging from the growing pile on the floor, I'd say I've misspent many a Saturday. But what choice did I have? As a new model you test and you test until you can replace those pictures with tear sheets.

By the time Marc's finished, my portfolio of twenty shots has shrunk down to four. Four pages filled, out of forty. I haven't been around long enough to realize that a variation of this happens every time you get a new agent—the by-product of some sort of Svengali complex—so I'm taking this hard.

"What's wrong with these?" I ask, holding up a few of the Fuhrmann/Whitman shots. Of all the rejects, these are the ones I'd most like to rescue, not only because of the pain procuring them but also because I look pretty, I think.

"Catalog," he shrugs. "Can't put it in your book."

This I didn't know. "Louis said I could."

"Ugh. Chicago," Marc mutters.

"Well, why not?" I huff.

"You just can't. It makes you look too commercial."

"But most of my clients *are* commercial," I say, confused. "And anyway, commercial means money and money is good, right? I mean, isn't the reason I'm trying to become famous so I can get even richer than if I was just trying to get rich, really?"

Marc does his scalp massage. "Emily, modeling is an image-based business," he says, kicking off a long-winded answer that uses the word *image* at least a dozen more times along with *aura, fantasy,* and *muse.*

"So you're telling me that catalog clients would rather see pictures of me as an Amish boy and have to imagine what I might look like in regular clothing than see pictures of me in an actual catalog, which requires no imagination, just eyesight?"

"Well, maybe not an Amish boy," he says, pointing to the floor. "But that's the general idea, yes."

My despair is interrupted by a gentle rap.

"Yes?"

Some models are so photogenic that when you see them in person, it's actually a letdown: Without the softening effects of the strobe and three hours of hair and makeup, they look wan, washed out, hardangled. Not Layla Roddis. She's standing in the door frame, her eyes more sapphire, her hair more golden, her skin more luminous than even the best photographer could capture. I'm dumbstruck.

"Emily, I think you know who this is," Marc says as my mouth hangs unhinged and Layla enters. "Layla, Emily just joined us." I note he leaves out the future star speech when speaking to the one person who actually is.

"Hey there." Layla yawns, then turns to Marc. "When's my flight?"

"Not till eight."

"Cool, 'cause I wanna go shopping."

Suddenly, Marc smashes his hands together like he's activating the Clapper. "Hey, I got an idea! Layla, you hate being alone and, Emily, I'd say you need some new clothes—why don't you go together?"

Layla's expression makes it clear she doesn't mind being alone all that much.

"It'll be *fun!*" Marc presses.

I hold my breath. Layla looks at me, then at Marc, then at her purse. "Okay, fine. Let's go."

I'm going shopping with Layla Roddis! I feel dizzy and stunned but I've had this sensation all day so maybe it's just LA—well, that, or else I'm starting to experience the side effects of caloric deprivation.

Layla saunters toward the doorway. I stumble behind. When we burst into the bright sunshine, I half expect a driver and stretch limo to be waiting, but the ride is a Porsche 911, license plate "Blueeyz."

Cool. "That your nickname?"

Layla shakes her head. "My boyfriend's. Nicky. It's his car."

Wow. I know who Nicky is—Nick Sharp, the movie star famous for playing a bad cop, an even badder drug lord, and a slew of other ne'er-do-wells—*everyone* does. They have matching tattoos for Christ's sake and, soon, double billing on a movie he's producing, but I'm not sure if I'm supposed to know or not know, if you know what I mean, so I just say "oh" and get in the car.

Layla puts on a pair of l.a. Eyeworks sunglasses—the latest brand; I have to get some—and starts driving.

"Have you lived in LA long?" I ask.

"Two years."

Layla depresses the tape player button and turns up the volume.

"Is this Bon Jovi?" I yell.

Layla nods.

"I haven't heard it before!"

"It's not out yet. Jon sent us an early cut."

Oh my God, she knows Jon Bon Jovi! I better buy this, too, when I can. I stare out of Blueeyz, happy as a clam despite my now roaring stomach, which reaches peak volume right as the tape player switches sides.

"Sorry," I say sheepishly above the gurgling. "I'm a little hungry, I guess."

"Well, you're doing Marc's fast so I'm not surprised."

I am. "How'd you guess?"

Layla emits a knowing laugh as she turns down the volume. "Because he makes everyone do it . . . including me."

"Oh." I'm unsure whether I feel better because this means I'm not especially fat or worse because this means I'm not special.

"In fact, here . . . mix this into your water."

Her hand extends behind my seat and into her Hermès tote bag, then flicks toward me. I open my cupped hands, expecting to see a special blend of vitamins, maybe even some uppers, but it's Metamucil.

"I always carry some with me. It fills me up. Usually, I mix it with Diet Coke. It hides the taste, I think. I have them all the time. Nicky calls it the Layla—like a cocktail."

"That's funny."

Layla smiles. She's friendly now, even chatty. I tear the packet open, slide the fiber into the bottle opening, and shake it up.

"But don't have more than four or five a day," she cautions. "Otherwise you'll be going constantly and they'll be runny—especially if you drink a lot of water. Which you should."

"Uh-huh."

I'm with Layla Roddis—*Layla Roddis*—and not ten minutes after meeting her we're talking about bowel movements: Shit! Why, we're practically best friends already. I wonder if I'll like Nick? I wonder who'll design the bridesmaids' dresses? Maybe I'll get a celebrity boyfriend, too!

Layla takes two hard right turns and pulls the Porsche into a vacant spot. We jump out. We're behind a white two-story building all covered in vines, the sign on it spelling the words *Fred Segal* in crazy red and blue letters. We walk through its entrance.

"Hi Layla, we've got some great new things on two!"

"Layla, I'm a *huge* fan of your work!"

"Hey Layla, what's going on?"

Oh my God. I glance back at the guy retreating into the men's section. My fingers curl around Layla's. "That was—was that Terence Trent D'Arby?"

"Yup."

"Cool!"

"I guess. Personally, I think he needs to rethink the hair."

I laugh—hard—and trot behind Layla up the stairs.

"Hi Layla!"

"Layla, I'm having a party this Saturday: 4787 Vista Del Mar. Make sure you come—and bring Nick!"

Again, I glance back. "Who was that?"

"Who knows?" Layla says.

Fred Segal is small. Small but well edited. We emerge near the sunglasses. Layla peels hers off. "Want these?" she asks, already sporting a new pair with a logo I don't even recognize.

"Yeah . . . wow, thanks!" I dump my Ray•Bans out of their case and carefully nestle Layla's rejects around the lens cloth.

Designer clothing comes next. "Ooh, pretty!" I say as she holds up a gray Versace.

"Pretty for you." Layla passes the dress over, followed by a gold leather mini. The saleswomen hover.

"Here, let me take that," says one.

"Diet Coke?" says another.

"Miss Roddis, I just got this in," says a third, holding up a full-length black dress. "It's Alaïa—you like it?"

Layla slides the new glasses onto her head. "I have it. Azzedine gave it to me," she sighs, turning back to the rack.

"Oh, then I'm sure it looks wonderful on you! We have it in yellow and navy, in case you're interested."

"Really?" Her brows lift. "Okay, I'll see the navy—and the yellow for her," she adds, grabbing a Diet Coke off the tray that's just materialized beneath her arm. I grab one, too.

"Excellent. They'll be in your rooms."

I smile. I don't really like yellow, but what do I know? "Hey Layla, any other diet tips?" I ask as our fingers work the racks.

"Well, I follow the Alkaline Diet—here." Layla hands me a brown leather dress.

"What's that?"

"Byblos."

"No, the diet."

"Oh." Layla picks out a pair of cream leather pants. I do, too. "You know how every person's body is a certain pH, like a pool?"

No. "Yeah."

Layla picks out a cream leather jacket. I do, too. "Well, with the Akaline Diet you avoid acidic foods," she says.

"Okay . . . Why?"

Layla passes me a pale pink cashmere sweater and then a white one. An attendant retrieves our piles. As we follow her into the dressing room, two giggling teenage girls stop Layla and ask her to autograph the *Vogue* cover. *Love, Layla* ♥ she writes, next to her cheek. "Acids can lead to fluid accumulation, slow down your metabolism—stuff like that."

"I see." I don't really but I'm willing to give her the benefit of the doubt. I enter my dressing room. Layla enters hers. Her hand comes through the curtain. "Here, pee on this strip of paper. It'll tell you the pH of your urine. Blue is good."

No wonder Layla carries a large tote. "Okay." I stuff the strip into my pocket. I'm sure I'll have to go soon—in the last half hour I've had two Diet Cokes and a water; the attendants are very attentive. "So that means what, avoiding tomatoes and stuff?"

"No . . . acidic foods aren't necessarily acidic in your body." Layla must be changing, her voice fades in and out. "Tomatoes are okay. So are oranges—all fruit is fine. Except cranberries. Oh—and prunes. Avoid prunes."

"Okay." That's probably for the best, what with all the Metamucil I'll be taking. I peel off my clothing and pull on the gray Versace.

"Eat kelp."

"Huh?" I peek around the corner. The Alaia's bunched around Layla's ears. "Oh. Here, let me."

"No, I got it!"

"No, here . . ." I twist Layla around. As I grab the fabric, I spot a six-inch black-and-blue mark on her rib cage. "What happened?"

"I fell," Layla says. Years later, I'll learn that this isn't true—that there were many bruises, many falls while she and Ol'Blueeyz were together. For now, I wince sympathetically. "Yeah, kelp. It's a seaweed," she continues. "I get it from a supplier. I'll give you his number—taa daa!"

The dress is on now. Layla spins. Navy fabric hugs every curve, accentuating her eye color. She frees her hair from her collar, it cascades past her shoulders. "Wow . . ." I whisper.

Layla shrugs. "It's okay, right?"

"Definitely."

I return to my dressing room. Turns out Fred Segal didn't have the yellow Alaia in stock. I settle for trying on the gold Versace mini. "So fruit, kelp . . . what else?"

"Peanuts—no, wait, peanuts are bad. So are cashews. Almonds and walnuts are okay, I *think*. You know, to tell you the truth, Nick usually orders for me so I'm not really sure. Oh, and no alcohol. Empty calories and it slows down your metabolism. But," Layla's voice becomes conspiratorial, "I drink whiskey. That's Nicky's rule: I can have whiskey."

Okay, obviously I can't lug a bottle of whiskey into the Columbia dining hall; I'll have to buy a flask. As for the rest—fruit, kelp, almonds—admittedly, it's not a lot to go on, but compared to my current diet of water and air, it sounds positively scrumptious, so scrumptious, in fact, that my stomach starts rumbling again just thinking about it. I distract myself by concentrating on the clothes.

And how. Layla and I try on everything in the store, it seems, a marathon fueled by can after can of Diet Coke brought to our adjoining rooms by the starstruck assistants. Everything the supermodel tries on looks like it was made for her—which it probably was—and everything she tells me looks "great" I add to my "yes" pile. By the end of our session we've come dangerously close to busting the seams of the dressing room, so I'm surprised when Layla emerges empty-handed.

"Wait—you're not getting *anything*?" I ask. My arms are so full, I can barely see her.

"Not yet. Nicky needs to approve everything, and it's just easier to do it here. We'll come back later," she explains.

I'm thinking Blueeyz has better things to do, then realize the prospect of having a supermodel girlfriend give you personal fashion shows is probably what motivated him to become a movie star in the first place.

So that leaves me. The salesperson beams. "Okay, Miss Woods, your total today comes to $2,150. How would you like to pay for that?"

Um, do you take flesh? My God, I've never spent remotely this much money on clothes in my life. As I dig through my backpack, my hand shakes. Nervously, I hand over my new credit card, the one Mom and Dad just got me. For textbooks.

"It's declined," she says a minute later.

My palms start to sweat. "But it's brand-new," I stammer.

Pause. "Your first card?"

I nod.

The saleswoman smiles. "Then you probably have a thousand-dollar credit limit," she says gently, talking to me like I'm four. "So we'll put that amount on the card and you can pay the rest in cash, okay?"

"I don't have $1,150," I tell her, vowing to get another credit card as soon as possible. "Maybe I should put back the gold mini," I say. And the pants. And the sweater.

Layla's lip juts. "But the skirt looked so good on you!"

"And it's gold— gold goes with everything," the saleswoman adds.

Layla nods. "Gold's classic."

"Like a hoop earring," I murmur.

"Exactly!" they cry in unison.

I finger the shiny soft fabric.

Layla pulls out her credit card. "Here. Let me."

"I couldn't!" I cry.

"Yes, you can."

"I'll pay you back."

"Of course you will," Layla says, handing it over. "You're with Marc Gold now. You'll be rich!"

Chapter 6

Lion Eyes

Sure enough, the very next day in Los Angeles, I'm working. "A good cash job" is how Jared puts it when I call to check in. The job is for a German catalog. Oddly, it's the closest I come to playing tourist, as the client wants the background of each frame to sing Holl-y-wood, so our location van hits all the major sites: Mann's Chinese Theater, Rodeo Drive, Sunset Boulevard (identifiable only if you stand directly in front of the street sign, which I do). It's hokey but fun, and they pay me $1,200 in cash.

We stop shooting when the sun dips low over the ocean, so heavy and red that colors start playing chameleon. I take a cab back to the agency.

Marc's in his office, his hand sliding into a bag of potato chips. "Don't wash your face," he instructs. "We're going to a party."

"Okay."

I've just sunk into a chair when Tanda, one of NOW!'s top earners, a girl with tawny skin and toffee-colored hair, pokes her head in. "Hey Marc, you ready?"

"One sec."

"'kay." The door closes.

Marc bites into a chip. *Crunch.* "What's wrong?" he asks with a mouthful. "You tired?"

I stare at him over the chair's armrest, which somehow I'm slumped against. "Yes, tired . . . and a little hungry."

Crunch. Marc frowns. "Hungry? You sure? Because fasting gives you a lot of energy, I've found, unless . . ." the creases deepen. "You didn't eat anything off the list, did you?"

"No, I've just had water and greens. In fact . . ." I force myself upright to gain the benefit of eye contact. "I think that might be the problem. I need tuna, I think, a little tuna. Can we stop for some on the way?"

Crunch. "On the way to the party?"

I nod, swallowing. I haven't wanted to resort to this: I've wanted to be above such a basic need as food, but today some primal drive for survival is kicking in and here I am, paws in the air, like one of those bizarre Sharpeis I've seen in the passenger seat of many an LA vehicle.

"We could"—Marc raises his eyebrows and speaks in that slow, exaggerated way that is, in fact, used when talking to animals—"We could get you some tuna."

My heart sings.

"It's just that . . ." *Crunch. Crunch.* "Preston is going to make you strip naked."

"Who's Preston?"

Marc shakes the bag to facilitate his chip selection. "The bookings editor at *Vogue*." *Crunch.* "A very powerful lady."

"And she'll want to see me naked?"

"Well, you might be able to leave on your underpants."

Well, that's something.

Nervously, I stare down at my body. A *Vogue* editor examining every inch of exposed flesh. I thought I already woke up from that nightmare. "When am I seeing her?"

"Next week. In New York. Told you I'd make you famous." The potato chip bag is empty now. Marc wads it up and throws it in the wastebasket, declaring the shot a three-pointer. "Provided you keep up the fast. Hey, can I have my commission?"

"Sure." Ignoring my whining stomach, I pull the cash out of my wallet and count out $240. Marc shoves it in his jacket pocket. "Thanks."

"And this is for Layla," I say, counting out another wad.

This goes in the jacket, too. "I'll see that she gets it."

I glance shyly at my nails. "So, Marc, does this mean you're my agent?"

"Of course, babe!"

Thank God. "Well, don't you want me to sign something?"

"Yeah, well, um, Emily . . ."

Knock. Knock. Tanda's back.

"One minute!" Marc cries. He points at me. "Because you need to change."

Puzzled, I look down at my brand-new cream leather pants and matching sweater. "But why?"

"Not sexy enough."

"But everything else is at the hotel!"

"I figured." Marc pulls a bag from behind his desk and removes a washcloth. "That's why I bought you a gift."

"Thanks," I say, realizing as I accept it that it's actually an eight-ounce article of clothing. "Though I'm not sure it will fit." I try to sound disappointed.

"It should. The salesgirl looked about your size. If it's too big, we can pin it and you'll get it tailored later."

I haven't worn terrycloth since I was toddling around in a onesie, and who the hell tailors towels?

Marc points to the bathroom. "Hurry."

The jumpsuit has a plunging V neck. Thanks to spandex, that miracle fabric, it fits: the way Frederick's of Hollywood—not God—intended, I'd say, seeing as there's no room for any form of undergarment. *No way.*

I step out of the bathroom. "Perfect!" Marc cries.

For *what?* Ayana's voice rings in my head: *Be a bitch.* "I'm not wearing this in public!" I snap.

"Now, Emily . . ." Marc walks up and encircles my waist. Close up, his copper-colored eyes are even more beautiful, reddish brown but ringed with gold. Like a lion. "Remember your goals?" he asks.

"Yes, but . . ."

"But nothing, Emily. Here in Hollywood there are no buts."

That much I do realize.

"If you want to rise to the top," he cinches my waist harder and sets his voice on auto-croon, "if you want to be like Layla, then you've got to trust me and wear this to the Chip Blitz party."

Hang on. "This is Chip Blitz's party?"

"Yeah."

"As in Chip Blitz, one of the most famous fashion photographers in the country?"

"I'd say in the world and I know Chip would prefer 'portrait photographer' or 'celebrity photographer' to 'fashion photographer' but, yeah, that Chip." Marc scratches his chin. "Oh, you didn't know? I thought I mentioned it . . . I certainly mentioned you to him."

Gasp. "You did?"

"Yup. He's dying for you to come. So, shall we?"

Preston. Chip. Minutes later, as we're driving down Sunset, I stare at billboard after billboard of those who've made it, or are trying to make it and suddenly, fame doesn't seem so hard to come by. It's right in reach, in fact; all I have to do is open my hand.

"Aaron, why *did* you name your new pilot after a zip code?"

"Here he is: the man behind *Pretty Woman!*"

"Girls, this way!"

Chip Blitz's foyer is packed with people, their meetings and greetings a cacophonous clamor matched only by the throbbing beat of the DJ's extended remix. Marc grabs Tanda's hand. She grabs mine. She's wearing a red lace-up dress so revealing that by comparison I need only a wimple and I'm off to the convent. As Marc pulls the two of us through the crowd, we're introduced as "Snow White and Goldilocks," "Jill and Sabrina," and, when his artistic references fail him, "arm candy," to the seemingly endless array of middle-aged men—all producers— who make our acquaintance. But if all that's missing from my getup are some ears and a fluffy tail, these men have a uniform, too, one that their extended ogling gives me ample time to examine: shirts, cuff-linked and initialed in a range of sherbet tones; pants, peg-legged and pleated; jackets, narrow-collared and linen. It's like being in a hall of mirrors with Crockett and Tubbs, only older and balder, their years in Tinseltown baked into their skin.

I tug Tanda's hand. "Is everyone gonna be this old?" I yell.

"Now, yes! Later, younger!" Tanda yells back. "This is the best time for networking, though; let's keep moving!"

As the hallway widens into the living room, a shapely redhead in front of me gasps and presses her fingers against her chest. "Oh. My. God—Jackie!"

No way. Jackie O?

It's nine Warhols of Jackie, not the woman herself, still I'm floored. By everything. Whenever I've been in fancy rooms before, they've always been grand in that crystal chandelier, Persian carpet, Louis the 14th/15th/whatever sort of way, like the lobby of a not particularly interesting hotel. But the floor of Chip's living room is dark ebony, so glossy that the white shag area rugs seem to float across it like leaves skimming the surface of a pond—an illusion of weightlessness the glass tables and Lucite chairs only maintain. White lights shaped like atom clusters dance overhead. Bright paintings and bold lithographs blast from the walls as if punched through them. Outside, I see the glimmer of a pool and, beyond, the shimmer of downtown Los Angeles. It's incredibly exotic, impossibly glamorous, like those destinations I've only read about: Bali, Tahiti, St. Moritz.

Tanda departs to work the room. I stay with Marc. I'm still taking it all in when another tanned, groomed man approaches us, this one younger and less pasteled, with a hawkish nose supporting a pair of thin black frames. Marc releases me and hugs him. "There you are," he exclaims. "Emily, I'd like you to meet Chip."

"Welcome!"

Chip asks the usual things: *Where are you from? Is it your first time here? Do you like it?* Through every response he grins agreeably, but his eyes roam around the room distractedly, making me feel rushed and tense.

"Emily got into Harvard," Marc says, when even the pretense of conversation begins to wane.

Harvard?

"Yeah, right," Chip chuckles. His eyes flick along the contours of my jumpsuit before jumping over to Tanda. "And that one's putting herself through law school."

For some reason, the two of them find this funny. So funny, they twist like wrestlers, clasping each other on the back of the neck as they gasp for air.

"So," Mark says as the guffawing has died down to more of a chuckle. He reaches for the nape of my neck and squeezes. "What do you think?"

Chip eyes me for a beat, then blinks. "Cute."

"*Cute?* C'mon, she's better than cute; she's perfect for your shoot next week!"

"For *Vogue*? You can't be serious . . ."

And, like *that,* I'm blinking back tears. *Cute?* What, because I'm dressed like a bimbo they think I'm deaf? And *Harvard*? Where did that come from? And "you can't be serious." I stagger off—I need to get away right this second—only to step on a foot. *Shit.* "Sorry," I gulp as an amber-colored drink splashes all over the white carpet. "Shit!" I say, this time out loud.

I bend over. I've gotten as far as waist level when an arm props me up. "Hey, don't worry about it," a male voice says. "It's a party. It happens."

"Okay . . . thanks." I bend down and dab at the carpet anyway. An attendant rushes forward with a cloth and club soda. As I ease myself upright, my gaze climbs the body corresponding to the foot and spilled drink. Jeans. Blazer. T-shirt. Grizzled beard. Chiseled cheek. Dark hair streaked with gray. Dark eyes. Richard Gere. *Richard Gere.*

"Hi."

Richard Gere. Richard Gere. Richard Gere . . .

"I'm Richard."

I stare into my cup. Hard.

"And you're?"

Oh my God. Say something.

Richard shifts his weight expectantly.

Say anything! Say your name! YOUR NAME!

"Emily." I treat my ice cubes to a dazzling smile.

"Nice to meet you, Emily." An attendant brings Richard a fresh glass. He swirls it and takes a sip, eyeing me over the lip. "Did I hear your friend right? You're going to Harvard?"

My tongue feels furry and thick. "Mmlph!"

"Congratulations, that's impressive!" Richard takes a sip and leans forward. "I wouldn't have pegged you as a Harvard girl," he murmurs playfully. Our eyes meet.

"Father Figure" isn't a particularly loud song. Still, I can't get my volume cranked up enough to compete. "That's funny, 'cause—"

"There's a professor you really should meet there, a friend of mine named Frederick Blauford who's done the most spectacular research on ancient Tibetan painting; I mean you really need to read his work. He, the Dalai, and I traveled across the Chang Tang for fourteen days— even sharing a tent during one or two hairy moments along the Brahmaputra, so when I say Fred's a good guy, I speak from experience. Heh heh. Great teacher, too, so I've heard. You should look into taking his class. You're about to be a freshman, correct? Do you know your major yet?"

I'm so focused on raising my volume that I yell, and what I yell is: "I'M NOT GOING!"

Richard Gere flashes his palm. "Easy!" he says. "Don't take Blauford's class if you don't want to. It was just a suggestion."

"No! To HARVARD! I'm not going to HARVARD!" I bleat.

His brow crumples. "But I thought you—"

"I applied, see, only I didn't get in."

Oh no. Shut up.

". . . I'm going to Columbia, actually. Not the country, the university. Columbia University. In New York City. Manhattan."

Shut up.

"Okay, yes, I'm familiar with where—"

"My Harvard essays were good. At least I thought so—well, actually, so did my English teacher, Mrs. Schwab. She thought the one about the toboggan showed real promise."

Shut up. Shut up.

"Toboggan," Richard echoes slowly.

"It's a sled."

"Yes, I—"

"But, well, math—it's not my best subject, especially all those trig problems: you know, sine, cosine—all that? *Totally* confusing. So I'm not going to Harvard. I didn't get in. I'm"—I giggle—"I'm a Harvard reject!"

Shut up! Shut up! SHUT UP!

When I've finally wrested control of my loose tongue by clamping down on it, I see that Richard Gere's jaw has actually dropped.

Perfect. I didn't get into Brown either, should I tell him that?

"Er, I'm sure you'll like Columbia—good luck!" Richard says, giving me that locked arm pat that really means *stay where you are or I'm calling in backup.* Once again, I fixate on my cup. When I next look up, Richard is gone: over and out and into the next conversation.

"Now what?" I mumble to my new best friend, the ice cube, who, sadly, won't be around for long, either. I think of Chip's voice—"*Vogue?*"—and feel a pang. Marc's nowhere to be seen. I spot Tanda "networking," though her position—leaning against the wall between two scoops of sherbet—makes her seems more like a cherry on their sundae. I head for the bar. There's a line. A guy near me raises his cocktail. "I'm Terry."

"I'm Emily." Terry's sunglasses are dangling around his neck, like Magnum P.I.

"Are you an actress?" he asks.

"No, a model."

Terry snickers. "Aren't all models wannabe actresses?"

"Um, I don't—"

". . . Or maybe I just think that because I'm a director," Terry finishes. He scratches his stubble, eyeing me appraisingly. "Hey, did anyone ever tell you look like Ally Sheedy? Because you do. Exactly. It's uncanny. I should know. Our movie just wrapped."

Wow . . . Ally Sheedy? I like her. "Thanks!" And he directed her? My heart flutters. "What movie?"

"Breakfast Club."

"Breakfast Club?" I pause. "Didn't that come out three years ago? And, wait . . . wasn't that directed by John Hughes?"

Terry tugs at the collar of his denim shirt. "Well, actually on that movie I was a grip, but I'm about to direct a short film that you'd be perfect for—will you read the script? It's called *Peepsh* . . ."

Suddenly, I decide I'm not that thirsty after all. I circle the party in search of Marc. I spot Julian Sands and Charlie Sheen, but no agent. I walk upstairs and down a long hallway. Between one set of doors, a guy and a girl make out. In front of another door two girls argue. I'm about to turn around when the arguers split apart. As one tears past me, the other pushes open the door.

In the dark room, a television's bluish, flickering glare illuminates a woman lying on a bed. It looks like she's fallen and shattered. Her long black hair is fanned around her. Her long dark dress has cutouts shaped like shards of glass. From an exposed sliver of pale, creamy flesh, Marc is doing a line of coke.

The girl holding the door shifts impatiently. "You coming in or what?"

"No," I say. No, I'm not. I need air. I rush down the stairs, through the living room and out the glass doors, past the water, past the garden to the lawn's edge, where I place my hands against the smooth steel railing and look out. The canyon spills beneath me, dark and fragrant. Beyond it wink the lights of Los Angeles. It's a familiar view, the mirror image of the one I had two days ago, only it's the inhabitants and not the vista I find confusing now. *Is Marc signing me or not? Is this a party or an audition? Why exactly am I in LA?*

"There you are! Emily!"

I turn around. Marc's standing behind me. Behind him, the pool stretches in both directions, bursting through the greenery with the brilliance of a sparkler.

"Right here," I mutter.

Marc juts his lip. "Babe, what's wrong?"

I decide to ignore the coke and focus on other issues. "So, I flunked the audition, didn't I? No interest, is that right?"

"What?" His head gives a puzzled shake. "Emily, I told you already, I want to represent you!"

"No, I mean this party. Meeting Chip."

"This wasn't an audition!"

"Marc . . ."

"You're wrong," he says quickly. "Chip liked you."

"Just not for *Vogue*."

Marc's still standing a few feet away from me on the slate path, his need to protect his white linen pants outweighing any need for physical contact. I watch him try a few responses in his head. "No," he finally goes with. "Not yet. But Chip's funny like that; he needs to get to know a girl first, sometimes. We'll work on him, take him to dinner, get him to shoot a test on you. It'll work out. You'll see."

"But how? When? Chip lives here. I'll be in New York next week."

"I think you should stay."

I stare across the expanse of green. Charlie Sheen's now standing on it. As he turns to the girl beside him, it looks like he's whispering in Marc's ear. "But what about college?" I whisper back.

"Go in a year," Marc says.

"You can book me from here, I know you can."

Marc's shaking his head. "It won't work. I need you here, full-time, so I can watch over you. Teach you. Be your mentor, your counselor, your trainer . . ."

Great. More training.

"You can do so well at this," he continues. "You and I together. I'll take you straight to the top."

A breeze lifts, then dies. I'm staring at the ground when Marc decides to go for it, rolling his pant legs and treading lightly, his footsteps producing silvery wells in the lush green lawn. We turn toward the view. "See those?" he asks. His fingers wrap around mine, pointing our hands past the lights of Los Angeles, into the sky. "I can make you one of those. A star," he breathes. "Just like Layla."

I look up, pondering fame of cosmic proportions. A few stars twinkle in response. "I'm not as beautiful as Layla," I murmur. I know this much is true.

"I think you are," Marc says, the only thing he can. He lowers our arms, but keeps my fingers encased in his grip. "You'll be great at this, Emily, a great model. But it has to happen now."

"Now?" I echo.

"Yes, now. This year."

I free my hand. "But I'll only be twenty-one when I graduate."

"Twenty-one is too old—way too old, Emily, you know that," Marc replies. "It has to be now."

Twenty-one has never seemed that old to me before, but as I look at Los Angeles, it seems far—impossibly far—and, though I search the horizon, I catch no glimpse of it.

"Emily . . ." Marc slides behind me. "You told me you wanted to be famous. Well, here it is. Right here. Stay and let it happen to you."

I close my eyes, imagining what fame must feel like: cascading water, warm but not too hot, the temperature of your skin.

"And if I don't?"

"Then I can't represent you. It won't work."

My eyes, when they open, are swallowed by the canyon. "Why did you tell Chip I got into Harvard?"

"Better school," Marc says. "Remember what I told you, Emily, it's all about marketing, about self-promotion. But you'll get it. You'll learn."

I feel the heat of Marc's body, his hands sliding down my arms, his fingers encircling mine. "And I'll be the one to teach you," he murmurs. Nuzzling my ear, he pulls me tight. "What do you say, babe, shall we reach for the stars?"

How do you know whom to trust? It's a hard question, I think. Until now, my world has mostly been a safe haven, inhabited by people I know. That's what happens when you're one of 8,311 people living on a lake. But then, one day, I got on an airplane and here I am, with Marc Gold, on a cliff. I close my eyes and I stay. I stay and let it happen. I let Marc kiss me.

Marc kisses me for a while. He has me backed against the rail, his hands skimming the contours of my jumpsuit when something—I'm not sure what—makes me stop and look up.

It's Tanda, beside the pool, staring at us. When I look at her, she looks away.

"Never mind her," Marc says, seeing. "Tanda's nothing, a tacky whore."

I take a stab. "But you dated her."

"I wouldn't say 'date.'"

I stiffen.

"Aw, you jealous, babe? Don't be! You're my baby. You're my star!"

Then again, sometimes you just know. I lift Marc's hands from my body and push off from the railing. I'm going to Columbia University. It's what I want. It's the right thing to do.

Besides, Columbia is in New York City. I can get rich and famous there.

Chapter 7

She's a Bitch Girl

Snap	*Francine's*
Elite	*Wilhelmina*
Ford	*Women*
Liquid	*Zoli*
Factory	*Click*

I stare down at the list that Louis has just jotted on his napkin. "So you're saying these are the only agencies that matter in New York? These ten?"

"Right now, yes."

"What about the rest?"

Louis takes a bite of his eggs, chews, and rests his utensils in the tray. "Some use the word *model* loosely—very loosely if you know what I'm saying. As for the others . . . let's just say model with one of them and you might as well add 'waitress' to your job description because that's all you'll ever be."

I pry my glass of water from the soggy airplane napkin and take a sip. When I returned from LA empty-handed except for luxury fabrics and some hefty credit card debt, it was time for Plan B. I was going to need a New York agency, that much was certain. But which one? How would I find it? I was nervous and scared until Louis came to my rescue. Instead of driving up for a late August holiday in Door County (Wisconsin's Riviera, known for its boiled fish and cherry pie), he would, he told me, come to New York and assist me in the process of finding an agent. "After all, cookie," he said with a smile. "It's the least I can do for the girl who put Chicago Inc on the fashion map."

Other than the "cookie" part—ever since Marc's starvation diet got me to 120, I've found the nickname unpalatable—I was thrilled. I'll have an ally! By my side! I threw my arms around Louis with such vigor I nearly suffocated him. I was worried my parents would freak—they were supposed to drive me—but then fate intervened. Tommy's opening game takes place tomorrow. They would be able to attend. So now they're there and I'm here, up at thirty thousand feet with my mother agent, strategizing how to best accomplish our mission.

"So ten agencies," I say. "That's how many models?"

"Well, let's see. Ford and Elite are the biggest, and they have a couple hundred girls apiece, I'd say. The rest are boutique agencies with . . . hmm . . . roughly forty to eighty girls each, so that means that the grand total of honest-to-god fashion models in New York City is somewhere shy of a thousand," Louis calculates.

"A *thousand* girls? That's a lot!"

"You think?" Louis swirls his coffee and takes a sip. "Remember, Emily, that's not just girls from New York City or even America—that's every girl from around the globe."

"What do you mean? What about Paris?"

My agent's nose wrinkles. "Paris? Forget Paris. Paris is good for haute couture, something that three ladies in Texas with too many dollars and not a lot of sense actually purchase. No, there's only one fashion capital on this planet and that's New York. If you're a top girl, or even close to it, you *have* to be represented there, whether you're Spanish, Swedish—even Latvian. New York is where it *all* happens. So, looking at it that way, I'd say one thousand is not a very big number, it's pretty tiny. In fact . . ." his fingers rap against my book. "I'd wager it's harder to get into than that place."

I look down at Louis's pointer, now partially obscuring the C of my *Columbia Guide to Incoming Freshmen,* and give a derisive snort. "What? I have to write an essay on how to walk-step? Ace an interview with Lagerfeld?"

This is rewarded with a teasing jab. "Okay, right, no application to fill out or anything, but in terms of acceptance rates, yeah, I'd say it's harder to get a New York agency," he says. "Much."

My sneer evaporates. I make a mental note of the location of the barf bag. Clueless, I was nervous; informed, I feel ready to upchuck.

The details that follow do little to ease my nerves. There are dozens of agencies, only ten that count, and only two ways in: by invitation— our situation, thanks to the New York agents who, like Marc, saw my face in various places and tracked me to Chicago Inc—or as a walk-in. The latter sounds like a real nightmare. Few agencies have open castings and then only for a couple hours a week, resulting in ninety-minute lines simply to submit a picture and some contact information. The thing is, the picture—most likely a bad black and white taken by the sort of photographer who papers phone booths with ads reading *Professional Headshots Only $150!* (*plus film and development costs)—gets tossed in the trash; the *real* screening process occurs while the girls wait. All it takes is one junior agent's swish of the head to see if anyone standing there has a chance. They rarely do. "Maybe one girl a year is found that way, *maybe,*" Louis emphasizes, shaking his head at the inefficiency of it all, "but she'd have to have been hiding under a rock. No, what with modeling scouts working for agencies in every corner of the globe, I'd say the days of undiscovered beauty are over."

My water splashes against the tray. "But what about contests? Can't you get an agent from those?"

"Oh, cookie." Louis runs his hand over my hair, which, thanks to the plane's Saharan climate, has taken off on a flight of its own. "Those contests are just marketing ploys—promotions that have the added benefit of generating a bit of cash for the agencies—nothing more. First, the agencies that run those charge hefty fees for the girls to enter, to get the proper photos taken, et cetera. Second, who's participating? Most entrants already have an agency: usually the one throwing the contest. And trust me, if the girl is that great, no agent is going to have her waste time prancing around in a bathing suit in some Latvian shopping mall when she could be earning him dough in New York."

So we were back in Latvia, and things weren't sounding so good there. "But the girls that win get contracts worth like, $250,000. How ugly can they be?"

"They're not ugly, but they're not superstars, either. The whole thing is a scam. I'm sorry to admit this, cookie, but we agents are little more than glorified middlemen—critical to your success, yes, but still middlemen. We introduce you to clients and then take 20 percent from your earnings, add a 20 percent surcharge to their bill for our troubles and that's it: point, period, end of paragraph. No agent, nowhere is going to give you a paid guarantee that you'll work when they have no control over the outcome—that's just bad business! If you read the fine print on that $250,000 contract, I guarantee you'll see that all it says is that the winner has guaranteed agency representation while she makes $250,000, *if* she makes $250,000. If she makes zero, boo hoo that sucks—not their problem. Plus there's the winner's curse."

Instantly, my head fills with images of serial killers choking tiara-clad contestants with Chanel chains. "The winner's curse, what's that?"

"That the winner never amounts to anything. Ever. I'm telling you, if *Vogue* hears that a girl's won one of those contests, they're not even gonna want to see her, much less book her. They know she'll be too commercial-looking to ever be a real star. Same goes for *Mademoiselle*, Saks Fifth Avenue, L'Oréal. She'll be lucky to work for Penney's. Anyhow . . . why are we even talking about this? It's not your concern. You're going in the best way possible: through the front door."

As I lift the orange garnish off Louis's tray, I'm grinning. Louis might not be the toughest negotiator, but he sure does understand the modeling business inside and out. Thank God he's here to protect me.

The captain comes over the loudspeaker. "Ah, folks, air traffic to La Guardia is looking mighty heavy," he says in the cowboyish growl of pilots everywhere. "The good news is we're in a holding pattern riggght over the Big Apple."

Muttering, Louis looks at his watch. I stare eagerly over his shoulder. There it is, immediately off our wingtip. New York City.

Last year I came here with my parents, the city serving as gateway for my East Coast College Tour (eight schools, three days, one rental car). But I've never seen it like this. Up close. A fleet of buildings, silver and gleaming.

Gasp.

Louis looks at me, his eyes smile. "Wanna switch?"

Settled in the window seat, I literally press my nose against the pane. Louis orients me. We're nearing the southern tip of the island, heading straight up the Hudson. The first thing I notice is the water. *There's so much water!* And not a lot of wind, either, for the surface is steamroller flat. In the bright sun, it looks purple, iridescent even, like a soap bubble or the underside of tin.

"The Statue of Liberty, see it?" Louis says. I can't at first, but then—*oh, wait, there she is!*—so small amid all the barges and ferries that she appears to float haphazardly, like an errant tub toy.

I laugh and squint and laugh some more; what have I been so afraid of? From where I'm sitting Manhattan is so small. A tiny little thing. A wee amusement. I'm bigger than all of it. Wall Street? It would come up to my waist. The Chrysler Building? I could stare into its windows, bend back the tip, and peek inside. Central Park? I could brush the treetops with my fingers and dip my toe in the pond. The city is here, right here! My playground. I just can't wait to jump into it.

And then we land. In not-so-quick succession Louis and I claim our baggage, hail a cab, and ride through the Midtown Tunnel. We're running late—that holding pattern—which means we have just enough time to store our bags and freshen up in the public restroom at Louis's hotel (the Royalton, which has handleless sinks and gigantic wing chairs) before continuing on to our first stop.

Our taxi creeps along Madison Avenue, slow enough to evade a breeze. Jesus, it's hot! We lower our windows. "Whoa, whoa whoa sweet child o mine," Axl Rose cries from the rear speakers, trying but failing to drown out the guy jackhammering to our left and the two cab drivers—either in a dispute or a discussion, it's hard to tell—on our right. Against a building, a man with a maroon tux and surprisingly advanced sound system is singing "I'll Take Manhattan" into a large mike. He is largely ignored.

"Hey look, a shell game!" I cry in wonderment. "See those break-dancers?"

"Is that Corbin Bernsen?" Louis asks.

"Where?"

"Over there in the acid-washed jacket."

I lean out the window, trying to find the famous person in the crush on Fifty-seventh Street, but all I see are Japanese tourists with Tiffany bags.

"Oh, wow, a homemade unicycle!"

"Free Bernhard Goetz!" some protesters yell. "Free Bernhard Goetz!"

"Who's that?" I ask.

"Dunno," Louis says.

"So, what's the story with this place . . ." I say, finally tearing myself away long enough to glance at my Filofax, which up until now has done nothing but make my right thigh extra sweaty. "Francine's?"

Over the course of the next few blocks, as office buildings are replaced by chic stores, and even chicer pedestrians, Louis rattles off what he knows. Francine is the owner. He's spoken to her once or twice on the phone, "including once about you." She'd modeled in Paris during the sixties before opening an agency in New York, "so she can relate to what you girls are going through." She's been here awhile but has always kept her operation small, a real boutique with a "homey, familial feeling" and she's known to prefer natural beauties. "Like you, cookie."

We're stopped at a light. I look left. In a boutique window between two mannequins sporting oversized houndstooth sweaters, black stirrup pants, and large-brimmed black hats, I study my reflection. "Natural beauty," what does that mean? Camera-ready natural, which takes two and half hours if you're lucky, or fresh-from-the-shower natural? Because, with my spicy lips slicked with gloss, a single coat of mascara, and large quantities of sweat-absorbing powder, I'm somewhere, hopefully not hopelessly, in the middle.

Hang on. A woman in several layers of pastel gauze, faux pearl necklaces, and a large floppy hat affixed with a cabbage rose is strolling up the sunny side of the street, her right hand holding a pink leash attached to the collar of an Abyssinian that's slinking slightly but otherwise unfazed by the surrounding cacophony.

"My lord."

Louis glances over, then flicks his wrist. "That's nothing. In this town I've seen people walking with ferrets, snakes . . . cockatoos."

"People walking their *birds*?"

"Yup."

"Down the *street*?"

Louis chuckles. "Not on a leash, on their shoulders, silly!"

"Oh alrighty then, because for a second I thought that was strange."

"Trust me, Em, after one year in this town, you will have a completely different definition of normal—why, you might even do some strange things yourself!"

I jab my thumb in the direction of the cat. "Not that strange."

"Hey, this is New York," Louis says. "Anything can happen."

Francine's is another of New York's surprises: the place is cozy. The small, low-ceilinged lobby is painted a deep hunter green. Ficus and rubber plants soften each corner. The reception desk is a knotty pine. The lamp is made from an old butter churn. Hanging above the couch is a framed poster of a quilt. In fact, the only indication that we're standing in the entrance of a modeling agency is the unusual number of international fashion magazines strewn across the coffee table.

At the sound of our names, the receptionist, a friendly fortyish woman with cropped brown hair and white T-shirt under an ecru sweater vest, visibly brightens. "Emily! Louis! Francine's been expecting you! Go right in."

We do. The booking room is also small, with the same green walls and pine furniture as the lobby, albeit humming with activity. Phones purr constantly. A radio plays George Michael. Two agents kneel in front of an armoire, the doors thrown wide as they sort through and rearrange portfolios, while the rest sit at the ubiquitous circular table going through the now familiar motions of spinning the charts, picking up those purring phones, and selling.

"Only one girl—are you sure? 'Cause I have this great new Swede . . ."

"She's nineteen, cross my heart."

"The red-eye? You must be *joking*. Katja would break out in *hives* if I even *mentioned* it."

"You sure? 'Cause she's got legs up to your eyeballs . . ."

"Oh, for beer, really? For all of Europe? Okay, okay: she's twenty-five, cross my—waitasec. Girls! We're roasting over here: WILL YOU MOVE ALREADY?"

Startled, I look from the agent—a twentysomething guy wearing navy linen and too much hair gel—to the far end of the room. Two models, both brunettes, are facing the air conditioner side by side, their hair blowing, their black skirts flapping like flags. One sweeps her hair up, as if forming a bun, then lets it fall. I don't need to see their faces to tell that they're laughing. I step closer.

"Of course she's blonde, she's Swedish!" A second agent, roughly my age, smiles in my direction: *Nice earrings,* she mouths.

"Thanks," I say, touching my finger to one of my oversized blue hoops. As for her, only her right lobe is adorned with a large pearl, either a response to this spring's *Vogue* spread in which the mono-earring look was sported on eight pages by Christy Turlington, or because she's working the phones, I'm not sure which.

"Business class? You must be kid—"

"GIRLS!"

"Catherine, I'm very sorry, can you please hold for a second?" The third agent, her hair streaked with silver, taps her hold button with the end of a pencil. "Olivier," she says evenly. "The girls can't hear you. If you want them to move, you'll have to walk over and ask them."

"Fine, Pupa. Fine," Olivier grumbles, checking out my legs but otherwise ignoring me as he walks past. "GIRLS!"

"*Psst!* Emily!"

Louis is waving at me from the other side of the armoire. As I approach, I realize he's standing between two composite racks, staring at a field of framed photographs.

"Look at these girls!" he murmurs.

Yes, look at these girls. Natural I'm not sure about, but beautiful? Definitely. There are covers from French and American *Elle*; *Harper's Bazaar* and *Harpers & Queen*; *Mademoiselle* and *Madame Figaro*; *Moda* and *Mirabella*; *She* and *Lei* interspersed with some of this season's most coveted campaigns: North Beach Leather, Christian Lacroix, Anne Klein,

Caché, Ray•Ban, Princess Marcella Borghese, Revlon's Unforgettable Women—two of them—Giorgio Beverly Hil—

"Enjoying the view?"

I am, so much, in fact, I'd almost forgotten who we'd come to see. But the woman I turn to face is Francine, I'm sure of it. With her large, almond-shaped eyes and surprisingly full lips, she's pretty, but the dead giveaway is what lies beneath. After forty, only a former ballerina or ex-model could pull off white leggings with such aplomb.

We exchange hellos. Francine gives us a quick tour, including introductions to bookers Pupa, Francesca, and Olivier, before leading us to her office. There are two chairs in front of her desk. I walk toward them, dropping my backpack as I prepare to take a seat.

"*Attends!* Emily. Let's have a look!"

Amelie, ave, luke—despite her years in New York, Francine's French accent is as thick as triple-cream cheese. I spin around. The head of the agency has closed the door, her hand still on the handle.

"Would you remove your jacket?"

And yet she seems to have acquired a New Yorker's no-nonsense attitude. *Good. That's good,* I think, as I oblige and unbutton, her eyes traveling up me, down me, and up me all the while. *Exactly what you want in an agent, especially in Manhattan, a no-nonsense town.*

Louis reaches for my jacket: a white double-breasted Donna Karan selected during a last-minute shopping expedition down Chicago's Magnificent Mile (none of the things I bought in LA were "quite right," he thought), and I'm stripped down to the coordinating navy-and-white-striped strapless minidress.

My prospective agent leans back against the door, thus elevating her chin and turning her eyes to slits. I don't know where to look, so I stare at her feet. She's wearing boots the color of the carpet, a beigy sand, that crush loosely around the middle of her calves like paper bags. Mine are a bright royal but otherwise identical.

"Love your shoes!" I exclaim. Common ground at last, thank God! For a second there I was feeling uncomfortable.

"*Non,*" Francine says.

She isn't talking about the shoes.

"*Non.* She's very different from what I was expecting," Francine continues, now staring solely at Louis. She breezes over to her desk.

"In fact, I have a girl who looks just like her, Yvonne Bellamont. You know her?"

I don't. Louis seems to. "No comparison," he says quickly. "Totally different."

"You think?" Francine says in that tone that means *you're wrong*. She picks up the telephone. "Olivier, bring me one of Yvonne's cards, will you? I want to show these people what she looks like."

These people? I look at Louis. He squeezes my hand.

"Even better," Francine says. She hangs up.

Silence. To the left of the desk is a bulletin board jam-packed with photos and invitations. Thick paper in black or silver has jazzy pink lettering spelling out snippets like "Kelly and Calvin Klein invite you to . . ." which overlaps with "New York Screening of *When Harry Met* . . ." which overlaps with a picture of Francine hugging Mayor Koch.

The door opens. It's not Olivier.

"Voilà! Amelie, Louis, this is Yvonne. Girls, you look alike, *oui? Oui!* Yvonne: Go stand next to Amelie."

I recognize Yvonne from Neiman Marcus, *Mademoiselle,* and most recently, the front of the air conditioner. She's beautiful, but I'm sure I can speak for both of us when I say *non,* Yvonne and I do not look that much alike. For starters she has green eyes and then there's her haircut, a long bob. Okay, aside from our irises maybe we do have similar coloring, but so what? Aren't there enough jobs in this town for the two of us?

"Stand profile," Francine directs.

We face each other. Yvonne giggles.

"See? Luke at their noses and chins. Very similar."

"What about the shape of their faces?" Louis rebuts. "Emily has a square shape, Yvonne more of an oval."

"Heart," Yvonne corrects, then giggles again. Oh this is all fun and games for her, and why wouldn't it be? She already has her agent. I stare at her toes and ponder stepping on one.

"And they are the same height . . ."

More giggling, then Yvonne yawns and says, "Francine, can I go now? I have an appointment with Marc Hispard in twenty minutes."

"*Alors,* Marc? *Pour* Elle? *Alors, vite! Vite!*"

Francine scoots Yvonne out the door briskly yet affectionately, the way you might a puppy, then, once again, stands in front of it.

"You see my dilemma, Amelie? What do you think, too similar?"

I decide that Francine's full lips are pure collagen and that I hate her. I don't respond.

"Not at all!" Louis counters. "Yvonne is a lovely girl but, Francine, you cannot be serious. Her skin, well—look at Emily's! She's got tiny pores. Perfect for beauty!"

Francine's head tips back. "Let's ave a luke . . ."

"You should have sold yourself more! You didn't even try!"

Louis and I are exiting a deli with two large iced coffees, mine in jeopardy as I stomp down the sidewalk. "Why should I? When you were doing such a stellar job!" I hiss, evidently more than a little bitter. After the skin examination, we spent ten more minutes in Francine's office, ten minutes that boiled down to this: her saying she already had an Emily Woods and Louis saying she didn't.

"It shouldn't have just come from me, Em!"

"Why should I have begged her to take me?"

But she didn't release us, either; Francine just stood sentinel in front of her office door, squinting and challenging until finally, the real Emily Woods had had enough. I grabbed Louis's hand, said we'd be late for our next appointment, and barreled on past. It was humiliating.

"Because that's what she wanted, Em!" Louis cries. Coffee spurts from the hole in the lid, narrowly missing his shirt. "Not to beg, I wouldn't say that, but to sell yourself, to point out your assets!"

"I'm not a Ginsu carving set, Louis!" I snap.

"I know you're not—"

"I hated her! She sucked!" Tears build.

"Okay . . . okay."

Louis directs us toward a concrete railing encasing what apparently qualifies as a New York City garden: a bunch of scraggly trees surrounded by scraps of garbage. Gingerly, we take a seat. "It's okay, Em," he soothes. Louis's tone is reassuring but his eyes are squeezed into slits. His hair glows. He pats it. "We have other appointments. We'll just go on those and see what happens."

So that's what we do. We go see Liquid, Factory, and Snap. I'd like to tell you about each in detail but, already, they've blended together.

I wasn't expecting this. When I heard about these places, I figured each had its own vibe, as distinct and unique as an aisle in Sam Goody. Francine's, home of those natural beauties, would be Country: freckle-faced girls with long flowing hair and earth-toned dresses. Liquid, New York's edgy agency, would be Punk: frightfully skinny girls with lots of eye makeup. Snap, the eclectic agency, would be Indie: exotic beauties in a spectrum of shades and shapes.

I was wrong. Sure, Snap represents a smattering of celebrities—or really, the children of celebrities—which added some famous, if less photogenic, genes into the mix, but beyond that, every agency had a re-markably consistent blend of girls: mostly white; heavily blonde; tall, thin, and chiseled. Then again, this is 1988, only a couple years after Kim Alexis and Christie Brinkley dominated fashion's real estate and makeup artists slapped concealer on Cindy Crawford's mole. Exotic isn't—not really. Even Ayana, my favorite African bush baby, isn't. Her nose is narrow. Her lips are thin. Her hair is long and smooth. I mean my God, slap a blonde wig on her and some blue contacts and you've got Kelly Emberg with a really good tan.

It wasn't just the girls who were similar; the agencies were, too. If the place was on the Upper East Side, like Francine's, the rooms were small and the floor was carpeted, usually in a soft pastel. If it was in the Flatiron District—and that's as far south as they went—we were in a "loft" or a "raw space" and the floors were hardwood. In either case, the décor was typically chrome and black leather, the lighting track or café style—nice but not too nice, nothing to distract from the main attrac-tion: that wall of girls. As for the bookers, it turns out that every agency has a Pupa, Francesca, and Olivier. Sure, their ages and gender might vary, but the essential personality types don't. When I test this theory on Louis, he laughs.

"That's because every agent wants to mother you, be you, or fuck you."

After a beat, I say, "Thanks, Mom."

Louis laughs. "You're welcome."

So the models, the interiors, and the bookers aren't that different. Which leaves the owners.

I know each meeting with an owner was a business meeting, but it felt like a date—or what a date would be like if the guy stared openly at your pores, ducked down to examine your legs, and blatantly checked out your chest—all while you're trying in vain to make eye contact as you ask the tough questions like, "What is your commission structure?" and "Where do you see my career going over the next two years?" Or maybe this is what dating in New York is really like.

Each of these meetings sucked in its own special way. Patrick, the head of Factory, was keen to take me on . . . so long as I agreed go to Europe for two years to build my portfolio, a common next step to be sure, but one I'd already decided against. I declined. The fact that he refused to shake our hands and kept wiping every surface down with moist towelettes (including my portfolio) simply made the decision that much easier.

Mary, the head of Snap, a tough-talking woman I could easily picture pulling a knife out of her heavily laced boot, offered to represent me . . . so long as I underwent a serious image overhaul. "I'm thinking jet-black hair, I'm thinking lots of leather and chains. I'm thinking we must find your inner demon," she said repeatedly. Not diva: demon. I'm thinking no.

Martyn and Julee of Liquid were enthusiastic and filled with praise. "You have a timeless quality that's just so *now*. Classic, but not cookie cutter. Versatile," Martyn cried in a typical sound bite. "I see you doing *Vogue*. I've got three girls in this month's issue—did I mention that? *Bazaar*, but only with Puhlmann or Duran. *Elle*, you're not really *Elle*, though I think Tyen would like you. *Glamour*, only sometimes it can be too matronly so we'll have to cherry-pick. *Mademoiselle* . . ."

It all sounded great. But then Martyn kept going to the bathroom, returning with a nasty case of the sniffles, and Julee kept tripping as she darted in and out of her seat. At lunch they couldn't keep track of their own orders. Sure, the entrées seemed strange to me—chili infusion? blackened Cajun? and what the hell is mahimahi?—but there were only four to choose from. Plus they ate there every day. Yes, Martyn and Julee were either clinically insane or highly fucked-up. I dumped Liquid.

So, the upshot is that I'm 0 for 4 and it's late in the game. Which brings us to the present.

I shift in my seat. "Louis, maybe we should go back to the hotel now. I need to be on campus soon."

"This won't take long, I promise." Louis's eyes scan the buildings. "Four . . . twelve . . . twenty-two . . . Okay. Great, here it is. Okay, thank you. THANK YOU!!"

Our cab driver is either ignoring my agent or is lost to the siren call of Debbie Gibson, for we continue down Eighteenth Street just as "Foolish Beat" reaches its thundering climax, sailing past our destination and stopping in the middle of the next block, but only after the two of us scream at the top of our lungs and pound the Plexiglas divider.

"This town," Louis huffs, and not for the first time today. As we retrace our path, he starts to tell me about agency number five, Chic.

"It wasn't on your list," I point out.

"That's because it just opened. Besides, I didn't know if Byron could see us, but I called him during lunch and he was enthusiastic, so . . ."

I dodge a woman carrying several black shopping bags.

"Barneys, what's that?"

"A department store right down the street."

Oh. I make a mental note. "And Byron?"

Louis ticks through a list. "Owner of Chic. Elite booker for several years. Half-Samoan. Gay. Tall. Really good-looking. Former model."

I grimace.

"Not like Francine," he adds hurriedly. "Look, I know Byron pretty well. He's a good guy and the buzz is that Chic is going to be invite only, no walk-ins—very exclusive. Most people think it's the next big thing."

"I thought NOW! was the next big thing."

Louis shakes his head. "NOW!'s hot now. Chic will be hot a year from now."

And why did my agent want me to sign with an agency that will be over before my freshman year is? I wonder—wonder, but don't ask. I'm getting déjà vu from all the hype as it is. Instead, I glance at the entrance, a nondescript door sandwiched between a deli and a copy shop, issue a sigh of protest, and mutter, "Fine. But let's get this over with as soon as possible."

☆

If Byron is tall, dark, and handsome, I don't notice: I'm stuck at the tiara—a crush of metal and rhinestone rising and winking above a mass of dark curls.

"Oh, Emily, I forgot to tell you," Louis whispers as man and head-gear get closer. "You never went to Los Angeles."

Huh? "Why?"

"You just never went, that's al—."

"Louis! Emily! Welcome!"

In sort of an East by way of Chelsea greeting, Byron puts his palms together and bows, lids fluttering, before leaning in to give the inevitable double kiss. As his head zooms toward me, I realize the tiara contains some sort of crystal pendant, mainly because it swings into my eye.

Umppph! I fold in half.

"Oh honey, I'm so, so sorry! My crystal!" Byron exclaims over and over, seeming genuinely surprised that a heavy pendulous object does, in fact, swing. The let's-be-friends hug he gives proves nearly as perilous, so, as soon as I'm released, I step back slightly, out of charm's way, then stare longingly toward the exit. *Get me outta here.*

We cross a long, open room, emphasis on the open. There is no café lighting, only naked bulbs. The stain on the hardwood floor is from a thousand spills, not a fine mahogany finish. Every piece of furniture—two tables, six chairs—is collapsible. The wall of girls contains four photographs, none of them a cover. The bookers are odd-looking: Jon, we soon learn, a pasty middle-aged man in a paisley shirt and octagonal glasses, and Justine, a short, wide woman with green-tipped hair and the weary swagger of a long-haul trucker.

Get me outta here.

We get to the "seating area." I slump into a chair.

"You all right?" Louis mouths. I scowl.

"Want anything, Emily?" Byron asks.

Like what? There's nothing here. "No thank you."

Byron sits down next to me and places his hands on the table, palms flat. His fingers are long, smooth, and bejeweled with what I think are mood rings but will soon be identified as "sensitivity crystals."

He's wearing a black tunic with flowy sleeves. His skin is the color of caramel, his eyes a deep velvet brown. Long lashes, thick brows, wavy hair, full lips, and a wide jaw. Handsome? Yes, and yet his finest feature can't be seen. Words aren't spoken so much as poured. They spill out— smooth, rich, and melted. Like warm butter. Or chocolate.

"Look, dear, I know it's been a long day for you," Byron soothes, "so I'll get right to the point. I know Chic doesn't look like much yet. We don't have many girls. I'm sure you're wondering why you're here."

Exactly.

"If I may, I'd like to give you some reasons. I was a model for ten years, mostly here and in Milan. After that, I was a booker at Elite— first the men's division and then the women's. Say what you will about that place, John Casablancas really revolutionized this business. Before him, agencies were nothing more than finishing schools, and you models were nothing more than pretty girls earning pocket change. Now you're contracted professionals making serious money. And I get that— I get that difference. I get how to maximize your value, to really sell you. It's in my bones."

I've just read the profile of John Casablancas in *New York* magazine, forwarded to Mom by some helpful co-worker from the women's shelter. In it, the forty-five-year-old agent defended his marriage-busting relationship with sixteen-year-old Stephanie Seymour by saying things like "I fed on her" and "She opened up new doors." "If you even meet that man, you're going to community college," Mom warned me.

I lean forward. Byron purrs on. "At the same time, I'll never forget what it was like to be a model, to go on casting after casting and have people study every page of your book and scrutinize every pore while you're standing there wondering if it's all gonna pay off. I remember how even when it does pay off, the fears don't vanish; they're just replaced. You start wondering whether you're being managed and marketed properly, whether you're making the most money you can in the short time you have to make it.

"That's why I approach my models the way a coach approaches a professional athlete. Not a sports agent, mind you: a coach; because you and I, Emily, we're on the same team—at least I hope we are . . ." Byron's fingers press into the table. He stares steadily into my eyes. "Emily Woods, I don't need to look at one photograph to tell you that I want to represent you; I feel it in my gut. And I promise you, if you give me the opportunity to be your agent, I'm going to devote all my time and energy to advancing your career. I'm going to be your partner every step of the way, from redoing your book to getting you your first contract. It's the only way to do it—the only way we can both win." He smiles serenely, presses his palms together, and bows his head. "So how does that sound? Are we on the same wavelength?"

I blink several times and sit up in my chair. The fact that Byron's swami act is more than a tad annoying suggests we're not, not entirely. Still, the man *sounds* relatively sane; in fact, he sounds fantastic. For the first time since we landed, I grin. I like what Byron's offering. I like Byron.

When Byron looks through my portfolio a few minutes later, it's with the air of collaboration. When he asks me about school, I can tell he really cares. "I have a mixer tonight," I say chattily.

"Well, I'd love to take you two to dinner before."

"No, the mixer's early. In fact . . ."

As I rifle though my backpack to locate the lone slip of paper in a sea of crap, items spill onto the table: Filofax, 35 mm camera, a coaster from the new Hard Rock in Chicago, Evian, a sunglasses case . . . "Hey, these are nice," Byron says, opening the last and lifting out the frames.

I can't resist. "Layla Roddis gave them to me."

The glasses clatter against the table.

Oh shit.

Byron leaps up and jabs a reproving finger toward Louis. "Don't tell me you took her to see Marc Gold!" he shrieks.

"She needed representation on the West Coast, Byron, nothing personal," Louis says smoothly, though my eyes detect a slight flush creeping neckward.

I'm not the only one.

"Bullshit!" Byron shifts his weight. The crystal rocks back and forth, back and forth. "Don't even *try* telling me her little visit there was for the LA market: there is no LA market—THIS IS THE FASHION INDUSTRY! What the fuck did you send her to that oversexed, over-coked hetero mongrel for?"

Well, when he puts it that way, I want to know, too.

"Now calm down!" Louis says, to both of us.

"No, *you* calm down! I can't believe this! I've been calling you about Emily for months—"

For *months*?

"—and you fuck me over, you . . . you *whore*!"

"Don't you call me a whore!" Louis shrieks, now rising to his feet as well. "You're just pissed that that *'oversexed, overcoked hetero mongrel'* represents Layla and you don't. You lost her to him . . . GET OVER IT!"

Uh-oh. Two sets of hands hit two sets of hips.

"Er, let's not resort to name-calling, guys. We don't want things to get out of hand, now do we?" I say, apparently under some delusion I'm chaperoning recess.

Two sets of eyes turn to me.

"The important thing is I'm here now . . ."

Actually, the important thing is they're about to get into a catfight.

"And for whatever it's worth, I really didn't click with Marc, I found him . . ." *What? What?* "Gross," I finish, the dumping motion I make with my hand casting aside not only Marc but all men who have the audacity to be heterosexual.

Byron bites his lip and stares sullenly at his sensitivity crystals, which are now glowing a rusty orange.

". . . And, um, I'm on the East Coast, so really I want someone here anyway.

". . . And I *love* New York!" I know this statement can't fail.

Nothing. Seconds tick by. I'm about to back out of the room slowly when, in a low voice simmering with fury, Byron says, "You know the real reason has nothing to do with Layla and everything to do with your *take*."

"That's not true!" Louis cries.

"It *is* true," Byron says. "And Louis, you're getting five."

"Seven!"

"Five."

"Se—"

I shove my hands out. "STOP!" I screech, then "Byron? Excuse us a second." Locking my fingers around Louis's forearm, I pull him across the room until we're flush against the double-height windows. "What the *hell* is going on here? Five what?"

Louis presses his palm and forehead flat against the pane, body language that the pedestrians six stories down might interpret as *Look out: I'm jumping.* "It's seven, not five," he sniffs.

"Seven *what?*"

"The mother agent fee. I get 7 percent of agency earnings, not five. Byron's just a cheap bastard!" Louis clutches my hand. "Come on, Em, let's go. I never should have brought you here to this—this *asshole!*" he says, glowering over at Byron, who, far from being equally ruffled, is in the process of fielding a call at the booking table.

Hang on. "Louis, you've been negotiating your take?"

"Of course," he says.

Of course. No wonder he gave up Door County. I'm such an idiot. "What about *my* take?"

Louis sniffs once more, then, his grooming instincts resurfacing, starts removing shed hairs off my collar. "I told you already: That's a done deal. Nonnegotiable. It's 80 percent of the day rate."

Nonnegotiable. Right. Just like his finder's fee. I replay the events of the day given this new information. It affected what—who we saw? The order we saw them? How long we stayed?

How long we stayed.

"Louis, who else is giving you seven?"

Louis resumes his forehead press against the window. I squeeze his shoulder.

"Come on, Louis, tell me. Marc Gold and who else?"

"No one. Well, Francine said she would but . . ." he pulls back. "You know what? I don't think Chic is the right agency for you after all. Let's get out of here. We'll get our bags. Check in. We'll spend tomorrow at Ford, Elite—wherever else we decide."

Elite. And risk being maimed by my mother. Besides, boutique agencies are less mainstream, more exclusive, and have a superior model/booker ratio, making them more suitable for a full-time college student . . . at least that's what Louis told me. Then again, the man also told me that coming here was "the least he could do," so who knows what the truth is? I can't trust him. He lies! "You shit!" I holler.

Louis gasps. "Cookie!"

I duck his outstretched hand and start furiously circling the seating area, my jaw clenched, my fists balled. In this business, everyone's working an angle. EVERYONE! Isn't that what Laura told me? Ayana, too? I learned this lesson once, though obviously not well enough. I don't need to learn it again! I'm going to be steely and tough. I'M GOING TO BE A BITCH!

Yes, I am. Suddenly, I know what to do. I stop in my tracks. My hand grips the folding chair. I smile. "You're right, Louis, let's go."

Louis looks like he's been pardoned by the governor. "Oh good!" he exclaims, underscoring this with a little leap. "I need a drink and a shower in that order. Then dinner, French maybe. There's this great place on Prince Stre—"

"Oh!" My hand flies to my chest as I attempt a lighthearted chuckle: *silly Louis*. "I'm not going *with* you!"

The smile fades. "You're not? Why not?"

"Well, for one thing I have this . . ." I pick up the invitation and hand it over. Louis smooths it against the glass.

Feeling Overwhelmed?
Carman Hall Frosh: Cut Columbia Down to Size at our **Meet 'n' Greet**
Just Before the Inaugural Bash 5–7 P.M., VAN AM Courtyard

"And, oh dear—" In a move taken straight from my Milwaukee modeling days, I raise my wrist and study my watch face "—would you just look at the time? It's five already and I'm blocks away. Gotta dash!"

I start tossing my things back in my backpack: Filofax, camera . . .

Louis steps toward me. "But you don't even have representation yet!"

Coaster, Evian . . . "Oh, that's okay," I say breezily. "I'll get it later!"

"L-later?"

"Later." I deposit my glasses in their case, and close it with a resounding snap. "After all, what's the rush? I live here now, and thanks to you, I have a list of all the great agencies, so I'll know just where to go." I close up my backpack, slide my arms through the straps, then do a little shimmy to center it.

"But—"

"Bye Louis!" I give him a double kiss, turn away—"Oops!"—turn back. "I'll just take this" and snatch the slip of paper from him. "Have a good flight back!"

"Emily!"

I start walking toward the door. *Step one, two.*

Byron hangs up the phone, then leaps away from the booking table. "Emily! Louis? What's going on? Where is she going?"

"I told you already, I've got that mixer!"

Step three, four five.

"What?" he cries.

"That mixer! At school!" *Six, seven, eight.* "Nice meeting you Byron, I'll be in touch—bye!"

Nine, ten. As I turn to wave, I see that Byron and Louis have migrated to the center of the room and are now standing side by side, eyes bulging, mouths open—in other words, exactly where I want them.

I touch my finger to my cheek. "That is . . . unless Byron would consider 15 percent."

"Fifteen percent? I can't do that!" he yelps. "I'm a start-up!"

"And I'm a college student. I've got tuition to pay."

"But . . ." Byron thrusts an arm toward Louis. "*He* wants seven!"

I shrug—"Well, then, we're at an impasse!"—and do another one-eighty. *Eleven, twelve, thirteen.* "See you around, I guess, Byron. Good luck getting started!" I'm at the door now. I turn the knob and swing it open. A blast of unconditioned air hits me.

"Eighteen!" Byron calls.

I close my eyes and take a deep breath. "Nope, fifteen! B'bye!" The door closes behind me. I leap forward, press the elevator button, and start humming Hall and Oates. *She's a bitch, girl . . .*

The elevator clanks as it speeds up the shaft.

. . . And she's going too far . . .

And nothing.

Oh God. Too far? I went too far. The clanging gets louder. A green light flicks on. The elevator shudders and is still. Slowly, the door groans open. A bike messenger stands in the tiny space, his earphones emitting a tinny beat.

He raises one earphone. "You in?"

"Um . . ."

"Um yes or um no?"

I went too far. The door starts to close. I stick out my foot. It flies back open. I step inside. "Shit!" I cry. My fist pounds the wall. "Shit, shit, shit!"

"Down girl."

The headphone settles on his ear. I hear Tracy Chapman and then—right as I'm reaching for the door close button and trying to ignore the constricting sensation deep in my throat—Byron. "Fifteen percent, renegotiable after one year and that's my final offer!"

Yes! I smile and pump my fist. The bike messenger extends his palm. I high-five him and step off the elevator.

"Okay," I say coolly. "Tell me where to sign."

Chapter 8

Hello, My Name Is Bimbo

I race out of the agency entrance and leap into the air. I did it! I got representation in New York City, the toughest modeling market in the world!

At least, that's what Louis told me. Again I feel a stab of betrayal, or maybe it's the pang of recognition of my own stupidity. It never occurred to me that Louis was getting paid to deliver me. How dumb was that? What, did I think he was some kind of fashion fairy bestowing telegenic girls on deserving agents? But I showed him, didn't I? I got the agent that I wanted for the rock bottom rate of 15 percent!

I must be giddy to distraction because I get pinged from—whoops!—a man with a short sleeve oxford and bulging briefcase to—pardon!—a guy nursing a dachshund from a water bottle to—sorry!—two girls carting an easel.

But enough of this. I'm late for school.

I march to the end of the block, the intersection of Eighteenth Street and Sixth Avenue. When I spot a cab speeding steadily up the street with its sign lit—the indication of availability, I learned from Louis—I raise my hand.

Zoommm.

O-kayy. Good thing there's another one coming straight up the middle.

Zoommm.

"Tax-eeee!"

Dashing nimbly between a garbage can and a green delivery van, a woman manages, despite two bags of groceries, a purse, a child's yellow backpack, and a child, to flick her wrist northward. A cab on the far right cuts diagonally across two lanes of traffic and comes squealing to a halt inches from her navy pump. She whips open the door and speeds off.

Hmm, okay, louder and closer. I follow her lead and step right onto the street. *Oh my.* Cars are right next to me. I raise my arm, stretch out my fingers, and issue my first Manhattan battle cry.

"Tax-eekkkkk!!!"

Something hits my ass so hard that I careen forward until— splat!—I'm halfway up the hood of the green delivery van, my palm and cheek pressed flat against its surface like a very large, very unhappy hood ornament. And someone is yelling at me.

"Very bad you! You very bad!"

Ummph. I swivel my head and find myself nose to nose with an angry Chinese man.

"You step in front of me. I hit you!" he yells, not bothering to adjust the volume for proximity. "You very bad!"

"Sorry . . . I'm sorry," I stammer. Where did he come from? How could I not have seen him? I uncurl my palms and attempt to push myself up but I can't move; whatever hit me is still there. I drop my chin only to discover a bicycle tire and heap of twisted metal between my legs. Steaming chunks of food are splattered all over the street. Something brown and goopy trails down my thigh.

"Very bad," the man says again.

"Christ Almighty! What did you think you were doing?" a woman screeches.

Everyone's concern is touching. Really. I slide down the front of the van, careful to avoid the bike, the puddles of food, and hoist myself around. Pedestrians have stopped to observe the scene, including a frizzy-haired woman, her gift-with-purchase tote bag swinging wildly from her shoulder—the screecher, who I now realize is screeching at the man. "You were going the wrong way! And now this girl is covered in General Tso's Chicken!"

Chicken? How can she tell it's chicken? And who, exactly, is General Zo? It's all so incomprehensible. Finally, the delivery man turns and starts dragging the mangled remains of his bike down the sidewalk. I feel terrible. Maybe he was going the wrong way, but I should have looked.

"Sorry!" I yell out one last time. "I'm really sorry!"

He turns and scowls. "You very bad!"

After this, I have no problem properly hailing a taxi. I slam the door shut. We speed from the curb, the mangled remains of a meal crushed beneath the tires, and cruise north.

I chose Columbia because it had two unbeatable things going for it: It's in the Ivy League and it's in New York City. Actually, this isn't strictly true; as I let it slip in Los Angeles I also applied to Harvard and Brown but didn't get in, making it as much the admission officers' decision as it was mine. The funny thing is, when I got those thin envelopes I didn't care. In fact, it was almost a relief. It was as if they knew up there in New England that it just wasn't the place for me, that it was too cold, too remote, that I was meant for bigger, brighter things.

And now I'm here. Columbia University's class of 1992 numbers just over a thousand. As I step out of the taxi and onto the sidewalk at 116th and Broadway, I feel like they're all around me. Students carrying bookstore bags and slices of pizza. Students unloading milk crates and futons and halogen lamps. Students—

"Excuse me, do you mind moving out of the frame!"

—getting their photos taken, getting hugged, getting teary as their parents wave good-bye. Students wearing shirts emblazoned with everything from Greenpeace to Polo ponies paired with either cutoffs or chinos.

Oh shit.

I sneak a glance into the window of a partially unloaded Oldsmobile

Cutlass to confirm the bad news. My hair is Studio 54–ready, only a tad limper than it was at 6:00 A.M. this morning, thanks to considerable teasing and a quarter can of hair spray. The large navy and rhinestone hoops that were such a hit with Pupa hours earlier are still in place, as is most of my makeup, including the lip liner and smear of gloss that make my lips look full and puffy. My white linen blazer is off, thanks to the brownish smears all over the front of it, and I'm clad in the striped strapless minidress. It reaches the top of my thighs. And then there are the blue boots with the stacked heels.

Barbie's Evil Twin does the Ivies.

Shit. My heart starts racing. My stomach knots. I'm a freak all over again. Not Cheese Curd but cheesy. What was I thinking? Fuck punctuality—I was going to be late anyway! Why didn't I just swing by the Royalton and pick up my duffel bag? Why? *Why?*

Shit. Shit. Shit. I turn toward campus just in time to see a girl in frayed denim shorts and a Dukakis '88 T-shirt tape a flyer announcing the Democratic candidate's New York City visit to an already blanketed lamppost. Is it my imagination, or does she glance at my legs and smirk?

She smirked. Definitely. I glance at my watch. The Meet and Greet started forty-five minutes ago and is only scheduled to last two hours, which means that traveling fifty blocks downtown and back up would be . . . pointless.

A guy in a Bart Simpson T-shirt glances at my legs. A girl in tie-dye eyes my blue boots. My heart rate continues to climb. *Okay calm down, Emily. Calm down. This is not a crisis, just an outfit.* I'll just check in and go straight to my room. I shipped some stuff. Maybe those boxes have arrived . . . or my roommate is here . . . or I can borrow a sweatshirt from someone on my floor. It'll be fine. Really.

I skulk under the banner, follow the arrows to the big white tent, and get in line for incoming freshmen, last name M–Z. Five minutes later and I'm in front of "Kath," who's sitting next to several stacks of paper and a plastic file case.

"Hi, I'm—"

Kath puts a finger to her lips and gestures through the tent flaps, only I can't see beyond the wall of people standing or hear anything other than the occasional twang of a microphone—grating even here—and some guy saying, "Okay, what room do we have next?" in an extraperky master-of-ceremonies baritone.

"Last name?" Kath stage-whispers. Her T-shirt says Sherwood High Honor Student in fuzzy white letters.

"Woods. Emily Woods."

Kath's hand shoots up: I'm overwhelming her. "One-oh-one-fiveB," she murmurs finally, her Bic pen running over my last name several times with practiced precision before her chair slides toward the file case.

"Thank you Kelly from Poughkeepsie!"

People are clapping. I crane my neck.

"That's strange," Kath mutters.

My head snaps back. "What's wrong?"

"The key is missing," Kath says.

"The *key*?"

"Ssh!" The manila folder marked 1015 is already upside down. Kath gives it a firm shake. Nada. "Let's see," she murmurs, eyeing the front. "1015A Serena Bechemel, *check;* 1015B Mohini Singh, *check.* Hmmm . . . Maybe there were only three keys? Maybe I gave yours to one of them by mistake? I'm not sure. Well," she finishes brightly. "Get a roommate to let you in tonight. Tomorrow just show your student ID and they'll give you a copy at the security desk."

Oh no. No, no . . . "Kath, I really need to go to my room now," I say in a voice that is decidedly not a whisper. "It's vital."

"And we'll get you there. The student intros are almost over . . ."

"*When?*"

I lean forward, Kath leans back. "Here. Donna can help you." Her palms flatten against the table. "*Psst!* Donna! *Don*na! This is Emily Woods, 1015B."

A girl standing at the periphery of the tent cups her ear. *What?*

"This is Emily Woods."

What?

I walk over to Donna and give her the information myself. She slowly scans her list. We're outside the tent now; I can finally see the action. At least two hundred students are gathered around a small courtyard, their attention fixed on the man behind the mike on the steps of Carman

Hall. "C'mon guys, give it up for the awesome foursome of 418—Brad, Juan, Aniruddha, and Randy!" he croons. There's a smattering of applause.

"Isn't Jed good? He DJs our radio station," Donna whispers admiringly. "Oh, 1015? Oh bummer! Your room went already," she continues.

"Bummer," I say. Thank the lord. "Listen, I really want to get to my room."

Donna flips to a blank sheet of name tags and writes EMILY W. in extralarge letters. "Grab a seat," she urges, slapping it on my lapel. "You can go in a minute."

"Really?"

"I promise."

I nearly hug her.

"Sit right there and I'll tell you when." I follow Donna's pointing finger to the vacant spot on the lawn. It's not in the back . . . still, it's a seat. I creep toward it, sliding past students, every single one of them in cotton and denim and eyeing me suspiciously. Sinking to the ground, I breathe a sigh of relief. I'm just being paranoid. Everything is going to be just fine.

Applause. "Okay thanks, Aniruddha!" Jed says. "Okay, people! You made it through the *meet,* now it's time for the *greet.* We've got subs, soda, Columbia's own Killer Bee Gees behind the mike, and don't tell Mom but Sigma Nu has sponsored a keg—"

"Wait!" Donna extends her arm. The clipboard rises in the air like a flag. "There's one more!"

No.

Jed holds up his hands. "Hold on, folks, we've got one more."

The crowd groans then starts chanting. "Keg! Keg! Keg! Ke—"

"Emily Woods!" Donna yells. "1015!"

No. This isn't happening.

"Keg! Keg! Keg! Ke—"

"Come on, keep it down! Emily Woods, where are you, you little latecomer you?"

"Right here!" Donna shouts.

You know how in movies everything gets blurry and slow and all you hear is a rushing sound and a few mangled words that sound like they've been spoken by Jabba the Hut? Unfortunately that doesn't happen. Everything is crystal clear. Every one of Jed's stupid comments, all two hundred people staring my way, resenting me instantly, urging me to hurry up so they can get plowed. Donna bending down to help me stand.

As Donna's fingers encircle my wrist and pull, I stumble over the strap of the backpack. As I keel forward, I can feel my minidress riding up in back. I tug it down. Maybe no one saw.

"—Hey, it's Tuesday!"

"—Why, she's ass backwards!"

Oh God. Oh God. I feel my cheeks turn scarlet. I tug down my hem again. I got dressed a lifetime ago it seems. What have I got on down there? The day-of-the-week panties Christina got me as a joke, I think. Is that right?

"TGIF!" someone screams.

Yup.

"Fri-day! Fri-day! Fri-day! . . . "

Just let me die now.

"Quiet down, people! Get over here, Emily of 1015!" Jed hollers.

My hands are shaking when Jed thrusts the mike into them.

"I'm Emily Woods. I'm from—

"Fri-day! Fri-day! Fri-day! . . . "

"Oklahoma!" a girl with a partially shaved head yells. Several people chuckle and clap.

"—Wisconsin." I step away.

"Whoa there!" Jed yanks me back. "Not so fast, pardner! We need at least one other personal tidbit—what have you been doing this summer?"

I blink and stare out at the sea of faces. Now is probably not a good time to speak of a summer getting my brows plucked, fasting, and standing in stilettos.

"Wo— working in fashion," I finally offer.

"Fashion, well, that explains the boots. Thank you, Emily. Now, everyone, the moment you've all been waiting for . . ."

Everyone makes a mad dash toward the festivities. I stay put. I'm right back where I was before. Class oddball. And I'll never get a second

chance to make a first impression, that much I know for certain. *Perfect.*
I rifle through my backpack, locate my Evian, and guzzle.

"You sure gonna need something stronger than that," a syrupy
voice drawls.

I drop my chin, vaguely aware that my mouth is forming a soft O
but unable to contain my surprise at the sight: a platinum blonde pushing six feet and two hundred pounds. A tangerine silk scarf peeps boldly
from a fuchsia collar, as do her ebony roots. Her pink sandals are encrusted with red, green, and blue crystals. Her makeup application makes
mine look like an outline, and she's wearing enough Giorgio Beverly
Hills to scent the entire 90210 zip code. A *blonde Delta Burke* is how
she'll later describe herself; somehow, it will be an understatement.

"Jordan," she says holding up a minibottle of Wild Turkey. "917B.
One flight down."

"Emily. 1015B," I say.

"So I heard."

I grab the bottle. "I haven't been to my room yet," I say, twisting off
the top. "I'm going right now." *And never leaving.*

"What for?"

I take a long swig, then make a sweeping gesture toward exhibit
A: me.

Jordan snorts. "What, because of little miss punk rocker's comment? Oh please. Anyone who has taken a razor blade to the side of
her head should not be dispensing fashion criticism. *I* think you look
fabulous!"

"Thanks," I say. Anyone who takes her color cues from a Popsicle
box should not be a trusted fashion critic, most likely. Still, it's nice to
have *someone* on my side.

"Besides, you've already flashed everyone," she adds. "What's the
point of changing now?"

My mouth forms that O again. And then I start laughing. So
does she.

"So, 917B huh?"

"Yup. And Emma Lee, don't you forget it," Jordan grins. "'Cause I
just may be the only friend you've got."

☆

ROOM MEETING
SATURDAY 5 P.M.
DON'T BE LATE !!!☺

"Okay guys!" Serena's eyes flick from a yellow notepad to Mohini and then to me for precisely 1.5 seconds apiece. "Glad you could make it."

"It's our room," Mohini points out.

"It's now the end of the first week," Serena continues steadily. "Before too much more time has passed I wanted to touch base regarding our décor. It's getting a bit eclectic."

Earlier discussions revealed that, while both of my roommates were valedictorians, only Serena was class president, too, making her the natural organizer. Now all eyes turn toward her contribution—a pair of gold and pale blue brocade chairs that look like they've been shipped straight from Versailles though in actual fact are from her vacation home in Southampton, Long Island, casualties of her mother's decorator—before sliding over to the room's other contenders: a pair of kelly green beanbags courtesy of Mohini's rec room. My contribution? Zip. I couldn't fit anything on the plane and it was too expensive to ship.

"So, bergères or beanbags," Serena murmurs.

That just about sums things up. Unlike some freshman roomies who roam the campus in tight herds, lacking only matching jerseys to proclaim their team spirit, thus far we three have remained as far apart as the points of a triangle.

Let's start with my roommate in 1015B, Mohini Singh. Mohini's from Cape Canaveral. Her father started working for NASA not long after graduating from Punjabi University at the ripe old age of sixteen. Like father, like daughter. Within hours of her arrival, Mohini's bookshelf was crammed full of lighthearted fare like *Pinch Technology Understood, Thermodynamics Today,* and my personal favorite, *Partial Derivatives Made Simple.*

"Actually they really *are* simple," Mohini assured me after I protested the title, which lay open on her desk because she'd been perusing it until 3:30 in the morning with the aid of a miner's headlamp. "Partial derivatives are simply the derivatives of a function holding one variable constant. They came in handy in N-dimensional Calculus."

Right.

On the other side of the common room, we have Serena Bechemel, or Pixie, as her friends from Groton keep calling—and calling—her, presumably because she is the size and temperament of one, I don't know; I've barely seen her. All she's done all week is whirl into her room, change designer shoes, and whirl out again—well, that and she's from Manhattan.

"So. . . ." Serena tucks a bobbed, raven lock behind her ear in order to facilitate eye contact. "Let's select one or the other, don't you think?"

"I like the beanbags," Mohini says, diving into one for emphasis.

An almost imperceptible ripple snakes across Serena's brow. "You do? That's a pity. The bergères take up less floor space and offer much more lumbar support."

My hand skims the wood. "They are pretty . . ."

"Aren't they? The pattern is lifted from an Aubusson my mother has in the morning room. I was hoping to get that, too, but Alberto—"

There's a thundering rap. Serena collects herself—no doubt it's another high school friend eager to reminisce how much better life was at boarding school—and opens the door.

The voice is gruff. Male. "Is this Emily's room?"

"Um . . ." Behind Serena's puzzled face pop the heads of not one but four guys, all craning to get a look in.

I walk to the door. "I'm Emily."

"Kevin," the lead man says. "How's it going?"

"Fine," I say, though in fact, I'm thoroughly confused: I glance past Kevin to the other three and realize there are more—many more— guys, spilling off the landing and down the staircase.

Kevin extends a meaty paw. "I'm a friend of your brother Tommy's. Met him at football camp this summer. I play DT for Columbia."

"Great," I say cautiously. I still don't follow . . . did he have to bring over the entire defensive line just to make this connection?

"So, Emily," Kevin wedges his foot against the door. "Tommy tells me you model."

Pause. After the Meet 'n' Greet, I zipped my designer duds into garment bags and made pit stops at The Gap and Benetton. I stopped wearing makeup and starting wearing ponytails. When pressed about my "job in fashion," I describe a "roving internship." In short, I've tried to redeem myself as best I can for a girl who's now named after her panties. Modeling, I had convinced myself, would be my dirty little secret.

I was wrong. "Is that right?" Kevin presses.

I nod. It takes Kevin awhile to register the gesture; he's too busy undressing me with his eyes, as if hoping to peel me down to something worthy of the *Sports Illustrated* swimsuit issue.

"Cool," he says at last, then, "Can I see your book?"

My *book?* "I don't have it here," I lie.

"Well, any modeling photos then."

"I don't have any."

"Not even one?"

"Nope."

"Not even a Polaroid?"

"Nope."

"Not even your card?"

My *card?* Jesus. Did Tommy leave anything out? "Nope."

"Well then . . . maybe later?"

I'm sure a great beauty like Jackie O or Grace Kelly would find a way to let the team down gently, flirtatiously, so they would walk away shaking their heads and saying, "That Emily, she's a real class act." At the football games, they, not I, would be the fans, hollering and waving, while I smiled back from a specially reserved seat.

Only I'm not such a beauty. "Maybe not," I say, my punctuation the door hitting its frame at high velocity.

It's Serena who breaks the ensuing silence. "So, you're a model?"

"Does that mean fashion model?" Mohini asks.

I start talking about football, how the only book a team with a forty-four-game losing streak should be focusing on is a playbook, but the more I talk about Columbia's roster and its injured tight end and its weak passing game and all the other stuff Tommy teased me about before I arrived here, the more my roommates want to talk about my career. Finally, I capitulate. "Okay, shoot."

"Do you do print or runway?" Serena asks.

"Both—at least I'd like to. There's not that much runway in the Midwest, so we'll see."

"What do you do with all the clothes?" Mohini asks.

"You don't get to keep the clothing," I say, which, as far as I'm concerned, isn't all that tragic. How many pastel tracksuits does one person need?

Mohini frowns. "So you get nothing?"

Actually the perks are considerable, or so I'm learning: haircuts and highlights at salons like Bumble & Bumble and Frédéric Fekkai for the price of the tip, waived initiation fees and discounted monthly rates at the best health clubs, 10–15 percent discounts at designer boutiques, comped food and drinks at trendy restaurants. "We get a few deals."

"*And* entrance past the velvet rope at just about any club in town," Serena adds with the air of a New Yorker who had witnessed this occurrence long before I came onto the scene.

"Do you have to diet?" Mohini says next, her eyes widening at the mere prospect. Despite going through a bag of Milanos during every late-night study session, my whiz-kid roommate weighs well under one hundred pounds, and that's including her Coke-bottle glasses.

"Unfortunately."

Speaking of food, the consensus is that even discussing decorating our room has been such hard work, we simply have to have some right now. We order pizza. Jordan wanders in and joins us. My roommates fill her in.

"But Em, *we're* not football players," she points out. "Can we see your book?"

"Nope."

"Some poses then?"

"If I'm not sharing the recorded version, I'm sure as hell not sharing the live."

Serena tosses her crust and balls her napkin. "I did some modeling once," she offers. "For a charity event my mother hosted one summer—"

"Lemme guess, Rina: in Southampton," Jordan interjects.

Serena gasps. "Omigod, rude!"

We freeze.

"No one calls me Rina—Serena, either! It's *so* horsey! Call me Pixie, *please*! Anyway, my mother? Well, she hired this runway expert who told us to walk like this . . ."

Our roommate leaps up, nearly upending the pizza box, sashays and twirls. The sight of her determined stare and sucked-in cheeks sends the three of us into hysterics.

"Oh come on! I know I'm short," she says, not getting it, "but I had heels on—really high ones. like *this*—"

Pixie runs into her closet, returning with a pair of heels. Soon, one pair turns into four. The shoes are accompanied by several wigs and sunglasses from Pixie's accessories area ("closet" or "drawer" each being too limiting a term). Jordan gets her bottle of Wild Turkey and her makeup. Mohini puts on her miner's helmet, which we decide she simply has to wear with my white Frederick's of Hollywood jumpsuit stuffed to Dolly Parton dimensions. Everyone starts doing shots. The girls across the hall come over . . . and that's how we end up throwing Carman Hall's first all-night rager.

"This is awesome!" Pixie screams at 10:00 P.M. after a succession of running leaps into the beanbags has resulted in an explosion of white pellets all over the floor and into everyone's drinks.

"Awesome!" Jordan yelps at midnight, pushing aside the curls of her rainbow clown wig as she boogies down with two guys who, in an alleged reaction to the black light they've supplied, have stripped down to their tighty-whities and are bobbing along as best they can to "Red, Red Wine."

"Awesome!" Mohini cries at 4:00 A.M., the headlamp and the jumpsuit now accessorized with a skull and crossbones earring and Pixie's E.F. Mutton stuffed lamb moments before she pukes in the trash can.

I puke, too. We all do. Even so, I have to agree. College is awesome.

Thanks to the football players, my secret's out. So I'm a model, so what? On a campus full of accomplished brainiacs, I don't expect anyone to notice much, and certainly not care, which makes what happens next that much more surprising.

Bouquets of flowers appear on my doorstep with phone numbers attached. Singing groups, flush from the excitement of Rush Week, serenade me in the courtyard, the dining hall, and, on one particularly mortifying evening, the main reading room of Butler Library. Two fraternities call to ask me if I'd participate in rose ceremonies—whatever those are. I decline these invitations, say no to the dates, and flee from the singers, but there's no escape.

Off campus, either.

On Fridays, I don't have classes. I do appointments. One morning in October I'm on a go-see (the same thing as an appointment, so called because you "go" and "see" a prospective client) for *Seventeen* magazine when a guy starts following me. His arms are filled with roses wrapped in newspaper. At a red light he pushes them against my chest.

"Take these," he says. He's somewhere in his late fifties, grizzled and wrinkled, including his suit, which looks like it hasn't been spending its evenings in its closet.

". . . Please."

Everyone is watching. My cheeks feel hot. A thorn presses uncomfortably against my chin. I shift my feet, then open my arms and smile. "Thank you."

Serenades, flowers—so much attention. But then . . . a senior anthropology major calls to interview me about the modeling industry. Minutes into the conversation, her thesis is clear: There are "striking parallels" between the current fashion industry and child labor abuses in nineteenth-century industrial England. When I tell her I disagree and point out what I consider to be rather large differences—I'm an adult, I get paid a lot of money for what I do—she gets irritated, tells me I'm part of the "cycle of abuse," and hangs up. A girl I've never met walks up to me at a party and drunkenly confesses she detests me because her boyfriend finds me attractive. This happens twice.

But back to those appointments. Nowhere I've been before has prepared me for the streets of New York City. I don't mean storied boulevards like Wall Street or Forty-second, I mean the smaller streets, the ones that are less busy, the ones where men say things that no one else can hear.

Sometimes the comments are nice, almost hokey: *"Hey beautiful!"* or *"I must have died and gone to heaven!"* or *"You're giving me a heart attack!"* More often they're commanding: *"Smile!"* or *"Say hello!"* over and over until I react, getting angry— *"Bitch!"*—if I don't. But worst of all are the men who follow me down the street telling me what they'd like to do to me, their voices soft and low, like we're already lovers.

Even that guy with the roses. When I accepted them, he smiled. A couple people clapped. But when the light turned green and I moved to go, he reached out and grabbed the edge of my shirt. "Cunt," he spat as the fabric slipped through his fingers.

Yes, so much attention. Before I got here, I thought I could keep my worlds separate. I'd be Emily Woods, model/student. I pictured myself whizzing like Wonder Woman from glamorous photo shoots to Ivy League lectures and back again, my JanSport a jumbled mix of subway tokens, Filofax pages, composites, and textbooks.

But real life isn't black and white, it's shades of gray, like the Wisconsin winter sky. I'm the Model Student, no hyphen required. I'm the Model Student, whether I like it or not.

Chapter 9

Princess Imaliar

The only place I'm not getting attention is the only place it counts: the studios. No one is interested in my portfolio. No one. "Oh, so you're a beginner," they say. "And from the Midwest, how nice. Come back and see us when you've got more experience, 'kay?"

Test pictures from small markets like Chicago don't cut it in the fashion capital, I've learned. This is a standard-issue problem. So is the solution: Go abroad. Cities like Milan, Sydney, and Paris all have many more fashion magazines per capita, certainly per model, than New York. So a model who signs here often does what Patrick at Factory suggested I do—skip town. One year overseas, maybe two, and a girl has the requisite tear sheets complete with the appropriate backdrops—sipping espresso on a cobbled street, mincing down a wide Parisian boulevard, nuzzling a carefully disheveled beau. The girl then dashes back to New York where she is suddenly regarded as an exotic, international jet-setter, thus kick-starting the third and most lucrative phase of her career. Because you see, New York isn't where you build a book, it's where you show it off.

But I just signed on to spend the next four years at Columbia reading books, not building them. This worries me. Not Byron.

"We have a small window of opportunity," he tells me in late September, his fingers pinching a mere inch of air. "You're still brand-new and everyone loves a new face. More than that, they love thinking they've *discovered* a new face. All we have to do is get them to think Emily Woods is the hottest, newest face in town, create a feeding frenzy, and the book you've got will work just fine."

This sounds great. "And if it doesn't?"

Byron's lips press together. "Positive karma please."

"Sorry."

That was two months ago. And just when I've concluded that my stars are not aligned, it all starts to change, beginning one crisp morning in early November when I walk into Chic.

I close the heavy door. Byron catapults from his seat.

"Emily, name an Indian tribe! All I can think of is Winnebago and that's all wrong!"

"Hmm, let me see . . ." I unzip my jacket, my brain channeling sixth-grade social studies. "Hopi . . . Sioux."

"No and no. Not pretty enough."

Byron spins on his heel and starts pacing. He's wearing a white poet's shirt, which billows when he walks. Between that, his usual jewelry, and the long flowing mane, he looks like the male lead in a Harlequin romance.

"Chippewa?" I offer. "Cherokee?"

"Cherokee," he repeats happily. "Cherokee's good." Justine and Jon nod in concurrence. Byron starts pacing again. "Okay, back to the name."

I drop my things on the couch and walk toward the booking table. The agency has changed considerably since its days as an empty box with collapsible furniture. Steel gray walls rippled with white, as if carved from the finest Carrara marble, surround a suite of dark leather furniture. A series of spotlights with royal blue shades hang overhead, their cords bobbing antically along the ceiling like bouncing balls. Underfoot lies a plush area rug: gray with blue, black and white triangles and squiggles. And, just opposite, is the beginnings of what Byron calls his "trophy wall": four framed prints featuring two of the agency's seven girls, a cover and a campaign apiece.

I roll back a chair and slip in next to Jon. "What's going on?"

"Shh!" Byron shushes me in a decidedly unswamilike way before raising his arms to the ceiling "Princess, Princess . . ." he intones.

"Lotus Blossom!" Justine says.

Byron shakes his head. "Too Thai."

"Tiger Lily!"

"Too martial arts."

"Runningwater!" Jon exclaims. Justine and Byron look at him.

"Well then, how about . . . Fallingwater!"

Byron mulls it over for several strides. "Yes, Fallingwater," he says at last. "I like that! It sounds familiar. It sounds . . . right."

Justine nods.

"The thing is . . ." Suddenly Byron fingers his chin like a worry bead. "The thing is . . . should she even be a princess? Is she princess material?"

With a synchronized swivel straight out of a Broadway chorus line, all three agents turn and stare. At me.

"What?" I say uneasily.

"She needs bronzer," Justine says.

"Bronzer, definitely," Jon echoes.

My eyes dart back and forth and down to the table. Shortly after joining Chic, Byron decided that until I have better photos, I shouldn't waste money on an expensive composite, which typically has one head shot on the front and anywhere from one to four shots on the back, all in color. I agreed—after all, it's the model, not the agency, that pays for these babies and they cost over a dollar a pop. As a result, my cards come from the copy machine, their shoddy quality dressed up by Jon's florid script penned in metallic ink. Today, dozens of the latest version are fanned across the center of the table, only as I study them I realize they're blank beneath the headshot: They're naming me.

Byron's behind me now. His hands run through my hair. "Should we darken this?"

"Hmm, to a soft black?" Justine says.

"Or chocolate brown?" Jon says.

Okay, *enough.* I push Byron's hands away, turn and face the three of them. "What's going on?" I ask, feeling this to be a very brave question; unless I'm a new Disney character, the answer is bound to be disturbing.

Byron beams. "Great news, Emily! You're on hold with Thom Brenner for Franklin Parklyn Sport. It's national. Billboards, print ads, the works."

What? Thom Brenner is a legend, the desert series he did for Donna Karan credited with putting the designer on the map. And now he's working with Franklin Parklyn, the man who's considered the next new thing in American fashion, "the next Calvin," as *Elle* called him and . . . me? "Wow. Great!"

Byron seems to think so. "This is it, Emily!" he bleats. "This is what we've been waiting for."

"It's paying $60,000," Justine adds.

I repeat this number slowly. *Sixty thousand dollars*—that's nearly three years of tuition and living expenses right there. Plus I'll be in magazines and on billboards. Me! On billboards. I'll be famous. I'll be a star.

The hands return.

"So . . . soft black or chocolate brown?"

Giddily, I tip my head back. "Why do we have to dye my hair?"

"They think you're an Indian." Byron says. "Anyway—what color?"

Hang on. "An *Indian*?"

"You know, an American one."

"An American Indian, why would they think that?" I say slowly. "My name is Emily Woods."

"Only half-Indian," Byron amends. "On your mother's side."

"Could she still be a princess if she was only half-Indian?" Justine asks.

I'm still processing the line before. "Wait, Byron . . . you told them I was half-Indian?"

"I'm writing!" Jon calls out.

"Byron?"

Byron strides toward the window. I look over at Jon, his brow furrowed as he folds over a copy of my new composite: a test shot of me smiling in a white sleeveless shirt, my cherry-tipped fingers caressing the brim of a jauntily perched captain's hat. Inches away from its embroidered gold anchor, the word *Fallingwater* emerges in elegant script. When Jon's finished, he pouts. "It just seems plain somehow without the princess part."

"Yes, too plain." Byron gives the skyline a dismissive sweep, as if disgusted by a city littered with Fallingwaters, then turns to face us. "But maybe that's because we don't know the Indian word for 'princess.' Maybe that's it." He looks at me. "Emily, don't you study this sort of thing?"

Sigh. Since I started school, for every useful piece of information I've provided (the French word for lamé, for instance), Byron has identified several areas of astounding ignorance: the history of silk, the number of calories in seven and a half peanuts, the correct genders of the hairdresser Oribé (male) and the makeup artist Bobbi Brown (female). And now Cherokees.

"No, I don't know the word for princess," I tell him.

"Columbia," Byron mutters, making a soft clucking sound at the thought of thousands of dollars going to waste.

"Well, maybe you can just tell them about your royal heritage," Jon insists. "You know, work it into the conversation."

"Good idea!" Byron steps forward. "That works!"

"What royal heritage?" I say. "What conversation? With whom?"

Justine yawns. "Thom, the Franklin Parklyn people, the ad agency— the usual."

Wait, what? "You want me to tell a roomful of people that I'm half-Cherokee?" I can feel my heart rate rising, along with a sense of wonderment that within five minutes I've been whipped into a frappé-like state of apoplexy.

"Sure," Byron shrugs, "why not?"

Why not? *Because . . . because . . . it's wrong,* I think, though I don't say this for fear of sounding too midwestern, a faux pas Byron puts on a par with Lycra bicycle shorts encasing cellulite-rippled thighs. But while I'm composing an alternate response, part of my brain takes Byron's side of the argument. *Well, why not?* Who would know? It's not like I'd have to swear it in writing or anything, and . . . *I'll be famous.*

"Look . . ." Byron presses. "Just tell them about your mother. . . ."

Who certainly has weird traditions.

". . . life on the reservation. . . ."

We have a canoe.

". . . the ways of the Cherokee," Jon adds.

And a loom . . .

"It's like acting," Byron says.

"Yeah, acting!" Jon echoes.

This brings me back. People have accused me of being a lot of things, but never a thespian. I don't even toss off a white lie with aplomb, let alone an elaborate charade. "I don't think this is such a good idea," I say eventually. "I mean, I'll go see them, of course, but maybe it would be better if I was just Emily."

Byron looks crestfallen. "But it's down to you and an Italian!"

"And she looks Indian," Justine adds.

"Maybe if we left the princess stuff out?" Byron says.

"C'mon, how 'bout a quarter? Anyone could be a quarter Chero-kee," Jon presses.

I look around at them: three agents, their brows lifted, their chins cocked, clearly unwilling to let the dream die.

I'm not sure I can, either. "Okay, a quarter Cherokee," I say, "but only if it comes up in conversation."

Byron does a leap step. "It will come up!" Then squeezes my shoul-der. "I'll make sure of it!"

Jon starts writing P . . . r . . . i

"But no princess."

Byron looks at Jon, who crumples the paper. "Deal," he says.

"A Cherokee princess? You've gotta be kidding me," Jordan says as we cross campus.

"Just a Cherokee," I correct. "No princess."

"What do they care? I mean, I thought the whole point of model-ing was to dress you up in funny outfits. If Franklin Parklyn thinks you're right for the part, Franklin Parklyn should be happy with the real you, Cherokee or no Cherokee," she continues loyally.

"I'll be sure to tell Franklin," I reply. I'm trying to keep things light. Inside, however, I feel nauseous, a feeling I've had ever since I sat down in Contemporary Civilizations, Jordan glanced sideways, and gasped, "What happened to your *hair*?" because last night it was dyed a dark sable brown.

I couldn't care less about my hair—it's actually remarkably close to my virgin color—it's what's happening next that's freaking me out. The Franklin Parklyn appointment was delayed twice, Thanksgiving came and went, but now, at 4:00 P.M. today, it's finally going to happen. According to the option, the campaign is now shooting in early January—dates that correspond exactly with my winter break. Talk about karma. I could spend two weeks at a ranch in sunny Mexico shooting an international campaign with a legendary photographer, get paid $60,000, and not miss a minute of class.

I really want this booking.

The wind flares. Jordan joggles like a bird fluffing its down and puffs out her cheeks, which are crimson-striped with fuschia. "Christ, it's cold," she grumbles as we get caught up in the knot of students whirring in and out of Butler Library. "This weather sucks."

Jordan's from Demopolis, Alabama, a place where Jesus is the big man on campus, beauty queens reign supreme, and the hot club is the Rotary. In fact, it was the Rotary Club that gave Jordan her scholarship to Columbia. "Not for your typical reasons," she explained one night, "but to get rid of me"—a claim that, admittedly, seemed far-fetched until I heard the rest. During Jordan's senior year, she hosted a talk show for teens on the local airwaves. Called *Love Bites,* a double entendre meant to encompass both hickeys and "love bites the big one," the show focused on dating and relationships, but "not sex," she was warned. Jordan complied with this edict until one night, one "sl-ooww" night, when she fielded a call from a distressed teen who wanted to know if she should wear rubber gloves when giving hand jobs "like that gal in *Grease.*" The first sentence of Jordan's reply—"As a general rule men don't love the glove"—was enough to get her booted off the airwaves.

Booted far. Now, the self-described southern reject is in northern Manhattan, steeling herself against the cold by wearing a union suit under her mustard yellow coat, fluorescent green gloves, and royal blue scarf—outré clothes befitting a person who moments ago asked our professor if "Thomas Aquinas rhymes with penis."

"Actually, I'm going in here," I say.

Jordan squints up at Butler. "*Now?* Why?"

"I want to research Cherokees."

"You've got to be kidding me."

"Hi guys."

Mohini dodges a bulging backpack and squeezes next to Jordan, who rewards her effort by grabbing her by the shoulders and yelling. "Hini, spill everything you know about Cherokee Indians quick!"

"Cherokees live primarily in Oklahoma. They emigrated West on a difficult journey known as the Trail of Tears and they weave baskets," Mohini says with the unhesitating air of someone used to having her brain picked on a wide variety of subjects.

Jordan smiles triumphantly.

"What's this about?" Mohini asks.

"Emily has to pretend to be an Indian for Franklin Parklyn."

Mohini shoots me the same look she gives whenever I hang up with Louis or Byron: *I don't understand your kind.* "I'm sorry but . . . it's a modeling appointment, correct? Will they quiz you about your ethnic history or something?"

I giggle. "I doubt it."

Jordan links her arms in ours. "Well, come on then, let's eat!"

"Emily? You're up."

At 4:10 I follow a woman named Anne into the heart of Sopher Fitzgerald, the hip new advertising agency near Union Square responsible for 1988's hottest shoe, beer, and car commercials. After a series of twists, turns, and double doors, Anne stops walking, smiles, and says, "Here we are. Ready?"

"Ready," I reply, apparently unconvincingly, since Anne squeezes my arm and says, "You look great."

"Thanks," I say, grateful for the kind words. No sooner did I sign with Chic than I learned the way I'd been dressing for appointments was all wrong. "You look like you're trying too hard—stop trying!" Byron instructed one day at the agency. "Just look good! Casual but good!" Well, I had no idea what that meant, so I just started wearing a lot of black, including right now, only today Pixie insisted on adding a beaded belt on the grounds that "Indians love color."

"Okay, follow me."

Most go-sees are with a photographer or an ad agency or a magazine or a designer's assistant. Even if things go well, you'll be introduced to two or three people at the most. But a campaign appointment is different, and this is clear the moment Anne opens the final set of doors and steps into a small conference room where no fewer than nine people are spread around an oval glass coffee table.

I follow in her footsteps. A giant design board with photos of Indians in war paint, snippets of Navajo rugs, and feathers fills an entire wall. Despite the impressive view of downtown through the floor to ceiling windows, the room feels congested.

Anne clears her throat. "This is Emily Woods, a new model with the new agency Chic. We have her on hold for the Cherokee series."

"Hi!"

"Hello."

Smiles all around, including from Thom, whom I recognize from a recent article in *Bazaar,* thanks to his narrow face and trademark cowboy hat. Though his hands are crossed over his bony chest, he looks amiable enough, like a smiling scarecrow.

"Have a seat."

I sit beside Anne and continue to look around. Next to Anne is a guy wearing a black-and-white-checked sweater—another Sopher Fitzgerald employee, probably, as are the two women next to him. Next to them, a woman and man in earth-toned wools and a woman in black denim—Franklin Parklyn, Franklin Parklyn, and Franklin Parklyn Sport, respectively—then Thom, then a woman in front of the design board with large red spectacles, then a young woman who looks like her assistant, then several empty chairs, then me. The table is strewn with white china coffee cups. In the dead center is the dessert tray, mostly picked over except for several brownie crumbs, two kiwi tartlets, and a chocolate-covered strawberry.

Anne turns toward the Franklin Parklyn trio. "Now one of the exciting things about Emily is that she's part Cherokee."

The room stirs, giving the impression the walls are vibrating. Or maybe that's my pounding heart.

"A Native American!" gushes one Earth Tone.

"That is so amazing!" gushes the other.

Black Denim claps her palm to her chest. "I'm sorry," she breathes. *Sorry?*

". . . on behalf of my European ancestors, I'd like to say I'm sorry," she says. Her eyes are actually watering.

I take a deep breath. *Here goes.* "On behalf of my ancestors I accept."
Black Denim thumps her chest again. "Thank you!" she mouths.
"How did you ever find her?" asks an Earth Tone.
Anne beams at me. "My good fortune."
"What percent Cherokee?" Red Spectacles says.
"A quarter."
"A quarter Native American Indian, oh my!"
"That is just *amazing*!"
"I can sense your *spirit*!"
"On your mother or father's side?" Red Spectacles asks.
I practiced this one on the subway. "My mother's. It was her father,
he was the Cherokee."
"Emily also goes by another name, too," Anne says. If she was smil-
ing before, her grin is positively parental now. "Fallingwater."
"So lovely!"
"So picturesque!"
"I can just see her on the banks of the Colorado River!"
How about a river in Mexico?
"Fallingwater—isn't that a Frank Lloyd Wright house?" Red Spec-
tacles asks.
"Oh, you're right!"
"Oh, that's perfect!"
"Another American icon!"
"Where are you from?" Red Spectacles says. Maybe it's just my
nerves or the glint of downtown in her lenses, but I could swear the
vibe from her is hostile.
"Oklahoma, but we moved to Wisconsin when I was five on ac-
count of my father's work," I reply.
"Wisconsin? Just like Wright!"
"Maybe her ancestors knew him!"
"Maybe her ancestors inspired him! Tell us, Fallingwater," Black
Denim cries. "Is there a familial connection?"
"My mother grew up near Taliesin," I allow.
"So probably!"
"I'm sure of it!"
As Black Denim starts murmuring about how the American Plains
are reflected in the planes of my face, I smile into my hand. Bad liar,

who me? Not only am I Cherokee, but I'm now associated with one of the most famous American architects and everyone's eating it up like it's the last brownie.

Almost everyone.

"Tell us, Fallingwater . . ." Red Spectacles pushes back her chair, then proceeds slowly to the coffee urn resting on the sideboard. "How can you live in Wisconsin if you're ugvwiyu uwetsiati?"

Huh? "I'm sorry?"

Red Spectacles blows delicately on her freshly poured cup of coffee then takes a tiny sip. "Maybe I'm mispronouncing it: u-gv-wi-yu u-wets-iati."

Okay, that was slower, maybe, but just as incomprehensible. My palms prickle, my eyes dart.

Thom is stabbing a knife into a kiwi tartlet. "It's on the board," he says, depositing it onto his plate.

Oh, thank God. My eyes scan the densely packed inspiration board, looking for the words. . . . *the words. Where are the words?* Seconds pass. I feel nine sets of eyes on me. *Wait . . . what's that between the edge of an Ansel Adams landscape and the rooster tailfeathers?*

ᎤᎬᏫᏲ Ꮝ Ꮝ ᎤᎩᏟᏦᎠᏘᎲ Ꮐ

Is that it? What is *that?*

"What the hell is that?" Checked Sweater murmurs.

Anne tips toward his ear and starts whispering. Not softly enough. "I thought that Gwen said it was her name: Princess Fallingwater."

Yes!

"Yes, well, my family and I go back to Oklahoma regularly, but these days the role of a princess is largely ceremonial—mostly weaving baskets and being in parades and that sort of stuff," I say, hopefully with the jaded tone of a girl who has ridden on one float too many.

"Like Princess Di!" Black Denim cries.

"Exactly."

Thom swallows the last of his tartlet, takes a swig of coffee, and says, "Emily, we're shooting this little campaign of ours in January. Does that work for you?"

Is George Bush our next president? "Yup. I mean it's on my chart. I mean I think so," I chirp. Once again, everyone's smiling.

"I hope we can get her!"

"Incredible!"

"It's the least we can do!"

Red Spectacles holds up her hand. "Why isn't your name Mankiller?"

Now it's my turn to laugh. I emit a soft, embarrassed chuckle.

She waits.

"Um, that's a nice compliment. Thank you," I say eventually.

This is batted away. "Actually what I was getting at was: Wouldn't your last name be Mankiller, after Wilma Mankiller, the current Cherokee chief—that is, assuming by 'Princess' you mean you're a descendant of the chief and not Miss Cherokee, the actual Cherokee Nation title for the largely ceremonial role you just described?"

Suddenly, my mind's a blank.

Red Spectacles stirs her coffee. "But silly me, I spoke to Wilma yesterday. She'd never heard of a Princess Fallingwater."

The warm, expectant hum of the room chills to a brittle silence. Nine pairs of eyes circle the table. Make that eight. Red Spectacles continues to bore holes into me.

It's Anne who finally speaks. She swivels her head, her face pinched. "Emily," she says softly. "You *are* Cherokee, correct? Tell us at least that part is true."

Red Spectacles stares at me calmly, expectantly.

". . . Well?"

"Well, no . . . actually . . . I'm just . . . I'm just Emily. Emily Woods."

Thom roars and claps and for a second I think it's all going to be okay.

"So you lied," Anne says.

I look at the desk.

"That's a yes," Red Spectacles says crisply. "Thank you, Emily. You may go."

I don't move at first. I don't think my legs will support me. Anne flips open her binder. The noise is deafening.

My chair wheels whir against the carpet. The seat creaks when I stand. "Bye."

Silence. I close the door as softly as possible behind me.

Chapter 10

Ahh! The White Sand of the Caribbean

Reading Period: the official pause between the end of classes and the beginning of exams. The first time I saw it listed on the academic calendar, I smiled dreamily, imagining students ensconced in leather wing chairs, slowly turning the pages of the great classics in front of a crackling fire while, outside, snow piled silently against the pane glass windows.

Butler Library doesn't have fireplaces, they're a fire hazard. There is snow, *inside*, as all of the windows have been flung open as far as their lead casings will allow—part of the students' fruitless attempt to bring the room temperature down from its usual fetus-friendly levels. As for the wing chairs, they're here, albeit ringed with books, notes, and highlighters as forebodingly as Do Not Disturb tape at a crime scene. Truthfully? Reading is one ugly, crazed cram session.

"Ugghh!" I moan, having just done my fair share, speed-reading over two hundred pages of Spenser's *Faerie Queen*, an exercise that I would equate with getting a bikini wax on a bed of sharpened nails.

Jordan drums her hibiscus-colored talons against her open page.

"I'm tellin' you, darlin'.' You need to rethink your major. We don't read books like that in Econ."

"And I'm tellin' you," I rebut in my best southern twang, "don't even mention that class."

"Economics, economics," she chants like a spell.

"Shh!" someone hisses.

"Oh brother." Jordan lowers her voice to a whisper. "When are you leavin'?"

"Tomorrow morning. *Maybe.*"

Pixie looks up, her highlighter still moving across the page "And going where?"

"The Dominican Republic. *Maybe,*" I emphasize, crossing both sets of fingers; it's bad luck to assume you have a booking before it's confirmed and I certainly don't need any more of that, not after the Franklin Parklyn disaster two weeks ago.

Within seconds of my return from Sopher Fitzgerald, Byron called my room.

"What the hell happened in there?" he cried.

"They figured out I'm not a Cherokee," I replied, my cheeks still flaming from the humiliation.

"I *know* they figured out you aren't a Cherokee!" he snapped. "What I'm asking is *how?*"

When I signed with Byron, I was worried about his swami schtick getting old. This is no longer a concern. I swallowed and gave my agent a detailed account of the meeting.

"That's it? You could have recovered! You could have said that Wilma Mankiller was your aunt or that she got remarried or something!"

"She talked to Wilma," I reminded him.

"Well, something!" Byron insisted.

"Look, Byron, I'm sorry. But I wasn't supposed to be a princess, just a quarter Cherokee, remember?"

Byron exhaled, a gale-force stream shot right into the earpiece. "Emily, dear, there were so many things going on that it just slipped my mind—anyway, the way you handled it made me look bad, it made the agency look bad, and above all else, it made *you* look bad. There were nine people in that room who now think you're a liar and, frankly, that's gonna hurt your reputation."

Now I was beyond humiliated, I was devastated. I'd taken a $60,000 national campaign from a done deal to a career liability in under sixty seconds. "I-I'm sorry," I stammered.

"Don't be sorry, just move on to the next job," Byron continued, his tone suddenly silky. "And I know exactly what that's going to be. . . ."

Pixie's stippling my forearm with emphatic dots of yellow high-lighter. "Omigod, you're going to the Caribbean *tomorrow*?" she gasps. "In the middle of Reading Period?"

"Maybe."

"That's crazy! For what?"

"SSH!" A girl we're beginning to suspect of dwelling in the library raps one of the twelve empty soda cans lined in front of her and glares.

In the lowest voice I can muster, I give my friends the lowdown. The job is editorial for an Italian magazine called *Lei*. Sixteen pages of swimsuits shot by an Australian ex-pat named Teddy MacIntyre.

"Sixteen pages—is that a lot?" Jordan asks.

"It'd go a long way toward filling my book."

Pixie shakes her head. "I don't get it. How can they not know yet? I mean, the plane's leaving tomorrow morning. Don't they need to get you a ticket?"

"They have the ticket and hotel room reserved already, but it's re-served under Model X or some other pseudonym. When they decide on the girl, they'll call back and get the name changed."

"That's crazy!" Pixie cries. "How long's the trip?"

"Three days."

"And when's your first final?"

"Four days."

"That's crazy!"

"I think you covered that, Pixie Stick," Jordan says.

"Stop calling me that!"

"SHH!"

Pixie and Jordan shoot each other looks, their favorite hobby ever since the two of them started hanging out together, an unlikely oc-curence that began in October, when word of Pixie's summer love trian-gle tumbled across Columbia's campus along with the first autumn leaves. As it turns out, in late August, during a spectacularly ill timed ten minutes, Pixie had given Thor (aka the boyfriend of her best friend,

Aleksandra) a blow job in the bathroom of his family's East Hampton estate—an activity she might have seen to completion were it not for the fact that earlier that morning, Aleksandra had downed two espressos and two glasses of fresh squeezed orange juice; she had to pee. The consequences of getting busted were grave, of course: complete ostracism by both the Groton (Pixie) and Andover (Aleksandra, Thor) crowds. Pixie spent hours wailing under her covers—"but Aleks was *sleeping* with her Ecuadorian tennis pro three days a *week,* doesn't that count for *anything?*"—until I insisted that daylight had a lot to recommend it. Jordan, who, despite the occasional bonding moment, had previously found Pixie "a prissy art-obsessed chatterbox," finally found one attribute to admire: "So, she's a slut." Pixie, who'd previously had a problem with Jordan's packaging ("the girl looks like a firework and swears like a drunken sailor"), decided she was in no position to be choosy. And thus, a friendship was formed.

As Jordan returns to Economics and Pixie to Art History, I stare at my stack of books, trying to quell a rising sense of panic. Spenser is out of the way, but I still have Newton, Milton, Machiavelli, and Augustine, plus a long list of French grammar and vocabulary words, a good chunk of which I'll be reviewing for the first time. How did I get so far behind? When? I guess all the modeling appointments—not just on Fridays but between classes—all the beauty treatments, and all the testing I've been doing on weekends ate up more time than I thought.

I pick up Milton, then drop Milton. Somehow, I managed to get a 98 on my English midterm, the highest grade in the class. I'll be fine there. Better if I study the future tense.

Je parlerai
Tu parleras

Who am I fooling? I slink out.

The hallway is empty and silent, a wide swath of linoleum cut by the light of the occasional globe lamp, but as I pass each reading room I see that every seat is taken, every nose is in a book, and, suddenly, the corridor feels congested, the air thick, the globes like the weight of the world—of several worlds—of our future—bearing down on me. *I shouldn't be doing this,* I think. *I shouldn't be going away.* By the time I reach the telephone booth, I'm sure of it, and it causes a reaction I've never had before: *Please God, please make this option come off.*

"Congratulations!" Byron cries. "You booked it!"

If I thought the air felt thick before, it's now pea soup.

"Excellent, Greta! Excellent! Now spread those legs wider!"

I close my book and lean forward. Greta's knees inch through the soft sand.

"Good!" Teddy cries. *Click.* "Even wider!"

Greta's legs continue their course. Her torso sinks down. Her hands press against the top of her lightly tanned thighs. She tosses her head. Thick, golden tendrils flash in the sun . . . and scatter in every direction.

"Hair!" Teddy calls.

Greta's hair is tamed, only to rise with the next gust.

"Okay, work with it!"

Greta twists oceanward. Her hair billows back. Teddy runs to the edge of the surf, his finger glued to the shutter button. She smiles coyly at the camera, her finger teasingly tracing her suit seam.

"Good!" *Click.* "Yes!" Click. "That's it!" *Click. Click.*

When I met Teddy MacIntyre on a go-see, his studio walls were papered with covers of supermodels from the seventies: Gia, Iman, Janice. I was dubious—*Dinosaur!*—but Byron sold me on the love: "Teddy said you were a fresh face, a standout, a knockout, and that he had to work with you at once!"

And that's when I realized: Teddy's star may have fallen considerably—so what? Mine was stuck somewhere around tree level, if it had even risen that high; the photographer could still give me a boost. Besides, as Byron pointed out, the job was sixteen pages of editorial and only a seventy-two-hour time commitment. I could study on the plane.

"Okay, Greta, ramp it up! I want more attitude on these!"

But the only subject I'm cramming thus far is Greta. Blonde, busty, green-eyed Greta. Greta, the girl who's graced the cover of *Sports Illustrated*'s Swimsuit Issue not once but twice ("And God Created Greta," the latest headline crowed). I felt like a gymnast arriving at her first national meet only to discover she was following Mary Lou Retton on the vault. How do you top a ten?

"Film!"

Teddy tosses his camera to Lothar, his second assistant, for a fresh camera back. Greta squints. "It's bright," she tells him.

Teddy shakes his head. "We can't scrim you. Too windy."

She turns to Guiliana, *Lei*'s fashion editor, and on this trip, head stylist as well. "Can I have some sunglasses then?"

"Sorry, we're not using any for this story," she answers.

"A hat?" Greta tries.

"Sorry."

"A—"

"Christ, Greta, just cope!" Teddy snaps.

The girl's not being a prima donna; it really is bright. Bright and gusty. We left our hotel at dawn and took a fishing boat to this deserted cove. It was pleasant at first, but now the sun is in full force and the wind is blasting the powdery white sand into our eyes and mouths.

Teddy puts the viewfinder to his eye. "Let's go."

Greta smiles and tips her head back, a pose I used to think translated into *ooh that suns feels good* but I now see means *ooh my eyes are killing me*. A half-dozen frames in varying states of rhapsody and she segues into two other eye-averting techniques, the first, staring at a random speck on the beach, the second, staring at her suit, another pose I used to think meant one thing—*check out my fantastic body*—but can now rechristen: *oh dark Lycra boobs, you are so much more cornea-friendly than that nasty white sand.*

"Excellent!" *Click. Click.* "Excellent!"

The supermodel's sun maneuvers *are* excellent. Note that they do not include cupping one's hand like a visor and beaming, a pose I struck during my first and so far only time in front of the lens.

"What the hell is that?" Teddy hollered in response. "What is that hand doing?"

Oh. I moved the hand by my side to my hip.

"Not that one!"

Whoops. I moved the other hand to my other hip.

Teddy regarded this pose silently, which under the circumstances I took to be a positive sign until the camera peeled away from his eye. "Emily, this isn't a bodybuilding contest!" he screeched. "You're a model, now MOVE LIKE ONE!"

That's right, Teddy MacIntyre's a prick. Unfortunately, he just might be a prick with a point. To date, I've only done catalog or advertising, and posing for these can be summed up as follows: right foot forward, right hip jutting toward the lens, body angled slightly back and away—never full frontal: too wide!—then a series of smaller, synchronized variations: one hand on hip, one hand touching collar, or the John Robert Powers/Tami Scott/Mack Daddy of all poses: one hand in pocket. A couple of each of these with changing facial expressions—in camera and away, toothy and straight smile—and it's time to switch your stance to the left foot forward, or, if you want to go really crazy, to the move I tried next: a rocking walk step.

"Emily, why are you WALKING IN PLACE when you have A WHOLE STRIP OF BEACH in FRONT of you?"

. . . Like I said, these are all catalog moves. Posing for editorial is something else—what, exactly, I don't know, evidently, which is why I'm studying Greta so carefully.

"Done!" Teddy tosses Lothar his camera before announcing that he, Hugo (his first assistant), and Guiliana are going to check on the wind situation in the adjoining cove. Everyone else (besides Greta this includes Rowena, a Harlem-born, pot-smoking, wisecracking, gum-snapping hairdresser, and Vincent, the makeup artist I worked with at Conrad's) makes a beeline for the Styrofoam cooler under the tarp, where I'm sitting.

I open the cooler. The book I've been reading slides from my lap. "Ooh, what's this?" Ro says, scooping it and a bottle of water in one fell swoop. "Now, *this* sounds juicy!"

Ro's holding *Paradise Lost.* "Trust me, it isn't."

But Ro's already grasped that. "*Whom fli'st thou? Whom thou fli'st—* this is *not* beach reading!" she announces.

"I agree."

"Then what is it doing on the beach?"

"I'm in school."

"Emily goes to Columbia," Vincent explains.

"Columbia? Good lord, you're a genius!" Ro sputters.

I snort. "Right."

Greta, still donning a silver high-cut Claude Montana bikini, slides into a vacant spot on Ro's towel, then lifts the tome from her hands.

Earlier, when I was sifting through my pile of French vocab flashcards "for a class," Greta, who I know from the *SI* article to be a Czech native who speaks four languages and "dabbles" in a fifth—a European's way of saying she speaks a language better than the one you've been struggling with since seventh grade—was polite if not exactly interested. Now, when I'm reading a 281-page, seventeenth-century epic poem for a course at "Columbia," Greta seems impressed—smart, too, I thought earlier, but I don't ask where she's in school; I've never worked with a model who attended college for more than a year.

Ro pats her towel. "C'mon, Miss Genius, step into my salon. You're shooting next."

My face falls.

Ro frowns. "And I'd thought that'd be welcome news."

"No, it is . . . it's just . . . well . . . It's—I don't know what I'm doing!"

If I'd blurted this in the hope it would be refuted, I was wrong. "Don't worry, doll, you'll get better!" Ro says.

"Yeah, hon, it takes time," Vincent says. "Years even."

"I don't have years," I wail. "I have minutes!"

Maybe it's because I'm a budding genius, maybe it's because my disastrous turn in front of the lens makes me the unlikeliest of challengers—whatever the reason, Greta closes my copy of *Paradise Lost,* opens her mouth, and starts talking.

"Okay, Emily, the first thing to remember when you're shooting swimsuits is the client. If it's editorial you're shooting, is it for a male or female audience? Because if it's for women, there'll be a lot less of this"—Greta juts out her ass and wiggles it like all kinds of bunny—"and a lot more of this"—she pushes onto her knees and smiles.

Ro coats her palms with Phyto Plage and runs them through my hair to minimize flyaways. "So, boys sexy, girls sweet," Vincent summarizes.

"But I tried smiling!" I cry. "And Teddy just got mad!"

Greta nods; she expected this. "That's because you also need to keep in mind the country you're working for. This is *Lei,* which technically is Italian *Glamour,* but it really isn't like American *Glamour* at all. Italian magazines are *much* sexier, so much sexier, in fact, that I'd say a women's magazine there is the equivalent of a men's magazine here."

"So I should be sexier."

"Yes," Greta says. "Especially with Teddy. Teddy likes his editorial very hot."

"Particularly lingerie," Ro says.

"Unlike most gay photographers, who like their photos pretty," adds Vincent.

"That's because Teddy's Australian," Greta says.

"I thought it was because he's a sadist," Ro says with a wink.

"Really? I've always imagined him as more of a bottom," Vincent says.

"Bottom of what?"

Everyone turns. I'd like to get to the bottom of this but as I stare back at the three of them, I spot Teddy, Guiliana, and Hugo a hundred yards behind and closing in, so I clamp my jaw shut.

". . . besides, most photographers don't like too many smiles," Greta's offering.

"That's true . . . sometimes," Vincent says.

Ro nods. "It depends."

"But why?"

"Smiles are too hard-sell," Vincent explains.

"Too catalog-y," Greta says.

"Too desperate," Ro adds. "It's why girls never smile on the runway."

As Ro adjusts my part, I scroll through the lessons learned: Keep in mind the publication . . . and the country . . . and the photographer . . . who may or may not like a smile depending on his country of origin and sexual proclivity. *Ninety yards.* "Terrific," I grumble.

Once again, Greta takes pity. "Okay, Emily, you're in a swimsuit. You're on a beach. These are your options," she ticks off. "One: running or walking along the water. The photographer follows you, you follow him—either way, take a few steps and then twist around so he's getting you from all angles. Two: getting on your knees," she continues, ably demonstrating by sinking into the sand. "Photographers like this pose because they get a sliver of sand and sky and ocean in the background—it's a good crop—and you'll like it because it's the starting point for a ton of variations: You can be shot dead-on, or with your back arched and chin up, like I just did. You can sit. You can kneel. And then you can get on all fours—a popular position with the men's magazines."

"Especially gay magazines," Vincent says.

This is ignored. "Plus, from here you can do all the swimsuit strip poses."

Seventy. "Which are?"

"Tugging at the bikini bow . . . or the strap . . . or tucking your fingers into the bottom," Greta says, providing visuals of each and staying with the last. *Tuck* is the right verb; the model's fingers aren't jammed down her suit—that would be porn—they're just hidden to the first knuckle: enough to seem casual, breezy—a dude at a ranch contemplating roping a steer rather than a cover girl inches away from revealing a pube.

"I call that the is-she-or-isn't-she-going-to-take-it-off pose," Vincent says.

"It helps men relive their favorite strip club experience," adds Ro.

"Thus giving them a very happy ending," Vincent finishes.

Now *this* I get. "Eew!"

"Don't think about that while you're shooting," Greta counsels.

Sixty yards. Oh God. Oh God. "Okay, got that. What else?"

"There's the Hot Lava pose," Vincent says.

Greta grins. "Yeah, Hot Lava!"

Fifty-eight . . . "What's the hot lava?"

"It's my nickname for one of *SI*'s most famous poses. Wanna see it?" Greta asks.

Fifty-five . . . fifty-four . . . fifty-three. "Yes! YES! SHOW IT TO ME NOW!"

Vincent pats my arm. "Relax, hon, it's a modeling pose, not a cure for cancer."

"But it's gonna save her ass all the same," Ro quips.

"Okay, you start here . . ." Greta extends until she's flat on the towel, nose to the sky, her hands at her side. "Bend a bit . . ." Her thighs lift off the towel, curving ever-so-slightly for a more flattering profile. "Then—ooh, Hot Lava!" She arches her back, indeed as if allowing a steamy molten trail to pass beneath her lumbar region. I note the pressure points: shoulders, butt, heels. The pose doesn't look very

comfortable; it looks fantastic. "Now, the photographer might be strad-
dling you," she continues breathlessly, "but usually he'll be right where
you are."

Greta turns. Until now she's been going through the poses with all
the excitement of someone getting her calluses filed, but with Hot
Lava, she plays the part. And how. I stare. At her hair: Most blonde
models have trouble keeping it past their shoulders on account of the
twin perils of peroxide and excessive styling, but Greta's is thick, full,
healthy and thus worth way more than its weight in gold, as evidenced
by all the lucrative shampoo ads she books. At her eyes, which are
green, glowy, and frequently peeking from behind thick frames: the
sexy librarian in the matching bra and panties. At her mouth, which
was last featured in "6 Ways to Pack a Pout" in *Mademoiselle*. At her
breasts, which have sprung forth from countless centerfolds. At her
stomach, which used to appear in the Calisthenics section of ladies'
magazines before she got too famous for that. At her legs, which have
sold L'eggs, Around the Clock, and miles and miles of other hosiery. At
her slender hands and narrow feet. At inch after inch after inch of perfection.

Her mouth curves downward. "You okay, babe?"

I swallow. "Yeah . . . fine."

"What *are* you doing?"

What with all the heat radiating off Hot Lava, I forgot all about the
approaching trio. But here's Teddy, his tapping foot and testy expression
indicating that their twenty-minute search for a better climate was not
a particularly productive one.

"Stretching," Greta explains.

I smile. Greta winks.

And Guiliana summons me. I walk over to the makeshift changing
area—a smallish towel rigged to the top of the tarp—and step inside.
Christ. Not again. Teddy may have thought I was perfect for swimsuits,
but like I said, the man peaked in the previous decade. Guiliana, a
product of this one, is decidedly less enamored with me, specifically my
breasts, for at 6:00 A.M., she took one look at them and muttered,
"You'll be keeping me busy today."

I wasn't sure what Guiliana meant until I heard the thwacking wet-
paint sound the duct tape made as it separated from the roll. Then I

balked. "It only hurts when I take it off," she said tetchily. This was a lie. Trust me: There's simply no aspect of having two feet of duct tape attached to your breasts that would qualify as anything but painful.

But it does make them look bigger.

I peel off my shirt, lift my boobs, and mash them together.

"I heard they've come out with silicone," Ro says as Guiliana presses the end of the tape below my shoulder blade.

Vincent chuckles. "Yeah, hon, it's called a boob job."

"No, for *in*side the bra."

The tape wraps around and crosses my fiery red nipples. "Silicone pads—I've seen those," Greta says. "Lots of girls use them. Victoria's Secret *loves* them—uses them on almost every girl. They feel slimy. Girls call them chicken cutlets."

"Gross," I say, making a mental note to buy some.

Teddy lumbers under the tarp. "Jesus, come on, get Emily ready and let's go!"

I wish I could say things go smoothly from here. After all, I've just gotten tips from a master, a master who pointed out I'm in a swimsuit, I'm on the beach, and there are only so many options. But everything I do is wrong, from the moment I get to the "set"—the fifteen-yard section of beach that the assistants have painstakingly combed free of sticks, shells, and seaweed—and start posing. My walk is too much of a stride ("More energy!" Teddy hollers. "You're not walking the plank here!"). When I up the energy by switching to a jog, my pace is either too fast ("Freddy Krueger is not chasing you!") or too slow ("This is not *Sweatin' with the Oldies*!"). When Teddy suggests I lie down, I happily comply. But it turns out, despite the duct tape under my maillot, *Sports Illustrated*'s finest move isn't so fine on me: I'm too flat-chested for Hot Lava. I flail.

Teddy gets mad, then madder, then he blows: "EMILY WOODS YOU HAVE NO IDEA WHAT YOU'RE DOING!"

I'm recovering in my hotel room, when there's a knock on my door.

It's Greta, with a hibiscus in her hair. "What's up?" she asks.

I open the door wide enough to reveal the books and dirty dishes from room service blanketing my bed. Greta takes this as invitation. As she floats past, I'm enveloped by Halston mixed with baby powder. Her hem brushes my leg. Besides the flower, a burst of bright pink, she's wearing a gauzy white strapless dress and a pair of espadrilles in the lace-up style that was all over the runways for the coming spring.

"A few of us are going into town now," she says. "You want to come?"

"Thanks but . . ." I flash my flashcards.

Greta juts her lip. "We're only going for a little while—a half hour, an hour at the most."

"I'd love to, but I have exams starting in *two* days," I say, my voice rising at the mere thought of it. "I *have* to study now."

Greta stands in front of the bed, surveying the chaos. Her hands slide onto her hips. Her lips part, close, and part again.

"What?"

She picks up Machiavelli. "Oh, nothing."

"No, tell me."

The Prince collides into Galileo. "It's just, well . . . *if* you are so smart already, *if* you are a genius, then do you really *need* to study more? What's the point? How can you *get* any smarter?"

I could think of at least fifty ways lodged in the palm of my hand— plus all the books on the bed, plus my class notes, but I'm not sure I do. I'm staring at Greta. Greta, the pinup queen. Greta with the green eyes, eyes that are inches from my own and pleading. Greta, created by God. Who am I to say no?

"Five minutes," I tell her. "I'll meet you in the lobby."

The nightclub is filled with Dominicans, all men, or maybe it just feels that way, for the moment we enter the smoky, mirrored room everything stops and all eyes turn to us, the lust, sweat, and testosterone rising up and rocketing toward us with such force that I step back, my eyes averted, my palms clenched, as if hoping to deflect the blow. Greta, however, remains where she is, steady and erect, her chin up, her eyes forward—the figurehead on a ship, parting the crowd as we make our way across the room to the booth that has magically opened up in the far corner, the best seat in the house.

Hugo orders a round of tequila and beer. He's got calico dyed hair, big biceps, and sparkling white teeth. He's cute. Lothar, with his chin-length brown hair, shark-tooth necklace, and tanned, toned surfer build, is even cuter. And both of them are straight. Not that I'm surprised. The gayer the photographer, it seems—and I'd estimate at least a third of them are—the cuter and straighter his assistants. So where are all the gay assistants, then, with the female photographers? There's only a handful of those (Annie Leibovitz, Sheila Metzner, Deborah Turbeville . . .). With the straight ones, perhaps, or still in the closet, or, *perhaps* perhaps, cutting their teeth in another position, such as clothing stylist (where there's a 50/50 gender split but 99 percent of the men are gay), makeup artist (50/50 gender split, but 95 percent of the men are gay), or hairdresser (again 50/50 gender split, though oddly here, perhaps inspired by Warren Beatty, 50 percent of the men are straight and *quite* good-looking).

Cheers! We do our shots, chasing them down with the Presidentes. Guiliana leans sideways, Hugo slips his arm around her and I realize they're a couple, at least for tonight. The two of them depart to merengue. Lothar dances with either me or Greta, the alternate taking lessons from one of the hordes of willing instructors. A few more Presidentes and Hugo and Guiliana decamp to have sex. Several more turns, another tequila shot, and my head lolls against the back of the booth.

"Let's go," Greta says.

Oh good. Thank God. I pull my bowling ball brain upright.

"—This place is boring! Let's check out the one down the street!"

I groan.

"Ooh, baby!" Greta coos. "Baby!" A term of endearment she's been using since shot number three, possibly because she's forgotten my name. "Don't cry, baby!" She strokes my hair.

"It's late, we have to be up early," I manage. The rest comes out as a jumbled commentary running through my brain: *Paradise Lost* . . . Hotel . . . A half hour? We've been out much longer than a half hour . . . *The Prince* . . . Bed . . . I should have stayed in bed and studied. *Je finirai, tu finiras, il finira* . . . Galileo, Galileo, Galileo . . . .

"C'mon baby!" Greta's tugging me out of the booth.

"Gretanooo!" I whine, as we turn away from the door.

"I have to pee!"

The restroom line presents a great opportunity to snooze against the wall and I waste no time getting started. But then Greta's grabbing my hand and we're moving forward. Together.

"Gretaawha?" I cry though it's clear what; she's peeing.

I haven't peed in the same stall as someone since kindergarten. When Greta's finished and pulling her G-string over an area that's darker than I might have anticipated and heavily waxed, I think about how many *SI* subscribers would kill to be in my shoes right now. Thousands? Tens of thousands? Millions?

"Now you pee," Greta commands. I'm wearing the Frederick's of Hollywood jumpsuit that I threw in my suitcase on a whim and this makes mine a more complicated maneuver but with Greta assisting, I comply. As I'm squatting, my friend's nose is in her purse, her fingers digging.

"What are you looking for, a tampon?" I ask, perhaps a tad nervously; I'm not sure I'm ready for quite this level of intimacy.

It's not a tampon. It's a case of some kind, gold with a fan-shaped sapphire clasp that's now being undone by Greta's long, slim fingers. The lid clicks open, folding back to reveal a mirrored underside. Under that is a powdery white mound.

I blink. "Greta is that *coke*?"

"Shh!" Greta hisses, then, "Don't tell me you've never done it."

"Okay but . . . I've never done it," I say wide-eyed. Before I worked at Conrad's, I never knew of anyone who had even *tried* cocaine.

I've finished peeing and am adjusting the halter when "Eek!" Greta exclaims, squeezing me in a way that I fear will spill the drug, though she's careful to make sure it doesn't. "This is so exciting!"

Yeah, um . . . I stare at the mound. "You do this often?" I ask. I sound surprised and I am. I didn't notice any of the telltale signs. I didn't even have a clue.

"Noo! Just occasionally, recreationally—times like this."

Greta squeezes past me and sits on the toilet. It's a move that makes me fear for the health of her dress, but she doesn't seem to notice or care—she's concentrating on other things, like the miniature spoon now popping from a compartment like the toothpick out of a Swiss Army knife, which she uses to pile the powder; on the gold-edged razor blade she uses for chopping and shaping. And then—but only after those two instruments are carefully returned to their rightful place—on the tiny gold straw, which she extends toward me.

I recoil.

Greta's hand circles my wrist. "Oh, come on. It's so *fun!*"

"It's so *bad*," I retort.

The supermodel laughs, then bends down and puts the straw to the line. One long inhalation and she's arching back and pinching her nose. "Whe—eww!" she gasps. Her eyes close. A smile spreads. Her hands drop the case onto her lap and thrum the walls of the stall. "So good, so good, so good!" she pounds rhythmically.

When Greta's eyes finally flutter open, she looks radiant, ecstatic. "So good," she murmurs. "But nothing like the first time. The first time is . . ." Her hands stir the air, before falling to her lap. *There are no words.* "The best. Just the best. I still think about it."

My voice is a whisper. "You do?"

Greta parts her lips, runs her finger along her tongue, and plunges it into the coke. The white crystals wink against her tanned skin, like she's been dipped in sugar. "Just a taste," she murmurs. She gazes into my eyes. "A tiny taste."

I open my mouth.

Warmth. Rushing. Tingling. Roaring. I'm flying and I can't contain it. I open my mouth for more, Greta feeds me more, and then this stall can't contain it—can't contain me—and we're out of the stall, and Lothar's with us and we're out of the club and rushing through the warm, scented air, passing a bouncer and pushing open the door of another nightclub.

The moment we enter the smoky, mirrored room, everything stops. All eyes turn. Once again, the lust, sweat, and testosterone rise up and rocket toward us. Once again, Greta remains where she is: steady and erect, her chin up, her eyes forward. I do, too: *Bring it on,* I think, *Right here. Right now.* My friend wraps her hand in mine. "Ayyy!" she yells, raising our fists like a lightning rod. "Ayyy!" the men respond.

We dance and visit the bathroom and dance some more until the club closes. Somehow, we make it home. Back at the hotel, we skinny-dip, first in the pool—because that's the first thing we come to—and then in the ocean, where we bodysurf until we hurt, and then back in the pool again where we swim and splash until we're spent and shivering. "Brrr!" Greta hums in one long sonorous note until Lothar breaks into a cabana to procure a stack of fluffy white towels. We dry off and huddle on deck chairs, laughing, hugging, shivering.

And then Lothar's kissing Greta, softly at first, then more insistently until they're both cooing and murmuring and his hand is reaching into her towel. I tighten mine and prepare to go but as my chair creaks, Greta reaches and pulls me in and the three of us are kissing, our tongues intertwining in a way that you can't tell whose is whose and it feels funny and so we laugh, but then we stop laughing because it starts to feel good and then Greta's towel comes off and she's tugging at mine and hands are caressing and stroking and touching and it starts to feel very good.

"Loth?" says a voice. "Lothar?"

". . . Loth?"

"Shit!" Lothar bangs his fist against a chair back. Hugo's on the second-floor balcony, standing in front of their door, mostly undressed, shoes in hand, clearly returning from his night with Guiliana.

"Loth?" He knocks more loudly. He's locked out. "Hey, Loth, you there? . . . Loth?"

Hugo scratches his head. And then he spots us. "Jesus, Lothar, *Jesus!* What the *fuck* are you doing?" he hisses, though I have a feeling Hugo can see exactly what Lothar's doing, and this has something to do with why he's so pissed. "Get the *fuck* up here! It's 5:40! We have to load the equipment right now!"

No way. It's 5:40 in the morning? Not possible. But sure enough, as I race wildly about for my stripped-off clothing—not a simple task, it's strewn everywhere—I notice a thin yellow line pushing along the horizon. 5:40. "I have to be in Ro's room in five minutes!" I gasp.

"And I have to be in Vincent's," groans Greta.

I bury my head in the pile of extra towels, exhausted, suddenly, and regretting everything. *What did I just do? Oh God, I did drugs. Drugs! That was so stupid! What about my exams? What about this editorial? Stupid, stupid—*

Gold flashes in Greta's fingers. "Here, baby, to get us through the day."

This time, I use the straw.

And then I'm wide awake and ready to go. I race back to my room, throw water on my face, change into a fresh set of clothing, and am slipping though the ajar door at three minutes past the allotted time.

"Good morning, Ro!"

Ro yawns and pads to her closet. "I need coffee," she grumbles, shuffling her feet into a waiting pair of orange flip-flops. "A very large, very steaming hot cup of jav—oh well look who's gone and washed her hair."

Oops. When you're on a multiday shoot with a hairstylist, she'll usually ask you not to shampoo after the first morning unless you've worked out, and even then only if you *really* sweat. "Otherwise, we dirty it up with product, you clean it, and we just have to dirty it up again" was how one stylist once put it. "Grease is windproof" was how Ro put it last night. "Sorry," I tell her now. "I forgot."

Ro misses my excuse; she's too busy sniffing the air. "I smell chlorine," she announces. Grabbing a pair of cat's-eye glasses off the bureau, she steps closer. Her dark eyes widen, then blink. "Emily, did you just go *swimming?*" she says disbelievingly.

"Um . . ."

Another step. Ro's in front of me, now sniffing a limp lock of my hair. "Yes, you did. Why didn't you shower? Holy shit, you're as high as a kite!"

Oh God.

"Don't deny it!" Ro grabs my chin roughly. "Your pupils are the size of dimes!"

My racing heart accelerates even further. I'd heard that stylists could always sense if something synthetic was under the skin; the bobbed nose, the puffed-up lips, they just seemed a bit *off.* Evidently the same holds true for the bloodstream.

Ro releases my chin. Her head is shaking. "Emily Woods, don't start doing drugs now, you hear?" she says before marching me off to the shower.

After this, I expected the rest of the day to be a buzz kill. In fact it's the opposite. Thanks to Greta's ministrations, I feel so euphoric that when Teddy criticizes me, I don't get upset, I just get better. Even in the afternoon, when we stop using and the effects of the drug are starting to wane, that works for me, too. The fatigue makes me less spastic, more fluid, my poses more poised. "Good!" Teddy says in a voice scarcely containing his surprise. "Very good!"

It is good. But then the shoot ends, and we're en route to the airport and I'm crashing and that isn't so good. And then we're at the airport and all I want to do is curl into a ball but I can't. I really can't; I have school to think about—my exams. I simply have to study on the plane.

I pull Greta out of the check-in line. "Greta, I need some more."

It takes her a second. "Oh, no baby. I don't have any. Not here, no."

Bitch. She's holding out on me, I just know it. I grip her arm. "Greta, I'll pay you."

"Emily, I don't have it, I'm sorry," she says, shaking free. "If I did, I'd hand it over."

I gulp down two cups of coffee and two Diet Cokes, which I think will be enough to save me. It's not even close. I sink down, down, down, so far down I don't wake up until after touchdown, when the guy sitting in the window seat is climbing over me to exit. *Shit.* I go to my dorm and cram. *Shit. Shit.* I go to the library and cram some more. *Shit. Shit. Shit.* I pull an all-nighter.

It isn't enough. I'm a muddled mess. Una, who's Una—is she good or bad? And King Arthur, what are *you* doing here—don't you belong in question four? And who said this, Raphael or Gabriel? Oh, Gabriel. Gabriel! *Help me,* I think, as my pencil pounds against my blue book. *Help. Help.*

Chapter 11

Plain Cold Busted

Santa's on a domestic tear. At home in Balsam, sprinkled among the usual under-the-tree gifts (handknit wool socks, Birkenstocks in the latest shade of rust) are a pair of crocheted potholders, a yogurt maker, and a trio of unusual flours—amaranth, buckwheat, and spelt—perfect items for dorm living, all of them.

Unfortunately, I give as good as I get. Mom, always a sucker for the handiwork of hill tribe villages of northern Thailand, loves the Hmong pillow I picked up in the American Craft Museum gift shop. Other attempts are less successful. Tommy turns his nose up at a Giants sweatshirt ("*Why,* exactly, would I want to root for a *New York* team?"), Christina genuinely doesn't know what to make of the hat I give her ("Oh boy, a baseball hat covered with buttons!"), never mind that it was featured in *Vogue.* And then there's Dad. Included in his assortment of New York–themed paraphernalia is a T-shirt procured in Times Square proclaiming THIS IS NOT A BALD SPOT: IT'S A SOLAR PANEL FOR A SEX MACHINE. It was meant to be a joke. He actually starts wearing it.

Tommy and I get through these difficult times the way we always have: he by lifting massive amounts of weights, I by hanging out with Christina and then, after she's left for Captiva Island with her parents, complaining about how bored I am—behavior that backfires when Mom starts suggesting riveting ways for me to fill my time such as, "Say, why don't we break out that new spelt flour of yours and test it in this ravioli recipe?" Or "There's a fascinating article on counterculturalism in *The Nation*." Or "The shelter sure could use a hand cleaning out their basement."

"Fine," I say to this last one, mostly because I sense that I'm dangerously close to developing cabin fever.

"Okay, let's get a move on."

We leave immediately. In the car, Mom flicks on NPR. As the reporter with the porn-star-smooth voice talks about the Pan Am crash over Lockerbie, I stare out the window. Picture winter in Wisconsin and you just might imagine bucolic farmland blanketed by a thick layer of snow. That would be because you've never been here. True, it snows occasionally, but usually January is the way it is right now: gray sky, freezing cold, the fields barren and brown except for the occasional ice-coated cornstalk.

Mom lowers the volume. Her voice, when she speaks, is tight. "I noticed you received a letter."

Instantly, my heart rate starts to accelerate. Yes, an envelope—the tissue-thin variety that requires you to tear off the sides, then the top—arrived three days ago. I discovered it on the staircase. Where it remained. The following day, the letter appeared on my bed. I hid it in my nightstand drawer, but in the wee hours of the following morning, I couldn't sleep and so I rashly, stupidly tore it open. It's been in the bottom of my backpack ever since. "What letter?"

"The letter from Columbia."

"Oh. Right. Good news. I got in."

Mom doesn't even crack a smile. "Your grades, I presume."

"Correct."

"How were they?"

"Okay."

"*What* were they?"

"Average."

"Could you be more specific?"

"Mom! What is this, Twenty Questions?" I snap. "I told you they were fine! I don't remember exactly!"

"Then give me a ballpark."

It starts to mist. Mom flicks on her wipers. I eye the road wildly. We're more than five minutes from home now and moving at forty miles per hour; I am trapped.

". . . Emily, an estimate?"

"C's mainly . . . and a D+."

Mom has to swerve to avoid a mailbox. After the car straightens, I notice that her knuckles are white, her jaw muscles pulsing to the beat of her clenching teeth. For a long time there's silence, then, "Just wait until your father hears."

This is a crock and we both know it. My father, a subscriber to *High Times* magazine, is currently wandering around in a T-shirt announcing he's a sex machine. The appropriate motto for him—clichéd but true—would be "Mellow, Dude" if you were talking his language, "Chill Out" if you were talking mine. No, the disciplinarian of the Woodses' household is right here, in faded coveralls and a rapidly unraveling Katharine Hepburn–style bun, evidently content to fill the air with stock phrases as she struggles for something to say. Still, I try to look cowed on the off chance it will evoke pity.

And then I aim higher.

"Mom, the academics at Columbia are *tough*. I'm not sure I was ready for it."

"Then how was it that you got a 98 on your English midterm, the highest grade in the class?"

Fuck.

"In fact, that's the thing that astounds me the most," Mom continues. She's yelling now. "You got a C in the class—"

"A C+."

"—which means you must have gotten a D on your final. You, Emily Woods, getting a D in English; frankly, I never thought I'd see the day!"

A D– actually, though I won't know this until next week, when I collect my final from the cardboard box located outside my professor's office. The grade will be scrawled in red ink on the inside cover of the first blue book, and below it, a note: *You used to be my most promising student. What happened?*

The mist has turned into a steady rain. The wipers swish faster, Mom continues her rant. "Emily, you and I both know this report card has nothing to do with your raw brainpower and everything to do with your modeling."

Oh Jesus. "Mom, that's my *job*!"

"You're eighteen! Your job is to get an education!"

"Modeling's paying for my education!"

"It's also destroying it!" Her hands slam against the steering wheel once. "I mean Jesus, Emily, you got *terrible* grades." And again. "C's? And a *D*? Just *terrible*!"

"A D+," I correct—I need to cling to every plus I got—"In French," I add, because she's bad at languages, too.

Mom's voice is suddenly quiet, so quiet I can hardly hear it above the downpour. "You were doing so well," she says. "Whatever possessed you to go to the Dominican Republic during your study period?"

I freeze.

"I found the stub to a boarding pass on the floor of your room," she explains.

So she does go in my room.

"—I assume you went for a modeling shoot, correct?"

I can feel my mother looking at me but I still can't move. I'm pinned by a thought, irrational, perhaps, but potent just the same. *If she knows about the trip, maybe she knows about all of it. The drugs, too. Maybe she can tell.* This wouldn't be good. My parents believe that dope is a miraculous panacea that can heal the human body in wondrous ways. All other drugs, however, are evil. I'd be skinned alive.

"Emily Woods, don't throw away your life on modeling."

I exhale, relieved. "I won't, Mom, I promise."

When I say this, I'm sure, but I shouldn't be.

Drugs. Even as I thought the word, I felt a tiny prick of excitement. *Cocaine,* my mind had whispered. *I can't wait to try you again.*

Chapter 12

Put Out to Pasture

I exchange one cold climate for another and start my second term. The first Friday I'm back, I enter Chic.

"I'm sorry, did you say Cap D'Antibes or Cap Ferrat?"

"—Yes, of course: five feet, nine inches; I've measured her myself."

"—I need to change the first to a second on the fifteenth and sixteenth. The seventeenth is still a first, and the fourteenth . . . and the thirteenth if you happen to need it, but there is *no way* you can have this big a chunk of time on her, *just no way. Impossible* . . . Unless you confirm her at once."

My head darts around the booking table from Byron to Jon to Justine. *Whoa.* I haven't been inside Chic since before Reading Period. The buzzing phones, the harried bookers—for the first time the place has the vibe and energy of a thriving and happening agency.

"Cap Juluca. Oh. Well, that's much better weather, obviously, and it's a *perfectly* nice place, it's just that . . . well . . . Jade finds the poverty in Anguilla simply *too* depressing!"

Byron catches my eye and smiles. I smile back. He's wearing a brown shirt and matching suede vest the precise color of a Hershey bar and it suits him. I peel my arm out of the strap and spin my backpack to my belly. Inside is his Christmas present—nothing too fancy, just a card and one of those crystal pendants he's so fond of.

"Difficult? Who? . . . Oh, no, Carlyne! Look, darling, all I'm trying to say here is that you have a second option on Jade starting on the twenty-eighth. If you want the opportunity to confirm the time, well, I'd just think about another country, that's all, okay? . . . Okay, bye!"

"Well, hel-lo Emily!"

"Hi!"

As Byron pushes back his chair in preparation for his customary kiss-laden greeting, his phone buzzes. "Byron, Harriet from *Elle*'s on two," Justine informs him, running her hand through hair that's no longer green tipped but solid green, as if she's been held upside down over a bucket of slime.

"Regarding?"

"Jade."

"Ah." Byron digs for the chart he's just refiled.

I frown. "Who's Jade?"

"Jade's eighteen, half-French, half-Vietnamese. Showed up in the couture shows in Paris and every New York agent wanted her—I can't believe I got her!" Byron points. "Over there—well, hel-lo Harriet!"

I turn in search of a half-Asian, slightly pampered, Parisian sensation, but the only non-Chic employee I spot is the delivery guy from the corner deli, so I'm puzzled until my eyes hit the trophy wall, now a dozen photographs strong, including two covers of a girl with short dark hair and almond-shaped eyes.

As I'm studying the photographs, arms slide around my shoulders. Byron noses aside a lock of his hair. "Ten girls, two covers; Chic is really on the map now," he murmurs.

I fall against him. "It's exciting," I exhale. "So busy!"

"Byron, it's Leslie from *Self* on one!" Justine bellows.

"And Jean-Luc from Paris on two!" Jon adds.

I straighten. "Here, Byron, hand me my list and I'll get out of your hair," I tell him. After all, this is why I'm here, to say hello, certainly, but mainly to pick up my list of appointments from Byron. Every Friday he writes out the details for my go-sees with photographers, marketing executives, and editors neatly and sequentially, usually adding extras like a weather report, a miniature map—even a dumb joke or funny sketch. It's our weekly routine.

Byron points at the couch. "Here, Emily, grab a seat."

"Byron, line one!" Justine prompts.

"Hold my calls."

Uh-oh. I perch tentatively on the couch. Byron takes the adjoining chair, and then my hand.

"Look, darling, I spoke to Teddy about the *Lei* booking. He said you were quite stiff—"

"Teddy yells!"

"—Yes, yes, Teddy MacIntyre has a bad temper, but I told you that—anyway, *I'm* not yelling; I have great news! He said you *totally* blossomed under his tutelage and the film turned out *spectacularly!*"

Gasp. "Are you serious?"

"Of course I'm serious. You're getting eight pages—eight *spectacular* pages—I'm so excited and I think we should wait."

I wait for more. It doesn't come. "For . . . ?"

"The pictures. They'll be out in late April, possibly early May."

Justine tries again. "Byron!—"

"Hold. My. Calls!"

A cold chill comes over me. "Wait, Byron, are you saying that I shouldn't work between now and *May,* is that it?"

"April and absolutely not! If a job comes up, you should do it, depending on what it is, naturally. But Emily . . ." Byron leans over the armrest. "There haven't been a lot of jobs so far," he says gently. "Mostly appointments, correct?"

"Yeah but . . ."

"Byron!"

Byron releases my hand just long enough to give Justine a locked-arm block, then clasps it again. "Look, darling, it's up to you. You can either slog through the wet, cold New York winter with a book full of test pictures, or you can take a break and come back in balmy April, refreshed, ready, and with eight *spectacular* tear sheets in your book. Either way, I'm good to go. What's your pleasure?"

I stare at a black triangle in the area rug. If I don't get my grades up this semester, Mom has once again threatened community college, so no appointments sounds appealing—except for one thing.

"So, I guess this means we didn't accomplish our goal," I say quietly.

"Goal?" Byron says.

My fingers pull an inch apart the way Byron's did months ago. "You know, squeeze through the narrow window of opportunity, become the new face with a bad book, I guess it didn't happen."

Byron's on his feet now. He leans over and takes my face in his hands. "Oh, no, Emily, don't say that—I wouldn't! You got the *Lei* booking, didn't you? And, Franklin Parklyn . . . almost? Why, those are just the kind of jobs we were going for!"

I gaze up at him. "Really? They were?"

"Absolutely!"

"Byron!"

"WHAT!"

"It's Carlyne," Justine says. "She wants to know if St. Barth's would work."

"Of course it would! No poverty there! Emily, darling, trust me on this: You're great. I really believe in you; you're going to be a big star. But we need to introduce you the right way: with a bang. Because you never get a second chance to make a first impression. You can never be the new face twice."

I've heard this before. I nod.

Byron extends his hand. "So, until April?"

"Until April."

And then I'm on my feet, too, being kissed good-bye. I don't even think about Byron's present until I'm back on campus. Impulsively, I toss it high into the air. It catches on an oak tree and swings in its branches.

It's there still.

"I found another condom!"

Mohini extends her rake toward the roots of an evergreen bush. "Used?" she grunts.

Jordan pinches the offending item with her thick rubber gloves and wiggles it in the air. A milky white trail oozes out.

"That would be a yes," mutters Pixie.

The shelter-cleaning in Balsam must have triggered latent feelings of guilt, for not long after spring term started I marched into Earl Hall and signed up for "Modifying an Urban Landscape: Columbia Beautifies Our City" (yes, even volunteer work gets a colon on this campus). Mohini, Pixie, and Jordan signed up as well, or rather, I signed them up and cajoled them later with promises of fresh bagels and coffee—the least I could do once we found out our assignment was Tompkins Square Park, a forty-minute, two-subway, several-block commute to the opposite end of Manhattan, which means that on Sunday mornings we have to rise at 8:30 A.M. Which means that my friends now hate me.

And that was *before* we discovered our task. "Beautification" implies restoring some gem, polishing it like a tarnished tea set. But Tompkins Square Park is a dump—literally. For years the location of a homeless encampment nicknamed Tent City, the park was purged last summer at the behest of Mayor Koch. Riots ensued to no avail; Tent City is in ruins and now it's our job to remove the rubble. Since we started six weeks ago we've found Spam, hypodermic needles, safety pins, two dead cats, one live chicken, a box of dirty Band-Aids, a picture of Morgan Fairchild, a Bee Gees album, large bottles of Colt 45, enough soda and beer cans to circle the island, a very crusty diaphragm, and—and these are clearly more recent contributions to the rubble—condoms.

Lots of condoms. "This is the fifth one today," Jordan says, giving the latest addition to the tally an efficient shake before flicking it into her trash bag. "I think we're the only people in New York who didn't get it on last night," she grumbles.

"Speak for yourself," Pixie says.

"Wait, *you* did?" Jordan says. "With who?"

Pixie digs out a can from the base of a scruffy elm tree and holds it aloft. "Look, grape Fanta. That's a new one."

"Nope. Got it last week," I say.

"Oh."

Impatiently, Jordan spanks the earth with her spade. "With *who*?"

"Prowl," Pixie says under her breath.

Jordan's eyes widen. "*Prowl?* What the hell is *Prowl*?"

"Prowl's a lounge," I explain, though *hot spot* might be a more accurate term; with its swanky leopard print banquettes and stylishly framed pictures of big game cats, the new NoHo nightspot has recently replaced Limelight and Palladium as the place to be.

"So you slept with an entire bar. My, you've outdone yourself."

Pixie aims high with her middle finger. "*Bar-ten-der*, Jord. His name's JT."

Mohini sputters and blinks, evidently rejoining our orbit. "JT? Whatever happened to Zach?"

"The ferrets really got to me," Pixie says with a shudder. "And I understand that he was into the whole New Wave thing, but makeup really stains, you know? Anyway, forget Zach, I tossed him back and got another."

Mohini, Jordan, and I exchange glances. Since school started Pixie's been catching and releasing guys with such frequency that Jordan has coined a term for her victims: Pixels. "Clearly, I'm in search of a father figure and I have a tremendous fear of abandonment," Pixie explained one night (like any good New Yorker, Pixie's been in therapy since before she got her nose and teeth straightened). "And my mother's a *total* nut, so I have some passive-aggressive tendencies. Besides, thanks to the whole blow job incident, everyone thinks I'm a slut anyway, so I might as well enjoy the upside."

"Okay, so JT," Jordan prompts.

Shivering, Pixie gestures toward a patch of purple crocuses located several feet away in full sunlight. It's the first week of March, a time when being on the bright side of things makes all the difference. "Nothing to tell, really," she says once we've moved. "He's got brown eyes, blond hair."

"Age?"

"Thirty-three."

"Okay, so he's old," Jordan says. "Celebrity look-alike?"

"Daryl Hall."

"That means cute, yes?" Jordan turns. "Emily, you were there. Cute?"

"Yeah. He's fine. Great."

Jordan eyes me curiously before turning back. "Well, *was* he?"

Sighing, Pixie starts dreamily caressing a flower. She's wearing pigtails and pink pants and if I didn't know better, I'd say she was about to tell us about her latest Barbie and not: "He went downtown immediately." Pause. "Twice."

"Twice?" Jordan starts playing with her hair. "Twice is good."

Mohini flops onto her back, no doubt fantasizing about the astrophysics professor she has a massive crush on in spite of the fact he's forty-five, the father of three, and in possession of a potbelly that would give Winnie the Pooh a run for his honey. My friends all agree that the sign of a great lover is one who gets things going by going down on you—or at least offering to. "It's sort of like a waiter at a good restaurant asking if you'd like anything else," Jordan once explained. "Even if the answer is no, you appreciate the attention."

Not that I would know. To date, I've had nothing but dating disasters. First, there was Luke. Luke was tall and cute and on the crew team. Luke was also a slobberer. In fact, the first and only time we kissed, Luke slobbered so much, he actually licked the drool off my chin. He thought that was cute. Tom was great . . . until I discovered his high school nickname was Tom the Titman, his yearbook peppered with pithy quotes from classmates to the tune of "Never met a *pair* he didn't like!" and "He sure keeps *abreast* of things!!!" Charlie was sweet, so sweet he talked to his mother several times a day. She knew the names of his friends, TAs, and professors. Early one morning I discovered she knew about me, too. *All* about me. "Emily slept over again," Charlie whispered, clamping the receiver to his tousled bedhead. "And it was great, we—" I was out the door before he could scar me for life. So, while I've experienced a slobberer, a titman, and a momma's boy, I have *not* experienced orgasmic ecstasy at the hands of a skilled lothario.

"EMMA. LEE."

Huh? All three of them are staring at me. "What?"

"I asked you—twice—did you meet anyone last night?" Jordan says.

I look at Pixie, then at the dirt. "Not really."

"Not really is not no," Mohini points out.

"Exactly, Hini," Jordan says. "Come on, Emma, spill."

Last night, Jordan had a date and Mohini had study group, so Pixie and I made a plan to hit the clubs, that's clubs with an *s,* only our tour began and ended with Prowl, where Pixie made googly eyes, and JT made us an assortment of jewel-toned cocktails, all on the house. At 1:30 A.M.,

Ike, a friend of JT's possessing unwashed hair and the untarnished ego-
tism of someone who's been overly praised by his mother, showed up,
eager to discuss our next move. "Bed," I said, meaning I was going there,
alone, preferably right then, though even as I said it, I had a sinking feeling it wasn't true; Pixie and JT had just gotten to the hand-stroking phase;
my presence as wing girl would be required for at least another hour.

Ike simply laughed. "Looks like someone could use some perking
up," he said.

I knew exactly what he meant.

I followed Ike into the storage closet. Then I got cold feet. After all,
he wasn't Greta holding a pretty gold case in her pretty slim fingers but
a total stranger with greasy hair, a vial, and a rolled-up twenty—what
was I thinking? "No," I said firmly, "no, Ike. No thank you," only the
words never left my lips; instead, I watched silently as Ike made a little
white trail on the top of an extralarge can of maraschino cherries, my
racing heart eagerly anticipating the rush.

And that's when the door burst open. It was Pixie. "Omigod, what
are you doing?"

"Nothing."

The rolled-up twenty fell to the ground.

Pixie, suddenly as strong as a team of oxen, grabbed me by my belt
buckle and hauled me into the hallway. "Since when do *you* do *coke?*"
she panted.

I pause. The only person I'd told so far had been Christina.
"Coke—you mean cocaine?" Christina had gasped, which I took to be
a bad sign and it was; Christina was horrified. After that I vowed to
keep my little drug experiment to myself. The last thing I needed right
then was a lecture from Pixie; already I'd heard about the Groton friend
who's been in rehab five times, and counting.

Pixie crossed her arms. Her foot tapped the concrete. "Well?"

I pulled up to my full height. "Well, nothing," I said coldly.
"There's nothing to tell."

I say these words to Jordan now. Her response is similar, too. After
gazing at me for a beat, she says, "Fine. Deny it if you want to, Emma,
but there's more to the story, I just know it."

Chapter 13

Häagen Daze

"I got the *Lei*."

Byron has the disconcerting habit of never saying "Hi!," "Hello!," or even "Emily" when he phones, much to the bewilderment of Mohini, who's lifted the receiver to the tune of "Darling, I need you *desperately!*" "What are you wearing *right this second*?" and "*Please,* don't forget your sheer G-string!"

My breath catches. "How does it look?"

"Fabulous, darling," Byron purrs.

There is no qualifier. Fabulous, that's it. *Fabulous!* I start bopping around my room. "What do they look like? Tell me!"

"Let's see . . ." I hear pages rustling. "There's one of you walking on the beach in red. You're looking out to sea and squinting a bit—next time try to open your eyes more, dear—still, it's a good body shot and we can use it. There's another of you in blue leaping in the surf in profile; your ass looks great, so we'll use that, too. There's one of you in black. I'm not crazy about your expression but your boobs look surprisingly big—was it your time of the month? Anyway, that one's a yes.

And then there's one, a double page actually, of you in the surf that's very nice, very *From Here to Eternity* and my favorite shot of you ever!"

A double page spread? I upgrade to more of a leap. "And?"

"And, that's it."

Hang on. "Five? That's all? I thought I was getting eight pictures!"

"Always happens, Em," Byron says breezily. "Especially when you're new; Teddy told me you were a bit stiff in front of the camera, remember? Plus you seem to have worn only maillots and maybe they didn't need so many of those—anyway, Greta got the rest plus the cover, which is just beautiful! Did you see them shoot it? She's in this white bikini that's see-through, sexy, and just *so damn wonderful*! Eileen represents her, that crazy old bag—tell me, is she happy with Ford? Because I could do more for her, I think."

"We didn't discuss it," I say, trying to ignore the stabs of jealousy now piercing my solar plexus.

"Well, if it comes up at another shoot or something, be sure to let me know, I'd be forever grateful—anyway, Emily Woods, you have tear sheets!"

This is true. *Tear sheets. I've finally gotten tear sheets!* I resume my wiggle.

"So what are you waiting for? Get down here!" Byron cries.

"What, *now*?"

"Yes now. Come on! We'll rearrange your book, put in the order for your new cards—get you all set for your castings tomorrow."

Tomorrow. As in the day before finals. I picture my first semester report card . . . and then my mother's face. I'm not dealing with that again, no way, not for a bunch of go-sees. "Byron, I can't right now."

"No problem," he says. "Just come first thing in the morning."

"No, I can't then, either. I've got finals coming up. I need to study."

"Oh. In that case, I'll give you two or three castings: just the really critical ones."

"Byron, I can't."

It's quiet for so long, I'm about to check the line when Byron says, "How long are we talking here?"

"Two weeks."

"Two weeks?"

"Emmuhh!"

The cry is accompanied by a pounding on my door. "Emmuhh!" Then a shove. It's Jordan. "Christ Almighty, Emma, what *are* you doing? We've got to go to the dance *now*!"

Shit.

"Dance?" Byron bleats. "Did I just hear *dance*?"

"Er . . ." I jam my finger to my lips. Nodding, Jordan clamps her hand over her mouth and tiptoes out. It's cool. I'm about to close the door when Pixie bursts from the bathroom.

"Omigod, Emily. Get your *dress* on! And your *shoes*! And your *makeup*! We're supposed to be at the *ball* in *fifteen minutes*!"

I slam my door and press my back against it, the better to hear Byron say, "So you're going to a ball, well how nice for you."

"Tonight, yes," I admit. "But I do have exams."

The voice on the other end could freeze a Jacuzzi. "And I can tell they're a real priority, too. I thought you were excited about being one of the twenty girls that Chic represents, Emily. Evidently I thought wrong. Enjoy the ball, Cinderella." Click.

Perfect. I slide down the door until I'm puddled on the rag rug. Byron's pissed, really pissed. I'm being stupid. I should go on the castings—not all of them, just the critical ones. Two or three, just like he said . . . but when is it ever really two or three? And what if I get the booking, how do I say no then? No, I made the right decision . . . Did I make the right decision?

"Emma Lee, what in the lord's name are you *doing*?"

I open my door to Jordan: all peaches and cream and uncharacteristically coordinated in a taffeta and lace Jessica McClintock, a pearl-studded, princessy number complemented by a curled up-do containing white ribbon and baby's breath. And Pixie: clad in a shiny magenta strapless minidress, a quilted black satin bolero, cherry-red lips, and lace-up stilettos.

"Wow, you guys really went to town," I murmur. *On opposite sides of the planet.*

Jordan pats her hair. "Well, it *is* our spring formal."

"And we've only got ten minutes to get to it!" Pixie barrels past me. "What are you wearing?"

"Oh, I don't know. I hadn't decided."

"What?" Like a crazed squirrel, Pixie starts foraging in the recesses of my closet. Jordan meanwhile, has found my makeup bag and is now handing over various pots, wands, and tubes that I dab, wipe, and draw accordingly.

A muffled gasp ensues. "Omigod, Versace! Dolce! Donna! Ralph! Emily, when did you get all these?" Pixie cries.

I shrug. "Last summer mostly."

"I can't believe it. Most of them still have the price tags, too!"

Jordan drops a brush and runs over. "Let me see!"

The week after I signed with Chic, I made my first trip to Barneys and, boy, was it worth it. The place was fashion nirvana. Everything I had seen in the magazines was hanging before me. Ripe. Beckoning. Right in reach. And smack in the middle of its holiest of sanctuaries, the European Collections, there it was: the navy Azzedine Alaia Layla had tried on in LA.

"Care to try it?" the salesperson asked.

I fingered the price tag. "Oh no, I couldn't."

Oh, but I could. "You paid $1,200 for a *dress*?" Jordan screeches.

"It was on sale."

She doesn't seem to hear this. "$1,200 and you've never even worn it."

Pixie pulls it off the hanger. "Well, you're wearing it now."

"Really? You don't think it's too va voom?"

"Trust me: You could use some va voom," Jordan says with some heat on it. This semester, my friend's been dismayed with the "tragic decline" of my wardrobe to the point where lately she's been issuing comments like "Whoever told you sweatpants were a wardrobe staple should be shot," and, "There's this really cool invention you should try called a hairbrush." The thing is, Jordan's wrong. The more sweats and baseball hats in my wardrobe, the more I fit in. "I had *completely* the wrong idea about you—*completely*," a girl in Art Humanities told me one day after class, her head bobbing approvingly at my untied sneakers, untucked button-down, and stained Columbia sweatpants. "You're so . . . real."

Now, I tug the designer dress over my head. Alaia rarely uses zippers or buttons, instead relying on lots of Lycra and expert tailoring to get that fit-like-a-glove look, only—"Ugh!"—I'm stuck.

"Wait!" Several firm tugs and Pixie says, "There."

"Taa daa!" I twirl and wait for the rave review.

And wait.

"Wow, that certainly is form-fitting," Jordan says finally, "isn't it, Pix?"

"Certainly is," Pixie says.

"Oh God, seriously?" I jump up and down to get a peek in the mirror above my bureau, the longest one we have. "It looks *bad*?"

"No, no, good!" Pixie says hastily. "It's just that, omigod, you're right, it's very va voom."

"Too va voom," Jordan says.

"Considering it's for a school dance," Pixie finishes.

"Oh . . . okay," I say, preparing to take it off. After all, I don't want to be "Friday" again. Besides, all that jumping and my body's pounding like I'm wearing a tourniquet. I don't remember it feeling this tight in the try-on room, then again, I remember helping Layla with hers. Guess I've forgotten what high fashion feels like.

Getting out of the Alaia is a three-person job. "I'm screwed!" I wail as my friends stand huffing against the bureau, their cheeks pink, and I've gone through my closet, "I don't have as many dresses as I thought." Fortunately, Pixie does, including a variety in sizes larger than her usual two. "For fashion emergencies," she explains, "and I'd say we're having one now."

I dress, we dash—down the steps and into the night.

Six days, five exams, and one plane ride later, I'm worried that I'll never know what high fashion feels like again.

I'm standing in my parents' bathroom, watching as the metal weight glides across the doctor's scale with the unhampered ease of a speed skater. Last time I stood here, the skater clocked in at 120. Today, he's past that and then some and showing no signs of tiring.

125. I step back off and remove my Tag Heuer, another fall purchase and heavy—why, it's gotta be sixteen ounces at *least*. As I deposit it on the counter, I extend a tentative hand toward my reflection. Yes, I look a bit wider, but surely I'm just puffier? After all, I just got off a plane yesterday, and I'm sure a long, practically transatlantic flight like the one from New York is enough to add several pounds of bloat. Right?

Right. I step back on.

126.

127.

128. Time to remove the panties. I shimmy them off. I'm about to step back on when I breathe a sigh of relief: Of course! Mom and Dad, Luddites that they are, don't have a clue how to work a can opener, let alone calibrate a . . .

Oh.

129.

129.25

129.50

129.75 Okay, wait, I've figured out what's going on. And it isn't funny. There's something seriously wrong with me. Something medical. I have a thyroid problem or a tumor or—I have a cyst. Yes, that's it. I have a cyst the size of a grapefruit, the kind with hair and teeth growing inside it. And teeth are heavy, obviously, so *obviously* my cyst weighs ten pounds, maybe even fifteen, which means I've actually *lost* weight, and all they'll have to do is cut me open, scoop it out, and presto! I'll be as good as new.

. . . Except I'll have a scar and that means no more bathing suit or lingerie shots, which means less money.

130.

130.25

130.5 No, it isn't a cyst, it's my thyroid. I have a thyroid problem. It's sluggish, slow, retarded— it's *some*thing—because I ate perfectly all semester, I know I did. The exact same way I ate last fall.

130.75

Piña coladas . . .

131

Whole-milk lattes . . .

Petit fours. Crisp apple turnovers. Suddenly, images start to explode through my brain, as glossy and Technicolor as the photos at an all-you-can-eat smorgasbord: remembrances of things consumed. *Cherry strudel.* Who cares about madeleines—so small, so spongy—when the Hungarian Pastry Shop had so many other goodies? *Cookies, cake, pie.* Sure, I ate in the dining hall for the most part, usually at the salad bar, *which has great croutons and a yummy blue cheese dressing,* but I explored the neighborhood now and again, of course I did. After all, isn't that what college is about, broadening your horizons? *Beer bongs.* So I broadened—Chinese, Indian, Thai, *bacon and egg sandwiches from Tom's for the hangover,* Greek, French, Mexican—after all, I'm a child of hippies: I like ethnic. *Twinkies.* True, I went to Häagen-Dazs two or three times *a week* but that was more of a convenience issue really; the store is right across the street and a vanilla shake *double scoop or hot fudge sundae* makes such a fast meal *and an even better late-night snack.* And then there were all the holidays. Don't underestimate the trauma *joy* of celebrating Valentine's, Presidents', and Martin Luther King Day away from home for the first time—Easter, too, especially Easter. Why, it was only natural I'd stop in to Mondel's to buy my roommates *a dozen* cream eggs in an assortment of flavors *chocolate, vanilla, and coconut—they're all pretty good.* And what's an egg without a chocolate chick *or four* in white, milk, and dark because you don't discriminate on the basis of color? And those caramel-filled bunnies—so adorable! I just knew they'd love those, and if you're getting one, you might as well get a few *pounds*—and then some solid chocolate bunnies to keep them company and then some Cadbury creme eggs to show you're not a gourmet snob, which are not to be confused with the egg cream from Katz's, which goes really well with the . . .

Oh God. Oh God. Oh God.

I crawl into bed. I feel awful. Furious and disappointed with myself. How could I let this happen? How could I confuse dressing and studying like a college student with eating like one?

Because, in addition to discovering that the occasional pair of pajama bottoms were oh so comfortable against the lecture halls' hard wooden seats, I did study. Hard. I studied and learned about a lot of things: Plato and Pavlov, Virgil and Virginia Woolf; this past term is when I really I hit my stride, pushing myself to study harder, to understand better, to broaden and deepen my intellect to attain a level of knowledge beyond anything I could have possibly imagined.

How stupid was that? All those late-night cram sessions—and pizza—with my roommates and I forgot what was *really* important: my career, my dream, the pictures on my wall. Fall semester, I got bad grades and good tear sheets. This semester, I got A's and a big fat ass. There's no question which is worse. Everyone knows grades don't matter and, besides, isn't it much worse to fail at something easy? Yet here I am, an Ivy League student, letting something little like fat cells get the better of me. How could I let this happen? How could I have been so stupid, stupid, *stupid*!

"Em?"

It's Tommy. "What are you yelling about?" he yells. "What's stupid?"

Perfect. On top of it all, I'm now talking to myself. "Nothing."

"Em!"

"Emm!"

"Emmm!"

Previous experience has taught me that my brother will not enter my room. He is, however, more than capable of yelling until I capitulate and enter his. So I do. As usual he's reclined on his bench, pressing a bar of iron toward the sky.

"What's your problem?" he grunts.

"Nothing." I skirt around him and sink onto his water bed, which ripples alarmingly *because I'm so fat*. "I gained a few pounds at school, that's all."

Grunt. "How many?"

"Twelve."

"Twelve *pounds*?" Tommy raises his chin so he can see me. "You're kidding! That's a shitload, even for me, and I'm *trying* to gain weight!"

Everything that's available to throw on the bed, I throw. Then I curl into a fetal ball, a position that, given the current sloshing, feels positively embryonic. *Wait—I'M PREGNANT! Oh, no, not possible, I have my period—I HAVE MY PERIOD!!*

A pillow hits me in the head. "Em, don't worry about it. Taking off twelve pounds is no big deal. Football players lose that in a practice."

I sit up. "You're kidding, in a single workout?"

"Big guys," Tommy qualifies. "In the summer."

"Oh."

"Wrestlers drop weight quickly, too. Not that much in a day—they're puny, so it takes longer—but in two or three days, they can. Totally. They do it to make weight for a match."

And if they can do it, so can I. I rise to my feet. "How?"

Tommy starts curling a barbell. "I'm not sure."

I start pacing. "Think, Tommy, *think!*"

"Diuretics," he grunts.

"Uh-huh."

"Long saunas."

"Uh-huh."

"Often while clothed."

I swallow.

"And long workouts," he says. "Two hours minimum."

"A *day*?"

"Yes a day."

"Yuck!"

"Well, you asked," Tommy says. "If you don't like it, don't do it. It's your body."

My *fat* body. I spin on my heels. "Can you help me, T? Can you give me a regimen? Take me to the gym?"

His face falls. "Oh Em, I don't know . . . I'm kind of busy."

I can think of plenty of snappy comebacks to this one but I resist uttering them, probably because I'm now gripping my brother's shoulders, perhaps even shaking them a little. "Help me, Tommy! *Please!*"

"Jesus!" Tommy removes my hands, looks in my eyes, and sighs. "Okay. Be dressed and ready to go at 2:00 P.M. sharp."

In a nearly unprecedented move, I hug my brother, refusing to let go until he has deposited me in the hallway.

2:00 P.M. That gives me just enough time to go shopping.

Dexatrim, Diurex, Metamucil, I drop them all into my cart, plus the Diet Coke I'll use to wash them down. Of course, I'd do cocaine now; it's the best diet aid there is, but I don't know where to buy it in Balsam, and asking around seems risky. So I buy a pack of cigarettes and light one up instead. It seems like the least I can do.

Chapter 14

Lips, Boobs, or London

Jon squints sideways and fingers his sideburn, as if contemplating a Botero. "We could send her out and see what some clients think."

"Hmm. . . ." Justine mulls this over. "As sort of a test run?"

"Uh-huh."

"But which ones? I mean, we'd have to be careful."

I watch as Chic's two bookers scan a list of appointments, appointments that Byron spent the last week making, appointments I was going to go on before they laid eyes on me.

Despite Tommy's grueling workout sessions (seventy minutes of cardio daily, plus an hour of strength training designed to "target and destroy" specific muscle groups), copious pill popping, and an assiduous application of Alkaline Diet, not to mention upping my ciggie consumption to half a pack a day, I lost only four pounds during my week at home. Four out of twelve, which meant that when I got to New York—New York, where I'm supposed to spend the summer of '89 working as a fashion model—I opted for Plan B: hide behind figure-flattering clothing. But Byron saw right through my oversized Norma Kamali shirt.

"Hello, beauti—" he exclaimed, stopping midword when his eyes hit my midriff. Now, while Justine and Jon figure out what to do with me, Byron's pacing the hallway with a cigarette. I didn't even know he smoked.

"How about Lord and Taylor?" Jon says. "She has them at 3:00."

Justine shakes her head, which is now a deep purple, the precise shade of her top and lips, giving her the appearance of an overripe plum.

"Macy's?"

"Uh-uh."

"A&S?"

"Nope, none of those," Justine says. "Too much at stake."

"I agree."

Byron strides through Chic's entrance, his aura tinged with tobacco. That's not the only alteration. His hair is now cropped closely to his head. A diamond glitters in his ear. His ensemble of royal blue washable silk shimmers under the café lighting like pool tiles beneath a sizzling sun. Personally, I think it's a look best left to Arsenio Hall, but something tells me *his* appearance isn't subject to review.

Jon stares at his boss, surprised. "*None* of them? Then where can we send her?"

"Nowhere. No appointments," Byron replies. "I've thought about it. She's gonna get a bad reputation in this town."

A bad reputation. I stare in the distance, contemplating those words. Growing up, there had been times when I gazed enviously at the girls who had them. Compared to the rest of us, they seemed freer, bolder, less afraid. When they laughed, it welled up from someplace deep, forcing their necks back and their lips open wide. Of course, it was precisely this position that got them the bad reputation to begin with, but they didn't care, not one bit, and I envied them for it—and now I'm gonna get a bad rep because I'm a blimp?

"Then what's Plan B?" Justine asks. "Should I order the Optifast?"

"No, no . . ." Byron grabs my hand and leads me across the agency, past the trophy wall. I avert my gaze. Hanging dead center is the back view from my *Lei* series. As I discovered this morning, just the sight of my ass—so firm, so small, so frosted with sand—elicited a wave of nostalgia followed by a bout of nausea: That was me, before I was attacked by dairy.

We arrive at the seating area and sit, side by side, on the couch. In front of us are the requisite piles of fashion magazines, the normally neat rows in slight disarray thanks to Carmencita and Genoveva, the sixteen-year-old Spanish twins who just breezed out of here along with their entourage of relatives. Byron sighs, shoots an irritated look at the door, and starts fishing. When he finds the May issue of American *Elle,* he plucks it out, pages though it, and passes it over.

"Tell me what you see."

"Ashley Richardson and Rachel Williams sitting on a beach," I say immediately.

"Yes and . . . no."

Hmm. "A Giles Bensimon photograph?"

"Don't think like a model."

"Okay"—I'm not sure what this means—"two blondes?"

"Think abstractly."

Abstractly? Not a problem. I took art history this spring. I squint my eyes and tip my head. "Manet's *Le Déjeuner sur l'Herbe*—without the men in suits, obviously."

"*Manet?*"

"Seurat?" I counter. My class ended with the Postimpressionists.

"Not art!" Byron cries. His hands smooth his pant legs. "I see you."

Me? I pull the photo toward me and give it a closer look—not that I haven't seen it before. I study most fashion magazines, obviously, especially *Elle.* Everyone's reading it now (*Vogue* under that Grace Mirabella is just so *tired*) and while the magazine does show some career looks—big blazers over fitted vests and pleated pants, for instance—*Elle* is all about the beach. Swimsuits on the beach. Tube dresses on the beach. Miniskirts on the beach. Lycra, Lycra, Lycra. Thus, this shot of two models reclining on some sandy dunes in a black iridescent version of that form-fitting fabric is simply standard fare.

That's it. I snap my fingers. "You want me to wear more Lycra."

"No."

"Buy this dress?"

"Em-i-ly."

"Oh my God, you want me to go blonde!"

My agent closes his eyes and inhales, his nostrils flaring to maximize air intake. "Emily, look at these girls," he says, once he's returned, a hand now lifting to encompass not just Ashley and Rachel but the entire pile. "Look at their bodies. They're fit, sexy—"

"I told you already! I'm losing the weight. I promise!"

"—Curvy."

Dutifully, I glance down, though it's not necessary; like I said, I've seen these magazines, seen and studied them, and I know Byron's right. Cindy, Elle, Tatiana, Carré, and that new girl, Claudia—these girls are fit, sexy, and yes, curvy. But we're talking Modelville curvy, which means the same harrowingly skinny body only with two big boobs stuck to the front and, given the choice between Modelville "curvy" and Modelville "stick," I'll opt for the stick every time. After all, developing those perfectly placed curves would require an act of God or . . .

Oh.

"You want me to get implants."

The nod is almost imperceptible. "Little ones. To fill you out. Rebalance you. Like this—"

Byron's hand dips into his breast coat pocket and emerges with something dark. Two somethings. Two shoulder pads. Cupping a pad in each palm, he purses his lips and squints.

I fold my arms.

"C'mon."

"No."

"But you'll book swimwear and lingerie!" Byron cries.

"I do swimwear now!"

"Some."

But I was taped. Wait, I know, "I'll buy those silicone cutlets!"

"You could . . ."

Byron doesn't say the "but," but it's there, hanging in the air as he puts down the shoulder pads and pages through the *Lei*. He doesn't say a word as he finds my photograph and his thumbnail etches a crescent a half-inch beyond where my (taped) bust ends and tropical paradise begins. He doesn't say anything as he turns to the pictures—and cover—of Greta in skimpy bikini tops, too skimpy to be hiding a cutlet. He doesn't need to.

He raises the shoulder pads. "Here, Emily . . . let's just see."
I open my blouse.

Dr. Ricsom has slicked-back hair, well-moisturized skin, and mani-cured hands, which are currently assessing the volume and elasticity of my breast tissue.

I stare up at the ceiling, blinking under the bright lighting as I wonder whether it's purposely unflattering. The reception area was a muted blend of lavender, gray, and forty-watt lightbulbs, the lamp shades a soothing mauve. It was dark, but not dark enough to conceal the woman in black, blue, and bandages. I was about to turn tail and run when the nurse emerged though the recessed door and called my name.

"Miss Woods." Dr. Ricsom steps backward and peels off his latex gloves. "Yes, I'd say I can definitely make some substantial improve-ments," he says. The lid of the trash can snaps open and shut. "Would you like to tell me your goals?"

"Goals?" I shift against the papered table. "You mean . . . for my breasts?"

"Yes." He's by the counter now, flipping open a folder with my name on it. "Are you aiming for a certain look? A specific size?" he asks, skimming.

I hadn't gotten this far. "Bigger?" I say.

He laughs. The folder closes. "Well, in that case, let me tell you what I'm thinking: a D. Now, since you're a fashion model I'm erring on the conservative side," he says, hastily flashing his palm to ward off any impending objections. "But if you want to go bigger, we could."

"Bigger than a D," I say slowly.

"Bingo. You're tall, of course, with broad shoulders and a generous rib cage, so you could support a larger size."

"Is that an issue?"

"I meant visually. It's always a question of proportion, of balance, of finding the solution that works for you and your needs," Dr. Ricsom says. "And my professional opinion, based on hundreds of breast aug-mentations, is that a D would be the ideal size for someone with your physical charactcristics—especially after we throw collagen into the mix."

"Wait . . . you'd put collagen into my breasts, too?"

He smiles patiently. "No, Emily, the collagen is for your lips."

"My lips?"

His own curve downward. "Yes. Byron mentioned your lips, too— I thought . . ." He consults the folder. "Yes," he says after a beat. "Yes. It's right here. Top and bottom. Now, let me see. . . ."

Dr. Ricsom pulls another set of gloves from the dispenser. I recoil. "You spoke to Byron? When?"

"Yesterday. Of course I did. I talk to Byron before I do a consultation on any of his girls."

"But—"

"Don't talk now, Miss Woods. Just hold still. Okay, yes. Yes, I see what he meant. The top lip is quite thin. The bottom too, for that matter. Is there a shape you have in mind? An actress you admire? Because looking at these, I'd say we have an array of options. . . ."

Trudging across Central Park, I start breaking it down: (A) I'm a model, (B) I'm not physically perfect, (C) some of these imperfections can be corrected with surgery. And if A, B, and C are true, then D—or possibly a C, I haven't decided. Why shouldn't I? After all, it's not as if I'll be the first model to have plastic surgery. True, no one talks about it— we're supposed to be natural beauties, no effort required—but obviously it goes on, or else Dr. Ricsom wouldn't have offered me the "Chic Discount" (10 percent off one, 15 percent off two or more services). Besides, as Byron pointed out when he was studying my shoulder-padded chest, breast implants are a business expense, a tax write-off, and I'd make it back in spades—all in all, a small price to pay for big tits and a sexy pout.

I make it to the eastern edge of Central Park, cut up the zoo stairs, and dodge traffic. Pixie's mother spends every summer in her thirty-room Hampton "cottage" with her third husband, so my friend invited me to take "one of the extra bedrooms" in their apartment. On Fifth Avenue. With a terrace. By day, Pixie will be interning at Sotheby's and

I'll be modeling. By night, we'll be hitting the dance floor at Prowl, MK, Nell's, Area. It's going to be a fantastic summer.

"Hey there! How was your day?"

Pixie, prone on the sofa with a blue eye mask spread across her face and a chilled Yoo-hoo resting on a coaster, peeks out and hazards a limp-wristed wave before groaning and smoothing the mask more firmly across her temples. "Awful! Really awful," she moans. "I'm filing, Em! *Filing!* Can you believe it? I mean, I basically begged, borrowed, and called everyone I knew to get this job at Sotheby's, and I'm nothing but a glorified secretary! Considering I know more about the Neue Sachlichkeit movement than my boss does, I find this positively criminal, but I guess I'm eighteen and lots of people want to work there so you have to start somewhere, right? Right! How was yours? Anything exciting happen?"

"Um, well . . ." I beat a path toward the kitchen. "Byron wants me to get plastic surgery," I call out.

"Plastic surgery?"

"Yeah. Want another Yoo-hoo?"

"Yeah! I mean, no! Plastic surgery?" she hollers. "What kind?"

I rummage through the fridge. "Lips! Boobs!"

"You're kidding!"

"Nope!" I locate a Diet Coke and pull it out. "And the doctor thinks I should be a D. Can you believe that? A D!"

"You saw a doctor already?"

"Yup!"

For several seconds, I busy myself with procuring a glass and some ice. When I close the freezer door, Pixie's behind it, her face as animated as a stone, the blue mask parked on her forehead.

I nearly drop my drink. "Jesus!"

"Who did you see?" she asks. "What doctor?"

"Dr. Ricsom."

"Who?"

I tell Pixie all about my appointment with the plastic surgeon.

"'Bingo'?" she mutters. "A D? . . . Lips?"

Oh dear. I recognize that cheek sucking. "You disapprove, don't you? Okay, let me guess: You have a friend who's had five botched boob jobs, but, Pixie, I haven't said I'm doing it! I'm only *thinking* about it! Thinking! It's for my job! It's a business expense—who *are* you calling?"

"My mother. I'm getting a reference."

Pixie's mother is known in the society pages as Sandy Smythe, but everybody calls her Silly Sandy, the "silly" short for silicone. I rush forward. "No, Pixie! No!"

"No?" Pixie spins to shield herself. "Jesus, Emily, if you're going under the knife, it's sure as hell not going to be with a doctor who offers *volume discounts* from his office on *Central Park South*!" she shrieks. Her fingers stab at the phone buttons.

"Pixie, would you hang up and CALM DOWN? I said I'm CONSIDERING surgery, CONSIDERING, meaning I haven't decided yet!"

After an agonizing pause, Pixie hangs up.

"Thank you."

"You're welcome." Evidently deciding she needs one after all, Pixie pulls a Yoo-hoo from the fridge. "So, how long do you have to decide?"

Dr. Ricsom's receptionist told me he had on opening due to a cancellation, otherwise I would have to wait six weeks. "Thirty-six hours."

I'm coated in a chocolate spray. "*My God.* What are we standing here for? We've got research to do!"

Pixie offers to assist me—"We'll buy porn at the newsstand, no, wait, there's this club under the Queensboro Bridge"—but I have a better plan, one that must be implemented solo. One phone call later and the plan is in action.

Il Solero is an Italian café in the Flatiron District not far from Chic. Recently opened, it's good but not so good there's a buzz about it, pretty, but not so pretty that people linger long into their coffees, and so on Tuesday at 3:00 P.M. I find myself its sole patron. Greta walks in ten minutes later.

"Hey, baby!"

"Hey!"

The supermodel has the day off, she'd said on the phone, so Greta's casually dressed in a white cashmere crewneck and faded, torn jeans. Her hair has a hastily pulled ponytail. Her face is un-made-up. She looks fantastic, of course, but as I hug her in greeting she feels surprisingly frail, and as I pull back, I notice the dark crescents under her eyes. "Yuck. I'm so jet-lagged," she says, pulling back her chair.

Ah, no wonder. "Why?"

"Just got back from the Andes."

We stay on this awhile: the Andes, and then exotic destinations the wide world over. I don't have much to contribute, but Greta, by the sound of it, has spent the last two months on most of the mountain ranges in North and South America, their rocky, arid climates creating believable backdrops for the autumn clothing that's shot this time of year.

After this, we touch down in the Dominican Republic, briefly, a light rehashing, mostly reduced to a string of single-sentenced reflections like "Teddy was weird," and "Merengue dancing was a blast."

"So . . ." Greta slices a sliver of chicken. "Good trip," she concludes.

"Yes, it was."

"I'm glad you called."

"So am I."

Greta takes a sip of water. I take a deep breath. We've talked a lot about a little and lunch is almost over; it's time to get to the point.

"Greta, since I last saw you, I've put on some weight."

Greta's lips curve, into a sympathetic smile as she waits for me to continue. Oh, right. She knows this, of course, just as I noticed her frailty, her purple circles. Self-consciously, I pluck at the sleeves of my shirt and edge my seat closer to the table before continuing. "And now I have to lose the weight or else . . . um . . . or else um . . ."

Jesus. This is harder than I thought. Harder and dumber. What was I thinking? Because it's not as if we discussed them! Greta didn't even make the most offhand of offhand remarks about them! I only know because I saw . . . and felt . . . so I thought . . . but I was on . . .

But Greta's staring at me. "Or else I have to get implants," I finish.

She shifts in her seat. "And you thought I could tell you what they're like?"

"Yeah." I grab my water and start guzzling it. This was a huge mistake. *Huge.*

Only Greta is transformed. "I love them—*love* them!" she gushes. "I. Love. Them!"

The model jiggles her bust. The waiter lucky enough to witness this occurrence is holding a pitcher that, after a few trips of the nipple, is flooding my glass, plate, and lap.

"*Alora, alora!* I'm sorry! So sorry!"

Greta watches our red-faced waiter run off for more towels and napkins. "See?" she says. "That never would have happened before. I used to have one of those athletic bodies—totally flat!"

"No way, seriously?" I pick endive off my pant leg.

Greta lifts an untouched dinner roll off her bread plate and tears it. *Thwack!* The unlucky half ends up on the tablecloth as a pancaked, pulverized lump. "Like that."

I glance down.

"Oh please, baby, you're a whole roll at least!"

Thank God for small favors. "And now? You're a . . ."

"C."

"Not a D?"

My lunchmate nearly topples over. "A D . . . of course not! A D! Why, I'd never be able to fit into the designer samples with a D, which means I could kiss show season good-bye—*and* editorial, since it's the same samples as the ones on the runway, and that would *ruin* my career. Don't tell me you're considering D's!"

"Of course not."

Greta makes a show of dabbing her brow. "Get yourself up to a C cup at the most, that's my advice—but definitely get them! You'll *love* them! They're *such* a great investment! Get them and I'll tell Julie Baker about you and she'll book you for *SI,* I just know it! I bet we'd be sent on the same trip. Ooh, that'd be so fun! And just wait until you meet Walter Iooss. He's the *greatest* photographer! He'll shoot doubles of us! It will be *such* a blast!"

"Sounds it," I say, though I'm not thinking about doubles at all but about me, solo, on the cover. I'll look busty and sexy in a white bikini that's sheer, but not too sheer—just enough. I'll be smiling softly, knowingly. My hair will be blowing. The sky will be orange and pink. *Sports Illustrated* it will say in the clouds. "Love 'Em in the Maldives," it will say next to my crotch.

"Of course, the recovery process hurt like a bitch," Greta says.

Oh. "It did?"

"Oh yeah. My boobs killed—*killed*!" Once again, Greta smashes the beleaguered roll. "I was on massive amounts of painkillers for over a week. It took three weeks for me to go without wincing, five for me to be able to hail a cab. It was *terrible*!"

It sounds it. "And now?"

"Oh, they don't hurt now."

"No . . . I mean, how do they feel now?"

"Well, my right one is a bit numb, which is odd because that used to be the more sensitive one. The doctor says the sensitivity might return with time, but if it doesn't, it's not too bad, I guess, I mean I still feel *some*thing."

Greta illustrates this point by tapping a teaspoon against the nipple, a gesture that results in a crash somewhere in the vicinity of the kitchen. "Other than that, nothing," she continues. "Just the scars under my armpits. But you can hardly notice them, and they always airbrush them out anyway."

Useful information, all of it, but I still don't get it. "But how do your breasts *feel*? Heavier than they did before? Harder?"

"They feel firmer."

"A lot firmer?"

"A bit firmer."

"What's a bit?"

Greta bites her lip and stares into the distance, evidently trying to recall LBBJ—life before boob job—which I'm beginning to see as a more momentous schism than the leap from B.C. to A.D., then shrugs. "Dunno," she says. "You tell me."

As Greta steers my hand, I look over and spy the entire waitstaff of Il Solero busying itself with the polishing of a single spoon. *Sorry guys. The show's over.* I slide my hand into hers. "Here. Come on."

The bathroom is one open square—easily big enough to accommodate two people doing whatever it is they feel like doing, such as Greta throwing her Maud Frizon purse onto the floor, pulling her arms from her sleeves, unhooking her bra, and saying, "Touch them."

I jab a finger into Greta's boob. It springs back.

"Not like that; it isn't Jell-O!" she chides, though her breast, is in fact, wiggling. "Emily, you want to know how they feel? Then *feel* them!"

I reach out and squeeze. *Boing!* It's firm, it's hard, and for a second I get the sensation I'm clutching one of those tension-relieving balls you find near the checkout counter—and then the breast is gone, Greta's ducked into a squat, peeling apart the handle of her purse and digging furiously.

The case is silver and slightly battered. I wonder what happened to the gold one, wonder but don't ask; I just do my usual drill of watching and waiting as the cocaine is scooped out, diced up, and spread into long thin lines. Greta doesn't even notice my silence; she's gone again, in my sight but not here. Or maybe I'm the one who's left. I've become a speck. A fly on the wall. Nothing. And only after my friend has snorted up three of the four lines she's laid out on the edge of the white ceramic sink do I return, a fact she acknowledges by extending the silver straw.

"Here, baby," Greta says. "For you."

"Occasionally," Greta had told me. "I do coke *occasionally.*" And I had believed her. Only now I don't. Why? What's the difference? A few lost pounds? Twenty hours of lost sleep? Silver not gold? It's ounces and inches and colors. It's nothing. But it's enough, enough for me to believe that while Greta might be from God, she's no angel. She's just a girl with enlarged pupils and a sniffly nose. A girl who's wan and sunken, too tiny for her implants. A girl you'll never see in a *SI* reunion issue, not five, not ten, not twenty years from now. Because Greta will disappear.

Greta rises and moves toward me, the straw dangling from her fingertips. When she speaks, her voice is a teasing purr. "Come on, baby, you know you want it. You liked it so much before. It . . . and me."

I refuse the coke. The kiss, I accept out of pity.

"I'm not getting the operation."

Byron's brow wrinkles. His mouth opens in protest. I don't wait for the sound.

"Look, I'll do the stick-thing instead. I'll get the extra weight off right away," I aver. "Optifast, the Beverly Hills Diet—whatever you want."

As my agent stares, I meet his gaze, still adjusting to how his cropped hair makes his eyes seem larger and more penetrating.

"London," he says finally.

London? Most diets are named for places you might actually wear a bikini, not locations where you dine on dishes with alarming names like "Toad in the Hole" or "Spotted Dick" . . . or maybe that's the point. "What diet is that?"

"It's not a diet, it's a country," Byron says flatly. "If you don't want to get the surgery, then it makes sense for you to work there for the summer. They like the pear shape in London: you know, Fergie, Dame Edna, that sort of thing."

Justine looks up from a chart. "Dame Edna's Australian," she says.

"Dame Edna's a man," I say, to me this the more relevant point.

"Who cares?" Byron cries, exasperated by our niggling. "The point is you'll do well in London. You'll be a star."

"A star?"

Things happen quickly after that. Justine and Jon make a flurry of phone calls to agency heads and travel agents. I go home to break the news and pack.

Everyone's okay with the change of plans. Pixie's sad at first; soon, however, she becomes reflective: "Maybe it's better you don't get your boobs done while you're a student because you might have gone from 'Friday' to 'Jugs.'" Dad, after showing off the cordless phone he finally got around to installing ("Okay, I'm on the porch. Okay, I'm on the dock now—can you believe that, Emme? The dock!"), says, "London? Wonderful! Why, it's everything you've been studying. Why, it's the Dickens!" a pun he finds so pithy he repeats it. Even Mom—though I suspect she's simply basking in the glow of my 3.6 GPA—sees my trip in a positive light. "Immersion in a foreign culture is always mind expanding."

All of them are okay with my spending the summer in London. On the plane ride over, I decide I might be okay with it, too. In fact, it just might be the perfect solution. Not only is London a cool place: exotic enough to require a passport, but not so exotic that I'll actually have to practice any of my foreign language skills, but it's a fat place: the land of scones, roast goose, and Yorkshire pudding—pudding of all kinds, actually. Pud-ding: Even the word conjures images of guts bursting over belts, mushy love handles, and saddlebags rippled with cellulite. Yes, my pear shape will fit just fine in London, and when it goes, so will I. It's like I've signed up for one of those vacations advertised in the back of magazines that promise pounds lost amid majestic scenery. Maybe I didn't ring in the summer of 1989 in anticipation of Fat Camp, but now that I'm going, well, I'm going to make the most of it.

Chapter 15

Measuring Up

"ello?"

My duffel plops loudly against the stone floor. "Hello? . . . Anybody home?"

I've followed my instructions to 55 South Clapham Common, an address that from the outside appeared to be an elegant town house. Inside, however, it's classic college dorm. A University of Miami sweatshirt hangs from a peg. A hot pink beach towel dries over the banister. Three pairs of Rollerblades are piled atop a row of sensible English footwear.

A tall man with graying temples descends the staircase. "Finally, a brunette!" he cries.

"Glad to provide a little color," I say to . . . Vidal Sassoon?

"Edward Jones," he chuckles, extending his hand.

"Emily Woods."

I've never had a landlord before. I was expecting Mr. Roper, and while Edward might be his contemporary, on the ensuing tour I find him much more amiable and decidedly less lecherous. The house is

pleasant, too, nice in fact, a mixture of white slip-covered couches and
ebony colonial furniture that is both more elegant than the foyer promised and several notches above what Byron told me to expect (model
apartments have a reputation for being total dumps), which only adds
to my feeling of good fortune.

"What's that?" I ask, pointing to a supersized contraption near the
kitchen.

Edward grimaces. "A pay phone. After the last batch of girls left, I
got stuck with three pages of calls to Spain. Cost me two hundred
pounds."

I whistle.

"Exactly. Only, this new one is a bit of a pain—I tell you what: Be
a good girl and I'll let you use mine," Edward says, finishing off the
offer with a quick wink.

"Thanks!"

The tour includes the fridge—the models' shelf empty except for
one and a half bottles of champagne and several boxes of what looks to
be the English equivalent of Cap'n Crunch—then concludes in the
back hall, with Edward opening the door to reveal a scruffy patch of
grass and two blondes in deck chairs.

"Emily Woods, I'd like you to meet Vivienne Du Champ and Ruth
Foote."

At the sound of Edward's voice, the two stir slightly, like lizards
cooled beneath an errant cloud. "Mmmmnnnn," whines the dirty
blonde on her stomach. The honey blonde lifts up her eye shade and
looks at me.

"Ruth, Emily here is from—"

"America," I announce.

Edward chuckles. "Yes. So are they, dear. What state?"

Americans? Oh. For some reason, now unclear, I thought I'd be the
only American model in London this summer, making me both a novelty item and instant success. I'd pictured myself strutting into an appointment wearing something faintly patriotic, like Halston or Bob
Mackie, and being immediately recognized. *USA! USA!* they'd yelp,
rushing toward me and sniffing sharply, as if inhaling the bracing scent
of coffee. If I have to live with two blondes this summer, can't they be
Swedish . . . Swedish and so-so looking?

"Wisconsin," I mutter. "Hi guys."

"Hey."

Ruth flicks her cigarette on the ground and adjusts the bra of her bikini, which honest to God is itsy-bitsy, teenie-weenie, yellow, and polka dot.

Edward tenses. "Ruth, haven't I asked you to please use an ashtray?"

"Sawry, Edward, I forgot." She pouts prettily. "I'll go get one."

"Never mind, darling," he softens, "just remember next time, okay? Anyway, as I was saying, Miss Foote here's from Scranton, Pennsylvania, and Miss Du Champ here—"

"Ugghhhh!"

Vivienne rises on all fours and flips from stomach to back, her unhooked bikini top trailing limply behind as if it too is recovering from a midday siesta.

"Miss Du Champ . . . er, here is . . . is from . . ."

"Osceola, Florida." As Vivienne extends a well-oiled arm toward a packet of Marlboro Lights, her bikini top slithers to the ground.

I look at Edward, who's now the color of a well-cooked beet. "Well, I'm sure the three of you have lot to talk about, so I'll just leave you to get acquainted!" he cries. The door closes with a resounding whomp.

Vivienne stares after him. "That guy is such a motherfucking wimp."

Edward's wrong; I have absolutely nothing to say to Scranton or Osceola . . . except, "Can I bum a cigarette?"

Ruth thrusts the pack forward. Vivienne tosses me a ribbed gold lighter. For several seconds we puff away, they taking the measure of me and I of them. With her plush red cheeks, freckled nose, and strawberry-blonde lashes, Ruth reminds me of a sexed-up Holly Hobbie doll. Vivienne is less ingénue—decidedly less ingénue. Her hair cascades in dark gold ringlets, her eyes park behind oversized tortoiseshell shades. The bottom half of the bandeau bikini she's currently wearing is a solid black, as is the straw hat she's gingerly affixing to her head with the assistance of carefully polished nails. *Veronica Lake,* I think, *Hollywood Starlet.*

"Ruth, you're burning," Vivienne says.

Ruth gasps and starts buttering her body with SPF 4. Vivienne turns. "How long you staying for?"

"'Til August, I guess."

"It's slow here in August," she grunts. "Slow here now."

"I've been here three weeks and I've only worked twice," Ruth says softly.

Vivienne nods. "Yeah, Ruthie here isn't working very much."

"That's too bad."

"I'm not the *only* one," Ruth rejoins. She's done greasing up. The bottle of sunscreen slips between the chair slats and onto the ground, her fingers occupied with peevishly plucking the bow of her bikini bottom. "Lots of girls aren't."

"It's true," Vivienne says.

Perfect. I'll be fat and *unemployed.*

"*I'm* really busy, though," she continues. "Doing lots of killer jobs."

"That's wonderful."

"Yeah, London really works for me."

"Uh-huh."

Vivienne's tongue peeps between her lips, revealing a fleck of tobacco. Lightly, she touches her index finger against it and flicks it away. "Do you like to party?"

"Um, yeah," I say. "Sure."

"Where?"

"You mean here?"

"Yeah," she says. *Duh.*

"This is my first time here."

She crosses and recrosses her legs. "Oh," she says. "Well. Where have you been: Tokyo?"

"Nope."

"Paris?"

"No."

"Milan?"

"Uh-uh."

"You've never been to Milan?" Vivienne repeats. Clearly, I've misheard the question.

"No." I stare down at my suede loafers. They're not that old, but in the bright sunlight they look scruffy, matted even. "I've been . . . at school."

"School?" A crease disturbs her brow. "Where?"

"At college."

"Yeah . . . *where*?"

"Columbia."

Vivienne's lips drift apart like I've casually mentioned a recent so-journ on Venus or Mars. I suppress a smile. Trumped her at last.

"College is for idiots," she says.

Oh. Well.

"I mean, don't get me wrong. I was there a couple years ago, and it was fine and everything, but then I got scouted and. . . ." She settles back into her chair, her arms folding onto her hat. "Now I just can't imagine going back, you know? Life is *so* much more interesting than school."

"Yeah," I say. I hate her.

In my room, a mattress has been plunked unceremoniously on a bare floor. I lie down. At school, my dorm room walls became an all-purpose repository, every square inch jammed full of delivery menus and the occasional incriminating photo, making this tiny space tucked beneath the eave seem that much emptier and quiet.

"I am not homesick. I am not homesick," I whisper until my eyes flutter shut. When I wake up, it's dark. A strange sound drifts under my door. I walk to the landing.

"You okay?"

Even before Vivienne whips around to glare at me, her eyes as narrow as the crack in the bathroom door through which I'm peering, I realize that she's fine, that this is all part of her plan, that I'm the one who's fucked up.

"Idiot!" she hisses. The door slams shut.

I climb under the covers, stare at a spidery crack in the ceiling, and listen to the muted sound of her puking.

The following morning, Vivienne and I are united by a common goal: pretend as if nothing's happened, which I manage to do even as she consumes a plate piled high with bacon, eggs, and buttered toast. Around nine o'clock, the three of us take the tube to Bond Street, South Kensington, to the offices of Début, our London agency, they for a casting, I to meet Siggy, vice president of Début and wife of the owner. "She's the real VIP there," Byron explained before I left. "Be sure to get on her good side."

During yesterday's flesh fest, I couldn't help but notice that my two roommates look a lot more like Twiggy than Fergie. I'm sure it's an aberration, but I've decided to hedge my bets by wearing an oversized black sweater and black leggings. The problem is, it's warm, "unseasonably warm," Edward noted, so by the time we've ascended to the second floor of a stodgy gray building that looks like every other we've passed, I'm coated in a light sheen of sweat.

"This is Début," Ruth announces.

I dab my sleeve against my forehead and look around. The agency is one long, open room. In contrast to the double-height windows, ornate moldings, and twin marble fireplaces, the bright molded plastic furniture looks temporary and flimsy, like something constructed out of cardboard by a giant toddler.

"Which one is Siggy?" I whisper; any louder and things might topple.

Ruth twists me toward a small office that's been snipped out of the corner. Behind a glass wall, I see two arms gesturing frantically amid a swirl of smoke. "Right in there," she says. She squeezes my arm. "Good luck!"

"Thanks!"

Vivienne's lips twitch. "Stay cool."

I consider rejoining with "Don't upchuck," but I'd have to live with the consequences so instead, I cross the room, tap my fingers against the glass door, and say "Siggy?"

An arm shoots out from the miasma, gesturing for me to enter. Ever since Byron first told me Siggy's name ("like 'Jennifer' in Icelandic!"), I've had a mental image of Snuggles, the fabric softener bear, taking charge of my modeling career in London. "Book Emily!" Snuggles says over and over, his blue eyes blinking creepily. But as the smoke seeps out and the air clears, I see that while Siggy may have the eye color, she's small and wiry, with spiky hair that sticks in every direction, and possesses the addled air of someone who spends quality time playing with sockets.

"Have a seat," Siggy mouths. She's on the speakerphone. "Si, Gianni, si!" she exclaims, along with a string of Italian I don't understand.

"Lotte!" She bends toward the microphone like she's paused in a dance number—"Lotte!"—springs away from the desk to plug a teapot into the wall—"Presto!"—scoops Nescafé and sugar into a cup—"Lotte!"—pours the boiling water—"*Vogue!*"—stirs it, and drinks it down, the cigarette never leaving her hand.

I look through the glass wall. The room is filling up for the casting. A smattering of girls, each the most beautiful you've ever seen, mill about the room, chatting.

"*Ciao!*" Siggy clicks off the call and catapults out of her chair. "Star-making. Emily! Welcome!"

I smile. *Star-making. My turn.* After kissing hello, I settle back into my chair, waiting for the new agent pep talk. Unlike the whole agency search process, experience has taught me that these little chats can be quite pleasant—veritable lovefests, in fact. Specifically, I'm looking forward to the second chapter in Byron's rousing *Hail Britannia* speech, which should begin with Siggy saying how lucky they are to have gotten me to London.

"Byron called me last week to tell me you were coming," Siggy says.

. . . *What a great addition I am to their roster of talent.*

"And I said, 'Byron! We already have lots of girls here this summer.'"

. . . *How unique I am.*

"Especially lots of Americans."

. . . *How much they are looking forward to furthering my career.*

"But, well, we owed him a favor. After all, he sent us Susie Bick."

Susie Bick?

"And the Californian wasn't really working out, anyway."

Californian?

"So we decided to squeeze in one more."

One more?

"Which is . . ."

Me.

"You."

Great.

"So." Siggy leaps up. "What is the expression? There's no room at the inn? That's funny because . . ."

And like that, Siggy's gone, out her office door and out of range.

Through the glass, I see her zipping between clusters of girls like some hypercaffeinated elf. *No room at the inn? What's she talking about? Jesus.*

I stagger after, losing Siggy in the tall, willowy forest.

"Siggy, am I still on option?"

"Siggy, where's my check?"

"Siggy, when's the client coming?"

"Sigg-gee!"

A tiny hand waggles above the shiny tresses. "This way, Emily! This way!"

I follow in Siggy's footsteps down a long narrow hallway I didn't even notice earlier only—Hang on—the booking table's the other way. "Where are we going?"

If an answer to this question is given, it's lost amid the clacking heels and continuous patter. "Hasn't been here very long . . . is really quite professional," I pick up as Siggy's legs continue to churn like eggbeaters. "Seems to be honing killer instincts . . . going for the jugular . . ."

Are we talking about a tiger cub here? A baby anaconda? But the room we stop in is small and cramped, with a square card table and matching foldout chair that's currently being occupied by a twelve-year old girl.

Siggy flings her arms up. "Here we are!"

"Here where?" I say. This is no place I want to be.

The button blue eyes fasten on mine. "Emily, haven't you been listening? Entr'acte! This is Entr'acte!" Blink. "I told you there was no room at Début."

Oh. Right. No room at the . . . Which means I'm in . . . "What?"

"Entr'acte! It's French!" Siggy trills. "From L'Entr'acte: the interval between the acts of a play. It's Début's new division for new faces!"

"Wait . . . you're putting *me* in new faces?"

"I am. It's a great place for you to develop!"

No. Suddenly I feel flushed.

"And build your book!"

No. I look around, at the lone dingy window, at the freebie calendar featuring an unpicturesque scene of the Thames, at the prepubescent girl now smiling up at me.

Oh my God.

"Emily? I'd like to introduce you to Samantha, your booker!"

No. This cannot be.

"She's really up-and-coming . . ."

And I'd say she still has a ways to go. Sweat trickles down my neck.

"Hi, Emily! I'm Sam!"

When Sam beams at me, I don't get the impression I'm placing my book in the hands of a consummate professional, one who will streamline the path down London's serpentine alleyways and through the back doors of its finest fashion houses. But maybe that's because, in a country whose entire philosophy toward dental care can be summed up as "If it can chew, it's good as new," I've found the one person with braces and she's my agent.

"Sam doesn't have many girls yet, so she can devote most of her attention to you . . ."

"Wonderful." I wipe my brow.

"And really focus on setting up quality appointments."

"Mmm."

The trickle has turned into a river, now wending its way down my spine and puddling against the seam of my underwear. The room, the girl—I seem to be having some sort of internal meltdown. I glance at Siggy, whose eyes are traveling from my moist upper region on down. *Shit.* In my shock I've forgotten to strategically position my modeling portfolio against my midsection. Quickly, I shift it back into place.

"It's warm out today, isn't it?" Siggy says.

"A bit."

"Hmmm, yes. And you're overdressed." Siggy's hand swats my portfolio aside like it's in danger of stinging her. "And a bit hippy, too, I'd say."

Shit. Shit. Shit. I hop backward, clutching the hem of my sweater. "I just gained a bit at school," I squeak.

"Should we measure her?" Sam asks.

"Let's!" Siggy cries.

Thanks, Sam. "Look, Siggy, there's no need. I know I'm overweight. In fact, I'm already on a diet!"

Siggy ignores this. She's too busy hopping around the room, opening and shutting drawers with gleeful abandon. "Where's the tape measure, Sam?"

"Siggy, listen to me: I've lost five pounds already, nearly six!"

"It's behind the door, Siggy!"

Thanks, Sam. "Siggy?"

". . . Siggy?"

Siggy swings the door half-closed. "Aha! Here it is!" she exclaims perkily.

"Siggy?" My voice is now on a different register altogether. "Siggy, I'll be back to normal in two weeks!"

"Come along, Emily." She holds out the yellow tape like she's sporting a leash. "Just a quick squeeze round the hips."

Blink. "Come along now."

". . . Come on, let go."

When I finally look down I realize that, somehow, I'm pressed against the filing cabinet, my fingers curled around its handle in a vise grip.

"Em-i-lyyy! . . ."

I stare back at my adversary, the dislike coming on so strong it forms a metallic taste on my tongue. Or maybe that's blood. Those eyes, that stare . . . God, she really is . . .

"Okay, Snuggy," I release the handle. "Sorry. I mean Si—"

A loud, high-pitched squeal fills the room. "Snuggy! Brilliant! *Love* that!" Siggy exclaims before emitting a violent peal of laughter. Maybe I'd find it funny, too, were it not for the fact that my beary good friend is simultaneously pulling the tape measure over my sweater and around the widest part of my ass. "Thirty-seven," she calls out to Sam, frowning. "That's too big!"

Thirty-seven? "Yes, that would be, but I think they're really a bit smaller than that, see—"

"Here she is! Siggy, we've been looking all ov—"

Two of the willows—Début girls, as I now think of them—rush into the room, size up the situation, and stop.

"Thirty-seven inches!" Siggy thrusts the tape measure sky-high on the off chance they've missed it. "Those are awfully wide hips!"

Briefly, I spot two sets of very wide eyes before the redhead pulls the door shut.

Let me die now.

"Lotte had big hips when she first came here, but she's six feet and has a C cup," Siggy continues. "Anyway, she's thin now—not too thin! Curvy. Perfectly proportioned."

I haven't the slightest idea who Lotte is, but that's not stopping me from hating her. "Great," I mumble, retreating toward the file cabinet. "That's great."

"It's all about inches and stones, Emily. Inches and stones."

Huh? "Got it."

"Good. Glad we understand each other." Briskly, she loops the tape measure back over the door hook. "Must get back to work now Emily: Star-making! Star-making!"

And I hate this word, too, since clearly the star she's making isn't mine. "Okay, Siggy."

"Snuggy!" She cries. Her footsteps ring down the corridor. "Snuggy! Love that! It's brilliant!"

Sam grins tinnily. "Brilliant."

Brilliant. I'm both fat and unemployable.

I walk the streets of London, going where I'm not sure: here, there, anywhere, just as long as it's away from that place.

A few minutes of aimless wandering and I'm completely lost, having left my *London A to Zed* on the card table. *Brilliant again, Em,* I think as I collapse onto the steps of a building entrance. My head hurts, I'm hungry but I shouldn't eat, and I need a cigarette.

"You all right?"

A hand grazes my shoulder. I startle, then sigh. It's the redhead from Début.

"Yeah, great," I grumble. "I'm just . . . lost."

"Already?" she says gently.

I follow her gaze to two leggy girls exiting a building not fifteen feet away from us. Somehow, the realization that I've tried so hard to get away, only to end up right back where I didn't want to be, tips me over the edge. Tears spill out. I crumple over my knees.

"Look. Oh, hey there . . . look . . ." I feel her crouch next to me. "Siggy's a bit tough at first but she softens up after a while, you'll see."

"She stuck me in Entr'acte," I sniffle.

"What's Entr'acte?"

Terrific. "It's a pause, a rest, a seventh-inning stretch. It's a *fucking potty break* and Sam is supposed to be Cujo and go for the jugular, but she looks like *fucking* preteen and Snuggy? What's *that* about? Entr'acte SUCKS!"

I'm not sure this description has clarified things, but I'm not sure I can offer a better one. I sit there, heaving.

"Well, look at it this way: a debut is something you can take or leave, but *nobody* can live without a 'fucking potty break.'"

I laugh and look up. "Emily," I say.

"I'm Kate."

Kate and I go for tea at a little café that reminds her of a place she frequents in Paris. We order: Earl Grey for her, coffee for me. I'm still in a crappy mood so Kate starts things off. She's British, nineteen, with honey-hued eyes and an aquiline nose and I know her. I know her face. She's known—not famous, but almost. She's dressed eccentrically in a flowy floral blouse, striped cotton scarf, and really dark jeans, and sitting there, under the low-beamed ceiling, surrounded by geraniums, lace curtains, and chalkboard menus, listening as Edith Piaf croons and Kate speaks liltingly of her boyfriend and his band, and her flat and five dogs, I start to feel not so bad then better.

"When did you move to London?" I ask.

"Three years ago, when I was sixteen. I had come down from Manchester for a school trip and Siggy walked up to me on the tube."

My coffee splashes over the rim. "Siggy," I mutter.

Kate flakes apart her scone, smearing the largest chunk with jam and cream. "Look, she'll come around to you, I know she will. She was very sweet to me when I first moved here, like a second mother. That's worth waiting for, mind you; she's very good at her job."

Great. Siggy's very good, meaning good enough to separate the Entr'actes from the headliners. Given this, what chance do I have of doing well here? Why even bother?

"I don't want to be here," I blurt. I didn't know this was going to pop out, but I don't take it back. It's true.

"Don't be silly," Kate says. "You'll do well here. I know you will."

I push back my chair. "Allow me to recap recent events," I begin. "I gained twelve pounds in one semester of school. My New York agent essentially tells me to lose it or use it—the latter with the assistance of silicone and collagen. When I decline, he sends me to Siggy, a total nut job who kicks things off by telling me she doesn't want me, then proceeds to march me off to a closet inhabited by a brand-new braced-faced agent, and then measures me. So at this point I'd say, no, it's not looking like I'll work well here, or in New York or anywhere. I'm a disaster of a model and I want to quit the business and go home!"

When I finish my diatribe, my heart is skittering in my chest. From excitement. Everything I said is true. *I could just quit. Right this second.*

"Emily, you're being silly," Kate insists. "You're the spitting image of Yasmin Le Bon and everyone in England worships her."

Yasmin Le Bon is one of the world's top models—and that was before she married the lead singer of Duran Duran. She's practically English royalty. I toss my locks. "No . . . really? You serious?"

"I am," Kate says. She pats my forearm. "Look, just lose a pound or two and you'll be fine, I promise."

Right on cue, my stomach growls. I still don't have any cigarettes. I ask Kate for one. As she starts sifting through her green shapeless tote, its contents spill onto the table. "Wow . . ." I pick up her copy of *Satanic Verses.* Thanks to the fatwa against Rushdie, this book has been this season's hottest accessory, but the binding on Kate's actually looks cracked. In fact, judging from her dog-eared page, she's almost finished. "You're reading this? What do you think of it?"

Kate grimaces. "Convoluted. Overrated . . . you?"

"Haven't read it," I say, flipping the pages to see if that's likely to change. "I'm reading *Jude the Obscure* right now."

"Oh God. Now, there's your trouble. No more Hardy; he's way too bleak!" Kate cries, her hand slapping the table like she's just issued an edict. After draining her tea, she lights two cigarettes and passes one over.

"Thanks." I take a long drag, eyeing Kate through the swirl of smoke. As the nicotine floods my veins, I feel a dizzying rush of relief. And gratitude. "Why are you being so nice?"

"Because most models think Hardy is a pair of amateur sleuths—okay, that and I have a weak spot for people crying on staircases," Kate says. Her eyes twinkle. "Come on, stay. Stay and we can hang out together. It'll be such a fun summer!"

Kate's nice, too nice for me to even care that she's a Début girl the approximate width of a toothpick who's currently polishing off her second clotted cream–filled scone. I break into a smile.

"I'll think about it."

Lying in my room that night, I do think about it. A year ago, the *Milwaukee Journal* ran a story on the front page of the Style section. *Balsam High Grad a "Model Student"* the caption read. The text— several columns that continued on page 14—included quotes from Dale and TAMI! saying they "just knew" I'd make it. Even Conrad went on the record: "A timeless beauty," he called me, citing my "flawless skin" and "sculpted features" as particularly winning.

Our dining room table really filled up then. So did our answering machine. Friends from Balsam ribbed me with breezy comments like "We knew you when, Em!" and "Autograph, please!"

But if I go home, what would the headline be now? *Model Student . . . "Outgrew" the Stage? . . . Went from Dairy Dream to Dairy "Queen"? . . . Packed It On and Packed It In?*

The thing is, there wouldn't even be a headline. If I go home, I'm just one more girl spending her summer on the dock, and there's nothing newsworthy about that.

I want to fit in, but I want to be somebody, too. I'm finally ready to be somebody.

It's dark, but the moon is round and heavy, not quite full but full enough to help me in my task. It takes awhile, but I take my time. I don't want to rush it. I want it, no, I *need* it, to be just right.

When I finish, I look up, at Cindy and Tatiana, Carré and Elle, Claudia and Ashley and Rachel. They're all here. Watching over me. Keeping me company.

What is it that Mom always says, *Do it and do it well?* Well, girls, I'm gonna join you, just you wait and see.

Chapter 16

Fielding Dreams and Siberian Queens

Every morning Sam gives me a list of appointments. It doesn't take me long to discover that London is a big, big place, the territory I cover far and wide. But while Siggy is allegedly overseeing my schedule, there doesn't seem to be any rhyme or reason to the order of things. At 10:00 I see a photographer in Soho, two tube trains and a half mile walk from my 10:30, a studio in Camden, which is conveniently located on the other side of town from my 11:15 on Oxford Street, which is one block away from where I began.

But I'm going to make it here, I've decided, so I rise to the challenge with a frenetic intensity. SOHO–CAMDEN–SOHO? No problem, Sam, these boots are made for walking. NOTTING HILL–KENSINGTON– MAIDA VALE–SOHO CITY–KENSINGTON? Okay, Sam, I've got my Evian. CITY–COVENT GARDEN–CITY–KENSINGTON–CITY? Got it, Sam: I know all the major public restrooms. KNIGHTSBRIDGE–MARYLEBONE–SOUTH KENSINGTON–CAMDEN–CHELSEA–ISLINGTON? I'm not a chicken, Sam, in fact, I own these streets. KENTISH TOWN–CLERKENWELL–COVENT

GARDEN—PIMLICO—ST JAMES? I'm a secret agent, Sam, a bad-assed American model prowling through the city on Operation Tear Sheet! SOHO—LAMBETH—KNIGHTSBRIDGE—VAUXHALL—SOHO—ISLINGTON—SOHO—LAMBETH—SOHO? What's that you say, Sam? London calling? Her Majesty's Secret . . . I can do it, Sam, I can do it! I'm the baddest! I'm the best! Just call me Double oo fat ass and PLAY IT AGAIN!

Two weeks of this and I have zero jobs. Zero. (I did get optioned to shoot nurses' uniforms with a photographer in Marylebone, but it released. I cried.) Both of my feet have blisters in every place you can get them and several that I didn't know you could (between the fourth and fifth toe, what's that about?). When I blow my nose, my snot is a grayish black. On the plus side, I'm minus three pounds, thanks to mastering the model's ability to walk, smoke, and ignore crippling stomach pains all at the same time.

"I feel like I'm getting the runaround," I grumble one evening back at the town house, having just capped off another day on the streets with a jog around Clapham Common, a public space about as picturesque as its name. "Literally."

Vivienne pauses. The brush of her nail polish wavers in the air. "You may be."

I pause, too. "May be what?"

"I heard they did that," she says.

"Did *what?*"

My roommate runs a leisurely finger down the length of her big toenail. Waiting for her to supply some nouns, I gulp some water. Through the bottom of my glass she looks like a Renoir: Girl with Pedicure. "Gave girls—some girls—the runaround," she offers eventually.

Wait. *"What?"*

"You know . . ." Her ankle circles the air, either an expansive gesture or a nail-drying technique, I'm not sure which. "Send them to lame clients, out-of-work photographers—that sort of thing."

My mind skips to the white-haired photographer I saw this morning in Kentish Town; the layer of dust on his photos was so thick that at first I mistook it for a soft-focus finish. "What could possibly be the point of that?"

"Why, isn't it obvious? To get rid of them."

Get rid? "B-but why not just tell them to leave?"

Vivienne looks at me like I'm from Milwaukee. "Well, that would be awkward, wouldn't it? For Début to call your agent in New York and tell him, 'Um, actually we think the girl you sent us. . . .'"

"Sucks," I finish weakly.

"Sucks," she confirms. "No point in pissing them off, not when the next girl they send over might be a real star." The fingers flick inward: *like moi.*

I soft-punch a sofa cushion. While some modeling agencies, like Elite, are in the process of building an international network, most have informal alliances that operate via a barter system: You send a few girls our way, we'll send a few yours. Models pay for all expenses they incur: airfare, lodging, portfolios, prints, long-distance phone calls, even photocopies (an agency will advance you the money, but that's about it), so taking on girls is a low-risk proposition—all this I knew, but . . . a runaround? . . . To get rid of me? "Why, that's horrible!" I exclaim. I haven't even earned back the price of one-way ticket, and now I'm being stuffed with a round-trip?

"Sorry," Vivienne says, not sounding particularly so. "It's just how it is."

After a fitful, nicotine-infused night, I rise early, and march straight to Siggy's office.

The head of Début is on the phone, of course, babbling away in some language I don't understand, so I park myself in one of the chairs opposite her desk and adopt a don't-fuck-with-me posture.

Siggy hangs up. "You seem peeved."

Peeved? "I'm not 'peeved,' I'm pissed as hell because my appointments are *total crap!*"

Siggy leans back in her chair. Her hair is even more tufted than usual, as if she slept upside down in her Bat Cave. "Are you telling me you won't do appointments?" Blink.

"No, I—"

"Because you need to go on appointments to work, Emily."

"I realize that, it's just—"

"You Americans, you never want to do the legwork," she says, giving her own two an admiring glance before continuing. "You're just a bit lazy. It's all that TV, I think. Or maybe your diet."

Wait, who is she calling lazy, me or my people? "*I* am not lazy, Siggy. I just want to work," I inform her. "It's been two weeks and I still haven't earned a dime."

Blink. "It's pence here, Emily. Not cents: pence. You're in England now, where it will take awhile for your career to get going."

"I don't have awhile, I only have a couple of months!"

"Exactly. You Americans," she begins again. "You never want to waste time."

And why, exactly, is this bad? I'm annoyed now—this conversation has geopolitical overtones that I didn't anticipate—and I'd like to express this by insulting Iceland, though truthfully, and perhaps because I am American, I know nothing about the country.

"No we don't, Siggy—"

"Snuggy," she corrects.

Grrr. "Look, *Snu*ggy, all I know is that you're giving me bullshit appointments: You're giving me the runaround and I'm sick of it!"

"Oh . . . that." Siggy swivels away, fills the kettle, and swivels back. "Well, you weren't ready for real ones."

Blink.

"You were fat: thirty-seven inches, as you might recall, though I must say, you're looking a bit better now."

Seconds pass. Steam billows in the air. The kettle makes an empathic click. "The Snuggy Diet!" she cackles. "The Snuggy Diet!"

" 'The Snuggy Diet.' Can you believe she said that? 'The Snuggy Diet!' "

". . . Kate?"

Kate's eyes remain firmly closed as Violet, the aptly named makeup artist, smooths out the creases in her soft black eye shadow with a blunt-tipped brush. I've just joined my friend in a location van that is parked (via special permit) directly across the street from the British Museum. Once she finishes the last shot of a six-page *Harpers & Queen* spread, the two of us are going shopping at Camden Market.

"No." Kate's eyes are still closed. Her hand wafts toward the museum. "Have you been inside yet? It's really amazing."

"Not yet—and what's with the nickname? Have you ever had someone *make* you use a nickname?"

". . . Kate?"

". . . Well, have you?"

"No. You really should go inside," she says. "In fact, you could pop in right now while I'm shooting. You won't have too much time, of course, just enough for a highlight. The museum has a fantastic collection of Egyptian art, the Elgin Marbles—"

"Maybe some other time," I say noncommittally. After all, there's Egyptian art at the Met, and I saw the Elgin Marbles on a slide in art history class. "Doesn't that sort of defeat the purpose of a nickname? To *make* someone call you something?"

"Yes," Kate replies, though perhaps with less gusto than I would like.

Violet turns. "Emily, would you mind moving over a touch? You're blocking the light."

I move two steps to the right, unsure why Violet's being so sensitive when the pictures are in black and white. "And Nescafé? Who *drinks* that stuff anyway? It's disgusting!"

"Emily . . ."

Kate rises and adjusts her black velvet Katharine Hamnett catsuit. Her blaze of hair has been minimally teased, her full lips given a neutral glaze, her eyes rimmed with black—*the* look for fall 1989, and she's wearing it well. Stunningly well. Kate sighs. "I just hate to see you so upset, that's what," she says. "You're taking this conversation with Siggy way too personally."

"How can I not take it personally? It's *me*!"

"It's you and it's not you, you know?"

Now it's my turn to sigh. Why is it that the British end every sentence with a question?

Guy, the stylist, guides Kate's feet into a pair of zebra-print ankle boots and zips up the sides. "Ouch, these are high." Kate totters in a tight circle as she studies the boots in the mirror. The theme of the story is animal prints so she knows they're bound to be a focus, along with the belt that Guy's now selecting from a stack more than two dozen deep, all of which were messengered over to the *Harpers & Queen* offices by designers dying to be featured in their pages . . . and then worn by the editors after-hours.

"All right, I like the pony hair. And we should stick with the zebra theme to avoid jungle fever so it's either this one . . . or this one," Guy says, proffering two from the pile.

Kate doesn't hesitate. "This one has a better buckle."

"I agree but *that* one's from Harvey Nichols," Guy says, after checking the labels. "And the editor's been *insisting* I use them, so that one it is."

"Ah, the power of advertisers," Kate murmurs. She stares at her feet. "You know, these are growing on me—any chance of a good deal?"

"Doubt it," Guy says, shaking. "They're too new. Too hot. But maybe I could swing it if you're willing to pay retail."

"Which is?"

"£275."

"275 *pounds*?" Kate cries. "Buggers! Who makes them?"

"Manol— "

"Okay, enough with the shoes!" I say crossly. We're getting way off the topic at hand—me—and clearly, no woman's going to pay so much to be in pain. "Kate, what did you mean 'it's me and not me'?"

Kate sighs. "I mean, this job is just about your face and body, Emily, not your soul."

I roll my eyes. "Kate, if you mention Buddha right now, I'm leaving the van."

Actually it's Kate who leaves the van. A photographer's assistant guides her down the stairs to the museum plaza, a background of nothing but sunlight and stone edifice (and thus another ideal choice for a fall fashion spread shot in the height of summer). Now, why a woman would be prowling around a cultural institution in a catsuit and stiletto boots is a question that no one is concerned with—least of all the dozens of tourists currently using their Instamatics to chronicle Guy adjusting the selected belt around Kate's nonexistent hips, Violet doing her final, *final* touch-ups, and the photographer reviewing the layout.

Only *I'm* not buying it—any of it. *Just my face and body, not my soul?* What a crock! Who cares about my soul? No one can see it. No, what matters is Siggy. Stupid *stupid* Siggy and this stupid, fashion-challenged city. In New York, a newly shorn Linda Evangelista is steadily gaining momentum, Claudia Schiffer is the new Guess? girl, and Naomi Campbell—a Brit—is getting a lot of work in the pages of American *Vogue,* which just dumped Grace Mirabella in favor of a new editor: Anna Winwonderful, who also happens to be British and also had the good sense to get out of Dodge and go where things are happening. They aren't the only ones. British designer Katharine Hamnett explained her decision to move her fashion shows to Paris in the latest issue of British *Vogue* by saying, "London is out of the way and shabby. It's all to do with wrong investment. Paris has gloss."

London isn't fashion challenged; it's fashion fucking Siberia. What the *hell* am I doing here?

Obviously, I called Byron and tried to ask him this very question—I've tried to ask him many questions since I've arrived, starting with the subject of pears—but he just said, "Darling, hang tight" before "jumping off" to "catch the coast."

And now I'm sitting in a mobile home on the island of nowhere. I storm outside and skulk around the plaza, scaring pigeons and tourists alike until Kate's done, changed, and we're sliding into the bucket seats of her red MG.

"Listen, Emily—" Kate veers sharply into the left lane, squeaks past a semi, and veers back. "I'm going to Manchester next weekend. Tranquill's playing in their favorite pub. It should be a great show. Want to come? It won't cost much; we can stay with my mum."

Noel, Kate's boyfriend, is the lead singer of Tranquill, an up-and-coming rock band known for their gritty sound and extended guitar riffs. I haven't seen them perform yet. "Maybe," I say. "If I don't have a job."

Kate laughs. "Emily, it's the weekend. Not many bookings on a summer weekend in London—SHITE! FUCK OFF YOU BASTARD!"

A startled driver turns as white as his Fiat.

"Would we drive?" I ask.

"No, train probably, why?"

"No reason."

"You should come, really. It will be great! Ice will be there. . . ."

Oh, right. Four-fifths of Tranquill is single; Kate's sure there's a match there somewhere—in fact, she's putting her money on Ice, the lead guitarist. The statistics certainly work in her favor. Models and rockers are the peanut butter and jelly of coupling: Mick and Jerry, Keith and Patti, Billy and Christie, Yasmin and Simon, Axl and Stephanie, Michael and Brooke—the list goes on and on. Even Ruth is dating, or should I say screwing, Stu Burges. Yes, Stu, the rasp-voiced rock legend who's currently married to one supermodel he left another supermodel to be with. I groan audibly. "Kate, I already told you: The whole rocker thing is *such* a cliché."

Kate exhales sharply. "Oh. A cliché. Well, I see."

"Sorry," I mutter not altogether unconvincingly.

Her fingers drum the steering wheel. "You know, Em, Siggy wasn't entirely wrong."

"Meaning?"

"You *are* impatient. You want things to happen and you want them to happen *now,* during your summer vacation, but life doesn't always work that way . . . on a schedule. You need to give your career a chance to develop. In the meantime: Relax! Enjoy yourself! You're young, beautiful, and spending the summer in London—what's so bad about that?"

"London is out of the way and shabby."

Our MG nearly rear-ends a Jaguar. "*What* did you just say?"

"I didn't. Katharine Hamnett did. In *Vogue.*"

Silence. Even the next two lane changes occur without comment, then: "You know Emily, what I said that day we met? I take it back. I think maybe you should go home after all."

"Maybe I will."

When we arrive in Camden, we decide to split up, a decision I'm totally fine with: Between her weird wardrobe and her *que sera sera* attitude, *Kate's* the one who should be the child of hippies and I should be getting six pages of *Harpers & Queen,* and I don't see any point in hanging out with her a minute longer. I wander the market alone.

Camden Market's a browser's paradise: a collection of indoor and outdoor stalls offering a little bit of everything: music, clothing, and collectibles from practically every era. I see none of it, only the red of my anger and the green of my envy. I'm not thinking about Kate now, I'm *past* Kate. I'm thinking about last summer. Last summer was different. Last summer I made $80,000 and was headed up, up, up the Hollywood Hills, straight for the stars. And this summer, if I hadn't fucked things up so royally, I'd be in New York living on Fifth Avenue with one of my best friends. Even two weeks ago—even then—if I'd made better choices, I'd be pushing my new C/D cups toward the camera in a skimpy swimsuit instead of hauling my ass all over this dirty, depressing, disgusting—

"Hello, dear." A wrinkled woman in a blue, moth-eaten cardigan, its sleeves stuffed with Kleenex, cups my elbow. "Are you looking for something in particular?"

"Uh . . . no, just browsing, thanks," I say automatically, as I focus. I'm in a bookstall, standing directly in front of a bin of eighteenth-century novels.

"Oh, you're American!" she gasps. "Well, let me see . . ." She raises a tissue-filled fist. "Over there I have Cooper, Hawthorne, James, Twain, Whitman. . . ."

I peer into the bin: Swift, Goldsmith, Sterne, Sheridan, Shelley. "That's okay, thanks; I'm happy here."

She smiles. "All right, I'll leave you to it then, dear. Let me know if you need anything."

"Thanks."

"So, you have a thing for the Brits."

I look up to see the man behind the Scottish accent: Tall. Midthirties. Dark eyes. Unruly hair. Unshaven cheek. Jeans. Raincoat. Gorgeous.

"Who doesn't?" Nervously, my fingers crack a binding to the title page of *Tristram Shandy.* When the comeback doesn't come, I look up. Great. Just great. He's gone. Can *nothing* go right today?

I shiver as if to shake off the slight, then start perusing books in earnest. I keep finding gems: a *She Stoops to Conquer* with an interesting font, a not-so-scary illustration of *Frankenstein,* a Mrs. Malaprop putting her foot in her mouth yet again, and "ooh!" *Evelina.* I read this last summer. I laughed. I cried. I couldn't put it down. I pick it up.

"Fanny Burney? Did you just squeal about Fanny Burney?"

Be still my beating heart. The guy's back, this time smirking from nineteenth-century poetry.

I return the smirk. "Don't mess with Fanny," I say. "I like Fanny."

"I wouldn't *think* of messing with Fanny," he says with a mock seriousness that reveals just how dark and delicious his eyes are.

I can't think of anything else, clever or otherwise, so I pick up Richardson. After reading one of a gazillion scenes in which Pamela narrowly escapes with her virtue, I move on to Fielding. A hand touches my back.

Ah! Oh. It's the bookseller.

"You've got *Tom Jones,* have you, dear?" she says, smiling down at my find. "That's quite a classic."

"It is," I say, and, because I'm being watched, "Bucolic and bawdy —what a beautiful combination."

The bookstall owner flashes that delighted smile that says young people aren't *all* bad. "That it is, dear. Shall I wrap it up?"

The book has a loose binding, unfortunately. I point this out and ask her if she has any other copies.

"Oh no, I don't. I'm sorry, dear. *Tom Jones* is difficult to come by," she says, "but I do have *Amelia* and *Abraham Adams* somewhere if you're fond of Fielding. . . ."

"No, thanks. Just *Tom Jones.*"

She laughs. "Love the cads, do you?"

"Let's hope not."

I settle for *Evelina.* As the bookseller rings it up, I twist around in anticipation of flak about cads or Fanny but, alas, the great Scot is gone.

Maybe it was my firm tone, maybe it was my firmer abs—some aspect of my showdown with Siggy must have been effective, for my appointments improve, and lo and behold, I get my first booking, a fashion spread for the *London Times.* Oddly, it's a surf story, so I spend the morning frolicking around a photographer's studio in a black and lime green wet suit trying not to whack Chester, the stunningly pale male model from Leeds, with a long board. Newspaper is the worst: It pays editorial-type rates, yet because of the poor print quality you could never use the photos in your book, even if you wanted to.

Still, "you'll get some exposure," Sam points out as I drop off my voucher. "And £300, that's got to be good for something—oh, and Em, love, don't forget your package."

"What package?"

Sam's masticated pen points to the top of the filing cabinet where, sure enough, there's a brown paper package tied up with string. I pull it down. It's heavy. On the top is written:

Miss Emily Woods, Entr'acte

"Fancy writing!"

Kate pushes a floral teapot out of harm's way before digging through the hastily replaced tissue. "Four leather books!" she exclaims. "No, wait—one book, four volumes. *Tom Jones*? Ooh, I love *Tom Jones*!"

"So do I!"

"The movie's good, too," Kate continues. "Hey, did you know, *it won the Oscar for best picture,*" we finish in unison.

Kate and I giggle. About thirty minutes into my solo tour of Camden Market, I felt terrible about our fight and ran off in search of her. In fact, I was so happy to reconvene, I told Kate that the odd, white Courrèges dress she was in the process of trying on was "stunning." Her hand flies to its bodice. "Emily, this is the third edition," she says slowly.

"I know."

". . . printed in 1749."

"I know."

". . . which means it's *very* valuable!"

"I *know*!"

She looks up at me, astonished. "And you have no idea who sent it?"

"No idea!"

"No card?"

"I didn't see one."

"Why, there *must* be." Kate picks up volume one and starts gingerly inspecting its pages. "Do you have *any* clue?" she asks. "Any at all?"

I tell her about the bookstall.

She dumps the box upside down and gives it a shake. Nothing. "So you bought a book. . . ."

"Yeah, *Evelina*. But it cost £8; nothing like this!"

"*Evelina?*" Kate gives a puzzled shrug. "I've never heard of it."

"But the Scot did," I remind her. "He knew it was written by Fanny Burney."

"The Scot—cute?"

"Yeah. Older, but cute. No, gorgeous."

"Give me a visual."

I provide Kate with the basics but she still doesn't get the picture so I succumb to a celebrity comparison. "He's a cross between Cary Grant and Sean Connery."

"Okay yes, I'd say that qualifies as gorgeous. Well, obviously he sent it," Kate says, "this Sean Grant—"

"I prefer Cary Connery."

"This Cary Connery character. He just asked the bookseller for your information."

"But that's just it!" I exclaim, so abruptly that everything on the table jumps, along with the couple behind us. "I didn't give her my information!"

"Are you *sure*?" Kate says skeptically.

"I'm positive! I paid in cash—only £8, remember? And anyway, I would have given her Edward's address, not Entr'acte's—*never* Entr'acte's; I still can't stand to even mention that name when I *have* to!"

"Do you have the *Evelina*?"

I pull out my new purchase. Kate rifles through it. "So, the only two people there at the bookstall that day were . . . ," she pauses to read the bookmark. "Edwina Semple, the owner of *A Page in Time*, and Cary Connery. It's got to be one of them."

"Perfect," I snort. "The way my summer's been going, I now have to deal with an eighty-year-old named Edwina sending me expensive presents."

This is rewarded with an eye roll. "Emily, it's the Scot. Trust me. He tracked you down somehow, I'm sure of it." Kate's hand trails slowly over the soft leather, her fingertips tracking the thick gilt lettering. "And right before your birthday, too. If this is what you get as the opening gambit, just imagine what your next present will be!"

Chapter 17

Tarting Around

I don't see Edward slip into the pantry, just emerging seconds later, with a raspberry tart, round and gleaming, its crisp, golden crust ringing row after row of ruby red berries glistening under a light glaze and dotted by the occasional candle.

"Beautiful!" I gasp.

"Happy birthday!" Edward places it before me. Everyone sings. As I blow out the candles, I see Ruth's lips move, counting. "Wait, you're not . . . are you *fifteen?*"

"No, Ruth."

"I ran out of candles," Edward explains, his fingers swooping to remove them.

"Oh," Ruth says. "Well, how old are you?"

"Nineteen."

Vivienne's sandals clatter against the tile. Her bare feet slide onto an empty seat. "My New York agent always says, 'No cover by twenty-one and you're done,' so you've only got two more years to make it."

Ruth gasps. "No way! My agent says, 'Cover before twenty and you'll work plenty!'"

"I've got three covers!" Vivienne says.

"I've got two!"

When my roommates have finally broken from their bear hug, Ruth pats my shoulder. "Don't worry, Em, you've still got a year."

"And here's a good way to get it started . . ." Edward plops a dollop of freshly whipped cream next to a fat wedge of tart and slides it across the table.

I stare at the plate. *Whipped cream + extralarge slice = 1,000 calories = nearly ⅓ pound.* I can no sooner eat this than guzzle a vat of bubbling lard. "Um . . ." I struggle to swallow, already feeling the load spreading across my hips, thighs, and ass. "Too big!" I finally sputter, sending it back. "Much!"

"I'll take it!" Vivienne says, taking it.

Edward cuts me the requested sliver. "Ruth?"

Ruth shakes her head and lights up.

The first thing I feel is the soft crush of the berries. The liquid releases, flooding my mouth with a tangy sweetness. As I reach the satisfying crunch of the occasional seed, I'm hit by the next layer: a smooth, rich custard, lightly flecked with vanilla bean, chased quickly by the nutty, buttery crunch of the pastry. It's the best thing I've tasted in a while, a *long* while in which the highlights have included undressed salad, one pack of smokes per day, and Dexatrim chased down with a little Metamucil—the Metadex mocktail, as I like to call it. The edge of my fork slices into the pastry, readying another bite.

Vivienne dips her fingertip into the whipped cream and deposits it into her mouth. "So, Emily, how's the diet going?"

My fork hovers. "Great."

"Really? You've lost weight?"

Bitch. "A little."

"How little?"

"Four pounds."

"And you've been here how long?" Ruth asks.

"Almost three weeks."

I thought I had my weight loss under control; Ruth, evidently, thinks otherwise. She leans on her forearms, arms jutting like chicken wings. "You should get a lot of sleep. That's what my agent in Philadelphia told me to do—smoke and sleep a lot."

I drop my fork and reach for the cigarettes.

"Try eating a single food," she continues. "Like lettuce. I had a roommate who did that once: ate one head of iceberg per meal. Lost a lot of weight."

"I bet."

"Or all fruit."

This is more of a food category but, "Uh-huh."

"Meat."

"Ruth!" Vivienne shouts just when I was despairing over how much of the food pyramid we'd yet to scale. "Don't be an idiot, *please*. Haven't you ever seen those potato ads? It's all about complex carbohydrates now. Who eats meat to lose weight?"

Yeah. We stare at her pityingly.

Ruth frowns down at the table. "My mom did that," she murmurs.

"Well, was your mom a model?" Vivienne rebuts, knowing as I do that Ruth's mother works at the Plus-is-Us dress shop in Scranton. "Anyway, *you* do it. All you eat is Cap'n Crunch and that's carbs."

"Yeah, but it's one food."

"Yeah, but—"

"Guys!" I hold up my hands. "Thanks. I got it."

Both of them shrug: *Suit yourself*. As Vivienne continues to wolf down the tart, Ruth pushes away from the table and approaches the big phone. "Hey, Vivi; Stu call?"

"Nope. Kenny?"

"Nope."

Vivienne flicks her ponytail in exasperation. Kenny, Vivienne's boyfriend, is the leading scorer for the Miami Heat. A few days ago, the two of them got into a fight. No one knows what happened, other than her screaming "Psycho" into the phone, pausing, then finishing up with "psycho, psycho, psycho!" Evidently, he disagreed with the diagnosis.

"Goodness!" Edward exclaims. "A basketball star, a rock star . . . what's your boyfriend do, Emily? Is he a movie star? A—what do they call them—a Brat Packer?"

"I don't have a boyfriend."

"Maybe you'll meet someone tonight," Ruth exclaims after a beat. "On your birthday!"

"Maybe," I echo. But I have no doubt. It's my nineteenth birthday; I'm going out to party and I want Cary Connery as my gift.

Our first stop tonight is Tramp. I must confess, I don't love the place. Tramp is "members only." Now, in New York, such a term refers to bad aviator jackets that should be airlifted, stat, onto the backs of needy kids in a distant land. In London, however, "members only" translates into a private club that routinely rejects the more charismatic party-goers in favor of two kinds of patrons: the pasty crowd (well-bred but congenitally doughy upper-crust types with bad breath and lead feet) and the modelfuckers.

The modelfuckers. I'm sure I don't need to explain the term, so let me explain the type, because a couple of varieties frequent London.

By day, banker modelfuckers—investment bankers, particularly traders and brokers—race down the street to hand you their business cards. This is done with the nonchalant efficiency of a guy in a sandwich board passing out flyers for a lunch special. By night, these bankers—note the *s*, bankers always travel in packs—become deadly predators, their bloodlust hidden behind whimsical wardrobes of brightly striped Turnbull and Asser button-downs with French cuffs linked by hot and cold water taps, pieces of candy, or pigs. Once the banker modelfuckers have got you cornered—and they will—they break out the battering rams: the names of their employers (but only if it's Morgan Stanley, Goldman, or Lazard) and the provenance of their MBA (but only when it's Harvard, Wharton, Stanford, or NCIAD). After they've stormed your gates, they start ransacking your treasure chest to see what you've got: "What type of modeling do you do?" they ask. If you want to get rid of them, the answer is simple: "I shoot catalog for Kmart, but only when I'm lucky." Trust me: Even the fattest, baldest, most vertically challenged banker is convinced he can do better than that.

If on the other hand, you wish to toy with them, tell them you "just got back" from a shoot for: "lingerie" (bonus points for mentioning "La Perla," "Cosabella," or "Victoria's Secret"), "swimsuits" (be sure to include the word "centerfold," "tanga," or "topless"), or any pairing of "campaign"/"commercial"/"contract" with "Bain de Soleil"/"Nivea"/ "Coppertone." Once you've done this, you've got a brand-new puppy dog just begging for his leash.

And then you walk away.

Tonight, as we whisk down the dimly lit staircase and into the nightclub, it's clear we're up against modelfucker type number two, currently spread thick as treacle across the down-filled couches: the royals.

Royal modelfuckers seem to be a specialty of London, but we're not talking House of Windsor here. They're not from England, nor are they necessarily royalty: They're the grandsons or nephews or second cousins of the royal family of _____ (insert name of oppressive Arab dictatorship here). Like the bankers, the royals travel in packs—even larger packs—and are most readily identifiable by their custom-tailored suits (where the last button of the sleeve is *always* left undone just because it can be), their ascots/cravats/accessories in jewel-toned silk, and their copious gold jewelry. Like the bankers, the royals are extremely good at cornering you; unlike the bankers, the royals don't ask you about the type of modeling work you do; in fact, they don't bother to ask you much about anything at all. They just like having you in their orbit.

Sigh. Yes, these are the modelfuckers, but don't let the name fool you. While plenty of models will let these men buy them champagne by the magnum and coke by the gram, the only ones going home with them are either desperate or Russian—the Russian girls date anyone with money. Still, I'm thrilled to see them. In fact, they're why I'm here. Model-fuckers are where the models are, and where the models will be, I hope, I *pray,* one very handsome Scotsman waiting to take me away.

Only I don't see him.

"Yummy, Cristal!" Ruth exclaims, recognizing the bottle despite heavy shades and dim lighting. Ruth's wearing leggings in a cherry red webbed with gold and as she gestures they shimmer like the scales of a tropical fish. "Want some?"

I nod vigorously. Ruth procures the flutes. The two of us join the models circling a brass and wood butler's table already crammed with half-consumed cocktails and ashtrays and lean in.

"She's in St. Tropez," a girl with a sleek bob says, "shooting a Dolce & Gabbana campaign."

"No. No. That's finished," an Asian girl insists. "She's in Paris shooting *Vogue* in studio."

"French *Vogue*?" asks a Wonder Woman clone.

"No, American. With Meisel."

. A collective gasp, the sort normally associated with fireworks, ensues.

"Who are we talking about?"

Sleek Bob arches an expertly tweezed eyebrow, astonished at my ignorance. "Why, Lotte, of course."

Of course. Lotte. Why wouldn't we be discussing Lotte? Lotte's the It girl of London, which of course means she's skipped town.

After Lotte, the conversation has nowhere to go but down the food chain.

"Siggy makes me go with her when she gets her hair cut and then ignores me," Ruth says.

"Me, too," Sleek Bob exclaims. "Only it's her pedicure!"

"Manicure," Wonder Woman says, wiggling her fingers.

Everyone titters. Let the personal horror stories begin.

"—She canceled a booking because I wouldn't date her brother."

"—She moved a girl into my apartment who stole all my stuff. When I complained, she told me it was about time I got a new wardrobe anyway."

"—She told me my photographer boyfriend was a loser who'd never make it."

"—She told me I should fuck a photographer to help my career. I was fifteen."

"You think those are bad?" The champagne sloshes in Sleek Bob's glass. "She booked me a job on the day of my grandmother's funeral! Advertising!"

"Awful!"

"How terrible!"

Nobody asks Sleek Bob whether she did the job or not; nobody needs to. I just hope it went national.

Excellent. An audience who feels my pain. "Well, this isn't as bad as your story," I say, giving a nod to Sleek Bob and her dead grandmother. "But," I raise my voice so it can be heard above Bobby Brown, "Siggy put me in Entr'acte. And measured me!"

The circle shudders.

"Entr'acte? How old are you?" wonders Wonder Woman.

"Nineteen."

Silence. In other words, too old to be a new face.

"Well, *I* would just leave," Sleek Bob says.

The others look away, even Ruth, who develops a sudden interest in her right kneecap. My cheeks burn.

"More champagne?"

The bottle zooms in front of my eyes enticingly. *Why not?* I certainly need it. I extend my glass then turn to acknowledge the source . . . none other than a smiling, breathless Kate.

"Surprise! Happy birthday!"

"My godddhiiii!" I nearly drop my flute, then throw my arms around her, thrilled. "I thought you left for Manchester!"

"We decided not to leave until tomorrow morning, which is brilliant; I can help you with your quest. That is"—Kate ducks her head and lowers her voice—"unless you found him?"

"Oh, *please,*" I say, surveying the modelfuckers du jour, which, according to the patter, includes an arms dealer and his retinue of bodyguards. If only that meant we were safe. "Cary Connery is a cut above this crowd."

"Well, then . . ." Kate smiles and juts out her elbow. "We'll just have to find a better one!"

On the passenger's seat of Kate's MG is a present. "For you," she says.

Oh boy. I tear off the tissue to find . . . a used jacket. "Don't you just love it?" Kate enthuses. "I can't believe I came across it! It's YSL from the seventies—a design called 'Le Smoking.' I think it will look great on you!"

"Yeah . . . It's terrific . . . Thanks," I say. Kate has the oddest taste.

We head toward Café de Paris, a giant club near Leicester Square with a copious VIP area that serves as a holding pen for actors, musicians, and models. (Since the feeling is usually mutual, we generally refer to the species known as "celebrity modelfucker" as "dates.") Noel and the rest of Tranquill will be here tonight; Kate surmises Cary Connery will be, too.

The line in front of Café de Paris extends around the corner, but when you're a model breezing up to the velvet rope with another model, a bouncer is little more than a warm and fuzzy welcome mat. The rope unclips, the doors part, and Kate and I slip into the main room of the club.

With its gilded mirrors, iron balcony, and crystal chandelier suspended over the dance floor, Café de Paris looks nothing like a Parisian café and everything like the ballroom of an eccentric aristocrat who's thrown open the doors of his chateau for his thousand closest friends, currently getting down to "Bizarre Love Triangle" by New Order.

"Goody, I love this song!"

I grab Kate's hand. As I pull her through the throng, the chandelier flicks from green to blue. Sapphires cascade down the walls and over our bodies. The DJ plays a lyric, then cuts the sound and lets the crowd fill in the rest. "Every time I . . . SEE YOU FALLING! I get down . . . ON MY KNEES AND PRAY!"

The two of us find room to move. I throw my arms in the air and arch my back. The air is rank with cigarette smoke, sweat, and in certain directions, the pungent aroma of pot. I twirl. Punk is dead, but tell that to the guy on my right with the Billy Idol boots and the fishhook in his lip. On my left, a gaggle of girls in stonewashed jean minis and ankle boots pass around a fifth of vodka.

A guy in a baby bonnet, Peter Pan collar, and leather hot pants grabs my hands. We go down, and up, and down again, in keeping with the lyrics until the song ends and the lights dim. For several seconds, it's quiet. Fog billows out of the side vents, clouding the air and pushing the cigarette smoke into thin ribbons until it feels like we're floating inside a marble. And then—

"Life is a myst-er-y."

The crowd roars. "Madonna!" the girls scream. Kate accepts a swig of their vodka and passes it to me. "Happy birthday!" they cry. Fishhook lets out a rebel yell and tosses me in the air. I laugh. I soar. I smile: I've been nineteen for almost a day, and *finally* it's getting fun.

We dance until we're sweaty and thirsty and not in the mood for The Bangles. As we make our way toward the VIP room, the chandelier fades from pink to purple. I tip my head back and feel the flecks of light ripple over me. "Please, oh please, let something wonderful happen on

my birthday," I whisper, only it doesn't feel like a wish so much as a har-
binger. Kate, Madonna, vodka—my faith has been restored. By the
time we get to the VIP area, I'm sure of it: Something wonderful is
going to happen tonight. I can tell.

Only Cary isn't here either.

"It's early yet," Kate reassures, ushering me over to the velvet banquette that's occupied by the band. I meet Tranquill. Noel has strange
patches of facial hair and the stringy, underfed bod of rockers everywhere, but his impish grin is irresistible and I can tell he clearly worships my friend. She slides next to him. Ice has his tongue down the
throat of some Jody Watley look-alike, so I squeeze in next to the drum-
mer, Little T, a pockmarked shrimp with thick lugs of steel piercing
each eyebrow and a watch encased in leather. "Hi."

I'm wearing a form-fitting hot pink mini-dress. Little T plucks the
fabric like a chord and laughs hysterically.

Okaay. I decide to embark on a walking tour of the VIP section. It's
crowded, with plenty of dark corners. I poke my nose into all of them.

At first, when I realize that absolutely, positively Cary Connery is
not on the premises, I try to rally. *Emily,* I think, *it's only a guy you've
seen once. You didn't even speak. Today is your birthday! You're nineteen!
You're having fun! You're a VIP!*

Back in the banquette, Kate and Noel make out. Whenever a new
song comes on, the other band members issue a collective groan before
launching into a detailed discussion of how much better the tune
sounds when performed by someone I've never heard of in the basement of a place I've never been to. When Kate comes up for air and
more champagne, she fills me in on the rest of the VIPs. This is when
my rally officially ends. A guy from *EastEnders*—what's *EastEnders?* A
member of Burning Spear—who are they? An un-made-up Adam Ant?
Diana Ross's stepdaughter? Dana Plato? Who cares? Who cares? Who
cares? These aren't VIPs, they're *nobodies.* Nobodies doing nothing. Nobodies going nowhere.

At ten minutes to midnight, I realize that even if Cary were to materialize, it's too late: I no longer want to see him. My hair is flat, my
fuchsia lips have long left their mark in other places. No, that ship has
sailed and I am most definitely not on it: I am sunk. I hunker against

the red velvet, guzzling champagne and reveling in my funk until Little T pulls me outside to show me something.

It turns out to be his hard-on, still in his pants but he's willing to change that.

"No," I say. The rest of Little T stiffens. "You suck," he informs me. I point out that this is precisely what I'm not doing and leave. No one even notices, of course; I'm as nobody as the nobodies I've left behind.

By the time I get back to the flat, I'm sure of this.

The remains of the tart are in the refrigerator, tightly shrouded in plastic. I break the seal and cut a generous slice. The whipped cream is a little runny. It will do.

I finish this piece and have another. It slips down my throat.

And then I walk into the bathroom—the downstairs bathroom, well out of earshot—and jam my finger in my mouth.

Nothing.

I push it further, only I gag and recoil so I try again, and again, for longer and longer until, finally, I start to retch. Islands of partially chewed raspberries soon float in a peppermint pink sea.

I stop then. My eyes are wet, my esophagus burns. It feels like there's vomit up my nose. I want to finish the job, but I can't.

I can't even do this. I can't even make this happen.

Chapter 18

Christmas in July

Only things *are* happening. Kate was right about me doing well here. As the pounds continue to come off, the balance tips in favor of work. I shoot suits for Debenhams, evening dresses for Marks & Spencer, and tops, appropriately enough, for Top Shop. My bank account is filling up and I can put aside money for school. The problem is I still haven't gotten anywhere, not really. I still don't have any new editorial and without that, I'll return to New York with the same old book—a summer in London and nothing to show for it.

"Can I see the magazines now?" I ask Sam.

"Soon," she replies. "Very soon."

And then, in the middle of July, I get my most plum job of the summer, the holiday advertising campaign for Garhart, a posh jeweler on Regent Street. It pays well, but even better, it's being shot by Kip MacSwain, described by Sam as London's most famous fashion photographer under forty, a man whose work has graced the pages and covers of *Harpers & Queen, Marie Claire, Tatler,* and countless others.

"What's he like, anyway?" I ask Marco, the makeup artist, a portly man with a goatee, as he preps my skin with concealer.

"Kip?" Dab. Dab. Pause. "You mean you've never worked with him?" Marco says. "Then how'd you get the booking?"

"I saw Garhart's."

Marco nods—this makes sense—and bends forward to examine the sides of my nose. Jewelry shots are essentially beauty shots. Whenever you're homing in on the head, every stray hair needs to be plucked, every pore filled, every blood vessel lightened. God forbid you have a zit, because you'll get sent home, and that cold sore could cost you a forty-thousand-dollar campaign. "If Kip likes you, he's excellent to work with," Marco is saying. "He gives direction, but not too much; he never likes to shoot more than three or four rolls, even for advertising. His beauty light is phenomenal: really flattering. Girls *love* him."

Great, but this begs a question. "And if he doesn't?"

"He can be a royal pain in the arse."

My stomach constricts, and not just because the only thing I've put into it in the last two days was leafy. Photographers have been known to walk into hair and makeup, decide they don't like the look of a girl, and send her packing, particularly if an important job is on the line. What if Kip takes one look at me and decides he'd rather not waste the film? I'd get a cancellation fee, sure, but that would be small compensation for total and utter humiliation—and that'd be *before* I sat down with Siggy.

Steps ring in the hallway. My heart pounds, but it's only Penny, the Garhart's rep, a redoubtable woman in a chartreuse skort, breezing in to provide shot direction to Marco, Celeste (hair), and Miriam (stylist), which means, two hours later, I've got a gold lamé bow on my head (festive; shows off earrings), red lips (you always get red lips for the holidays), and a high-necked ruffled taffeta blouse in a kicky Stewart plaid (this, I can't explain).

"Oh my, someone's got the Christmas spirit," Miriam murmurs as she plucks my neckline and fluffs my sleeves, which rise off my shoulder with the subtle curve of a ham hock.

"Ho, ho, ho."

Miriam smiles. "Let's pin you on-set," she says, walking out.

"Wait, what about pants?" I ask. I usually wear pants at Christmas. In any case, I don't swan around in sheer hi-cut briefs, which is the only thing I've got going on south of my belly button.

Miriam turns. "Do you want them?" she says, frowning at my crotch. "The shot's cropped, and it'll be hot under the beauty lights."

I definitely want something more substantial than nylon. After further discussion, I pair the taffeta shirt with my own jean shirt and scuffed tennis shoes and trot onto the set.

"Walking in a Winter Wonderland" is blasting from the stereo; it feels more like Santa's Workshop. One assistant carefully sprays fake snow on the panes of a window that's suspended in the air courtesy of poles and clamps. Another decorates the on-camera side of a balsam fir with crystal icicles and silver balls. Kneeling in front of a (real) marble fireplace is the third assistant, whistling while she works first foam, then silver and red presents into a green velvet stocking. A fourth lights candles along the mantel. And yonder, just outside of cropping distance, a goldfish swims agitated circles in a glass bowl next to an architectural model of the Tower of London and a giant ball of rubber bands that are all swaddled in a plush bearskin rug—Kip's stuff making room for the holidays.

"Emily's ready," Miriam prompts.

Penny spins. "Fetching!" she cries, tapping a faux gift against her chin as she takes in my top half. "You're ready for the emeralds!"

Advertising clients are always "thrilled" or "upset," there's no middle ground, so I'm perfectly happy to have Penny infused with the holiday spirit, even if it means I look like an FAO Schwarz grab bag. While I absently crinkle my gold bow, a security guard hoists a briefcase that's been shackled to his wrist onto a nearby table. Penny unlocks it, raises the top, and pulls a pouch from one of several foam compartments. Two items plink into her hand.

"First, we have the earrings: twenty pear-shaped emeralds, 288 round diamonds Girandole style."

Penny holds an earring aloft. Everyone gasps. It's delicate yet stunning: an upside-down candelabra with flickering green flames.

"And then we have the ring." Another pouch opens. "A thirteen-carat cabochon emerald flanked by two pear-shaped diamonds, mounted in platinum."

"Gorgeous!" Marco says. "This stuff must be worth thousands," Celeste murmurs, whispering the way one does around expensive things.

"£400,000 for the set," Penny says.

Okay, I don't think *I'd* sell for £400,000. I slip the ring on my finger and let it catch the light. It's beautiful. It's breathtaking.

"It's not for you, dear. The ring's for Flora," Penny says.

Huh?

"Flora's the hand model, dear," Penny says, seeing my bewilderment. "Obviously hands are *vital* to the Garhart campaign and we didn't know if yours were any good, plus it's *critical* we have someone who knows how to work a cabochon—all those flaws, you know. So we booked Flora." Penny shakes her palm encouragingly.

I want to wear the pretty ring! Reluctantly, I slip it off. Penny slips it onto her pinkie. "I assume you've worked with a hand model before, Emily, correct?" she asks.

"Of course," I say. I haven't. I have no idea what's about to happen.

"Flora?"

A petite woman, nondescript except for a pair of white, elbow-length cotton gloves, approaches.

"Emily, this is Flora," Penny says.

"Nice to meet you."

I extend my hand. Flora looks as horrified as if I had licked her. She also looks pissed. Once my limb is shunned as if it were emitting a foul odor, she peels off the gloves to reveal another, shorter pair underneath. "I thought I was doing singles!" she cries. "My booker said *five singles!*"

Singles? "Of your hands?" I ask.

"Well, I am the hand model!" she huffs.

Dear God, you must be joking.

"You have five shots, Flora," Penny says levelly. "Two with Emily and then some insets."

"Insets?" The gloves cross and disappear under the armpits like they're going into the Witness Protection Program. "I don't *do insets*. I did Cutex!" Pause. "I did Ovaltine!" Long pause, a drumroll, and . . . "I'm the *Palmolive Girl!*"

I can't resist. "Don't you mean the Palmolive hand?"

Flora turns on her heel. "I'm leaving!"

Despite this promising statement, what Flora actually does is flounce off to call her agent, who must have told her to suck it up for, moments later, the two of us are in front of the snowy window. For beauty shots, the lighting is so precise that a model is typically seated, and so it is now. I'm on a stool with my legs spread extrawide, Flora crouched between them, her degloved and bejeweled right hand delicately resting on the white reflective board that's spread across the table in front of us to bolster and even out the illumination. She's still upset, in fact, she's squawking in a way that even Donald Duck might find unintelligible, and I think I'd better change this; after all, in addition to being situated inches from a region I'm rather partial to, it's about to be my face in Flora's hands.

"Your hands—how do you keep them so perfect?" I ask. And I am curious. Flora's hands *are* perfect: smaller than mine, the fingers long and thin, the nails ten perfect ovals of glossy, festive red, the skin free of any blemishes whatsoever. Flora, it seems, has never had a scratching fight or a bug bite she couldn't leave alone, or gotten her hand slammed in a car door by her brother.

"I wear gloves 24/7/365. And my husband does all the house and yardwork."

"Wow," I say. Flora's husband must have a hand fetish.

An assistant hangs up the phone. "Kip will be here in five!" he shouts, a pronouncement that sends the other three springing into action. I glance at the clock, surprised. Apparently, if you're London's leading fashion photographer under forty and give great beauty light, you get wealth, fame, and the ability to show up on set at eleven.

"Girls, can we get a Polaroid? Hand on cheek?" Penny asks.

Flora fingers travel across my face until the assistant shouts "Good!" The strobe fires.

"Are you a foot model, too?" I ask Flora. It's awkward to make small talk with someone who's practically humping you. It's even more awkward not to.

Gasp. "A foot model? Why, I'd never!"

The Polaroid is examined. Miriam approaches the set brandishing a pair of scissors. "We want to see a touch of cuff in the shot," she explains. She's just sliced the taffeta from around my forearm and is in the midst of double sticking the sleeve to Flora's when the door slams.

"Jiminy Cricket, it's Christmas in July!"

"Kip!" Penny cries.

I look up and everything inside me jolts—on the outside, too, evidently, for the chair lurches—because Kip MacSwain is Cary Connery.

"Watch the hands!" Flora squeals.

I manage to plant my feet and flatten my palms but I'm shaking. Kip is Cary? I can't believe it. I can't believe he's here.

"Kip!" Penny throws her arms around him, and then: "You've got Flora and Emily on-set."

"Hello, Flora. . . ."

The hand waves. Kip struts toward us. "Hello, Miss Woods," he murmurs. A sly smile spreads across his lips. "Or should I say Fanny?"

I had given up hope. In fact, tomorrow I was going to take *Tom Jones* up to A Page in Time and tell Edwina I'm not that kind of girl. But it's him, the great Scot, bending across the set in a black polo and jeans, looking tanned and rugged and much more handsome than I remember. His dark hair is still endearingly unruly. His brown eyes glitter in the beauty light. His lips are enticingly full.

I take a deep breath. "He-llo," I finally manage. "Thanks for the book. I love it."

Kip reaches out and ever so lightly skims my cheek, *which I'm never washing again.* His smile broadens. "You're welcome. I'm glad you liked it."

"Book? What book?" Flora says.

"So you *do* know Kip," Marco says.

"Fanny?" Celeste says.

"Okay, Emily!" Penny cries, eager to convert this badinage to her company's bottom line. "We want these energetic and flirtatious. It's Christmas morning! You've just opened your present and you're as pleased as punch!"

I look in the lens and beam: *piece of cake.*

In fact, the day is a total nightmare. A few shots into the roll, it becomes apparent that Flora's booker gave her a different directive, or else the hand diva came up with it on her own—either way, she's treating our shot as her single, my face as her prop. She pushes my cheek right. I pull it left. She pushes it up. I pull it down. Finally, my neck hurts and I have no choice but to "nibble" on her finger during my "coy and delighted" look. Flora retaliates a few frames later by having her pinkie "accidentally" catch against the inside of my nose as we move into the "fondle the earring" pose. After my nose stops bleeding and I've changed shirts, I have the set all to myself. Kip's sent her home.

But there's still trouble in Santa's Workshop. Around noon, Penny morphs into "upset" client, a pendulum shift that manifests into a conviction that no shot is "quite right," which translates into shooting each set of jewels with three different shirts and two different hairstyles just to make sure we've "covered" it. Marco spends the rest of the day cleaning crusted blood from my nose (makeup artists routinely play mom: removing eye goo, picking food out of teeth, and wiping noses but trust me, having one's nostril picked repeatedly in front of eight people, including the person you have a massive crush on, is an entirely new level of humiliation). Worst of all, we are subjected to six hours of Christmas music looped around only one extended mix tape that is heavy on the Chipmunks.

It's a nightmare. It doesn't matter. I'm on cloud nine and every time Kip smirks or winks—no, every time he even *looks* at me—I float even higher. Marco has to take down the blush a notch or two and my eyes are a bit watery because for the first time in my career, I'm looking into the lens feeling what I've only ever pretended to feel: Energetic. Flirtatious. Pleased as punch.

When the booking is over, I know what I want to happen and I'm willing to wait for it: I walk back to the dressing area and call Sam with the day's report. I make tea. I slowly remove my nail polish, even though it's the usual neutral. I brush my teeth. I gargle. By the time I walk back on-set in my jean skirt (now more appropriately paired with a white tank top), Louis Armstrong is playing. Two assistants scurry about, snuffing out the candles, removing the ornaments, rolling out the bearskin rug. Kip is seated at his desk rifling through a stack of mail. Everyone else is gone.

I wander over to the tree. The branches have dropped and opened. "You should leave this up," I say, inhaling as I stroke the soft needles. "It smells so nice."

"Does it now?" Kip rises and walks over to where I'm standing, close enough that I pick up a second scent: sandalwood entwined with a little spice. As he touches a branch, his fingers brush against mine.

"Maybe I will," he says. He turns to survey the room. "I should let these guys go anyway; it's Friday."

I smile. *Yes, send them home.*

"Nice to see you again, Emily." Kip clasps my hand, walks back to his desk, and gives his full and loving attention to his pile of mail.

A handshake? I race toward the Underground, stomping as much as my rubber soles will allow. *A handshake?* What is going on with this man? First, he flirts from the poetry section. Then I get a book. Then he books me. Then . . . *a handshake? A handshake.* Jordan says no man buys a girl an expensive gift unless he wants to have sex with her. Pixie says older men like to take their time pursuing. Kate agrees with both of them. And then, *a handshake?* . . .

I look the wrong way, realizing my mistake right as a car beeps. I jump back. *A. Hand. Shake.* I wish Kate were in town. I wish I were on tour with Tranquill. Maybe I could be. I'll just call her hotel and hop on the train.

The car beeps again. One long beep. Then another. I twist. *What the—*

A vintage Mercedes convertible pulls beside me. It's Kip. "I've decided I'm not done shooting you, Miss Woods," he says. His eyes are obscured by shades but he's grinning. A dimple dots his chiseled cheek. A 35 mm camera dangles from his neck. He pats the red leather seat. "Care to jump in?"

I do.

We take pictures all over the city, sometimes at the big tourist attractions—Westminster Palace, the Cavalry Guards, St. James's Park—places I keep meaning to visit, but somehow never got around to—sometimes at more obscure places: a bench, a phone booth, a lamppost. At sunset, Kip shoots me on a bridge overlooking the Thames.

And then the sun sinks, the lanterns flicker on, and he puts the camera away.

"There," he says. "That's that."

My hands are as they were: behind me, on the balustrade, a breeze fluttering in my hair. Kip steps closer. I tilt my chin up. *Now. You can kiss me now.*

"You hungry?"

We walk a couple of blocks to a tiny Italian place, the kind with the red-and-white-checkered tablecloths, drippy candles oozing from the top of old Chianti bottles, and braids of garlic on the wall. "Order something good," he instructs. "And not in model portions."

"No, no, I still have to lose a couple pounds," I protest. "I'll have a salad."

"Oh no you won't."

Kip orders pasta and tiramisu for two. I swoon. As he refills my glass of wine, I ask him the question that's been on my lips for weeks. "How did you find me?"

"When you opened your knapsack to pay, I saw your portfolio."

"So you *were* still there!"

"In seventeenth-century poetry."

"Clever!"

Kips smiles. "Wasn't it?"

"Very." Suddenly, I stare at my plate, feeling shy. "I thought I was never going to get the chance to thank you . . ."

"Oh, Emily, I'm sorry I took so long," Kip rejoins quickly. "But for the last two weeks I've been in Tanzania shooting—"

"Shooting?"

"Girls, not game."

"Good."

Kip's leg wraps around my calf, pulling me closer to the table. To him. "Africa—you ever been?"

I sigh dreamily. "No, but I'd love to."

Over our entrées, Kip tells me about the Ngorongoro Crater, the tents they slept in, the game they spotted. Their campfire at night. The stars.

"So many stars. The sky is thick with them, thick and heavy," he says. "You can feel them pressing down on you, like you're part of it, like you're part of the sky."

I close my eyes, for a moment, seeing this. "I haven't been any-where, not really."

Kip's fingers lace into mine. He raises them to his lips. "Oh, you'll go places, Emily Woods. You're beautiful and smart and that's a killer combination," he murmurs. Ever so lightly, his tongue trails along each knuckle, moistening the space between.

Emeralds, stars, Kip now gnawing at my thumb; I'm dazzled. When dessert comes, Kip feeds me the tiramisu, breaking frequently to brush the hair off my face and run his finger down my neck.

And then we're on the street. My body is warm and humming. *Now. It's going to happen now. He's going to kiss me now.* His arm slides down to the small of my back. He pulls me against him. "Let's go see the lions."

It's misting and windy, so not many people are lingering in front of Lord Nelson's column at Trafalgar Square or near the four bronze lions surrounding it. We walk to one of them. Kip hands me his camera.

I laugh. "Oh, no. You're not serious!"

Kip's response is to jump onto the base of the statue and extend his hand.

"You're crazy!" I cry.

He takes the camera, then, "Come join me."

The lion's back is wet and slick. As Kip takes it by the tail, I move to the middle. Once my legs are wrapped around its belly, I stick my face toward the sky.

Kip looks through the viewfinder. "Beautiful!" *Click.*

A few frames, and I'm leaning back. My head is on the lion's mane. My thighs grip its flanks. The mist turns to rain, hitting my face, my arms, my legs, and dampening my shirt until it's pressing against me like a second skin.

"Gorgeous!" *Click. Click.* "Just like that!"

Above me I see Kip, the sky, and the stars. "Emily the lion tamer," he says and we kiss.

The bearskin rug is much softer.

Chapter 19

The Big O . . . My God

" I still don't get it. Why all the focus on virginity?"

Over the faint transatlantic hiss of the phone line, I can hear Jordan taking another bite of cereal. "You mean when the real milestone's the orgasm?" she asks, and not very chipperly. Kate's away on a booking and I had to talk to *someone*—it was all I could do to wait until it was morning in DC. Unfortunately for Jordan, I only waited until 7:50 A.M. On a Saturday. To talk about orgasms.

Evidently, I'm not done yet. Shifting my weight, I slide to the other corner of the phone booth. "Yeah. I mean, I realize that men come pretty much every time, but shouldn't we women care more about our first orgasm with a guy? Orgasm—your orgasmity," I say, testing the term.

Jordan swallows, then sighs. "Okay, leaving the whole issue of pregnancy aside, wouldn't orgasmity be something you'd *gain,* not lose?"

"Exactly! Something positive, which is so much more fitting! I just gained my orgasmity!" I announce, and not just to Jordan; all Londoners within earshot pause and cock their heads, like they just heard the twelve o'clock whistle. "I feel like I've discovered a whole new world, a world of pleasure and joy and pleasure—"

"You said pleasure."

"—a world where only good things happen, over and over again, hour after hour!"

"My God, Emma Lee, how many orgasms did you have?"

"You mean last night or this morning?"

Jordan's spoon clatters against the bowl. "Stop! And kindly remember who you're talking to, I beg of you!" she cries after a second crash suggesting something hitting the floor.

Jordan is currently dating Ben, the guy she took to the spring formal, only Ben's in Ecuador this summer, a long way from her job in Senator Covell's office, and so the two of them adopted a "don't ask, don't tell" policy. It didn't take long for Jordan to decide that the person she most wanted to utter nary a word about was Evan, Senator Covell's hot page. Problem was, Evan wasn't so hot between the sheets. "He told me sex is overrated and that, given the choice, he'd rather curl up with a Bob Woodward book—I mean, who says that?" Jordan shrieked last week, furious even in the retelling; clearly she'd been hoping for a different kind of page turner. And that's been as steamy as DC's gotten all summer.

"Don't worry, Jord. Your time will *come*."

"Pathetic!" she snorts. "The hot Scot . . . dare I ask if you'll see him tonight?"

"Not till Monday," I reply. Unfortunately, Kip had to go out of town for a job this weekend, which is okay *only* because I need time to physically recover. "What are you up to?"

"Oh, you know me, soiree at the big house with George and Babs—oh, shit, I'm being paged!" Jordan exclaims. "Can you believe that? And on a Saturday morning, too!"

"Aren't you glad you're already up?"

"Shut up."

When Monday evening rolls around, Kip and I don't even make it out of the studio. In fact I'm still in the foyer when Kip presses me against the wall.

"Hello, you," he says, putting his nose to mine.

I'm too excited to speak, so I answer with a kiss. We keep this up, first gently, then more insistently, until our mouths lock together, our hands touch and we stroke and probe and our clothes seem like bandages—tourniquets—and I want them off at once. I unbutton Kip's shirt, pausing halfway down to press my lips against his chest and inhale his warm, spicy Kipness.

Kip's fingers plunge into my hair and tip my head back. "Come with me."

Kip growling anything in his deep Scottish burr makes me weak in the knees—especially when it's accompanied by a tug toward the bed. Only we stop outside the darkroom.

I groan and bite his ear. "You're *such* a tease."

"Patience, darling; good things come to those who wait," Kip murmurs, punctuating this promise with a caress to my ass. His foot pushes open the door. "I just thought you might be interested to see how I spent my afternoon, that's all."

As my eyes adjust to the small, warm room, I see the clothesline and the two dozen black-and-white photographs drying on it: me in two sizes, large and larger.

"I printed these as a start. There were many other good ones." Kip's arms wrap around me. "What do you think?" he whispers into my hair. "Do you like what you see?"

In the photographs, I still have on most of my makeup from the Garhart's shoot: heavy, glam, I'm £400,000-pound-worthy makeup. My hair, though windswept, still has the controlled curves that can come only from the hands of a skilled professional. And yet, they're me. Emily. An Emily I've never seen before—sexy, seductive, womanly—but still Emily. Do I like them? Yes, very much. "They're so . . . real," I murmur.

"They're so beautiful—like this." Kip's fingers curl around the edges of one of the larger photographs: a close-up from Trafalgar Square. In it, my hair swirls against the lion's mane. I look radiant, expectant, alive. This was moments before our first kiss. "Emily the lion tamer," he whispers.

Kip releases the photo. The clothesline bobs, causing every photograph to quiver. I'm wearing a sundress. He pushes the hem to my waist. His hands trace my thighs: up and down again and again until all I feel—think—is this. This feeling. I arch against him. "Emily, we make a good team, don't you think?" Kip says, his lips pressed against my pulsing jugular. His finger slips under my panties.

I moan.

"I'll take that as a yes . . ."

My dress is off now. Kip remains behind me. His hands cup my breasts. His mouth tends to each link of my spine down, down, down, slowly, slowly until he's lying on the ground and pulling me to him, to his face. My knees slip past his shoulders.

When his tongue touches me, I shudder.

Kip pauses and looks up. Above him, all he can see, is me. Me and me and me. "I just called your agent," he whispers. "I've got you on hold next week for a *Harpers & Queen* cover."

"Oh, *Kip*!"

After, we take a bath, scramble some eggs, and make a fire. On the bearskin rug, Kip reads Wallace Stevens aloud. *Pink and white carnations, fire-fangled feathers, ambiguous undulations*—the words pour over us. Our bodies are tucked together, our limbs braided and curled, a knitted layer against the outside world.

I'm in love.

You know how they say one good thing happens and everything else falls into place? Well, it's true. I'm in love. My chart continues to fill with bookings. And something else is happening too. Here, in London, I'm really learning how to move.

Whenever you see models in those made-for-TV movies, they're always doing these big sweeping poses: leaping, spinning, jumping, springing; it's like a bad outtake from a *Thriller* audition. In reality, modeling is a lot less dramatic. This I knew, of course, along with the basic angles I gleaned from Conrad, and swimsuit poses I picked up from Greta, but this is only the half of it. No, the hard part is making it real. Do a bad job and you'll look like one of those cardboard cutouts next to the beer cooler at your local 7-Eleven—stiff and cheesy—and you won't work a lot, no matter how stunning you are.

Do a good job, however, and it's completely different. You're no longer the model showing off the pocket feature of the Dacron house-coat but The Woman. The Woman Whose Linen Never Wrinkles, The Woman with the Chic Little Black Dress. The Woman with the Perfect Shade of Lipstick. She's relaxed, confident, and beautiful and everyone wants to be her.

And I am that woman, I mean, sometimes. The shoot with Kip must have kick-started something, because now, whenever I walk on the set and strike a pose, I feel just like that—relaxed, confident, and beautiful—and when I look in the lens and the photographer's saying, "Yes Emily! Yes!" and clicking away, I know that I'm good at my job and that this is what I was meant to do.

So I'm busy. I still haven't gone to see the magazines ("Soon, I promise," Sam says), but they're starting to come to me. Within days of learning of the upcoming *Harpers & Queen* cover shoot, I get my first editorial booking of the season: a fall outerwear story for British *GQ* that's being shot on Hempstead Heath.

GQ is a men's magazine, obviously, which means that I'll be a prop. This comes as no surprise. The men's magazines use women as props far more often than the other way around. As I see it, there are two reasons for this. The first is that men have no imagination. They need to be face-to-photo with a babe ogling a jacket/suit/whatever in order to imagine it happening to them. The second—and more important—reason is that guys like looking at pictures of babes.

The *GQ* story is six pages. I'm in two of them, which are: one, me perched on a fence in a skintight black velvet dress and heels, while Armin (steely Swiss supermodel) stares contemplatively across the heath, one arm snaked around my leg, the other in the pocket of his Barbour jacket, as if retrieving a pipe; and, two, me in a black velvet cat-suit (similar to the one Kate wore but with a plunging neckline) staring up at Armin (adoringly? awestruck? satisfied? We try all these and more) while Armin laughs, his brow perfectly cocked beneath his wool cap and coordinating peacoat.

Looking at the Polaroids, part of my brain, the part that has been stretched and flexed for several months at an Ivy League institution, says that it's wrong to be portrayed—objectified—like this. But then I get real. I've got two more editorial pages for my book—*two!* Plus, Kip MacSwain, the man I adore above all others, is going to shoot a cover on me—*a cover!* For the first time since I've arrived in London, I feel like I'm moving forward. Building momentum. Going someplace. Going up.

This is the kind of news that must be shared. I rush straight home from the shoot and place a call.

"That's great, Emily!" Byron says. "How many pages?"

"T—"

"JON TELL MARIO HE HAS A FIRST ON LISCULA!"

". . . LISCULA!"

". . . LIS-CUL-A! . . . GOT THAT?" Byron yells, our connection so good I'm sure they got that in Wales. "Sorry, Em. How man—A FIRST! A FIRST!! . . . Sorry—what was I saying?"

"The number of pages," I say crisply, "is two. Plus the cover."

"Two? That's it? What are they?"

I start to describe the shots for British *GQ.*

"Great," he says again when I've gotten as far as the heath part. "You fat?"

"N—"

"TELL MARIO TO HOLD—OKAY? EMILY, YOU FAT? . . . Sorry, you fat?"

"No, I've lost about ten pounds!" I cheer. "Almost there!"

"WELL, I'M A BUSY MAN, TOO, JUSTINE. TELL HIM THAT . . ."

"You sound busy," I say pointedly.

"God yes, we have thirty girls now, Em—thirty! Two more as of this morning; I'm so busy dealing with all the bullshit I can't even see straight. So two pages . . . that's it?"

"Plus the cover."

"It's a cover *try,* Emily, you always say cover *try.*"

"Sorry, cover *try.*"

"I'm just saying that in case you don't get it. Magazines always shoot several girls for every cover—five or six is pretty common—and most of those are cover girls of issues past, making it virtually impossible to nail one on your first try. . . . Anyway, that's *it?* Two pages plus a cover try—that's *all* you've got?"

Speaking of bullshit. "Well so far, yes, but I'm really starting to work," I tell him. "I'm really getting momentum here. Just ask Sam."

Pause. "Who's Sam?"

Wait, *what*? "Sam. My agent."

"Is she new?"

Is he kidding? "No, Byron. Sam's the head of Entr'acte. Anyway, about my momentu—"

"Entr'acte? *You're in Entr'acte?*"

Jesus.

"Two pages plus a cover try and it's almost August," Byron mutters. He seems to be talking to himself now. "London shuts down in August."

I feel my heart start to fibrillate. Or maybe it's the nicotine. "What do you mean, 'shuts down'?"

"*You* know, Em, it's England. *Europe.* Come August, the entire continent takes off, especially the fashion industry. Anyone who's anyone will be in Capri, or Cap d'Antibes, or Monaco. I'll be on Monaco myself. On Valentino's yacht."

No, I don't know. Valentino? "Not me," I blurt, suddenly panicked. "I'll still be here."

"Not working, you won't—well, the first week of August you might, but—"

Now it's my turn to yell. "'NOT WORKING!' What are you TALKING about? NOT WORKING! Why didn't you TELL me?"

"I'm telling you now."

"But I haven't even been to the magazines yet!"

"WHAT? THEY BOOKED ESTELLE? HAVE THEY SEEN ESTELLE LATELY? SHE'S AS BIG AS A HOUSE! Well, you saw *GQ* and *Harpers & Queen,* didn't you?—"

"No! Both of those came through photographers I already worked with. I did catalog with the *GQ* photographer and I'm dating the *Harpers & Queen* photographer—Byron, you've gotta help me! You've gotta tell Siggy to send me to the magazines!"

"Who?"

He can't be serious. "SIGGY! THE HEAD OF DÉBUT!"

"No, the PHOTOGRAPHER! WHAT PHOTOGRAPHER ARE YOU DATING?"

Geez. "Kip MacSwain." Despite the circumstances, I find myself suppressing a smile: *Kip!*

Gasp. "You're dating Kip *MacSwain*? Jesus, Emily, why didn't you

say something! Kip's *huge*! JUSTINE, JUSTINE, I'LL HAVE TO
CALL HER BACK! How long has this been going on? Has he booked
you yet?"

"We did advertising for Garhart's," I say smugly: *Kip!* "Hey, maybe
we could use those . . ."

"Not jewelry. No way: too fuddy-duddy. Any editorial?"

"No, but he shot eight rolls on me all over London, and oh Byron,
I can't wait for you to see the film. It's beautiful! The best shots of me
ever taken."

"Emily," Byron says. "I want you to listen to me carefully: *Screw*
test pictures, test pictures are a waste of your time. You need tear sheets!
The cover's a good start, but it's not enough: You've got to strategize and
GET MR. LOVER BOY TO SHOOT A STORY ON YOU IN A
MAGAZINE—ANY MAGAZINE—and you've got it made. Got it?
Gotta go."

Click.

You gotta be kidding me. I only have two weeks left to get all my
editorial? *Two weeks?* I just got momentum. I just endured physical
agony and developed a pack-a-day habit—speaking of cigarettes, I
think I'll have one—to lose ten pounds. Ten pounds for nothing. Ten
pounds for shit. *Bullshit!* "Arrggggggh!!!"

"Goodness," Edward says, entering the kitchen.

I twist and point. "Edward! This is very important: Where will you
be two weeks from now?"

"Hmm, let me see . . . two weeks?"

"Yes, come mid-August, where will you be?"

"Cornwall."

I slap my forehead.

"A little dull perhaps, but not that bad," he says evenly. "Though it
can get crowded at that time of year—it's peak holiday season and the
roads are packed!"

"It sounds like you had a rough day. I'm so sorry, darling."

Kip's words are chased by lips pressed against my forehead. When I
first arrived at his studio, I had another freak-out about having only
two weeks before London shuts down. Hearing that Kip'll be gone,

too—to Brighton to see his mother and sister—didn't do anything to improve my mood. But then the two of us landed on the studio's star attraction: the bearskin rug. One extended trip to Orgasmity later and, "It's better now," I murmur sincerely. "Much."

"Good." Kip's tongue traces my ear. "And remember," he whispers. "You still have at least one good booking left: our *H&Q* cover."

"True . . ." I say, though, admittedly, I've been less excited about this since my conversation with Byron. "How many girls are you shooting for that?"

"Several."

I prop up on my elbows. "How many several?"

"Only one who's special."

My response is a light kick, a move that causes me to wince more than my target; ever since the topic of my career has come up, I've felt quite queasy.

Kip chuckles, grabs my foot, and starts rubbing it. "If you want more editorial, Emily, you need to go for it. Talk to Siggy. Insist that she send you to the magazines."

Another showdown with Siggy? "Yuck," I mutter.

"I could call her on your behalf if you'd like."

And have the ensuing discussion about my love life? No thank you. "No, it's my career. I'll do it myself. First thing Monday," I grunt before rolling onto my back, puppy style, to make things easier for the masseur.

"Good. Remember to get tough with her, Emily, that's what she'll respond to. It's all in the approach—both with Siggy and the editors you'll be seeing. In fact . . ." Kip releases my foot and sits up. "I think we should practice."

I think I need a foot rub. "Nooo," I whine. "Later. This weekend."

"I won't be here."

"What?" Now it's my turn to bolt upright. *Mmph.* My stomach does another sour flip-flop. "But why?"

"Oh, darling!" Kip strokes my cheek. "Booking in Paris. But I'll be back late Tuesday, I promise!"

"Tuesday? But what if I've seen the magazines by Tuesday?"

"My point exactly. So let's practice."

Grrrr.

His fingers lace into mine. "Okay, lesson one—handling the fashion editors can be summed up as follows: Be rude, uncommunicative, and stupid."

"Very funny," I say petulantly. I can't believe Kip's going away. Again.

"I'm serious. The friendlier you are, the more you talk, the more desperate you'll come across, and trust me: The *worst* thing you can be in front of an editor is desperate. You need to act like you couldn't care less: Be sullen!"

"Who am I, Sean Young?" I grumble.

"You mean you *aren't*?"

I roll my eyes: The British think they're so witty. "Well, just how dumb am I supposed to be?"

"For starters, you should never utter the words *Columbia University,* or even *university,* for that matter. No higher education. It's the kiss of death."

"Right," I snort sarcastically. Actually, Byron told me this, too, but I thought he was just being his typical excessive self, and so at my very next appointment, when the editor asked me where I lived, the whole story came tumbling out. Come to think of it, I didn't get that job. "But why?"

"Simple. In order for an editor to book you, she needs to feel superior to you. You might be pretty now, she tells herself, but you're stupid and you have no future. Sooner or later, you'll lose your looks and she'll come out on top. You have to play into their prejudices to get the job."

Ridiculous, though, I must admit, it sounds a hell of a lot easier than speaking Cherokee. "Fine."

"Good. Now, let's practice. 'Emily' "—Kip's Scottish brogue elevates an octave—" 'tell me, where was this picture taken?' "

I flop my hair in my face. "New York," I say curtly.

"No: you 'dunno,' " Kip corrects. "Let's try another one. 'Emily, how long have you been modeling?' "

"Two years."

Kip shakes his head. "No: you 'don't remember.' "

"You're kidding."

"I'm not. Try again." Kip pulls me closer and starts kissing my face, throat, chest. "Emily, where are you from?"

Mmph. My stomach roils. "I feel sick."

"Is that a midwestern city?"

I stick out my tongue. Kip tries to grab it. I giggle and he showers me with kisses, which makes me laugh . . . and then feel sad. "We only have two weeks together," I murmur when we've settled down and my head's on his chest. "Less after we subtract the weekend."

"Darling, what if I cut my family visit short? Would that help?"

Would it! I raise my chin and look into his eyes. "How short?"

"Oh, to one, maybe two days. That way, you and I could go away."

"Oh, Kip!" Liberally, I sprinkle kisses across his cheeks, forehead, and nose. "To where?"

Kip shrugs. "You're the one who said you haven't been anywhere. Where would you like to go: France? . . . Spain? . . . Italy?"

"God, any of those but you'll have just been to France, so—Italy!"

Kip grins. "Consider it done."

And then we're kissing deeply, passionately. Kip slips onto his back. I slide over him. He grabs my hips, my breasts. Clothing comes off. I tip my head and rock back and forth, back and forth. My stomach rocks too, gurgling and switching to its own beat until it feels as if it's going to detach and roll under the couch.

"Mmph," I moan.

"Mmm!" Kip grunts.

"Mmph," I moan.

"Mmm!" Kip bucks harder. Sweat pours down his face.

"Mmph," I moan. "Mmph. I can't . . ." I gasp. "I don't . . ."

Kip gasps. "Yes, you can, darling! Yes you can! Come on, baby girl: Let it out! LET IT OUT!"

Right as Kip comes, I heave. Over everything. And that's pretty much all I do for the next several hours, until every stomach muscle's in spasm and the bath mat seems like a cozy resting place, the base of the toilet the perfect cool compress to my forehead. When I next awaken, it's Saturday afternoon and I'm tucked between crisp cotton sheets. On the bedside table is a rose, a bottle of seltzer, and a note.

Darling,
And I thought all that moaning was because of me.
Rest and dream of Italy.
Can't see you soon enough.

Love, Kip

Chapter 20

Call to the Majors

The mystery bug is not the best start to the weekend; it is, however, indicative. I don't get vertical and out of Kip's studio until Monday morning. 55 South Clapham Common is dark and silent, so I pad unimpeded through the house, into Edward's bathroom and onto his scale.

There it is, right under my nose: the number I've spent the whole summer chasing. Eight and a half stone.

I did it.

I stare at the number. I always thought that when I got to 120, I would do something: *I'll throw a party!* I told myself. *I'll scream with joy! Or, at the very least, eat some cheese. Some*thing. But now that I've made it, I'm . . . pleased. And that's it. After all, this number, this weight, this is what's expected of me; it's where I was before that was unusual.

They say that the camera adds ten pounds, but this isn't true, not necessarily. It depends on the lens, the lighting, the competence of the photographer, and a dozen other factors. Still, you have to be rail thin, anyway, so that the unthinkable—that one bad frame where your arm is mashed against your side or the hem pushes into your thigh, never occurs. And to get there—here—I've had to ignore what I look like in person and just focus on the scale, the number. It's black and white, so simple, and it tells me when I'm thin enough.

I'm thin enough.

I step off the scale and turn to face the mirror. It's not full length, but previous expeditions have taught me that, if I stand in the center of the room, I get a perfectly acceptable three-quarter view. I stare at my reflection. Truthfully? I looked better when I first got here, less gaunt. Healthier. Now my limbs look long and brittle, like tree branches silhouetted against the winter sky, my breasts like two bumps on a pile of sticks. I should be accessorized with a feeding tube.

It's going to look great on film.

The foreboding padding of Siggy's Thierry Mugler jacket, when coupled with her usual spiky hairdo creates the overall effect of pilot, enemy spaceship. Well, I'm armed and dangerous, too. I drop into a chair, pull out a cigarette, and flick my flame to the tip.

"Send me to the magazines."

Siggy turns, fills her hot pot, and turns back. *Blink.*

Okay, enough with the staring contest, you Icelandic freakazoid. I lean forward and drop one hand on the desk, reserving the other one for wild and erratic gestures. "Siggy, I'm going to give you a choice: Either you send me to the magazines right this minute, or else you measure me and then send me, but no matter how you slice it, I'm going to see them because it's August and I have less than two weeks here and I only have two pages and that's not going to cut it—not with Byron, *certainly* not with me. So make your choice and make it NOW!"

I'm still panting when Siggy says, "You have appointments at virtually every magazine in London starting in about an hour. Sam has the list."

You could knock me down with a feather. "Wow . . . Okay. Great."

"Isn't it?" Is she . . . she is . . . *smiling.* "When were you going to tell me your big news?"

Words have now failed me. I issue a puzzled shrug.

"Byron told me about you and Kip! That's brilliant news! Kip's a brilliant photographer!" After yelling this, Siggy's voice plunges to a whisper. "So tell me, is he as good as they say? Is he . . ." *Blink.* "As big?"

Okay, I think I've discovered something more unnerving than the staring contest.

I leap up—"Er, he's great . . . Siggy . . . bigger and better"—and run down the hall to Sam.

True to Siggy's word, Sam has a list of editorial appointments, the first one in forty minutes and counting ("I've been calling and calling you," Sam says, relieved). I collect the list and hustle out the door, still weak from the weekend and still in shock about what just transpired.

And yet the moment I hit the pavement, I wonder why I made such a fuss.

See, I've been on editorial appointments before and they go something like this: Your agent calls the bookings editor and tells her—it's almost always a her—that she simply *must* meet this hot, young, up-and-coming, *totally* special new girl. Of course, for an appointment to actually be made, the agent must be both familiar and reliable (one can only promise divine and send dreck so many times). If the agent is legit and the editor owes him a favor/has time on her hands/is new to her job, you're in.

This is all fine and dandy. The problem is what happens next. The bookings editor is the lowest on the fashion totem pole, meaning she's one or two years out of college and she sits in a cube. It's a nice cube, decorated with Mapplethorpe postcards of bodies or peppers or peppers that look like bodies, but still, it's a cube. You sit in a chair on the perimeter while she flips through your book, mainly turning the pages of what little editorial you have sideways in order to read the name of the photographer. In other words, to see if you're important enough to send to a senior editor. In other words, she can't tell herself. After that, she Polaroids you, takes a card, and you're done.

Byron said you can only be a new face once. What he meant was you shouldn't see the editors until your book is strong enough to separate you from the pack. Of course, this won't happen until you get good pictures from good photographers, preferably in good magazines. Only they won't book you until your book is good enough. . . .

At least, this is what it's like in New York. But after zipping around town for over an hour, then settling in for several more hours at the

Condé Nast building on Hanover Square, I'd say the drill is pretty much the same on this side of the pond. Throughout it all, I try to follow Kip's advice, but acting "rude, uncommunicative, and stupid" is harder than it sounds, and so at *Good Housekeeping*, I'm warm and gregarious—the busy young mother just thrilled by the prospect of turning festive dish towels into fetching kitchen curtains. At *Santé*, I'm vivacious and enthusiastic, my performance culminating with a loud "B-bye!" accompanied by a balled fist that's half wave, half rallying cry, right as I step onto the elevator.

I know that you can never tell how a go-see has gone, but I have a strong feeling about these: I came, I begged, and they sucked.

And then I have one appointment left. Only one.

But it's a big one.

"Emily Woods? Right this way."

An intern leads me through a set of security doors and down a hallway. As we pick up speed, the framed covers lining the wall start to blur: *Vooooggggguuuueeee,* the girls whisper through white teeth and perfectly plump lips. *Vogue . . . Oh God.* I bite my own pair and try to focus instead on the other view: cube city, which looks reassuringly similar to the other magazines where I just bombed, until we've passed through another door, then another, then into a conference room.

"This is Emily Woods."

The intern places my portfolio on a spear-shaped table, as spartan and sleek as the editor standing behind it, and exits silently.

"Hello, Emily."

"Hello."

The editor tucks a glossy blonde forelock behind her ear and opens my book. I hear my heart in my ears: *Vogue, this is Vogue.*

"You're American."

"Yes." I start shredding the nail polish on my pinkie. I'm sure I should be doing something but what? How do I act *Vogue*? I don't know, so I just stand stiff as a board, my face tense and drawn as I bite the inside of my cheeks and try not to vomit.

"What part of the States are you from?"

"Dunno."

She looks up. "I'm sorry?"

I'm sorry, Kip. "Wisconsin," I say, more loudly.

"How lovely!"

I stand a bit taller. When you're from a rural part of your own country, you're a hopeless hick doomed to a lifetime of blank stares or odd comments like "Why, you sure are a long way from home!" When you're from a rural part of another country, it's "lovely."

More pages flip. "And you're how old?"

"I'm . . ."

A silver-haired woman, discreetly pregnant in a black sheath, steps through a side door and approaches the table. "Nineteen," I say to both of them.

"Liz!" The editor hops backward. "I didn't realize you were here! Liz, this is Emily. Emily Woods."

. . . who can hardly breathe. *Please like me,* I think as Liz Tilberis studies me through sparkling eyes. *Please like me.*

She doesn't. Liz flips through my book for five, maybe ten seconds before snapping it shut. Her palm presses flat against its cover, as if trying to sink it.

Oh. Everything inside me crumples. The reason you can't tell how go-sees go is because usually even the no's will pay token heed to your photos, throwing you a consolation compliment, like *You have terrific legs* or *You remind me of so and so.* You only find out it's a no-go later, when no options materialize, or they say something to your agent like, "She's not for us." But *this is* Vogue: *the* one, *the* star-maker; I guess they don't have to play nice if they don't want to.

Only Liz is smiling. "We want to work with you," she says, the hand now giving the cover an affectionate swish. "*Vogue* wants to work with you."

"Can you believe that? Liz Tilberis, the editor in chief!"

I leap up and attempt a heel click, the Lucky Charms leprechaun being the latest of the many great movers and shakers I've fancied myself in the past hour. "It doesn't get any bigger than that, does it?"

"Bigger than the chief? No . . ."

Kate refills my champagne glass and tops off her own before placing the bottle back in the bucket. Kate's been in Portugal on an epic booking; I haven't seen her in weeks. We were supposed to meet at the agency and go for tea, but when I walked into Début, Siggy bounded out of her office, the Moet and Chandon already on ice; *Vogue* had called to option me. Now, she's off procuring a second bottle ("of something more fitting, like Dom or Cristal"), leaving Kate alone with my euphoria.

"I've never been so thrilled!"

I execute a slower twirl, a move that nonetheless sends my champagne sloshing dangerously close to the lip. I tried to play it cool—Kate's been in British *Vogue* three times already—until she recounted how after her first booking with the magazine she raced around London on the back of Noel's Harley, shrieking into the night. Since then I've been letting it all hang out. "I mean, I just feel like all this hard work has paid off—finally! Of course, I don't have a booking or anything yet but—"

Siggy's entering the room, the fresh bottle raised in her arm like a torch. "If Liz likes you, you're in. It's just a question of time."

"Time or timing," Kate says.

And, as it has become all too clear in recent days, both are working against me. "But I'm not looking for much: a page, a half a page—surely they'll shoot something like that in August . . ."

Kate glances at Siggy, who, after popping the cork, says, "Emily, I think you should consider staying in London longer."

I shrug. "Sure, if it comes down to it, I can squeeze in another four or five days—of course, that means not going home before school starts, which wouldn't make my parents very happy, but if it's a question of *Vogue* or no *Vogue*—"

Another uneasy glance. "Em, Siggy means longer than a couple of days," Kate explains.

Oh. I know where this is going. I slide into a seat. "Let me guess: you mean skip school. . . ."

They nod.

My college roommates flash through my brain. I feel a pang. "But I like school. I want to graduate!"

"I know you do." Kate slides into the chair next to mine and tucks her legs under her body. She's wearing white linen from head to toe, and somehow, even in this small, smoke-tinged room, manages to look like a walking perfume ad. "It doesn't have to be forever, just . . . doing what I'm doing: postponing for a year or two to see how it goes."

I drain my glass.

"Or even just a semester," Siggy amends quickly. "That's what Lotte did: She decided to stay after the summer ended. She lived with me. You could do that, too. Or stay at Edward's—whatever you'd prefer."

"What about next summer?" I counter. "I could work for *Vogue* then."

Kate brushes my sleeve, her eyes tender. "Look, Emily, it's like what we talked about before, how sometimes you have to go with the flow, seize the moment—"

"Make hay while the sun shines, strike while the iron is hot, yeah yeah yeah," I mutter, reaching for the bottle.

Without warning, Siggy squeals. Her hands smash together. "Why, Kip must be thrilled!"

I smile. *Kip!* "He doesn't know yet."

"Kip?" Kate says.

Siggy pushes the telephone across her desk "Well, what are you waiting for? Call him!"

"He's in Paris."

"What are you talking about?" Kate asks.

"Oh, you don't—why, Emily's dating Kip MacSwain!" Siggy cries.

Kate's mouth pops open. I wanted to spill the news to her myself but . . . I grab her shoulders excitedly. "Kip is Cary!"

"Cary?" Siggy says.

"Never mind." I smile at my friend. The champagne has given us all rosy cheeks, hers dotted by tiny islands of freckles, only she's blanched. "Kip MacSwain," she echoes.

Once again, and equally alarmingly, Siggy's hands smash together. "Why Kate, it's ten past six! What are you *doing*? You're supposed to be at Heathrow *now*! I will *kill* you if you miss this flight! So will Hermès!"

Kate sighs. Agents spend half their time making sure models make their planes . . . or dealing with the fallout when they miss them. But Kate's a pro. "I'll make it, Siggy," she reassures. Nevertheless, at Siggy's insistence she trades her flute for her tote. I follow her out the door.

"So Kip—can you believe it? You've met him, haven't you? He's cute, right? My description was accurate, right?"

"Yeah . . . *Emily.*"

When Kate turns around, she catches me bouncing up and down. *Vogue!* Champagne! Kip! "What?" I stop. "Is something wrong?"

"No, no." She shakes her head. Her eyes are glassy but she's smiling hard. "Kip's gorgeous. You're right. Very Cary Connery."

As we hug, my eyes go glassy, too. In fact, they well with tears. Kate's part of the fashion exodus; she and Noel will depart for Cannes straight from Paris. I don't know when I'll see her again.

I step back, jamming my fingers under my lashes. "I wish you weren't going."

"And I wish you would stay," Kate says, blinking rapidly. A tear escapes and runs down her cheek. Her foot hits a step. "I'll be at the Ritz in Paris for the next four days and Emily? I'll call you. We really need to talk. I—"

"KATE! NOW!" Siggy hollers.

"I'm going! I'm going!"

Halfway down the stairs, Kate grabs the railing and turns back. "Emily, I think you should stay. Stay and see what happens."

And for the second time, I look her in the eyes and say, "I'll think about it."

Over one final glass of champagne, Siggy talks to me about my career: building it, developing it, maximizing it. Once *Vogue* is in the picture, I'll be moved to the Début board, of course, and she'll oversee my career personally. "It will be my honor," she tells me.

When we're finished, I take a walk. It's dusk now, and people have someplace to be. The tired trudge of the overcoat and briefcase set; the purposeful gait of those holding theater tickets, or reservations, or the ingredients of an eagerly awaited dinner; the lilting tripping of bar goers, party hoppers, and young lovers—I bounce between all of them, golden-eyed, buoyed by a champagne bubble. *Kip!* I think. *Vogue! Début!* my pickled mind not able to wrap around much more than that.

But then . . . my feet get sore. By the time I sit down in a sandwich shop for some coffee and a green salad, I've sobered up and am thinking of other things: Should I stay or should I go? <u>Pros,</u> I write, my pen pressing heavily against the napkin. <u>Cons.</u>

When I emerge it's no longer dusk but dark. There are fewer pedestrians and more meanderers. But I am not among them; I know where I'm going. I slide into a phone booth and dial.

They both answer.

"Emme!" Dad says. "Great timing, I just got home from work!"

"What's wrong?" Mom queries. Of course she does. For reasons that have never been entirely clear—probably because they aren't rational—Mom hates using the phone. Give her the option of dialing or driving and she'll pull out her keys; "catching up" with a friend always involves a pen; and I have one word for telemarketers: pity. In fact, I've only called my parents once since I arrived in London: when I arrived to let them know *that* I arrived. Since then it's been tissue-thin airmail all the way, my mother's missives filled with Balsam Lake news: riveting information such as her ongoing battle with garden pests.

"Nothing is wrong," I tell her now. "I'm just calling to check in."

"Are you pregnant?"

"No."

"Are you in jail?"

"Mom!"

"People use the phone for lots of different reasons, Claire," Dad reminds her. "Emme just told us she's checking in. It's great to hear your voice, Emme! How is it over there: fantastic?" Dad twitters, yanging to Mom's yin by being extraperky.

I spend a few minutes recapping what I've covered in my admittedly sporadic letters—a glossy, happy tale involving a beautiful town house and three attractive women, all overseen by a kindly older man: Charlie's Angels; cue the catsuits but kill the crime-fighting part.

"Sounds like a hoot!" Dad says, before launching into his own series of sound bites: The posters for the state fair are a big hit. Tommy's doing very well in the preseason. Speaking of games, he's got to run—he and T are seeing the Brewers versus the White Sox but stay on and talk to your mother. Bye.

"Bye, Dad!"

Mom's voice is guarded, expectant. "Okay, what's wrong?"

"Nothing!" I chirp. I'm the perky one now. "How's your garden? Do you still have a slug problem? Is the beer working?"

"I'm back to the hat pins."

"What is a hat pin, exactly? Where do you find one?"

Mom sighs. "Emme, it's almost midnight for you. Don't tell me you called to talk about slugs and hat pins."

Well, who would? I squeeze my eyes shut and inhale deeply: It's now or never. "Mom, I'm staying in London for a while."

In the moment that follows, I can hear my mother breathing. I can picture her on a kitchen stool, her back straight, her head erect—a posture that's been perfected by years of yoga. She's been cooking, most likely, and so her hair is in a low, loose twist, secured by a well-chewed pencil. She's wearing clogs, jeans, and a T-shirt lightly dusted with herbs and bread crumbs. And she's staring at the surface of the lake.

". . . Mom?"

"I heard you."

"Aren't you going to say anything?"

"What do you want me to say?"

An ambulance races down the street, lights on, sirens off. I watch it pass, then smooth the crumpled napkin against the booth: Here goes nothing. "I'm not talking about staying here forever, Mom, just for a few months. Think of the advantages." (*One*) "I'll make lots of money and save lots of money."

"You can do that now."

(*Two*) "You won't have to help out with my tuition, not one cent."

"It's your education. We're happy to help."

(*Three*) "Staying in London will help me find myself, help me figure out what I want to do."

"That's what your twenties are for."

"Why not get a jump on things?"

"Why waste time?"

"It's *not* a waste of time!" I'm shrieking now.

So is she. "It *is* a waste! It's silly!"

I ball the list—why not? We're completely off the script—and toss it. It sails through the air, dive-bombing the tallest in a pack of guys, all wearing black lipstick. "Nice shot, love!" he calls out. His friends start ribbing and taunting. "Hit us again, love! Yes, love! Go on, love!"

"*Love?* . . . Emme? Who's saying that?"

"No one, Mom, just some guy on the street."

"You're on the street? Why? Emme, it's midnight!"

"Hit us again, love!"

"Emme . . . Emme are you drunk?"

Abort. Abort. I grip the receiver. "Mother, I'm staying in London and I wish you'd respect my decision," I say quickly. "I'm nineteen now. An adult."

"An adult?" Mom laughs shrilly. "Then you'll see that going along with this is one thing, Emme; respecting you for it, another."

Chapter 21

Caddington Bared

All night I toss and turn. Mom was such a bitch. I keep hearing her shrill laugh, until it's louder and louder—the maniacal cackle of the Wicked Witch of the West—and then the drone of the dial tone after I'd slammed down the receiver.

It's a bad evening, but when the morning comes, it fades away. I've got more important things to worry about, like my *Harpers & Queen* cover try.

A cover. Who doesn't dream of being on a cover? Who doesn't imagine what it's like to be the face that launched one thousand, no, ten thousand, no, one *million* sales? Who hasn't pictured walking into a newsstand and saying, "Hi. Oh, yes . . ." Tee hee. "That's me. What? An autograph? Why, of course I will! What's your name? Oh, another?" *Emily Woods*, I'd sign in my hair, just like that guy who hides all the Ninas.

A cover. It's so exciting. The prospect of seeing Kip is exciting, too, and as I shower, change, and head for the studio I try to focus on these things—the exciting things—and not the other things, such as the knots up and down my midsection, which have formed for one and only one reason: because, unlike at a casting, no sentiment is spared on a photo shoot, especially one like this, there are too many dollars and egos on the line, so if this day doesn't go well, I'll know immediately.

When things click on-set, you feel it. The photographer shouts out "Good!" and "Beautiful!" and everyone's smiling, especially the client, who has a satisfied smirk from knowing he's the maestro who made it happen. Inquiries are made regarding your availability, and your agent calls to say you've been booked, not only for other jobs with this client, but for jobs with the photographer's other clients, many of whom you've never even met—all because they think you're fabulous.

When things don't click, the first thing you notice is the sound. Or rather, the lack of sound. No one is screaming with joy about the bigger picture; instead, they're huddled behind the lens, whispering about the minutiae. About you. This is the whisper campaign, and once it starts, it's nearly impossible to stop—not by you, anyway. You're trapped on-set, watching numerous pairs of eyeballs dart from one feature to another, overhearing just enough to know your fears are decidedly founded: *Is there a strand of hair poking out on the left side? No, actually I was looking at another strand, the one behind her ear. Her hair seems thin, wispy. What do you think of her eyes? Are they too strong? Not strong enough? Something's off—they look a tad small. Is it the eyeliner? Oh . . . it's her. Wait, there's something on her left cheek. No, my left. A mole? Can you cover it? Is the collar even? I don't know, it just isn't working. Maybe we should . . .*

The first few rolls are like this.

"Let's see . . ." Dee, the *Harpers & Queen* beauty editor, parts her assistants, pulls off her so-geeky-they're-cool glasses, and peers into the top of the Hasselblad.

"The collar's still uneven," she announces.

Miriam, the stylist, tugs at my neck. "Better?"

Sigh. "No."

"I'll crop it," Kip suggests.

"You can't. We'd lose the necklace if we crop and that would be a disaster; the message from up on high is that we need to use more jewelry."

Dee straightens and adjusts her skirt. Unlike her assistants—two horsey, preppy girls who seem entirely on par with *Harpers & Queen*'s target audience (readers who respond to headlines such as "Top-Secret Minutes of a Charity Ball Committee" and "Keeping a String of Polo Friends")—Dee's what you might expect in a fashion editor: model thin (why anyone would torture herself this way voluntarily is beyond me) and sporting a fresh-from-the-runway haircut: a boyish, heavily streaked style she feels the urgent need to frequently run her hands through. She also happens to be scantily clad in a tight Ungaro mini and pale silk top, the latter the tissue-thin variety that can only be worn with a judiciously chosen bra, only Dee hasn't bothered. Even from here, her nipples pop like raisins.

"Goodness, you're tense!"

. . . Which is why when Dee mock pouts and starts massaging Kip's neck and shoulders, I feel a potent urge to hit her.

"Emily, I need you in your exact position," Miriam reminds me.

I lean back and relax my fists.

"How's the collar now?" she calls.

"Fine, I guess," Dee says.

"Let's go to film," Kip says.

"*Wait!*"

Team Style descends. Celeste: "Drop your head back!" Miriam: "Not too far, I'm pinning!" Marco: "Eyeliner! Don't move a millimeter!"

"Okay?" Kip asks, three minutes later.

"Yup."

"Film!"

Kip and I vowed to play it cool today, to be "100 percent professional" in his words, "so that no one will get the wrong idea." Actually, they'd get the right idea, one underscored by the palliative blow job I administered early this morning in the dark room just a few feet from where I'm now sitting; but that doesn't count: No one was here to see it. Now, as Dee continues to fondle Kip's shoulder, I wish she had arrived early, or that I'd Polaroided it and could slip her the evidence—anything to stop this torture.

Kip's finger depresses the shutter. *Click. Click.*

I begin with a closed-lip smile. It's entirely possible my jaw is clenched.

"Okay," Kip says. *Click.* "Now, lower your chin."

I lower.

"Turn a touch more off-camera."

I turn.

"Her brow looks funny," Dee offers.

Bitch.

"Emily, relax your brow."

Emily. I relax it.

Dee frowns. "Hmm, is that better?"

Okay, ignore her, I tell myself. *Just relax. Relax and get this cover.*

Click. Click.

It's very important you get this cover.

"Okay." *Click.*

Cover before twenty and you'll work plenty.

Click.

No cover before twenty and you're screwed.

Click.

You have to get this.

Click.

You have to get this cover right now . . . now what are they looking at?

Click.

Is it the left eye? Because sometimes it doesn't open as wide in bright light.

Click.

Is—"Her smile looks crooked."

Click.

"Now she's not smiling at all."

Gee, imagine that. Kip steps away from the lens, and, after a moment of consultation, walks over and squats beside me so we're eye-to-eye.

"How are you doing?" he murmurs softly.

I turn my lips so they're off-camera, then hiss: "I'm ornery and horny. Which part would you care to discuss first?"

Kip's brow shoots up. He's smirking. "I'm confident I can take care of both those things later."

"For me or for Dee?"

The smirk fades. "Emily. Don't be absurd. Dee's got to be forty years old."

"Making her your peer!"

"You're being childish."

"Well, I *am* a teenager!"

"Listen to me, Emily," Kip says, his voice elevating to a low growl. "Dee is married with two kids; she likes to flirt a little, so I let her. It's harmless—and all part of being a fashion photographer, I'm afraid."

"You should be afraid," I snap, but there's no teeth in it. I'm mollified, partially by what Kip's just said, and partially because his hand has worked its way off his bent knee and is now tucked under the reflective board, gently kneading my thigh.

He leans closer. "You know the secret to a great cover?"

"Sleeping with the photographer?"

The fingers pinch. "No, darling, warm eyes. It's the single most important thing to remember, because eyes don't lie. When you're shooting a cover, you have to feel what you want to project—"

"Which is?"

"—Sexy but approachable. Always. Now close your eyes and listen to me."

I obey. Kip's hand works its way higher. "Emily. I want you to forget Dee, forget the collar, and just concentrate on the things you love, the things you love and desire most in this world. Things of beauty and truth . . . like the fact that I love you."

My eyes fly open and look into Kip's, which are all large and soft and liquid. "I love you," he says again.

"Oh Kip!" I whisper. "I do, too!"

"Ahem."

I flash Dee my biggest smile. When Marco comes over to blot me with a tissue—beauty lights are flattering but hot, requiring much base maintenance—he offers two additional tips for relaxing my face between rolls: one, puff up my cheeks and squish air around them between shots and, two, breathe in through my nose and out through my mouth.

These two tips plus Kip's three little words really add up. As The Cure blasts from the stereo, I stare into the lens, projecting sexy but approachable every way I can think of—an easy task because I'm feeling nothing but love love love. *Kip loves me!* The Cure fades into Don Henley which fades into Duran Duran *Kip loves me!* and, like *that,* it's my last outfit of the shoot, a sleeveless Genny dress encrusted with seed pearls and rhinestones and a pair of gold and pearl star-shaped clip-ons.

"Can we brighten her lips to a berry red?" Dee pipes up as I resume my position. The whisper campaign stopped awhile ago, and while Dee's still manhandling my man at regular intervals, I no longer care. *Kip loves me!*

Marco's in the process of mixing several shades of pink on the top of his hand when someone decides to kick things up a notch. "Woo-hoo!" Dee yelps as the studio vibrates with the first few notes of Tone Loc.

Marco's brush hits my lip. "Okay, hold very still," he instructs.

Wild thing . . .

Kip's hips start to gyrate. Dee shimmies on over and straddles his leg, a move that exposes even more of her thigh and gets those nipples standing stiffly at attention.

"Smile," Marco says, adjusting my top lip.

She loved to do the Wild Thing . . .

Dee bends lower and lower.

Wild thing . . .

As Kip raises Dee from her low point, his hand cups her ass.

"Kip, shame on you!" Dee exhales breathlessly as her hand grinds his hand deeper into her buttock. "*I,* a married woman!"

And clearly a skank.

". . . And *you,* a married man!"

What.

"Uh-oh," Marco says and not because the lipstick is on my chin.

". . . with a three-month-old *baby*!"

"WHAT!"

This time I holler it. Dee, reclined in another dip, tips her head in my direction. It is precisely at this moment that Kip drops her.

"Owww!"

"Kip, you have a BABY?"

". . . Kip?"

As I rise to my feet, pins pop from the dress. The tape unsticks. My chair rolls left and hits a light, which starts to quiver.

And then I'm pleading. "Please tell me she's kidding, Kip, *please.* Because you love me; you said you love me."

But Kip says nothing, nothing at all.

The dress is off before I've even reached the makeup room. I toss it into the corner, pull on my jeans, shirt, shoes, shove my bra into my backpack, and I'm out of there. I've gotten down two flights of stairs when I hear the door creak open above me. Feet clatter down the steps. My fingers grip the rail. It's Kip coming to tell me that this was all a big misunderstanding, that he's not married, that he doesn't have a child. That he loves me.

It's one of Dee's assistants. "I'm sorry," she says. Her brow is damp. Her chest heaves. Her palm meekly crosses the chasm between us. "The earrings. You need to return the earrings."

Kate exhales into the receiver. "I'm so sorry, Emily. I *knew* you didn't know. And I so wanted to tell you that day, but . . ."

Tears leak from my eyes, something they've been doing on and off—mostly on—for the past several hours. I blow my nose. When Kate first returned my call to the Ritz, she thought I had a head cold. If only.

"There was no time, I know. That's okay," I sniffle. Kate shouldn't feel bad; if she'd told me right before my cover try, I would have been like this *before* the shoot.

"Kip's a bad guy," she says.

"Kip's an asshole."

The facts my friend has provided go a long way to supporting my view. Kip MacSwain is a legendary modelfucker (evidently I didn't identify *every* category), a pastime he continues to pursue despite a yearlong marriage to an American model named Carrie (how ironic) and a three-month-old baby named Newton (named after not Sir Isaac or Fig but Helmut). Carrie and baby Newt are squirreled away in Hampshire, a town an hour outside of London "if you drive in the wee hours," Kate told me, a logistical inconvenience that conveniently facilitates the man's philandering, as he spends most weeknights "crashing" at his studio in order to avoid the "taxing" commute.

"Commute, my ass, I'll tell you what was taxing him," I say bitterly.

"Try not to dwell on it," Kate advises.

How can I not? For a minute it's silent as my leak turns into more of a flood—this the by-product of my brain flashing a picture of the bearskin rug. How many other girls have been spread across it? Gotten on their knees in the dark room? *Ugh.* "I feel like *such* a fool."

"You're not a fool," Kate assures me. "Look: I know you must be *killing* right now, but I hope this won't—I mean, I *wish* this wouldn't—affect your decision. You *will* stay here, won't you?"

"I don't know."

"Is the *Vogue* option still on?" she asks.

"I need to check."

"Well, check."

Vogue's still got me on hold, Siggy tells me when I call, only they've added time in early September. They'll shoot it then, she believes, "because every decent photographer is heading out of town now." *Every indecent photographer, too.* Siggy knew about Kip, of course; now she urges me to stay. "He feels terrible, I'm sure," she says, "and that's got to be worth eight pages."

At least.

Chapter 22

I Hate the Sunshine State

"So why'd you decide to come back?" Mom asks.

The two of us are in the kitchen in Balsam, she having recruited me to help her "cope" with her crop of zucchini. I pick up the peeler and shrug. "I decided it was a better plan."

"Anything to do with that guy shouting 'love'?" she asks.

Mom's wrong about the specifics, but the overall idea? Dead-on. But I don't want to revisit my experience with Mr. MacSwine. Not now. Not ever. "Not really."

Mom stares at the thick slab of green that I've peeled into the sink, and for once, she lets me leave it at that.

Christina, however, wants details, *lots* of details. After all, she's spent the summer working at Balsam Books and is desperate for new material. We're lying on the dock. I flip onto my back and am about to supply her with them, when I pause to light up. I have to; I can't smoke at home and I'm *dying*. "Oh boy, Em, you're *smoking* now?" Christina wiggles forward, her eyes instantly as round as the inner tubes floating behind her. "And what about the coke? You still doing that, too? Are you?"

Jesus Christ, I'm friends with Debbie Gibson. "No, no coke," I say, the wind suddenly knocked from my sails. When I finally give Christina the lowdown, it's a PG version, one that's not even close to the truth. After that, I avoid her.

One week of zucchini therapy (ten zucchini loaves, four dozen zucchini-raisin cookies, three zucchini lentil casseroles, and a large vat of tofu-zucchini "scramble"—all foisted on the denizens of the shelter, inspiring one patron to hum under his breath, "It's Not Easy Being Green") and it's back to school, where I'm grateful to be living with three roommates, Mohini, Pixie, and Jordan, roommates who do not puke—at least not more than the typical undergrad—or constantly call me an idiot.

Speaking of Vivienne, I left London so quickly, I didn't say good-bye to her. Ruth either. I didn't even see them. Later, I will learn that Ruth got dropped by both Stu and Début in the same week and disappeared. As for Vivienne, I'll never see her again, either, but later— much later—I'll spot her on the cover of *Town and Country* wearing white Vera Wang and six carats, the costume of her latest incarnation: fiancée of a financier. The only person I did get to part ways with was Edward. Over a quick lunch, he gave me a present from Harrods: two pairs of panties. "I noticed some of yours looked a little raggedy," he told me.

Like I said, it's good to be back. And yet my college roommates are the only people I want to see, or talk to. This includes Byron. He calls. I don't return. I know what he's going to say and, somehow, getting yelled at for skipping out on Siggy is a hardship I can't endure—not when I'm still reeling from the Dreadful Scot.

Because I am. Reeling. I spend a lot of time listless in bed, the layers of flannel and down muffling jagged, violent outbursts, puffy, gaspy confessions, and—and these are the ones that really hurt—those silent, dead-of-night tears, until my friends drag me out of my bed and into my sophomore year. Reluctant initially, I finally plunge into it. Distractions are what I need. The Take Back the Night March? I'm there. The Earth Day Planning Committee? I'm on it. Tailgates and football games and Halloween parties? What time do they start? I feel better: happier than I've been in a while, calmer and anxiety-free.

Except for one thing: money. I need the stuff.

The summer I modeled in Chicago, I made enough to cover my tuition and credit card bills and yet I still had enough left over to set some aside. That nest egg is gone now: London was less lucrative, especially since it ended earlier than I anticipated. I've managed to cover this year's tuition but that's it, there's nothing left in the coffer. So when the phone rings in early November, I'm all ears.

"Byron wants you to come in," Justine tells me. "He wants to show you something."

"Oh, really? Can't he dial his own phone?"

All ears but evidently still pissed. Correct, too, it seems, for Justine doesn't respond; she simply sighs and says, "How's Friday?"

I hesitate. But as I doodle daggers on a scrap of paper, my eye catches the corner of a credit card bill peeking out from under a pile: past due.

"See you then."

On the appointed day, Chic is thick with a plaster-dust haze and ringing with a commensurate amount of banging, pounding, and scraping. Something metallic and dangerous sounding whirs to life right as Fleur (eighteen, French, champagne-blonde) sashays past, her figure hotly pursued by a half-dozen eyes over face masks. Someone's gonna lose a limb here.

"Hey, Fleur."

"Ahh, Amelie . . ." Kiss-kiss. Fleur pinches the sleeve of my parka, currently bunched around my forearms. "I'd leave this on if I were you. It's *freezing* in there," she says, shivering for emphasis.

It's always freezing when you have no body fat, but Fleur's right; today is the coldest day of the season, the kind of morning that had Jordan reaching for her union suit and everyone else speaking wistfully of Berkeley—in other words, not the kind of day you want your windows wide open clearing the air.

I proceed inside. "Hey! What's happening in here?"

Byron's wearing a black wool sweater, black leather pants, and an olive cashmere scarf knotted around his head: warm, if perhaps a slight impediment to his phone skills. "Construction," he snaps.

Even with a parka on it's frosty.

"I see that," I reply in a similar tone. A dusty chrome chair sits near the booking table. I drum the back of it impatiently. "Is this what you wanted to show me? The construction site?"

"Nope." Byron exhales tiredly and reaches into a drawer. "This."

It's the latest issue of British *GQ*. I open it to the flagged pages: two photos of me with Armin, two black velvet, red lipstick, big hair, babe-olicious photos. I smile. I like them. "What do you think?"

"They're fine. Good. Good body shots," Byron says.

"Which one are you putting up?" I crane my neck. "Or did you already?"

"Nope. I have forty girls now, Emily, *forty*. The trophy wall is for covers only now. There were *too* many pictures the other way. My hands were getting paper cuts from changing them all. It was *too* much." Byron wags the pads of his fingers, though I know for a fact it's Jon who usually changes the photos, then jabs a digit toward me. "Besides, *you* haven't been here."

"I have, too."

"I meant in the agency."

I shrug.

Byron spins his chair to me and folds his arms, a gesture that corresponds perfectly with his irked expression. "Emily Woods, are you still a Chic model?"

"I think so."

"You *think* so? I have forty girls now, Emily, *fo*—"

Out it tumbles. "Yeah, I get it, Byron. You're busy: too busy for me, so you packed me off to London and then you ignored me!"

"That's not true! We spoke—"

"*Once!* After *I* called *you* several times!"

By now, I'm pounding the chair back. A cloud of dust rises. Byron wheels sideways to avoid it. "Look, Emily, I'd love to hold the hand of every girl I send overseas, but that's just not possible. Besides, I can accuse you of the same thing! *I* called *you* several times after you got back. You never returned any of them!"

"I'm in school in case you'd forgotten. Columbia."

Byron's lips tense. He pulls up to his desk. "So that's how it is. I see. You're letting girls like Fonya take your place. Okay, well, thanks for stopping in. Enjoy the photos."

Wait, no. *Money.* "Who's Fonya?"

"Fonya's an overnight success really. . . ."

Aren't they all? I scoff at this blatant attempt to make me jealous.

"Brunette, with dark eyes. From Miami."

Miami? Thanks to its reliable weather, abundant direct flights, and pastel art deco buildings—the perfect backdrop for any resort collection—Miami is rapidly becoming a fashion hot spot. But I mean *please,* everyone knows Miami models are C-listers at best, girls who scrape together a living by working for those German catalogs the size of phone books—the Germans *love* Miami—every page chock-full of deplorable fashion. New York talent is flown in for all the plum jobs. Byron will have to do better than this. I snigger.

"She's twenty-one."

I snigger again: *Twenty-one? Hag!*

"Her career took off in early September when a magazine was stranded without a girl. I faxed them her card. They flew her in for four pages."

Yeah. Yeah. Yeah. "Terrific."

"British *Vogue* certainly thought so. Then again, they had a certain look in mind: brunette, with strong brows and dark eyes, a girl they described as a young Yasmin Le Bon."

The construction, the chaos—suddenly it's all gone. I'm whited out. I stare into Byron's eyes, my fingers barely managing to tap my chest.

"Yes, Emily. They wanted you."

No. No, not *Vogue.* I didn't miss—"But Byron, why didn't you tell me? Why didn't you—"

Oh shit. Shit. Shit Shit.

"Call?" he finishes. "I did. Four times, as I recall. You never returned. *Vogue* was getting frustrated and about to go elsewhere, so I recommended another girl, a girl who *really* wanted the job: Fonya. That's what I'm saying. Some people have the drive. Some people don't. Obviously you don't."

No, no. This can't have happened. This isn't true. "Byron, I *do*—"

He fends this off. "No, I don't think so. You just told me you *think* you want to keep modeling: *think.* That doesn't cut it."

My heart pounds. I topple the chair. Fucking Kip! I should have stayed in London. Just toughed it out. After all, *I* was the one who met Liz Tilberis. *I* was the one she wanted. Fonya could have been—should have been—me. I plant my feet, my chest heaving. "You're wrong! You're just wrong! I do have the drive! I do!"

"Well . . ." Shrugging skeptically, Byron adjusts his turban, "if that's the case, then prove it."

"I will."

"Work hard."

"I *will.*"

"I mean harder than before." Byron eyes me soberly. "Emily, I know you like Columbia, but if you want to stay at Chic, you need to get one thing straight. You need to start giving me more time, a *lot* more time. You got it?"

"Got it."

"I mean it. You've got to go for it. *Really* go for it. No excuses."

I nod and place my hand on my heart. "You won't even know I'm a student."

In the weeks that follow, Byron gives me a busy schedule of appointments—grueling at times—but I never complain, not even once. I want it and I want it bad. The fury I felt that day in the agency doesn't fade; it grows and grows. Every issue of *Vogue* fuels it, the term "overnight success" feeds it, and every November cover with Fonya on it stokes the flames. There're plenty of those. On *Mademoiselle,* Fonya glows in red Anne Klein and rhinestones, on British *Marie Claire,* she's sleek in silver Mizrahi and a tight chignon, and on Italian *Lei,* she's the bombshell with sexpot lips and a plunging Versace. We do look alike, Fonya and I, though, honestly, her eyes are a bit squinty and when she arches her brows it looks like they're being yanked skyward by an invisible puppeteer. Other than that, she's not bad, I guess. She certainly is getting someplace: Fame. Wealth. Stardom.

But *I* was the one they wanted. Fonya could have been—*should* have been—me.

Okay, I really fucked up. Well, never again. *This time* I'm getting someplace, and *this time,* when I get there, I'm digging in my heels. No more stupid mistakes. No more backward slides. Only up, up, up— straight for the stars.

Modeling becomes my focus, my number one priority. I don't forget this, not at Thanksgiving, or exam time, or Christmas. Not at New Year's.

New Year's Eve. When the ball drops and the flutes clink, my resolution is simple: 1990 is going to be my year, whatever it takes.

Chapter 23

New Day Dawning

"Omigod, I thought I was going to have to give your seat to that annoying girl, but you made it!"

I slide into the chair next to Pixie, panting. I've been doing appointments. It took a cab ride, a subway trip, and a thousand-yard sprint to make it, but I made it.

"Okay, people!" Wenda, our professor, claps twice, then scans the classroom. "Welcome back to BBD. As indicated on the syllabi, today's discussion is a continuation of last week's: an examination of the female nude in Victorian painting."

a.k.a a second look at bad art, Pixie scribbles in the margin of my notebook.

At least you read enough to know that, I scribble back. I'm a bit behind.

Bewitched, Bothered, and Dead: Images of Female Repression seemed like a good idea initially; after all, it meets only one day a week and has provocative subject matter and minimal assigned reading, making it the ideal fifth class. However, some time after it became impossible for us to change our schedules without penalty, the course revealed its true colors: what Pixie and I charitably refer to as Boring, Brainless, and Dumb.

Wenda lowers the lights. "Let's begin with some slides. You'll recognize several of these from Dijkstra."

Di-What?

Our Textbook!!

Okay, perhaps more than a bit behind.

The slide projector sputters and blinks before blasting its first image: a very pale, very naked woman reclining in a field of flowers, surrounded by white doves.

"Women: See how they doze," Wenda intones somberly, today looking dressed for repose herself in a kimono jacket with bell-shaped sleeves and a pair of black satin shoes that seem suspiciously similar to bedroom slippers. Her eyes are even more sunken than usual, her body large and pillowy under the billowing fabric. In fact, the only thing alert about Wenda's appearance is her hair, a frizzled mess barely contained by a dirty rubber band. Taken all together, the woman is one Fashion Don't from hairline to heel.

The carousel advances to slide two: a woman collapsed on a bed, a hand fan inches from her splayed fingers, a sheet artfully concealing her nether region. "Perhaps you find these images soothing, peaceful even," Wenda continues. "But I see something else at work—thoughts?"

No A/C?

The fan vibrates?

I'm still covering up my snort of laughter with an anemic coughing fit when out of the corner of my eye a bright blur shoots straight up in the air. *God no.*

BBD is taught at Barnard, the women's college affiliated with Columbia. There are three Columbia students in the class, and while Wenda is inherently suspicious of two of us ("Why coed?" she asked Pixie and me, using that falsely neutral tone normally reserved for questions like "Why the NRA?"), the third Columbia student and sole male, Patric, a wisp of a guy currently dressed for success in red suspenders, red high-tops, and a porkpie hat, can do no wrong. Of course the teacher's pet for Women's Studies has a penis.

Wenda beams. "Patric?"

"I see passive, victimized creatures," Patric warbles.

"Excellent! As portrayed by the . . ."

As Wenda's hand wafts through the air, Patric's eyes follow it hungrily, like a dog in hot pursuit of a bone, until her sleeve gets caught in the slide projector.

"White male painters?" he finally guesses.

"Exactly! What I think you're also suggesting, Patric, is that these women are not simply 'asleep'"—Wenda finally wrests her arm free, only to start quoting the air—"but that their lassitude is so exaggerated, so *pronounced* it's almost . . ."

Posed

Artistic

"Vampiric?" Patric guesses again. Another safe bet: "vampiric," "sadistic," "misogynistic," and "autoerotic" being recurring favorites, particularly when applied to "Leda," "Ophelia," "Medusa," "Circe," or "Salome."

"Exactly, Patric! Excellent!"

As image after image of nubile, supine women floats across the screen, I start to feel sleepy myself, the power of suggestion working in tandem with my mad dash here. Pixie, on the other hand, starts thrumming her highlighter against her notebook. Besides our mutual grievances about BBD, my friend has one of her own: the quality of the art. "Lowbrow," she huffed last week. "Like students a hundred years from now studying Lladro."

Finally, she can stand it no longer. "Wenda?"

"Yes, Serena."

"While this art you're showing is certainly, um, interesting, I must point out that there are many depictions of active, vibrant, *erect* women during this time period, and much of it from far more influential artists," she says.

"Such as?"

"Well, Degas, to use an obvious example. His ballet series."

The kimono sleeves cross. "Degas? As in the Degas who painted women undressing?" Wenda smiles cruelly. "I'm afraid you'll have to think of a better example, Serena. Degas was a voyeur." Then steps behind the projector. "Now, as Patric so intelligently pointed out, the passivity of these female subjects suggests an inherent victimization—"

"But couldn't one argue that *all* painters are voyeurs?"

I smile into my hand: *You go, Pixie Stick!* Wenda, meanwhile, has the expression of someone who didn't realize the staircase had another step. "Some more than others, Serena; after all, Degas painted women undressing from the perspective of a man hiding in the closet—and I'm not being figurative. He was the *consummate* voyeur. Now, moving right along . . ." Her hand reaches for the forward button.

"But obviously the models knew he was there," Pixie insists. "Doesn't that render the so-called voyeurism as nothing more than an artistic gambit?"

"Not if as the viewer you're meant to perceive it voyeuristically," rejoins a girl in the second row.

"But isn't perception reality?" someone else asks.

"*No,* perception's perception. It's only reality if you choose to make it so," says a third.

"Are you saying reality's a conscious choice?"

Suddenly, we're having one of those discussions that's like a hypnotic wheel, going round and round and round without getting anywhere—in other words, everyone's favorite kind.

"Okay, people! Class!" Wenda yelps, eventually silencing everyone with her hallmark clapping. "I think everyone gets the gist of this discourse, so let me introduce a new twist. Specifically, let's compare and contrast the representation of women in fin de siècle art to the representation of women at the close of the current century. Aka, to our world today."

After rifling though a battered nylon briefcase, Wenda holds up stack of tear sheets.

Oh shit.

"That's right, people, though there have been several world wars . . ."

Like two. Serena looks up. *Oh shit!*

"And countless women's movements, I would argue that very little has changed. Women are still being depicted as passive creatures—victims, if you will, and I think you will once you see these—their primary purpose to entice and please the male viewer."

Wenda looks my way. Patric eyes me disdainfully, or maybe I'm just being paranoid. I slump down in my seat and take hasty and hopefully discreet swipes at my appointment-friendly cheeks, now no doubt doubly red. Am I in there? Tell me I'm not in there. That would be all I need.

Fortunately, the first shot is a photo of a guy feeding grapes into a girl's mouth. I don't know the guy, the girl is with Chic. "Thoughts?" Wenda says.

Patric raises his hand. He likes to get it way up high and shake it, a method frequently employed by second graders. Which gives me ample time to start talking. "Wenda, just because a woman is horizontal doesn't automatically mean she's passive."

"Perhaps," Wenda says. She looks surprised; I don't normally open my mouth except to yawn. "But the model is not merely horizontal, she's being fed grapes here—thoughts? Patric?"

"An obvious reference to Bacchanalia," Patric says. "The male god Dionysus getting the female drunk so he can savagely conquer her."

Savagely conquer? Give me a break. "One could just as easily argue this is a Roman goddess being tended to by one of her male servants," I retort.

"I see Bacchae," Patric insists.

"Livia, Caesar's wife," I counter.

"Who was a murderer!" Patric hisses.

"Making her an unusual victim!" I snap.

"Okay, people!" Wenda says to no avail; she's lost the reins again, only this time, I'm galloping right along. I'm irritated—I refuse to cede ground to someone who derives his fashion sense from a mime— but it's more than that; I'm defending my profession in a court of peers. "It's entertainment, not education," I say. "Fantasy, not reality." "Viewers can tell the difference." "Sometimes *Mademoiselle* is just *Mademoiselle.*"

"And sometimes it isn't."

A girl with a French braid and a stained sweatshirt purses her lips in a classic know-it-all moue. "Studies have proven that magazine images affect young girls' self-esteem. And consider the historical trends: Models and actresses are getting skinnier. For example"—she pauses before delivering the coup de grace—"Marilyn Monroe was a size twelve."

Oh God, not this again. "Yes, she was," I rejoin. "But do you know how small a size twelve used to be? The equivalent of a size eight today—maybe smaller. Sizes have blown up along with Americans!"

Patric practically lunges. "Emily, are you saying anorexia isn't a serious problem in this country?"

"No, it is. But in terms of the numbers it's not as serious as obesity, yet I don't see any photos of burgers and milkshakes in that pile."

Careful! Pixie scribbles. Wenda bridles. "Emily, I think the two issues are hardly comparable," she says. "After all, no young girl aspires to be a burger."

"Exactly, Wenda," French Braid says, nodding. "Young girls look at magazines in search of the woman they long to become, only to be rewarded with images of underfed *creatures* they can't relate to." Her eyes widen, perhaps even releasing a tear. "It's utterly demoralizing."

"Oh please."

Pixie breaks from her underlining of *Careful,* to launch her hand skyward. "I'm not sure I agree with that. People might grouse but I don't think deep down they really want models to be regular looking. I think they want them to be special, aspirational—"

"Exactly! Most of us are hypocrites, for example . . ."

After I blurt this, I slam on the brakes. I'm thinking of how to explain Queen's, a billion-dollar, catalog-only business that sells cheap fashions in sizes 12 to 44. They also happen to be a client of mine (but "only until you've got a better pool of clients," Byron stressed). "Why not use plus size models?" I asked the Queen's art director one day as yet another garment was practically reconstructed on my backside. "Aren't they a size twelve?" "We tried that," he replied. "And our sales plummeted." Queen's typical customer is a size 32—*a 32!*—yet she'd rather buy from a size 4 than a 12. Isn't dropping ten dress sizes aspirational enough? How do you explain that? It's an interesting story and it backs up Pixie's point and I should tell it.

"For example . . ."

But if I bring this up, then everyone would know I've worked for Queen's. Emily Woods: plus size model. *No way.* "I just think people are hypocrites, that's all."

French Braid smirks. Patric hooks his thumbs under his suspenders. "Is that so?" he says.

Fuck it. I'm about to dive in for another round when Wenda points to a girl in the back row, another girl who rarely speaks. "Dawn?"

When Dawn lowers her arm, her eyes are on me. "I have to say, Emily, I found your comments about hypocrites to be interesting, if not ironic," she says slowly. "Because I find the fact that you both model and take this class to be hypocritical."

Patric titters. Pixie slams her fists. "That was a low blow!" she shouts. "A LOW BLOW!"

Wenda flashes me a look that fails to pass for a smile. "That's right. All kinds are welcome in this class, Dawn," she says wanly. She claps twice. "People, I'm afraid that's all the time we have today. Remember, more Dijkstra due next week. The following week, we're going to the Metropolitan Museum to see some of these paintings in the flesh, as it were. Enjoy your weekend!"

"Omigod, that was totally uncalled for—totally!" Pixie screeches in the hallway. "Forget her. No, let's get her! C'mon, I'm in self-defense, you're tall: We can take her!"

"Fuck her," I say. I mean it. Fuck Dawn. Fuck Wenda. Fuck all of them. They see me as a model who's sold out? Fine. That's what I'm gonna do.

And this is when I go for it—I *really* go for it. I take every job I can get. I put on silk cocktail dresses and twin sets for Lord & Taylor, Macy's, and Brooks Brothers and take home $1,500 a day. I get optioned for L'Oréal and *Mademoiselle.* I shoot Christian Dior panty hose, Special K and book a two-page beauty story for *Allure.* "Maximize Your Assets," the story's titled. I certainly plan to.

I'm not the only one with conviction.

"Chic is now the most *beautiful* agency *ever!*"

With all my bookings and numerous trips, I haven't had time to stop in the agency. Now, there's a lot to see.

"It looks great," I tell Byron.

"Doesn't it?" In the reception area, a man in coveralls is stenciling an "H" on the wall. Byron taps the white space next to it. "Behind here is my new private office, which has a view of Eighteenth Street and a glass wall overlooking the agency, so I can keep an eye on all of you. Next to that will be the office for our new accountant—"

"Will that mean my checks will no longer bounce?" I interject, because that's been happening lately.

Byron exhales noisily. "Emily, dear, I told you already, that was an aberration—*both* of them—anyway, moving on to the décor. I just had the *strongest* urge for black and white and *clean, clean, clean*! like Geoffrey Beene's estate in Hawaii. You ever been?"

"Sure, right after I stopped by Oz and took a tour of Tara."

Byron rolls his eyes toward the newly installed recessed lighting. "Well then, picture this: white billowing curtains, zebra print rugs—real or fake, I haven't decided. The black-and-chrome sofa and chairs are staying *for now*. I'm still waiting on the Kouros chairs: black lacquer with a black-and-white zigzag print seat, a glass table for the corner *there,* and a fainting couch for between the two windows: white with black piping. Lining the hallway will be a series of black-and-white photographs; still lifes, I'm thinking, or landscapes: *not models.* Orchids will be everywhere, *white* orchids and some giant zigzag floor cushions scattered *there, there,* and *there.* What do you think? Timeless, right? And black and white was *such* a huge theme in the spring collections."

"Sounds great," I say, my head zigzagging along with his finger. "And—wow—that's a lot of changes, especially since you only redid it like, what, two years ago?"

"Closer to one but it's the nineties now, Emily: a new era! New era, new look!"

As Byron speaks, his hand sweeps the booking table, presumably referencing not just Justine, who is brightening the new decade with highlighter-colored hair, or Jon, who has taken to mixing loud plaids, but fashionistas everywhere. "It's *Vogue* now, not *Elle*," he continues. "And new faces in it. Girls like Tatiana, Claudia, and Cindy are on their way out—"

Hang on. "Cindy Crawford was just on the cover of *New York* magazine, a cover story devoted solely to her. The caption called her '*the* model for the nineties.'"

Byron shakes his head. "As I recall, it said Cindy was '*a* model for the nineties': big difference. In any case, *New York* magazine got the decade wrong. Cindy Crawford is an eighties girl. Sure, she'll make a fortune in advertising in the coming years, but *Vogue* isn't going to use her, not for much longer anyway. No, Cindy's peaked. These days it's all about the trinity. The trinity rules fashion. The trinity is it."

So fashion has found religion. I snort. "Next you're going to be telling me that God is the new black."

This is rewarded with a soft punch to the arm. "Don't be absurd, dear, everyone knows that white is the new black—*anyway,* of course you *know* I'm talking about Christy, Linda, and Naomi," Byron cries. "They're *everywhere*! But their reign will end, too. The question is: Who will replace them?"

I'd be happy to, of course, and I'm about to communicate this desire, when Byron clamps his hands over my eyes.

"Um, hey! . . . What?"

Byron's other hand starts propelling me forward. "It's a surprise."

When the hand comes off, I have a view of the trophy wall. At first I'm pissed: I know a little competition can be healthy, but staring at a row of Fonyas—aging Floridian, future star Fonya—is more than I can take. I grit my teeth . . . And then I see it. The top right corner, the January *Harpers & Queen* cover. I'm on it.

"Taa-daa!" Byron taps the frame. "Look at you!"

I look. I take in my hair, my face, my expression. I take it in . . . and everything inside me freezes.

"You like it?" Byron says.

"I can't believe it."

On the cover, my lips—a mauvy brown, not the berry—are parted and curled, not into a grin but almost, just enough to reveal the bottom half of my top teeth, which are whiter and squarer than usual. My skin, a warm honey beige, is poreless. The mole on my right cheek is gone. I've been airbrushed to flawlessness. And yet it's my eyes you really notice, my eyes that have it. They look willing, open. Alive. Warm eyes, just like Kip taught me.

I swallow, look away, then look again. To get the shot, I sat with my legs perpendicular to the camera, twisting for each click, a trick that keeps your expression fresh and uncongealed. I knew I'd hit my mark when—blast!—the fan kicked up the ends of my hair and my eyes hit the aperture dead center. And this is the result: Not-Emily but a woman, *the* woman who, at the sound of her name, turns her face into the breeze, knowing exactly who she'll see. The Woman Who's in Love.

I love you, Kip told me, *I love you.*

I pinch the bridge of my nose. "The shoot was for the December issue." I say quickly. "I thought I didn't get it."

"Sometimes when they take a bunch at once, they use one the next month," Byron says. "You got lucky. Here, look. We've already put it on your card."

Byron departs for the composite wall and returns. I stare at my card. Part of the magazine title has been lopped off to make room for my name. *Emily Woods* it says in my hair.

I love you.

I close my eyes.

"New era, new opportunity, new face," I hear Byron whisper. "Yours."

And yet . . . *A cover. I got a cover.* When I open my eyes, I'm smiling. Byron spins me around. We whirl through the empty space until I laugh with delight.

Thanks to my cover, the bookings start flooding in. I open the floodgates. Miami, Santa Fe, Santa Barbara, St. John, the Bahamas, Miami again. For a three-day booking, I return home with $6,120 in my pocket ($1,800 a day—that's my latest rate—times three, plus an extra $1,800 "travel time," less the 15 percent agency fee). Six grand for three days—and that's just for catalog.

"You're never here," my roommates complain as I'm lining mini shampoo and conditioner bottles from the Four Seasons (great mattresses), the Biltmore (great pool), and the Pink Sands (great beaches) along our stainless steel shelf. It's true. I miss hockey games and keg parties, study sessions and weekends doing . . . nothing. So what? When I'm alone in an airport, I can walk up to the newsstand, pull down a magazine, and find myself: in advertisements, in fashion spreads. I'm one of *those* girls now, a working model, a "rising star" according to Byron.

A rising star.

In mid-April, my professor for Earth, Moon, and Planets (read "science requirement") sits me down and informs me I'm "a nanosecond away" from failing. When I tell Mohini, my unofficial tutor for the class, she's unsympathetic. "That's because you're being an idiot," she says. "We all think so."

Comments like this clip my wings, but only a little. I curtail my travel just enough to pass the class. When school's out, I go home, but I keep my visit short and sweet; after all, I don't want to waste time, certainly not in a place that's so wrong it's not even referred to as the wrong coast, but merely the place you fly over to get to it. When I get back, and my taxi's picking up speed on the Triboro Bridge, I roll down the window, take a deep breath, and let New York in.

1990. This is my year, my season, my city. I can't wait to make it happen.

Chapter 24

Shoot the Moon

The elevator doors on West Eighteenth Street part, and I'm standing before a parade of girls. Girls lining the hallway and disappearing down the far stairwell. Girls alone. Girls with their mothers, their boyfriends, their twins. Short girls, tall girls, young girls, younger—every single one of them raking me with her eyes. And that's before I skip the line. "You're much prettier," I hear a matronly voice aver as I flick open one side of the new, glass Chic entrance. "*And* you're a blonde."

"Hello, this is Chic, *please* hold—HiEmilyByronwantstoseeyougoright in—How can I help you?"

Alistair, our new receptionist, is a recent Parsons graduate with a platinum pompadour and a penchant for vests. Waving hello, I glide past today's version (black and shiny with a faux watch fob and assorted buttons) and into the main room of the agency.

Nineteen ninety has been good thus far to Chic. No sooner was the last pillow plumped and plopped into place when Louis's prophecy came true: Chic became *it*, the hippest, hottest agency in New York—a transformation I could efficiently track in my interactions with other

New York models, which went from "You're with *what* agency?" to "Oh, right. Chic," to "Really? Do you like them? What about Byron? The bookers? 'Cause I'm thinking of switching." And many of them have: There are sixty Chic models by my last count. Sixty. I scan the composite wall, looking for my place among them: Dahlia, Dalila, Emma J., Emma T., Esme, Estella, Estelle . . .

Dahlia . . . Dalila . . . Emma J. . . .

Dalilia . . . Emma J. . . . "Al—lis—tair!"

Alistair does not ask "What?" He simply jumps and slides directly across the floor—an Ice Capades–worthy move that sends the zebra rug into a tailspin and has me leaping to safety.

"I don't see my cards! Where are my cards?"

"Relax, kitten, they're right in . . ." Alistair slides to a halt in front of a drawer I didn't even know existed. ". . . here. Here!" He hands me a stack of composites.

. . . Which I immediately clutch to my chest. Clients stop by the agency to pick up cards, bookers pull cards for mailings; if you're not on the composite wall, you might as well be modeling in Peoria. No thanks, I've already done that. "Alistair!" I blast. "What were *my* cards doing in *that* drawer?"

Alistair pats his pompadour, possibly because I've just sprayed spit in it. "Relax, kitten, don't be upset! You've been out of commission for the past few weeks and we were tight on space, so—"

"My cards were in a drawer! A goddamned *drawer*!"

Byron's desk is in front of the window, giving him a fetching backlight, especially now, when he's sporting khaki-colored cotton and a deep tan. His manicured hands hover in the space between us. "Emily, I'm sure Alistair told you it was only until you came back," he soothes, stroking the air. "I didn't want another snafu, like with Saks."

Oh, right. That. This past spring, Byron had gotten so used to me saying yes to every trip that he got in the habit of giving all my good clients a first option, meaning they could confirm at will. But after my Earth, Moon, and Planets conversation, I decided an upcoming trip for Saks to New Orleans was not in the stars, so I made Byron cancel it.

Saks was *not* happy. It only happened once, but still . . . "That's true," I mumble, mollified. "That was bad."

"That's okay," he says. "You're back now and that's what matters. I'll tell Alistair to put you front and center."

"With blinking lights."

Byron smiles, not a real smile, just a comma flipped sideways. "Right, Emily, listen, I've made some changes."

"I've noticed. Open castings? I thought you'd *never*."

His eyes widen. "Why not? It's hype and it's working! I'm getting great girls."

I eye the line dubiously.

"Not from *there*." Byron's head gives a dismissive shake just as a girl exits in tears, escorted by her mother, who's also in tears, and a new Chic employee whom I don't recognize. "But from where it really matters: out *there*." His hand does its usual skyline sweep. "Elite, Ford, Company—we're getting great girls. In fact, just this morning Svetlana switched from Elite and I'm *this* close to snagging Claudia."

"Claudia *Schiffer*?"

"Yes, Claudia Schiffer. Claudia." Byron sighs. I blink; for a second the guy looks straight. "I'm not taking *every* girl of course," he continues. "I'm only picking off the top girls. The best."

Last year, after going though all the heartache of signing with an agency, I learned that modeling contracts are essentially meaningless: No agency is going to hold a girl to the fine print if she wants to go (okay, maybe Claudia), mainly because no agency wants to be *held* to the fine print. Thus poaching and switching are rampant. "But Byron, you have so many girls now," I point out. "How many more do you want?"

"Oh, not many: seventy, eighty total. With the expansion we've got so much space now—"

"Except on the composite rack."

He laughs tightly. "Okay, yes, right, but we're fixing that. Plus I've just hired two new bookers, Stephan and Lithe—which brings me back to those changes."

Byron rises from behind the desk. He's wearing tall, stiff boots that creak loudly, as if protesting his tendency to stride. "Yes, yes I'm riding now," he says, seeing my gaze. "It's *so* invigorating! *Fantastic* for the thighs and seat—why, I'm hard as a *rock* there! Emily, I gave you to Justine."

It takes me a minute. "Wait . . . to *book* me?"

"Yes."

"But why? Aren't you booking girls anymore?"

"No, I am. Selectively." As Byron's pacing brings him near the glass wall, he lifts a leather crop from an umbrella stand. "But I don't have much time anymore, not with all this—" The tip slithers across the smooth surface, drawing a bead on the busy booking area and yet another girl leaving the agency crestfallen. "I only have time to focus on a few top girls. Special girls."

I can't believe this. "Byron, I've grossed $70,000 this year and it's only May and I've been in school—doesn't that make me special?"

Apparently not. "It's a good start." Byron's backlit again. I shield my eyes, trying to see his face.

"But not good enough for what: the top five? Top ten?"

My agent's silent. I continue. "So if $70,000 in five months doesn't cut it, what does? Eighty? Ninety? One hundred?"

Byron's fingers split across his forehead. "Emily, look, it's not only about money," he says. "It's about career path, too; I'm representing a certain *type* of girl now: a girl who does a lot of editorial, a girl who does a lot of high-profile campaigns: Versace . . . Iceberg . . . Vakko . . . Guess?"

"Like Fonya," I mutter bitterly. Fonya's the new Guess? girl. I saw the photographs last week. In them, she's standing in an apple orchard amid artistically positioned ladders and bushels, her body gussied, ging-hamed, and fringed. It's a look that might sound *Hee Haw* but wasn't—not on Fonya. She looked glamorous, dark, and glossy, like a fifties film star.

"Yes, like Fonya," Byron edges into his seat. "Girls of that caliber," he says. "Editorial girls. *Cover* girls."

"But I have a cover—and I did *Allure*!" I point out. After all, "Maximize Your Assets" should be out in a matter of days.

"Yes, you have *one* cover from *months* ago, and you shot *two* pages for *Allure,* but mostly, you've been doing catalog—which is good, I'm not saying it isn't," Byron adds hurriedly. "Especially when it's Neiman's, Saks, and Bergdorf's. Most of my girls would kill to work for *one* of them and you've done all three. You're a classic beauty, a proven earner."

I shield my eyes again. "But . . ."

"But I've made a decision. Look, Emily, it's been my pleasure to represent you, and I'll always be here for you, but I can't do it anymore. I'm passing you along to Justine."

When Byron leans forward, I can finally see his expression; he looks sad. He takes my hand. "Emily, I'm so sorry."

I came into Chic ready to tear ahead, but I seem to be sliding backward. Straight into an abyss. My throat tightens. "Justine's weird," I mumble.

"Justine's the best I have."

A tear slides down my face. Then another.

Byron comes around his desk and kneels in front of me. "Listen, Em, maybe if you start doing better . . ."

Better? I clasp his fingers. "How much better?"

"If you get three, no, two. Two more covers this summer, then I'll book you again," Byron says. He smiles. "How's that?"

"Great!"

"Things *we* book you for," he qualifies. "In other words, no *Vegan Life* or *Cat Fancy* or anything."

I hug Byron. Upon releasing me, he rises and plucks a black velvet riding cap off the console. "Now, I must get going and *you,* Emily dear, must go talk to Justine." He adjusts the chinstrap. "Because I just know that woman's got some fabulous ideas on how to develop your career."

You might think Justine's ever-changing hair color—currently a Grover blue—suggests a fun-loving, whimsical person, the sort of gal who likes to skip through Central Park in the pouring rain, lick lollipops, and dash off on spontaneous road trips.

You would be wrong. That's another blue-haired girl, perhaps, or another Justine. This Justine is weary, oh so weary. Always. It's as if powering that bright mop has sucked all her energy, leaving just enough for a mopey, floppy doll with the sour face and all the listless enthusiasm of Eeyore.

"Okay." Justine reaches limply for my portfolio. "Let's see it."

There is no exact way of structuring a modeling portfolio. Maybe that's the problem. Each booker is convinced she alone knows the magical arrangement of photographs that will lead to bigger, better jobs; everyone else is flat out wrong. True, there are a few common rules. If you're using more than two pages of editorial from the same job, the photos are broken up so their common origin is less obvious. Your portfolio should end on a high note and begin with a strong head shot, usually a cover if you've got one, otherwise, your best beauty shot. Yet even these rules are frequently broken.

Byron decided to put my cover in the middle of my book as a "pleasant surprise for the viewer." That said, my strongest beauty shot is in the front: the lion tamer from the Dreadful Scot. Everyone loves it except for me.

"You can keep this," Justine says, tapping it. "But the rest have to go."

Wait, what? "The *rest,* what do you mean the *rest?* Not my entire book!"

Yes, my entire book. "Well, you might be able to keep one or two from the London series," Justine allows after a beat. "But the others have to go—all the editorial, anyway."

"But *why?*"

Another weary sigh, this one tinged with impatience. "Because most of those pictures are from 1989. This is 1990—*June* of 1990. They're too old. Editorial has a three-month expiration date *max.* These are way past their prime. You'll have to test."

This can't be happening. *Test?* I'm all for getting new photographs. But *test?* "Byron told me I was beyond testing!" I say, my agitation increasing by the millisecond. "He told me that tests were a waste of time! He told me that last *year!*"

"Exactly: *last year.* Things change. Byron's not your booker anymore—I am—yours and the five others he just dumped in my lap. Along with the training of these two"—Justine's fingers limply encompass Lithe, who appears to be having issues determining which colored pencil to use on a chart, and Stephan, who's now looking close to tears himself as he passes a tissue box to a girl's boyfriend—"and I think you should test," she finishes.

Jesus Christ. "I understand you're busy, Justine, but if you book me some *editorial,* I'll have up-to-date pictures and we'll both be happy."

Sigh. "I would. But I can't. Not with this book."

We're in a standoff. Gnawing on a cuticle, I twist my head. Byron hasn't left yet; he's leaning over his desk, his riding cap still on, dictating something to a dutiful Alistair.

"Look, Emily, I'm not stupid. I know you want Byron to be your booker again and I'd love to get you off my plate, so what do you say we cut the crap, you do as I say, and I make you a star. Deal?"

My head snaps back. I take in the large eyes with the expectant expression, and for the first time in several minutes, I smile. "Deal."

Over the course of the next few weeks, Justine arranges a series of tests. I try to do things as she says. I *try.*

"This is Justine."

"I'm wearing a bikini," I say.

"Yeah . . . and?"

"It's made of paper."

"So?"

"A paper cutout . . . as in two circles and a triangle."

Silence.

"Don't you think that's odd?"

"I think it could be cute."

"Could be. For a four-year-old. For a nineteen-year-old it could be odd," I tell her. "And it is."

"I think it sounds cute." She sounds defensive.

"But not sexy. You didn't say sexy."

Sigh. "Emily, are you saying you want me to get you out of this?"

"Please."

"This is Justine."

"I'm dressed as a showgirl."

Sigh.

"With the feathers and everything."

"Good. This is good. It will give you a different look."

"I'm not trying to get a job in Vegas," I tell her.

"Who said anything about Vegas?"

"I did," I say. "Just now."

Justine exhales. "Emily, stop being so negative."

"I'm not being negative. I'm not. It's just . . ."

"What? . . . It's just what?"

"Well . . . there's pee all over my legs."

"There's pee? On your legs? Who p—on—ou—gs?"

"What?" I yell. "I couldn't hear you."

"What did you just say?" she yells back. "Emily? . . . Emily? Where are you?"

"I'm on the West Side Highway."

"You're on the West Side Highway? . . . In a showgirl costume?"

"Yup."

"Who peed on you? Never mind. Do you want me to get you out of this?"

"Please."

"This is Justine."

"NAKED?"

"Emily . . ."

"NAKED?"

"Emily . . .

"You didn't even *ask* me."

"This is not a test, Emily. I repeat: This is not a test. It's a job. It's *editorial.*"

"It's NAKED!"

"EMILY WILL YOU PLEASE KEEP AN OPEN MIND? WADE IS A GOOD PHOTOGRAPHER AND IT'S SIX PAGES OF EDITORIAL FOR A JAPANESE MAGAZINE!"

Jesus. For someone so slothlike, Justine is capable of spitting venom when she chooses. "No need to get huffy," I huff.

Sigh.

"The magazine," I say. "What's it called?"

"*I* don't know! It's in Japanese! Some sort of beauty magazine."

"Oh *really.*"

"Look, Emily. They want you to pose naked, but that doesn't mean you'll be naked in the photos."

"What's that supposed to mean?"

"YOU WON'T SEE ANYTHING."

"Oh."

"So, you'll do it?"

"Well . . ."

"*What?*"

"Nothing . . . it's just . . . well, the name of the beauty magazine, it doesn't translate into *Playboy* or *Hustler* or anything, does it?"

Another sigh, this one a long, drawn-out gasp that immediately conjures an image of Justine on the fainting couch, her hand pressed against her forehead like a beleaguered heroine on *Masterpiece Theatre.* "EMILY! It's not porn. These are artistic shots—artistic!" she emphasizes. "Just cut the crap and do the shoot FOR ONCE, okay?"

Click.

I put down the receiver and drum my fingers against its hard plastic before turning back to face Wade, his crew, and the shoddy décor of this room in the Chelsea Hotel. Sid killed Nancy here. When I heard that, I should have known that something was up; instead it took seeing the scant pile of accessories on the bed to clue me in. "Where are the clothes?" I asked, which led to Wade asking if I "had anything against nudity," which led to the phone call.

"All set?" he says now. As one assistant adjusts the lighting, the other—my stand-in—lies sprawled across the bed, his fingers curled upward, an ingénue in a Metallica T-shirt.

I lean against the bureau. No, I don't have anything against nudity, not as a general concept. I mean, if you want to go to a nudist colony, go; wear sunblock, and if you want to pose for *Penthouse,* super; I hope you become the Pet of the Month. I'm just not sure how I feel about nudity *personally,* or rather, my nudity on film, which seems anything but personal.

You'd think this would have come up before, but it hasn't, not like this. Sure, lately I've been doing more lingerie (Why not? The money's good and I book a fair amount of it—especially after I bought those silicone chicken-cutlet pads to ensure my cups runneth over), and for beauty shots I've had to bare my arms and shoulders, which has meant a scarf tied around my breasts. But this is the Chelsea Hotel, not Bergdorf's, and it ain't Avedon behind the lens, so I don't know what to think.

"Tell me the shots again," I say.

"You won't see anything, if that's what you're worried about," Wade assures me. I watch him flip open a battered camera case and fit a lens snugly into the foam womb. Speaking of Sid, there's something about Wade and his assistants—the long hair, the sinewy build, the wallets attached to their jeans with silver chains—that reeks of heavy metal. I feel like I'm locked in a bedroom with Mötley Crüe.

"Nothing here?" I point to my breasts.

"Covered."

"Here?" I point down low.

Wade looks at me, amused. "Emily! This isn't porn! You're not 'modeling'"—his crooked fingers rake the air—"You're modeling."

It's my turn to smile. I know what the bunny ears mean: models who work for *those* agencies, the ones with words like *escort* or *service* in their names. *Elite* not **elite.** In other words, not me.

"Think Helmut Newton, not Hugh Hefner. That's what I'm after," he says.

I think of those two, plus Justine. She's getting irritated with me. *Not sexy enough, not sexy enough,* she says whenever she flips though my book. Earlier this week, she got Byron to jump on her bandwagon and now there's a chorus of other mantras: I'm *too pretty, too collegiate.* "Don't you want to be more than that?" Byron asked me. "More than a pretty college student?" Of course I do. I want to be one of your girls, Byron. I want to be a star.

Besides these pictures are for Japan; no one will see them.

"No nipples."

Wade smiles. "Of course not, not if you don't want to."

"Okay," I say. We've struck a deal.

"In that case, you'd better take your clothes off now," he tells me. "We don't want any marks on your skin."

Ronnie, the stylist, hands me a polyester robe that's so well-worn and slippery it almost feels wet. Though it makes no sense, I slip into the bathroom to change. When I emerge, I see that Kelli, the makeup artist, has set up near the window, pushing back the grimy curtain to let in what little natural light there is on this muggy, sunless day. As "Livin' on a Prayer" blasts from a beat-up boom box, Kelli makes my eyes dark and smoky. When she gets them perfectly symmetrical, she smudges. "Bedroom eyes are always a little messy," she says. Once satisfied, she moves down to my lips. "Bite," she directs. "Again."

I bite until my lips swell. Kelli draws the top lip line well beyond my real one. Once she's filled the area with a matte burgundy (all makeup is matte now), I grab a compact and study them. They look symmetrical and full, as if carved from wax.

My hair is given a forties wave and then I'm ready.

Wade whistles. "Wow! Look at you! Dominatrix!" he exclaims, then, "Let's get started."

Wade pivots toward the window until all I can see is one silver earring and the back of his head. The others follow suit.

No big deal, my brain says, but my body is trembling. I undo the sash. The robe slips off my shoulders. It falls onto the pale blue carpet, just to the right of a brown stain that is almost in the shape of a puffy heart. *Nancy's blood?* I wonder. *Did she die here?* I inch backward onto the bed. "Do I go under the sheets?"

"No," Ronnie and Wade say in unison.

Okay then . . . I reach down, grab the robe off the floor, and cover myself from chin to calves.

"Ready?" Wade asks.

"Ready."

He turns and laughs. "Saving it for the last minute, are we?"

I feel stupid but I don't move.

The first shot has me in a pair of gloves. They're opera length. Soft black leather with scarlet cutouts running the length of them. Decadent, impractical. Sexy.

"Cross your legs tightly and twist sideways," Wade instructs. I do.

He clasps the edge of the robe. "You ready?"

My gloved hands cup my breasts. I nod. The robe slides over my skin and disappears.

"We need new music," Ronnie says.

Wade nods. "I'll change it."

It feels funny at first, being naked, that rush of air against newly exposed skin: like peeling off a Band-Aid. But only at first. After a roll or two, I start to relax. My legs remain crossed and turned (revealing my crack to an assistant, which I try not to think about), my upper body softens, my shoulders unfurl. I lean back against the headboard. I run the gloves across my face. I let Sinead's achingly beautiful voice wash over me. Wade was right: I can reveal what I want to; it's my show.

"Where are you from?" Wade asks when Kelli is reapplying the kohl to my lids.

"Wisconsin."

He laughs. "A nice, pure midwestern girl."

We work our way through the gloves, beret, and scarf; Sinead, Ella, and Billie. By the time we get to me on my knees on the bed, to the strands of pearls dripping down my back, I've embraced this moment, my role: Not-Emily but a woman who has done things—kissed in a café, danced on a tabletop, worn satin at a chateau, cried into her champagne.

A bad girl.

"Turn around," Wade says. And I do. The pearls slide over my shoulder.

"Fantastic," he breathes.

We begin with a headshot, the lens so close I can see the aperture opening and closing like a tiny mouth. I make an S with my body and give varying angles of my left profile—my better one—slowly drawing my chin u-u-p-p-p then d-ow-wnnn, my eyes always in-camera because it just feels right.

Click. "Beautiful!" *Click.* "So!" *Click.* "Beautiful!"

Wade kneels on the bed. I face the camera dead-on, my chin slightly elevated.

"Yes!" *Click.* "Sexy!"

Yes. Sexy. I thread the pearls through my fingers and pull them into the shot, caressing my cheek and lips, the way I might absently play with a strand of hair.

I'm a bad girl.

"Excellent!" *Click. Click.*

A siren. I open my mouth.

"Yes!" *Click.*

So sexy. Bring the pearls to my lips.

"Yes! Like that!"

And bite down.

"Yes!"

Wade shoots several of these, then hobbles backward until he's off the bed and several feet away from me.

"Lose the hand," he instructs.

The tape has stopped. The crew is quiet. As I drop my hand, the pearls click together like billiard balls, before settling against my breasts. I push my shoulder blades together and tilt forward.

"Beautiful!" Wade cries. "This is the shot!"

At school, there's this experiment we learned about in Intro Psych that shows if you ask for more, you get more. For instance, if you ask a person to give you $20, you might get $10, whereas if you had asked him for $10, you might have only gotten $7. Well, this is like that. Walking into this hotel room, I never thought about exposing skin. Period. But after hearing the word *nudity* and imagining myself sprawled spread-eagle in my birthday suit *Hustler* style, posing topless seems like a reasonable compromise. And truthfully? After all the swimwear and tank tops, the bras and briefs, the outfit changes and boob tapings in front of stylists and models, hair and makeup artists—it feels like I'm going just a little bit further: another twist, another turn. It feels good. No, that's a lie: It feels *great*. And with each click of the camera, with each cry of delight from Wade, it feels better and better until *I am a siren. I am sexy. Sexy! Oh so sexy. I am a vixen. A woman. I am powerful. I glow. Look at me. Look. At. Me.*

But then "Ughh!" Kelli shrieks. We follow her pointing finger across the street to the man on his balcony. Naked. Masturbating. He sees us cringing, smiles delightedly, and comes.

Jordan slides her money through the window.

"I still can't believe it costs $7 to go to a movie," she grumbles.

"Highway robbery."

We stopped after that. I scrubbed my face, threw my hair into a ponytail, and fled the hotel room.

Jordan takes her change and slides it into her wallet, which, in keeping with her wardrobe, is a subtle neon orange. "Harder to steal," she always says. "'Cause no one wants it," I always tell her.

In the elevator, Wade asked if I wanted to grab a drink. "Underage," I told him, then turned to walk down Twenty-third Street, my backpack slung over my shoulder: just another college kid going to the movies.

While we wait for soda and popcorn, Jordan, my roommate for the summer as well in a fifth-floor village walk-up, tells me about work. Though she hasn't ruled out a future in politics, this vacation she opted for an internship on the trading floor. So far at least, it's agreeing with her. "Made to trade," she says. "It's the perfect job for my ladylike disposition." Of course, the fact that Ben is spending the summer here interning at the International Rescue Committee helps, too.

". . . Can you believe that?"

"No," I say uncertainly.

I got here a few minutes early, so I went to the pay phone on the corner. "Good," Justine said, when I told her everything that happened. "It means you finally did something sexy enough."

We enter the theater. Usually seating involves protracted negotiation—Jordan likes the front, I prefer the middle—but today I say wherever and plop down in her first selection.

"You heard from Pixie?" Jordan asks. Pixie's taking art and German classes at the University of Vienna until August.

"No . . . you?"

"No. You know, for such a chatterbox, she's really quite a crappy correspondent."

"Yeah . . ."

Jordan pushes the popcorn toward me. "What's up with you?"

I push it away. "Nothing. Long day."

"Doing what?"

"A shoot in a seedy hotel room wearing nothing but pearls while a guy in the apartment across the street masturbated on his balcony—you?"

While I say this Jordan's eyes get bigger, then smaller, her hand cups her mouth and she tries not to laugh. I see her searching for the punch line.

"I know, I know: You hate it when this happens."

Jordan shakes this off. "So wait . . . seriously, you were naked?"

"Yeah, but you couldn't see anything."

"Really?" she says doubtfully. "Then what was the point?"

"Well, for one shot you could, but it was only my top half."

"So you were topless?"

"I guess."

"And there was some guy masturbating across the street from you."

"Yes, but he wasn't part of the shot!"

My heart races as I see things as described. Seedy hotel. Pearl necklace. Masturbator. "He just happened," I add, giving a dismissive wave that's more cavalier than I am right now. "You know, New York."

Jordan nods. She doesn't care about this part. "I thought you said you'd never pose topless."

"Did I?" I did.

"Yes."

"Well, this was different. It was . . ." I search for the word, ". . . artistic."

"Which part?" she begins, only I don't want to hear the rest.

"All of it," I snap.

The photos come back from the two tests. We don't use any from the paper bikini series—*please*—but Justine likes a couple from the showgirl shoot. In one black-and-white headshot, I'm gazing levelly as my feathery crown blows in a West Side Highway breeze. This gets paired with a full length of me strolling away from the lens, my sequins shimmering in the sun, the thin, spidery line of my fishnets running parallel to the thick, gray median. Cars rush past. I stare over my shoulder, my eyes narrowed, my jaw clenched.

"You look so evil . . ." Justine murmurs approvingly as she stares at the contact sheet. "Evil and tough."

"Scared," I reply, remembering the Snapple bottle filled with urine that, seconds later, was thrown at my feet by the driver of a Sleepy's delivery van. I'm sure it was an accident.

"Whatever." Justine grabs her grease pencil and makes two fat blue stars. "They're sexy, they're strong. They work."

Something's working. Whether it's the additional photos I can't say, but my career goes into liftoff. The *Allure* pages come out and get added to my book. L'Oréal decides I'm worth booking for a Studio Line print campaign. *Mademoiselle* confirms me. Saks decides to give me another chance. *Glamour* comes calling. Yes, three weeks in New York and I've done it, I've moved up to a higher elevation, a different perspective. I'm a known, working model making six figures a year. It feels fantastic.

And yet . . . I'm still not one of Byron's girls. I'm still not a star. And every time I walk into the agency, the buzz is about some girl who is. Fonya. Or the seventeen-year-old daughter of a Thai tribal leader. Or the 34–22–34 fifteen-year-old from Minsk.

"Jesus, how do you find them all?" I whisper one day when Byron and I have crossed paths in front of the trophy wall, where there are more *Vogue* covers and more faces I've only just come to know.

Byron shrugs. "Easy. There's no such thing as undiscovered beauty, not anymore."

Louis told me this, too. I stare at the floor, thinking about what lies six stories beneath us. There, in addition to the catcallers and freaks, walk the modeling scouts. While some are employed by specific agencies, most scouts are freelancers who find a girl, then go from agency to agency looking to cut a deal: bounty hunters who relentlessly work a territory. It doesn't take long to stumble across one. "Woods . . . Chic" the guy in Times Square mutters whenever I pass. He stands near the subway station, scanning the thousands of tourists in search of the one girl who will cover this month's rent.

So, there's no such thing as undiscovered beauty—maybe that's true. But what about discovered beauty? What about me? My eyes flick to the trophy wall. "I want another cover," I whisper, but Byron's walked away.

One week later, I'm back in Chic but focused on other things, like uncovering the reason Justine left a message insisting I stop by, and picking up an overdue check from Javier, our accountant.

Oh no. I stare at the dark office. "Don't tell me . . ."

"Hello, Chic. *Please* hold—YesEmilyyou missed Javierhetookoff-fortheHamptons."

"But it's two o'clock!"

"Butthetraffic'ssobad—How can I help you?"

Grrr. My lip is still curled when a girl runs past me, her face in her hands. *Huh?* Open castings are held on Tuesdays. It's Friday. "Alistair, what's going on?"

Alistair depresses a few buttons, rises, and leans forward until the bubbles embroidered on his red vest are flattened against the desk. "Bad news," he stage whispers. "Byron's dropping girls."

A cold chill runs down my spin. Dropping girls, I've heard about this. Periodically, agencies prune their ranks by cutting models, often dozens at a time. The rationale is always "underperformance," but no one's ever sure what the criteria are, because no agency ever shares it. It's rumored that "difficult" girls are always the first to get the boot—unless they're top earners, of course. (Note the "difficult" category includes everything from being pushy to pushing needles into your veins. Or mounds of coke up your nose. The thing I've learned about modeling and drugs is, do them a little and you'll help your career, do them a little too much and you'll no longer have one.) In a business where image truly is everything, getting dropped like this is tantamount to shaving your head or gaining twenty pounds: No good agency is gonna touch you.

So this is why Justine called me.

It takes forever to cross the main room of the agency; it's not long enough. I stand next to the booking table, my insides turning to lead as I watch four agents work the phones, waiting for the inevitable.

"Is that two stories, six pages each, or one twelve-pager?"

"—I suppose, but hasn't Hawaii been done?"

"—Of course she's professional; her affair with Ralph ended right when her contract did!"

"—Look, I told you: A perfume campaign with Petra is gonna run you $500,000—are you gonna cough it up or what?" Justine looks at me, issues a wan smile, and points.

At the door? The exit sign? "What?"

"—Are you kidding? You can't get *worldwide coverage* for the price of a ticket to Disneyland! Hang on—" She covers the receiver. "The light box. Go to the light box."

My whole body releases. "So I'm not being dropped?"

"Not today," Justine says. "No, you *to*day, in fact, *now* please, or else I'm giving the time to Donna." She pokes me. "Wade dropped off the contact sheets."

Wade? "But I thought that shoot was a job."

"He owed Byron a favor," she says vaguely. "In fact, he's offered to print a few for you before sending them off, so go take a look. There's one in particular that's great: very Jackie O . . . That's right, five hundred grand . . . good. I'm so glad. Now are you sure you need five days or could you shoot this in four . . . ?"

Negatives cover the light box, spilling onto the counter. There are at least a dozen rolls, but when I sort through them, I see that only one frame has been circled and starred, the indication that it's both Justine and Byron approved: me wearing the pearls.

I don't remember this in Camelot. In the shot, I'm eyeing the camera haughtily, almost indifferently, an expression that, when coupled with the necklace, contrasts startlingly to the paleness of my breasts, the darkness of my nipples, the seedy, barren room receding into the background.

Oh my. Taking the picture felt like one thing: an intimate moment in a small space with a few professionals. A blink of an eye, a wink of the lens. And then poof! Hours after I left it was like it had never happened. But now it's real. Very real. Me. Naked. In black and white.

If I put this photo in my book, we're not talking about one copy in one portfolio, but five copies in five portfolios—those duplicate books of mine that get messengered all over the city to be dropped into reception areas, peeled open on conference tables, examined at meetings, and scrutinized on desktops. And that's not including agencies in London or LA that represent me through barter deals, and as a result, receive packets of my latest pictures. Dozens of portfolios in all. One photograph exposed again and again and again.

No way.

I sort though the negatives, methodically moving the loop across the page in search of a compromise that's less compromising. Here, this one, with the gloves and just a hint of skin. How come no one starred this one? This one works.

"What about—"

I twist around. Four agents, working the phones.

"—So, North Beach Leather on Monday for $20K, got it."

"—You can't have her then. Elgort has her for the entire week."

"—I'm sorry, a fan club from *where*?"

"—A *Bazaar* cover, that's right. And she's only been in here a month! Isn't that a great fourteenth-birthday present?"

Four agents, working the phones. And just beyond, Byron's office, where Byron is wiping the cheek of a weeping Diana.

Justine replaces her receiver. "What about what?"

"Nothing," I say.

We put the photo in my book.

A few days later and it's the Fourth of July. I'm supposed to go back to Balsam, but I get a booking for three days of English catalog so I stay. New York is quiet. My friends are gone. I spend the better part of my birthday surrounded by foreign tourists at Barneys. When I get back to my apartment, I slowly peel the tissue from my latest finds. Lacroix, Versace, Ozbek, Roehm. I finger the feathers, run my hands along the hems, and hang the ornate finery in my closet.

Chapter 25

Dub a Rub Rub

"Okay, got it!" the photographer cries.

I start walking off-set.

"Hang on, you're stuck!"

Marron, the stylist, starts pulling my taped train, which is attached at regular intervals like an octopus's tentacles to the paper backdrop. "I need your slip, too," she says.

"And I need the veil," adds Aaron, the hairdresser.

"Do you think it's bad luck to be a bride so many times?" I ask, ducking and weaving as I try to hold my head up while stepping out of a hoopskirt-like contraption.

"Depends how many grooms you've had," Marron says.

"Hmm . . . I'd say at least three dozen."

"You're screwed."

Aaron spins my face away from the stepladder on which he's standing and tugs what has to be the thirtieth pin from the comb of the veil. (Bobby pins are like the clowns in the car: just when you thought

there couldn't be any more . . .) "Christ," he mutters as the art director approaches. "If she tells me to change the hair one more time,
I'll scream." His arms swing like a toy soldier's. "Up, down! Up,
down!"

But the art director is looking at me. "Emily? You've got a call on
line two."

"Thanks."

I don't bother to ask who it is; there's only one person who knows
I'm spending the day in a Queens warehouse as a bride-to-be.

"Hi Justine."

Justine's not one for small talk. "You got confirmed," she grunts.

"For what?"

Or, really, for talk of any kind. "The music video."

But at this moment I couldn't care less. I jump up and down until I
nearly trip over my train. The music video's for Down Under, an Australian pop duo who on this continent is known rather than famous,
and the pay will be terrible: one, two hundred dollars at the most, but
every model wanted this gig because it's a Thom Brenner video . . . And
I booked it! I can't believe it. The audition was by invitation only, only
the invitation had already been extended to 435 people before I signed
in, with dozens entering in my wake. Besides, the last time I was up for
a Thom Brenner job, I was busted for not being an Indian. I didn't
think I even had a chance.

"Getting this booking was tough, Emily . . ."

"I know!" I swish my white gown. My four-carat cubic zirconium
engagement ring sparkles in the light.

"Know? You couldn't possibly," she sighs. "But Thom really wanted
Fonya so Byron pushed for a deal."

Oh. So Fonya's in it, too. My hand drops against the counter. "A
'deal'? You mean like a two-for-one special?"

"I wouldn't say that," Justine says, though she doesn't offer any al-
ternative interpretations.

I watch as the makeup artist ensures the other bride is truly blush-
ing. Remember those jokes that go "you're pretty . . . ugly," "you're
strong . . . smelling"? Talking to my booker is like that: feeling good
then bad within a short space of time.

Only I want to feel good. "Well, two-for-one special or not, who cares? I booked it, right?"

"Right," Justine says. "But Emily? This is important. Try to make sure our efforts aren't wasted. Try and get a lot of face time."

Two nights later, I go to an address in the Garment District, where a yellow school bus idles out front. Onboard, people are chatting chummily. I see several familiar faces, but no one I know, so I sit down in the first available seat and slide next to the window, feeling like the new kid at the School for the Telegenically Gifted. As others climb aboard, I assign them roles, too: the guy with the long blond hair? *Class stoner.* The girl with the skintight sweater? *Class slut.* Soon, the bus is crowded and noisy, with everyone talking about the big man on campus.

"Thom's such a genius!"

"Legend, really."

"Did you see the latest billboard?"

"Killer abs, man!"

"Where'd they get that guy—what's his name, Mar . . . Marco? Who's he with?"

"Shh! He's right behind you."

I flip around, casually looking for the latest guy to bare it all in Times Square but really, it could be anyone; every single guy behind me is pumped and chiseled, a perfect ten. . . . And I don't even care.

I don't care because male models are dumb.

Now, I realize we female models aren't exactly MENSA candidates ourselves, but still, I'll say it: Male models are dumb, and the reason is simple—money. Few male models make much of the stuff. Even the top-grossing guys, the ones you might know on a first-name basis, make less than your average female model, and most male models are far more obscure than that. Moreover, underwear ads notwithstanding, the vast majority of male modeling involves wearing a suit, which means a guy's career doesn't get going in earnest until he looks old enough to pull one off—usually when he's somewhere in his mid-thirties. Add these two pieces of information together–low pay and a late start—and you get a bus full of guys who were very lost in life until they realized they could fall back on their very chiseled buns.

Plus there's something off-putting about guys who routinely discuss brands of styling gel.

Plus, plus, I had a guy. The guy broke my heart, and I lost *Vogue*. I'm not making the same mistake again.

I face front and wiggle my knees until they're propped against the seat in front of me, looking up just in time to see the *class beauty* climb on board.

She sits down next to me. "I'm Fonya."

"I'm Emily," I say. A hush has fallen over the bus; I guess even this crowd is cowed by a supermodel.

"Nice to meet you."

Fonya smiles. She's prettier than I imagined. Her brown eyes are almond shaped but wide, too, like a fan. Her hair is dark and silky, her skin tawny and warm. Looking at her, I think of thick furs, rich woods, soft suedes: things delicate, expensive, and lush. So I stare at my knees. I feel nervous and this annoys me; after all, I could be—no, I *should* be—the one making *her* nervous. I should be Fonya. My jaw clenches in anger.

"Emily, you're with Chic, aren't you?"

"Yup."

"I thought so. I've seen your card in the agency," Fonya says. She flashes a shy smile. "That *Harpers & Queen* cover you did is really great."

"Thanks. I like your . . . covers," I mumble. Fonya would have to be nice, too, wouldn't she? And bubbly? It just kills me.

Her hand descends past her brown leather mini, surfacing with a Chanel bag. "Want to see my baby?"

"You have a baby?" I sputter. Fame, wealth, a kick-ass bod, and a child—how does she find the time?

But the photo she hands me is of a white tiger cub.

"Cute," I say. "What zoo is he at?"

"*My* zoo! Sorry: my wildlife center. I always forget that! It's on this land I bought in Florida." Fonya's shoulders flop casually, as if we're discussing a hammock, barbecue, or other routine backyard purchase. "That's Fondar. I just hope he gets along with Darya. Darya's our little lion—this one here. Isn't he cute?"

"Cute," I say again.

Now it's a stack of photos: a veritable ark. "All the animals live in separate pens, obviously, but the trick is the placement of the pens. Who's going where? See, I really, really want there to be a spiritual connection between the animals, 'cause that's important to their health and happiness. I wish I knew Fondar's astrological sign; does he look like a Sagittarius or a Capricorn to you?"

Yes, there is a God; Fonya's as dumb as a post. "I'm not sure," I say, grinning merrily. For the rest of the ride, I revel in every stupid utterance. In fact, I enjoy myself so thoroughly it seems like we're rumbling off of I-87 and down a twisting, overgrown driveway before my companion has even caught her breath.

The gravel crackles beneath our tires. The crowd stirs.

"Aww man! Not this place again!"

"I've shot three videos here already!"

"It's always freezing!"

"Yeah, freezing, man!"

Oh, this is an überlocation. Überlocations are places that are perpetually rented out for photo and video shoots. While most überlocations are little more than empty studios with a few architectural details thrown in—a fluted column, a bay window, a claw-footed tub—others are actual homes that the owners move out of temporarily in exchange for cash. In Manhattan, there are certain überlocations of the latter type you work in again and again, all really posh. The double-wide brownstone off Gramercy Park with the elevator, garage, and wrought iron detailing. The apartment on Fifth Avenue with the view of the reservoir (nice, though I swear the reason this one's so popular is because you run into Paul Newman on the elevator). The all-white artist's loft in SoHo. Being a stranger in someone's home is well, strange. Everyone sits around cattily evaluating the décor and examining the personal artifacts that have been stashed away, though never well enough, while they speculate on how the fortune was won and—because we're there—lost.

These are the interior überlocations. There are exterior versions as well, ones that feature New York City as backdrop. Now, obviously, there are as many of these as there are yellow cabs, yet, even in this category, there are a few standouts. The number one exterior überlocation, so popular that there are parking spaces for location vans painted on the pavement, is Bethesda Fountain in Central Park. Wander that way on an early summer day and you'll see a slew of photo crews swapping catered lunches, equipment, and industry gossip like they're vacation-ing in a particularly chic trailer park. Other contenders include the façade of the Metropolitan Museum (fountain, steps—the posh back-drop), the intersection just north of the Flatiron District (buildings, taxis—the urban backdrop), and Vesuvio Bakery on Prince Street in SoHo (picturesque, quaint—the charming backdrop).

A few more yards of asphalt and our yellow bus pulls to a halt in front of a Gothic mansion (dilapidated, covered in vines—the faded grandeur backdrop). Though a fleet of people meet us, there are a lot of us to be met. After I make the critical error of going to pee, I wind up on the tail end of the assembly line, and so it takes me nearly four hours to get coiffed, made up, and dressed (an extra hour because the head stylist decides I need *really big* hair). By the time I'm finally delivered to the set, it's 1:00 A.M. (we're shooting at night for the ambience), I've had three cups of coffee, and I'm feeling more than a little antsy.

So is Henri, one of the video's producers and Thom's right-hand man. *"Finalement!"* Henri gasps, eyeing me and my ensemble in one collective swoop. His fingers hover like hummingbirds, coming to rest on my sash. "No," he tut-tuts. "This is wrong. This is not how Thierry Mugler wanted it."

I glance down at my outfit. The sash is part of a patent leather trench coat, so it doesn't seem to offer a lot of options; besides, we're in a Gothic mansion on the Hudson. "It's not like he's gonna know," I stage-whisper.

Henri's eyes widen, so does his mouth. *Sacre bleu!* I think he's about to yell, or *Zut alors!* Instead what comes out is "Thi-erryyy!"

Thierry?

Thierry Mugler trots over. *"Oui?"*

Or we can ask the designer himself. That works, too.

Henri pecks reprovingly at my sash. "This isn't right, is it?"

Thierry cocks an eyebrow, looking very much the way he did in last month's *Elle* under the heading *"Vivre Le Sex!"* "She needs a beret," he announces before trotting off.

"Mais le sash!"

Henri's hand is still clamped over his eyes when a black beret is proffered and wedged onto my head. So much for the extra hour of hair.

A hairdresser is clearing a lock from above my eyebrow when Thom comes into view. "You," he says, pointing at me.

"Emily," his assistant murmurs.

"Emily. Follow me."

I'm working with Thom Brenner—*Thom Brenner!* I try to play it cool as I follow in the director's footsteps. We're in the heart of the house now, the central core. Gorgeous men and women lounge along the hall and up the staircase in poses of studied nonchalance, their taut frames leaning against wallpaper that has long since given up trying: its edges tattered and curled, its fleur-de-lis pattern darker in places where paintings once hung. On the fat swirl of the banister a half-naked Adonis perches, his skin glossed with a light sheen of oil. On the stairs, a couple coils, alternately swapping saliva and a joint. My God, roll the cameras and you'd have, if not a superior species, at least the makings of a great porn movie.

We stop on the underside of the staircase, directly in front of a guy with a straight blond pageboy, a navy cap, and pants with two rows of shiny buttons. "You," Thom says. "I want you on the floor kissing him."

Then again, maybe we're making it right now. *Kiss him?*

Thom heads toward the camera. "Places! Please!" he shouts.

Kiss him? I turn to look at the guy I'm supposed to kiss, realize with lightning-like clarity he looks exactly like the Dutch Boy Paint mascot, and whirl back around. "Wait!"

"Attends!" Thierry Mugler trots across the floor toward me, flapping both hands. *"Attends!"*

Exactement, Thierry. I break into an easy smile. The famous designer is going to be my knight in black spandex and tell Thom that my beauty, or at least his outfit, would be wasted on the floor.

"I don't think we need this after all."

Thierry plucks the beret off my head.

"Places! Please!"

Thom's behind the camera now, his large frame all but obscured by a tangle of steel and hot lights. As one hand grips a megaphone, the other rests on his cowboy hat, giving him the odd air of a rodeo cheerleader. "Boys and girls, listen up," he booms. "We have a long night ahead of us with a lot of scenes, so it's essential that we keep things moving on schedule. That means no rehearsals: I'm just going to start rolling tape. I've given you your specific role already. Beyond that, the direction is simple: Don't fuck it up!"

The hall echoes with laughter.

"Are we ready?"

"Ready!" the room cries.

"Good. Places! Please!"

People settle into position, including Dutch Boy, who pops a mint. I just stand there. Truthfully? When we pulled up and I saw the abandoned estate, I imagined a video filled with moonlight, overgrown gardens, and cobblestone paths. The film would be black and white, perhaps a little grainy, the clothing would be fine, and if there had to be a kiss, a girl and a sailor, the moment would be cinematic, truly elegant, like that Doisineau photograph that hangs on every dorm floor. And I wouldn't be the girl. *Kiss him?* You won't even see me.

I want—no, I need—a different kind of face time. I tip my head back. "Thomm!"

Fifty sets of eyes turn to me, including Thom's. "What?"

"I can't do this shot," I wail. "I'm supposed to get a close-up!"

Everyone, and I mean everyone, finds this highly amusing, and not just in this room: a walkie-talkie bleats a ripple of delayed laughter, tripping another cascade of guffaws along the hall. I feel my cheeks flame. *What have I done?*

"Well, I want an eight-pack." Thom emphasizes this point by lifting up his shirt and revealing his thin but untoned stomach, a move that produces both whistles and laughter. "We can't all get what we want, now can we?"

The stares. The guffaws. My hot cheeks. I lie down next to Dutch Boy.

"I have a boyfriend," I lie.

"So do I," he says.

Forty-five minutes of tonsil hockey and it's time for shot number two. We relocate to the ballroom. Of all the rooms in the mansion, here is where the toll of time is most evident. Strips of parquet have peeled from the floor. Yellow, toothy chandeliers hang slightly askew. The furniture is threadbare. The curtains miss entire panels. Wind whistles through broken panes. It's as if the house has been shaken, stirred, and left to rot.

Shot number two is girls only. Thom's idea is for the female models (all except for Fonya, whom I haven't seen since we arrived) to rise slowly in response to the music, then bump and thrust until we've worked ourselves into a bacchanalian frenzy. He juts a thumb toward me. "Except for you. I need you to sit this one out."

Perfect. I asked for a close-up and now he hates me. I sink into the understuffed sofa, trying to remain calm, and watch the girls dance. The music is the Down Under song for the video, of course. It's been playing since we first arrived. Five hours ago, I liked it. Now it's driving me nuts.

"C'mon girls!" Thom's carrying the camera on his shoulder, like he's shooting the bombed-out streets of Beirut or ambush footage of celebs caught leaving the scene of an illicit tryst. As the girls bob, he weaves between them. "C'mon, faster. Faster!"

The models move together like a flock of flamingos.

"Girls! I need you to let go!"

"Let go! LET GO!"

Let go? If only. Being a good model means that for each and every frame, you're carefully composed; even in "spontaneous" shots, you know where every part of you is, what's accentuated and what's hidden. But Thom's carrying a moving camera that's recording dozens of frames per second—how can you possibly stay ahead of that? You can't. There's bound to be frames where you're seen from a bad angle or where your scar is showing. It's terrifying and, truthfully? It's the reason that most models make crappy actresses. Emotions are messy, emotions are ugly; we don't wanna go there.

I must fall asleep, for soon I've plunged into a dream where Thom is urgently insisting it's time for my close-up . . . except it isn't a dream and it isn't Thom. It's Henri and he's shaking me.

"Emily, get up. Up! Thom needs you upstairs!"

"Whaa?" I wipe the drool off my chin. Shuddering, Henri urges me to my feet. I trail him through a succession of rooms, all empty until we hit the kitchen, where a pocket of people are hanging out between takes, some drinking coffee, some passing around a flask. Against the fridge, Dutch Boy is making out with someone who I'm guessing is not his boyfriend. Off the Formica counter, a guy dressed in a leather pea-coat does a line of coke. Henri stiffens. I brace for the requisite hissy fit. Instead, he springs forward and does a quick one himself.

And then we're off. We scamper up the stairs, down the hall, and into a room on the third floor where Thom and a dozen crew members are watching Fonya take a bubble bath.

"Voilà!" Henri says.

Thom looks up. "Ahh, Miss Desmond—"

The crew cracks up.

"—ready for your close-up?"

It's Henri who responds: "No. She needs a massive touch-up and jewelry just like Fonya's."

Fonya's ears are adorned with flowers made of faux diamonds, her hair is piled high and smooth, and a cigarette holder dangles from her slim fingers. Right as a stylist pinches similar earrings on my lobes, a makeup artist emerges from the other side of the toilet, brandishing a loaded lip brush. I dodge it.

"What's the shot?"

Thom shrugs: *Isn't it obvious?* "You in the tub with Fonya."

"Behind Fonya," Henri clarifies.

"Doing what?"

Another shrug. "Whatever works. Whatever inspires you."

I study the scene. This can't be right. My bath buddy is buck naked, in fact. "You can see her breasts."

"Not when your hands are on them," Thom replies.

Hang the fuck on.

Henri whisks off my sash and starts unbuttoning my coat. I look at Fonya to see if she has a problem with this, but she's pushing a bar of soap along the rim of the tub like it's her rubber duckie: I guess not. I do some quick mental calculations. It's 4:00 A.M., I have to be at a booking—a booking that will actually pay me something—in four hours, and clearly, given the poisonous looks Thom's now issuing, the man's never going to book me again.

I push Henri's hands away. "No. I'm not doing the shot. Sorry."

Before the bar of soap splashes into the tub, I'm in the next room, speeding toward the kitchen, where earlier, I noticed the pay phone that I'll now use to call a cab.

"Emily!" Henri's footsteps ring behind me. "Emily!"

Without warning, I'm slammed against the wall, my arms pinned. I gasp in shock and pain.

Henri's face nears mine. Sweat streams down his forehead. His collar's wet. His eyes are wild. "You little bitch!" he hisses, shaking me. "You don't walk out on Thom Brenner like that, you got it? Who the hell do you think you are?"

Saliva is sprayed across my face. I blink and twist.

". . . You are doing this shot!"

I find my voice. "No, I'm not."

"Yes! You are! Right now!"

"There are a lot of other girls downstairs, ask one of them!"

Henri's words tumble out, each coke-addled thought tripping over the next. "We want twins, or almost twins. That means you. You're a brunette. You look like Fonya. You're the only one here who does. Here, but not at the casting. At the casting we had *six* girls that looked like Fonya. *Six* girls who wanted this job. But we chose *you*. You know why?"

Oh God.

"Because your book was the sluttiest. Yes, that's right. You've done topless before, Emily, you can sure as hell strip down again. Especially for Thom Brenner. Especially for a key shot." Henri pauses to swallow. His breath is ragged. The sweat now seeping from his chest and belly, splotching the fabric of his designer shirt. "I'm not letting you wreck the shoot, do you understand? *Do* you? Or do I need to call Byron and inform him that Thom Brenner Productions will not be working with Chic models anytime soon because they're too fucking difficult?"

Difficult. A difficult girl. Byron would drop me for sure.

I look toward the bathroom. Thom's stretched out in the door frame, his fingers hooked over the molding above, waiting to see how it turns out.

I've already done it once. What's one more time?

In the bathroom, I peel off all my clothing. "Tell me," I say to Thom. "Tell me exactly what you want me to do."

Chapter 26

Twinkle, Twinkle

I lift the nude bundle off the lilac-colored tissue and dangle it over the table. "What's the G in G-string stand for anyway: Good? Garnish? Gee as in Gee whiz?"

"Gee as in 'Gee, honey, you're wearing dental floss.'"

"Lovely image, Jord."

"*You* brought it up."

Jordan takes a slug of light beer. We're sitting at the kitchen table in our tiny Village sublet, sweating profusely as our electric fan tries and fails to cool the humid mid-July heat. I twirl the panties. "Do you think G in G-string is the same as the G in G-spot?"

"Well, gee, Emma, I never thought about it but, no, I think the 'G' in G-spot stands for the name of the doctor, Dr. Graffenwhatever, who invented—"

"*Invented?*"

"Sorry, *discovered* the G-spot."

"Oh. Still, it's quite a coincidence, don't you think? I mean there are twenty-six let—"

But my friend's mind isn't on spelling, it's in the gutter. "Now there's a good research topic," she interjects. "Hi, I'm Dr. Graffenwhatsits, can I put my finger inside you in the interest of science?"

"Jorddd!"

"In fact, I bet this Dr. Graffenwhosie invented the G-string, too," she continues. "As a cover-up for his new find—you know, to protect it, to keep it warm."

Pause. "You mean like a muff?"

"Exactly. A muff. Heh. Heh. Hey, I don't know if I have a G-spot, do you?"

How do we get into these conversations?

"My God, how should I know; I feel like I've barely mastered the orgasm!" I retort. 'Cause it's true. That's the problem with magazines like *Cosmo*: You learn about all the things you didn't know you were missing. Like the perfect scented candle. Or your G-spot.

"I hear ya." Jordan drains her beer, then wipes a damp towel across her forehead. "Hey," she says, shifting gears, "you still haven't told me about the video. How was it?"

I launch into a colorful description of my make-out session with Dutch Boy.

"Oh God! No way! Eeww! Was it weird?"

"Totally."

"Were your mouths open?"

"A little."

"And that was . . ."

"Like sticking my tongue into a pile of raw organ meats."

"Lord!" She cries. "*Lord!*"

"Probably because Dutch Boy kept making googly eyes at other guys."

Now, Jordan can hardly breathe. "No, no! That's crazy!"

"You think *that's* crazy?" I say. Before I can stop myself, I tell Jordan about the tub scene.

"Wait . . . you took a bath with Fonya?"

"Yup."

"On camera?"

Shit. Jordan's eyes. Jordan's voice. They've changed. "Yup."

"So you were naked again."

Shit. Shit. Shit. "Well, people usually don't take baths in their ball gowns, now do they?" I snap.

"What were you guys doing?"

"You know, the usual."

Jordan shifts. "No, I don't know. The last time I took a bath with another girl we made our hair into devil horns and tried to drown our Fisher-Price people, Emma, so enlighten me. Did you wash her back? Feel her up? Did you *kiss* her?"

"Jesus, Jordan, stop attacking me!"

"I'm not attacking you, I'm just asking."

"Bullshit! You disapprove!"

"No, I'm just surprised—"

"See!"

"—Because it doesn't seem like something you'd do."

"Well, I keep doing things you don't expect, don't I? So obviously, you must not know me very well!" I say. I'm hollering now. "Besides, sometimes people have to do things they don't want to for their jobs. It's called living in the real world! Being a grown-up!"

Jordan takes a deep breath and runs her hands along the Formica. When things get heated, she slows down, way, way down, until she's the laconic southerner under the magnolia tree, a trait I find intensely irritating. "Maybe that's true," she allows finally, "but . . . a gay sailor? A nude photo shoot? Pretending to get it on in a bathtub with another woman? What's next, Emma Lee? A blow job on a casting couch? A striptease onstage so you can test out a few new poses?"

I snort. Jordan blinks. "I mean, I feel like I've got a front-row seat to a downward spiral."

"Enjoy the view!"

That was it, the end of the discussion. I was outta there within seconds. *Downward spiral?* Give me a fucking break. It was *one* photo shoot plus *one* video. *Two* things. And *two* does not a spiral make. Besides, Jordan should talk. Last summer she worked on Capitol Hill with a senator who, as she likes to put it, "poked my breasts as if they were paperweights." Oh, it bugged her, I know, but she didn't quit, did she? And this summer she's working on a Wall Street trading floor with co-workers who, from her descriptions, aren't exactly choirboys—not that she's a shrinking violet herself.

Yes, Jordan's talking total crap. And no, the girl doesn't know me, obviously, because the truth is I liked doing the topless photo shoot. It was sexy. It was fun.

The video not so much.

And, sure, okay—the shoot begat the video, I guess. I guess that's another truth.

I mull all of this over for a few days, and then walk into Chic with the idea of talking to Justine about *maybe, possibly* removing the topless shot from my portfolios.

"Hi Alistair."

"Hello, Chic? *Please* hold—well, twinkle, twinkle, little star." Alistair depresses a button. "She's here!"

Um. Okay. I high-five Alistair's outstretched palm, then jump: Byron's pounding his riding crop against the glass and waving furiously despite the fact he's got four people in his office and the telephone cradled to his ear.

I wave back.

"Emily!"

"Hey Emily!"

The twin models Carmencita and Genoveva have one hand clinging to each of my arms, the other jointly brandishing a glossy invite. "It's for our seventeenth birthday party!"

"At 150 Wooster!"

"Can you come?"

"*Please* come!"

"Wow. Gee, thanks, I'd love to." I look from one to the other, surprised. I'm not even sure who's who; before now, we'd barely exchanged two words—and that's among the three of us.

"Great!"

"See you there!"

Hmm, things are getting curiouser and curiouser. Tucking the invite into my new Chanel bag—a gift to myself for nabbing the video—

I manage to reach the booking table without incident, where, as usual, all of the bookers are on the phone, working their magic.

"I told you already: not the twenty-fifth or the twenty-sixth—they're taken! I can give you a third option on the twenty-seventh but that's it. You sure you can't do mid-August? Because Emily might have some time then . . ."

"—Honestly, I'm not sure it's possible to go from the Seychelles to Maui in one afternoon. My advice is: Swap some of the other girls around, because Emily's chart isn't budging—"

"—That's correct: Redken's got her for hair care, L'Oréal's got her for color, so if P&G wants Emily, it will have to be for skin and they'd better step on it—"

"—Yes, yes, I've got you down, I promise—sorry, can you hold? Emily!" Lithe's arm shoots out like she's trying to hail me. "Who's your TV agent?"

"I don't have one," I say. *TV? P&G?* Okay, seriously: Have I fallen down a manhole? Did someone lace my latte? Spike my Evian? Did I never even get out of bed to begin with?

"Emily's in transition with regard to her TV representation," Lithe is saying. "But why don't you tell me what you need? I'd be happy to help . . ."

I crouch so close to Justine, I'm practically sitting on her. "*WHAT is going on?*"

"Right . . ." Justine holds up a finger, then makes a series of sweeping slashes across my chart: *booked.* "Right, got it. Maui on the fifth through eighth . . . Yes, naturally the suite . . . Right . . . Got it . . . Okay, bye!" Click. "*You're* what's going on."

"You're hot, hot, hot!" Stephan shouts.

"Smokin'!" Jon cries.

Lithe grabs my chart from Justine.

"Great," I say. "But why?"

Shocked faces all around.

"You mean you don't know?"

"*You* don't know."

"Emily, how can you not know?"

"Emily!" Alistair's voice bleats from the intercom. "Byron wants you in his office at once!"

"... Yes, yes, she *still* gets out of bed for less than $10,000." Byron spins his chair, grinning. "*You!*" he mouths before turning back to the receiver. "I know: bitchy, but *really*, I could have *sworn* Linda's rate was *much* higher than *that*, couldn't you? I'm absolutely *certain* I could get her more. You *will* put in a good word for me, *won't* you? Anyway— gotta go. *Emily!*"

Suddenly, I'm seeing the red of Byron's riding jacket. "You genius, you! You're on *fire!*" He kisses me on each cheek, once. "Your video is the hottest thing out there!" Twice. "You're a star!"

"My *video*?" I reclaim my personal space. "But that's not even out yet!"

"And it's not gonna be," Alistair says, ushering in two iced waters complete with lemon wedges. "Not in the U.S. anyway."

Byron's nodding. "I've got *three* words for you, Emily dear, the *best* three little words you'll ever hear: MTV Video Ban. Apparently there's *one* bathtub scene that's *much* too racy for preteen viewing. Now, *personally*, I think it's *quite* tame. Then again, shoot a video with a gay production team and what do you get? Two Holly Golightlys going lightly at it!" After collapsing at his own wit, Byron continues. "But I say *thank God* for the Puritans because they're the *best* thing that could have happened to your career, Emily dear. *Really!* Because of the ban, the video's gotten press abroad. It debuted at number one in Italy, number one in Australia, and is selling like hotcakes on the black market in China ..."

"Wait ... you've *seen* it?"

"Of course I've seen it. Haven't you? Oh no, of course you haven't: your copy's right here." Byron lifts a cassette and waves it in the air. "Sorry, I gave Fonya hers and just forgot about you—anyway, why are we gabbing so much? Let's sit back and enjoy the show! Alistair, lights! Action!"

Across the room, a twenty-inch screen flickers blue and starts playing. The tape's been watched before, clearly, for it starts up right at the tub scene. Fonya and I spring to life in the sudsy water.

"Look at you!" Byron murmurs.

I step closer. The all-too-familiar Down Under song bleats softly from the television's tinny speakers. On screen, a pastiche of images: a long, dark hallway. Cracked tiles. A claw-footed tub. Bubbles sliding down a damp back. The camera zooms in on a hand. My hand. It's tracing Fonya's shoulder blade, chased by my lips.

"Sex kitten!" cries Alistair.

My lips are working their way up the nape of Fonya's neck, to her ear. My tongue flicks the diamonds.

"That is *totally* erotic."

That much I could do: the back, the neck, the ear. After all, when I was getting touched up and bejeweled, Henri had plied me with champagne (now that I had decided to go along with the shot, he and Thom were all smiles and very solicitous). A couple of glasses and I was good to go.

"You sexy thing!"

But those body parts, those were my limit. The things Henri and Thom wanted next: feeling up Fonya, pulling Fonya into me, turning Fonya's lips to mine—becoming, in their words "a predatory seductress"—these I was less keen on. Nor was I crazy about the final position as they described it: Fonya reclined in the tub, me on all fours on top of her, the water level inching down, down, down.

"Oh, the camera's coming around now. I love this!"

Henri and Thom were persistent. They wheedled. They cajoled. They emptied the champagne into my glass. "Okay, kiss her *now,* make love to her *now,*" they said.

Yet still I couldn't.

"Here it comes!"

"The best part!"

Oh, I didn't want to react that way. By then, I had realized that this was indeed the key shot of the video—why, just the amount of footage devoted to it made that clear alone. And it was just the two of us on-screen: me and a star. I would be basking in the glow. I would be seen.

Besides, I had done this sort of thing before with Greta in the Caribbean. The thing is: I was pretty fucked-up that night.

That's when I realized I could be again.

I gestured to Henri. He crouched beside the tub. "I need some coke."

"A Coke?" he said.

"*Some* coke," I corrected.

Henri got me what I needed, and it got me where I needed to go.

"This is the part here!"

"Yup, here, where your hands are on her!"

"You can see the edge of Fonya's nipple there. See? I'm sure that's why they banned it!"

"Or maybe it's because of this part here, where Emily's on top."

The closing shot of the Down Under video is of the two of us. Fonya's lying back in the tub. I am no longer the seductress; I am spent, satisfied. My head rests on her chest. The camera lingers on Fonya (who appears as she's been throughout: calm, quiet, pliant), then pans out. It is our faces filling the final frame: Fonya's and mine.

Byron pauses the video. "There! You like it?"

I nod slowly.

"Emily, you okay?"

"Turn around and look at us!"

When I turn, Alistair's grinning, Byron's beaming, and just beyond, through the glass, the bookers are frantically working the phones.

Six people working for me. All for me.

Byron extends his arms. "I didn't think you had it in you," he says.

I cross the room and fold into him. "Of course I did," I tell him. "It was a piece of cake."

In no time flat, I shoot four pages of "Glamorous Updo's" for *Glamour.* I get optioned by *Harper's Bazaar* and *Vogue* (yes, American *Vogue* is holding time on me and Fonya for a lingerie story to be shot by Shelia Metzner); I take my new $2,500 day rate for catalog to Maui, LA, and Scotland. I shoot advertising for eyewear, jewelry, bags, and belts. Mom wants me to come home for a visit, but how can I when I'm going to the Seychelles? The shoot is a print ad for suntan lotion. Never mind that I'm as pale as a New York City sidewalk; they'll just give me a deep, dark tan during the retouching process.

So much work . . . and these are just the American clients. Thanks to the video, I'm hot stuff in Italy, too, which means that I shoot one story for *Lei,* two stories for *Amica*—and I meet Alfredo.

"He's a legend!" Byron gushes after my first job with the photographer has confirmed. He's right. Alfredo Robano has been a top-tier international photographer for over three decades—an impressive feat considering these include the Studio 54 seventies and the Coke-Is-It eighties. *Vogue*s from around the globe; Revlon and Revellion; Anne and Calvin Klein; Christy T. and Christie B—Alfredo's worked with all of these and more, so many more that his trophy wall wraps around corners and extends up and down staircases. He starts booking me for everything.

Two weeks and $40,000 later, I go to Alfredo's studio to shoot another *Amica* story: six pages of "Night Moves," plus a cover try.

That's right: a cover try.

We shoot the cover late in the morning, after we've completed two full-lengths on another set. The timing is perfect: before my makeup has started to cake, but after I'm warmed and woken up, and it goes off without a hitch. Granted, I feel a bit nervous when I'm in the dressing room getting made up (and up: *Amica*'s never seen a set of false eyelashes it didn't glue on), but as soon as I get on-set, I relax. I like Alfredo. I like KT, Ingrid, and Eduardo, the hairdresser, makeup artist, and stylist he works with. I like Katarina, the *Amica* editor. Even Alfredo's wife, Alessandra, a top model in the early eighties cum hands-on studio manager—hands on because she wants to make sure she isn't traded in for a newer model—is tolerable. There is no whisper campaign. There are no "I love you's" or tears. It's just fun.

After the cover try comes shot number four: a Chanel dress made out of bronze lamé, spaghetti-strapped and short but with a floor-length train lined in red silk.

When I walk on-set, Alfredo whistles. When I get on the platform, he says, "Do whatever you'd like on these. Just keep moving and give me a lot of energy."

"Okay, in that case . . ." I turn to Rob, Alfredo's assistant.

Rob smiles. "One 'Diva Mix' coming right up."

"Thanks."

I step into the light. When I first started modeling, I was afraid of shooting in studio. On location, there are always things to feign enthusiasm about: *Look, puppies!* or *Oh my! A hot dog vendor!* But a white seamless backdrop is . . . nothing, just you and the lens.

Now, that's exactly why I love it.

The speakers crackle. Barry Manilow's sonorous voice fills the room: *Her name is Lola, she was a showgirl . . .*

I start rocking, slowly at first, trying to get a sense of how the dress moves and what it is that I feel like doing.

With yellow feathers in her hair and a dress cut down to there . . .

Eduardo belts the lyrics into his lint brush. Ingrid and KT bump their hips together. *Swish. Swish.* The fan rustles my train. I thrust out one arm and twist my head to the side.

"Perfect!" Alfredo yells.

She would . . .

And then it starts happening. The room fades away, or maybe I expand out of it, for I no longer feel the lights or the fan or the music as external forces, but as things infusing me from within. They become me. Crazy? Maybe. I don't know; I only know that with each click of the camera, with each blink of the strobe, I feel energized, electrified, until I'm larger than life, until I'm filling up this room, this studio, this city. Until I'm lit from within by a thousand watts. The most beautiful thing in the world.

The rest of the day is just like this. I know that I'm moving, but I couldn't tell you how. I'm on the cusp of something—something big, something great, maybe even the edge of a star. I prowl back and forth across the platform—my terrain—feeling strong and sleek, with the confidence of a rock star, only instead of thousands of screaming fans, I have the camera. Only that. I give it everything I have.

When the shoot ends I feel happily exhausted, but there's more to come on this magical day. The next stop is uptown, Pixie's twentieth birthday party, a luau in a penthouse.

Granted, this part has some prickly bits—seeing Jordan, for one, to whom I'm still scarcely speaking, and enduring budding financiers who think that cocktails taste best when imbibed between snippets like "Today's Pac-rim volatility presented a huge arb play," and "My God, that yen!"—but they don't affect me. I simply walk outside, squeeze between the potted palm trees, and lean over the balcony.

It's dark. The lamps are lit in Central Park, punctuating the inky blackness with their soft violet blooms. All is still, except for a few runners, and it looks like an illusion, a mirage to soothe Manhattan's weary denizens. It's beautiful but it's far. That's because I'm up so high, up in the stars.

That's right. For the first time in a long time, I feel like I'm soaring above the earth, that I'm bigger than all of it. And my life is perfect.

Los Angeles. Bermuda. Lake Tahoe. "Come home," Mom says, but I can't. Come late August I'm busier than ever, with another $20,000 to show for my efforts. I don't get the *Vogue* booking (I'm bummed but not devastated; they'll be back). I do, however, book "Operation Style," six pages of leggings, berets, and trench coats for *Mademoiselle*. And best of all? I get my second magazine cover: *Amica,* a three-quarter of me in white Moschino. I like it. The magazine likes it, too. They book me for more pages, including another cover try.

"So that makes two," I say, settling into a chair in Byron's office.

"One cover, one cover *try,*" Byron amends. "We'll have to wait and see the outcome."

"Fine. I'll wait and see about *that.*" Cubes slush through liquid as I use my iced coffee to gesture to the accountant's office, which is dark as usual. "But I'm tired of waiting for a check."

Byron does his best to look surprised. "Aren't we up-to-date with you?"

"You owe me $4,000—at least $4,000," I inform him. It would be more but I've gotten good at trapping Javier between the back stairs and his Maserati.

Byron is now playing with the phone buttons. "I can't help you with that. Not my department."

"But Javier's in Cap Ferrat."

"Only for two weeks."

"Byron, give me a break and pay me! I'm your latest cover girl—and one you'd hate to lose!"

I'm kidding but I'm not. I'm trying out the role of the petulant diva, the bitch Ayana tried to teach me to be. And it works: After a beat, Byron pulls open his drawer and cuts me a check, his Mont Blanc carving thin, dark ribbons into the pale green paper. He slides it across his desk.

I thought it worked. "Hey, Byron, this check is for $2,000!"

"Now we're even," he replies.

"Even, for what?"

"The 50 Chicest Girls."

The 50 Chicest Girls is the name of a marketing promotion that Byron cooked up earlier in the summer as a way of "reintroducing fashion to Chic." (Fifty is the new total of Chic models; twenty-five girls were dropped that day.) Turns out, naming the promotion was the easy part; Byron hasn't been able to settle on a format, and so over the past few weeks, his formerly Spartan office has been filling with sample calendars, desk blotters, playing cards, T-shirts, and pens to the point it looks he's been moonlighting as a novelty vendor.

I've been playing with a ring of sample key chains. As I drop it on the desk it jingles and clangs. "So you've settled on a design?"

"Yes, thank God. *Finally,*" Byron exhales. "We're going with a basic book format: soft cover, black and white. Simple. Classic."

"Simple, but it's costing me $2,000?"

"Correct."

"But why should *we* pay?" I say edgily. "You're making us do it. And it's for the agency!"

"But it benefits *you*—anyway," Byron leans toward me, his features suddenly lifted. "What's $2,000 when you'll be taking in $33,000, because Emily, dear, your commercial with Justin Fields confirmed!"

I race around the desk and hug Byron, nearly upending my beverage in the process, which would be appropriate. The commercial—I auditioned for it last week, had the callback two days ago—is for coffee, Italian coffee. I'm just the prop: The real star is Justin Fields. Justin, the big dog of the Brat Pack and one of Hollywood's "Hottest under 30," according to *People*. And $33,000? "That's excellent!" I pant.

"*Isn't* it? The client wanted to pay $28,000, but we insisted."

Another five grand merits another squeeze. When I've finally released Byron, he stays right with me, pushing aside a stack of T-shirts and settling against the edge of his desk. "You know, Emily, I've been giving it some thought and this commercial, the potential covers, the Thom Brenner video, they all work because you're hitting different media and different demographics, which is going to broaden your client base. Now throw next month's spring shows into the mix and you'll be face-to-face with the magazine editors, which means we'll get some winter issues and that means . . ."

Suddenly, Byron is plotting and strategizing, providing details about the commercial and other jobs on the horizon—both existing and ones he thinks I can finally take a crack at. We talk and talk—for twenty minutes until I realize the obvious.

"Byron, the commercial is shooting the first week of September."

"Correct."

"That's the first week of school."

"And that's a problem?"

I tilt my chin. During my query Byron's eyes have gotten steadily closer to my own. I meet his gaze. Dark. Earnest. Intense. Thirty-three thousand dollars, Justin Fields, the head of Chic acting like my booker for the first time in a long time—how could I have a problem with that?

"No problem," I say.

He squeezes my shoulder. "Great. That's *great.* Say, Emily, are you busy tonight because there's this *fabulous* party . . ."

Café Tabac might derive its name from the establishments blanketing every Parisian boulevard, but the place is anything but routine. In fact, in the summer of 1990, Café Tabac is New York City's hottest hot spot, particularly with the fashion crowd, which delights in taking refuge amid its silvered mirrors, raffia walls, and black-and-white prints: the colors of cool, tonight to be considered through a mist of melons and frangipani—the latest brand of perfume getting the chicest send-off.

I lift off the banquette, find my reflection, and adjust the strap of my silver Marc Jacobs.

"Omigod, I *so* love that!" Pixie yells.

As a matter of fact, I did have plans tonight. After spending a summer working on some new telescope she's dubbed the "Hubba Bubba," Mohini got back into town today. A bunch of us had plans to celebrate; the only thing we lacked was a venue. When Byron told me I could bring my friends along, it seemed like the perfect solution: great atmosphere, unlimited liquor, beautiful sights, sweet smells.

"That girl's lace-up shoes are *totally* cutting off her circulation."

"What circulation? She's too skinny to have blood in those veins!"

What was I thinking? My good friends spent approximately 2.2

seconds catching up—of course that was it, we've been in constant contact all summer—whereupon they immediately turned the full computational power of their oversized noggins to far more pressing concerns.

"That girl has the widest-set eyes!"

I shift my gaze from Liscula to Fleur.

"Bug eyes!"

"Seriously, I thought they'd all be prettier."

"Me, too!"

"Except you, Emily, of course."

"Hey, that guy looks *exactly* like the White Rabbit!"

Alistair approaches, pulling a handkerchief out of his vest pocket. "There you are, kitten! I've been looking everywhere for you!" he exclaims, dabbing. "Byron wants you to come. Come!"

Thank God, I was getting a headache. Pushing past my friends, I follow Alistair's blindingly blond head down and around a corridor until we reach Byron, clad in a suitably swanky blend of black Armani and pink linen. Byron kisses me, tut-tuts something about circulating, grabs my hand, and suddenly I'm here, there, everywhere at once, being introduced as "the other girl in the Thom Brenner video." Everyone's seen it, it seems, and they seem to like what they've seen. *"Brava! Brava!"* Isaac Mizrahi claps. "Ravishing! Just ravishing!" says Todd Oldham. Jay McInerney wants to take notes on my experiences, Grace Coddington wants to say hello, Oliver Stone wants to have a drink. Patrick McMullan fires off a half a roll: me, front and center.

The giddy greetings. The glitterati. Byron gripping my hand. It's a whirlwind. I don't make it back to my friends for over two hours, well after the party has started to disband and the heavy aroma of a thousand test sprays has been subsumed by the scent of cigarettes. My friends (with the exception of Pixie, who by the look of things is about to turn Timothy Hutton into the latest Pixel) have all partied and reconvened, and as I slip into the booth, it's Jordan, holding court, about to deliver her punch line to a rapt audience:

"So finally, I had to stop and say, 'Excuse me, but existentialism doesn't have a thing to do with longer hair!' "

Jesus.

The table erupts in laughter. Ben gasps and wipes his eyes on his sleeve. "He didn't really think that, did he?"

"I think he really did."

"Is he still here?" Mohini asks.

Jordan twists around and points at Jon, one of my bookers. I point at her. "What I don't get is why you were talking about existentialism in the first place."

Jordan eyes me over the edge of her cocktail. "It just came up."

"Oh right, of course it did."

"Bye Emily! Call me!"

I wave good-bye to Rachel Hunter, then Esme. Ben snorts.

"If that girl was any skinnier, she'd need to accessorize with a feeding tube!"

Hah. Hah. Hah.

I feel a flash of anger. My eyes circle the booth as if lassoing everyone tightly together. After all, it wasn't just me who thought coming here tonight was a good idea; all my friends did. And they appeared to have a good time, too. But I guess they have to trash it anyhow. Well, I've had enough.

"If everyone here is so stupid and awful, then why don't you just leave?"

My friends' jaws drop.

"Hey . . . no, Emily, we're just kidding!"

"Yeah, the party's great."

The forced smiles. The looks of concern. Fuck this, I'm outta here. "Later," I tell them, jumping up. I make it all of two feet before being held up in the crush of revelers waiting to descend the staircase. I've almost moved forward—it's almost okay—and then, a hand touches my shoulder. Jordan offering a sincere apology? Hini? I whip around. It's the fashion editor Polly Mellen.

"That's a nice shot of you," she says.

Donald Trump nods. "Yes, it's classy and elegant and I like it."

"Who took it?" asks Marla Maples.

I have no idea what they're talking about, none at all, until Polly's finger points to the staircase, to the spot where a dozen black-and-white photographs hang above the landing. I glanced at them earlier; they're the usual assortment of café fare: a boulevard on a rainy night; a still life with pears; a nude woman in pearls . . .

I see it. So do my friends.

"Is that . . . Emily?"

"No way!"

"Shh!"

It's time to go *now*. I push people aside and race down the stairs; I need air. Time to think. I need to clear my head. Outside, I run and I run. Later—one hour later? Two? Who knows?—I'm in Washington Square Park. I sink onto a bench and drop my face into my hands.

The dealers circle my bench. "Smoke, smoke," they hiss, and, "Tell me what a pretty girl needs!"

It's stupid to buy drugs here. Risky. It's a park, a public space, exposed, and who knows about the quality? The drugs are probably fake, or, worse, cut with something that will really fuck you up. Besides, I haven't done them in a while. I've never bought them for myself.

The cocaine burns the inside of my nose, but the pain feels just right. I pace in the park, circling its perimeter like a caged animal, then take refuge in a nearby diner. The customers are mostly NYU students. They keep coming in, in twos and threes, their eyes bloodshot, their faces red, not from cramming sessions—not yet—but from the parties celebrating the kickoff of fall semester. Their spirits are high. Peals of laughter fill the room.

I can't do this anymore. I can't live in two worlds.

Back on the streets, I do coke. I pace. Several hours later—how many, I don't know, I don't keep track—it's daylight. I work my way to Chic.

"Emily, there you are! I just call—" Byron takes in my smeared makeup and sequined dress and covers his mouth. "Are you all right?" he gasps. "What's going on?"

"A lot," I tell him. "I'm quitting school."

The head of Chic wraps me in his arms. He smiles. I smile back. And if, in the ensuing minutes of celebration, he notices that my pupils are too large and my nostrils are a touch swollen, he says nothing about it, nothing at all.

Chapter 27

Jive & Tackle

Da Vinci Coffee: "Dreamgirl." 30-second spot. Day 1 of 2. Location: Silvercup Studios. Director: Flavio Esposito. Hair: Rowena Jones. Makeup: Vincent De Longhi. Talent: Emily Woods, Justin Fields. Call to set: Emily Woods, 8 A.M., Justin Fields, II A.M. First Shot: 12 P.M.

At 7:00 A.M., I settle against the leather seat of the Town Car that's taking me to Silvercup Studios and rifle through the production notes yet again. The plot of the commercial is simple. It opens with Justin Fields dreaming about a woman. That evening, he goes to a jazz club and, there she is, his dream girl, singing onstage. Cut to the two of them nuzzling on the balcony of a New York City penthouse, throw in a few product shots of them exchanging simmering glances over steaming espressos—and cut! That's a wrap. There's no nudity. In fact, other than the cabaret scene, I don't even have to open my mouth, and even then it's just to lip-synch a song that won't even be heard on account of the sound track. As Justine pointed out on the phone last night, "This job is easy money."

Still, I'm nervous, and it's all because of Justin Fields. Growing up, I would see every single one of his movies. Justin was in all the expected places—standard Brat Packer fare—but always at the margin: the shy, sensitive one with a love for the heroine that was doomed to go unrequited because his soulful eyes and bow lips just looked so much better in angst. "Take me," I'd whisper, in the dark, to the screen. "Take me, Justin." I wanted to comfort him, to kiss the pain away—an urge I continued to feel even after pounds of pumped iron and a generous growth spurt ensured that Justin finally got the girl. And so, in *Peak of Interest,* when Justin played the young adventurer who risked hypoxia and frostbite just for the sake of one final tango on the top of Mount Everest, I became the dying female sherpa propped up in his arms. In *Well of Good,* when Justin-the-rookie-cop stumbled upon the angel who had tumbled straight down from heaven into a fifty-foot well, it was my wing he refused to let go of. And in *Hell's Bells,* when Justin married his high school sweetheart only to discover she was the spawn of Satan . . . well okay, here, I might not have identified so readily with Daemonetta, but tears streamed down my face when he drove the stake through her heart nonetheless. Yes, Justin Fields has always been my go-to movie star, and now I'm about to meet him for coffee.

I exit the limo in front of Silvercup Studios and am immediately greeted by Steve. "I'm the third assistant director," Steve informs me after he's tapped his clipboard and pulled a walkie-talkie out of his pants to let someone on the other end know that "Talent Two" has arrived. "My job is to escort you to the set, hair and makeup, craft services . . ."

"Craft services? What's that?" I say, puzzled. It sounds like a place where you can drop off half-knit mittens, partially glued ornaments, and other unfinished creative projects to be completed by a band of merry elves.

When a smiling Steve opens a door, the first thing I'm hit with is the smell of bacon: greasy, crispy bacon. Then I notice the chef in the toque cracking several eggs into a sizzling skillet. "Craft services is the name for catering on all film productions," he explains as we approach. "What are you in the mood for? Eggs? Waffles? French toast? Pancakes? Yogurt and mixed fruit? Sausage, egg, and cheese on a buttermilk biscuit? I just had that, by the way, it's really good, especially with a side of grits. Granola? Hash browns? Any of this?" The sweeping clipboard covers a dozen glass canisters positively brimming with licorice, Kit Kats, Oreos, Nilla Wafers, Tootsie Rolls, Jelly Bellies, and other sundries. "Or, if you want to wait an hour or so, you can have freshly baked chocolate chip cookies."

"Half an hour," the chef says. "And there are blondies, too."

Craft services is living hell.

I beat it out of there with a lone cup of Da Vinci espresso and two packets of Equal, vowing never to return, despite the desperate yowlings from my tummy. Fortunately, as soon as I get to hair and makeup, there's a welcome distraction.

"*Ciao,* Miss Genius!"

"*Ciao, bella!*"

It's Ro and Vincent, my favorite style team ever since our trip to the Dominican Republic. I hug them hello. Vincent's eating breakfast, so hair's first. Ro's just finished wetting mine down and is working a hefty dollop of gel through my hair (hairdressers on photo shoots use so much more product than their salon counterparts that the difference would drown them) when she pauses and leans over my shoulder. "What's that?"

I flash the book jacket of *An Inconvenient Woman,* by Dominick Dunne.

"Don't tell me you're reading that for school," she says.

"I won't."

Ro lifts a lock of hair, then drops it. "You have time to read trashy novels *and* do your schoolwork? What *are* they teaching you in that Ivy League then?"

"Nothing. I quit."

"*Whaat?*"

I shift uncomfortably, suddenly remembering the two nieces Ro's putting through college. "I dropped out of school."

Vincent grins. "Well, it's about time!"

"Vincent!" Ro whacks his shoulder. "How can you *say* that? Emily was at *Columbia!*"

"Exactly. Her *career* was going nowhere," Vincent rebuts. "No offense, Em, but Queen's and Brooks Brothers catalogs were one-way tickets to obscurity, not stardom."

"Exactly," I say.

"What, exactly?" Ro asks. "The girl's got other interests; the girl's a *genius!*"

"See, that's where you're wrong, Ro," I say, taking sides, albeit reluctantly. "At Columbia I was a below-average student, nothing special—certainly not a genius."

"But you liked school," she insists. "Your classes. All your friends."

My friends. The day I went to Columbia to pick up my belongings, I sat down in the common room with Jordan, Mohini, and Pixie and informed them of my decision to drop out. They seemed sad but they didn't say much: What was the point? I'd already seen the bursar; it was a done deal. Besides, as Pixie put it, "the writing was on the wall and we all know how to read." We simply hugged and said good-bye.

"We'll still be friends, right?" I asked. Tears coursed down my cheeks, which caught me off guard: after all, this was my choice.

"Best friends," Mohini assured me.

"I'll be back soon," I vowed, "And until then, we'll have breakfast every Saturday at Tom's Diner, right?"

"Right," Jordan said.

"I'm going back," I explain now. "It's not like I'm dropping out permanently."

Ro purses her lips. "Of course not," Vincent soothes. "In the meantime, you're doing videos, covers, and a commercial with Justin Fields: You're on your way."

The walkie-talkie crackles. "Is she on her way?"

Steve looks inquisitively at Jamison, the stylist, who glances at the row of buttons along my spine. "Five minutes," he says.

Steve echoes this. "Okay, but no more than that," he relays, closing the door behind him.

"God, these people: rush, rush, rush!" Jamison grumbles, though really it's been nearly four hours, long enough that my butt is sore from sitting. Film makeup always takes much longer than it does for print. The strong lights and larger-than-life close-ups require a heavy foundation that's several shades darker than your natural skintone (any lighter and you'll look washed out), which must be applied evenly over every square inch of exposed skin (any shortcuts and you'll risk "newscaster neck"—that dark face, pale neck combo that gets every paint professional worked into a tizzy), but today has been particularly labor intensive. Ro and Vincent derived their inspiration from *La Dolce Vita*, a look that dovetails nicely with the recent resurgence in sixties fashion, but the thick black eyeliner, false eyelashes, heavy brows, and pale lips took ninety minutes alone, as did my hair, an elaborate construction that has been backcombed, piled high on the crown, and blown out with the ends turned up. The style is pretty and it suits me, but as I stand before the dressing room mirror, what I can't take my eyes off is the dress. Skintight and floor-length in a black netting with appliquéd tone-on-tone vines blossoming in all the right places, it's a dress that doesn't allow for panties, or an extra pound, or a shy and retiring personality.

Jamison loops the final button, adjusts the neckline, and casts an appraising glance over my shoulder. "What do you think?" he murmurs. "You like?"

"What's not to like?" I exhale—I'm sucking in and breathing shallowly—"The dress is to die for."

"On you it is." He smiles and squeezes my hips. "You want it? I can call Sophie at Gaultier and get you a discount: thirty percent, probably."

I study the profile. "Thirty percent off what?"

"Six thousand."

I gag.

"Maybe I can get you 40 percent. Want me to check?"

I check out the rear view. Then the sides again. Then the front. "Sure . . . just to see."

The door opens. "Ahem," Steve says.

As we glide down the hall, my heart starts to pound: *Justin. Justin.* It's a matter of minutes.

In a studio the size of an airplane hangar, thousands of watts of light point toward a very authentic-looking jazz club with hunter green walls, vintage posters of jazz greats, gently worn banquettes, and a smattering of candlelit café tables, every seat filled by an extra. Set stylists dart about, providing this one with a drink, that one with a different colored tie. In the corner, two stagehands test the optimal level of atmospheric "smoke" . . . and that's just in front of the camera. Behind it crowds a horde of people in suits. I know it takes a lot of executives to make a commercial, but forty?

"Movie stars have a way of drawing a crowd," Jamison says, registering my surprise.

Right. This isn't Ex-Lax. A man emerges from the pack, short and slightly built, with a mass of dark curly hair, heavy rectangular glasses, and jeans that rise to his rib cage: Flavio, the director. I met him at the callback. A cigarette dangles from his stubby fingertips. "*Finally* she cares to join us," he says, flicking it. "Let's get her on the stage *now*!"

"Wow, he's in a good mood," I mutter.

"Rumor has it his girlfriend just left him, baby and all," Jamison whispers. "He's been in a foul temper all morning."

Great. That's great. I follow the third AD, who follows the second. Jamison lifts my hem. Slowly, we proceed up a side staircase until we reach my mark: front and center on the cabaret stage. As the spotlights are adjusted and Jamison trades my slippers for heels, I smile and give a small wave to the extras. Some smile, most look stone-faced, especially the women. Oh, right. These are all actors; I'm sure plenty of them really wanted to be in these stilettos, to earn this check.

Off-set, the horde of executives has split and gathered around two monitors. Flavio clears his throat. "Turn right!" he commands.

I turn.

"Left!"

I turn. A woman in navy pinstripes darts between some café tables, squats to peer at me, then darts back.

"Grab the microphone and pretend you're singing!"

As I do this, another executive sprints forward and back. The ones gathered around the monitors are now murmuring. I feel a fluttering of anxiety. *Perfect.* The Whisper Campaign has started before we've shot a foot of film.

A few more minutes of this and Jamison gives me his elbow. "Here, doll, right this way."

"What is it?" I ask. "Is it the dress?"

"No . . ." We're moving at quite a clip; I struggle to keep the thin heels from falling through the metal steps. "They love your look, *especially* the dress"—he shoots a silent prayer heavenward—"it's just that they decided they want different earrings—well, that and . . ." We enter the dressing room. Jamison closes the door and leans against it. "We need to take care of *that*." He points at my crotch.

Trust me: These are words and a gesture you don't want to see paired together. Ever. As I feel my cheeks darken, I step toward the mirror and study my pubic region for . . . what? A stray hair? Lots of stray hairs? But everything's obscured by a flower. "I can't see anything," I finally admit.

"Spread your thighs," Jamison says.

Ditto for these words. I part my legs. I see nothing and then . . . a faint line. *Oh God.* "Jamison, *please* don't tell me you could see my tampon."

"Only the string," he says.

"Well, I would hope—"

"—And only when you have a wider stance. It's those lights: so strong," he adds quickly. "Look, some of the ad execs felt it wouldn't be a problem—that you could just narrow your legs. But others felt that doing so would restrict your movement too much. The consensus was, it needed to be taken care of."

Okay, forget the loose bikini bottom on the beach when I was ten; a roomful of advertising executives discussing my tampon is without question the most embarrassing thing that's ever happened to me. "But, Jamison," I say, when I finally can, "if I take out my tampon, we'll have bigger problems than a piece of string."

The stylist shudders: tampons, blood—girls are so *icky.* "I never said take it out," he says hurriedly, as if I was about to send my tampon sailing through the air. "I said 'take care of it,' meaning the string. With this." He brandishes a pair of scissors.

"Oh . . . got it." I reach for them.

Jamison jerks his hand away. "Child, if you think I'm letting you bend over and mess up that perfect coif, then you don't know much. Because, God as my witness, I've experienced Ro's wrath and I have the scars to show for it. I'm not going down that road again."

Now it's my turn to shudder.

"Exactly." Jamison parts the blades. The sharpened steel glints in the light. "Hold on to the counter," he advises. "And you might want to close your eyes."

Postsurgery, I'm recovering onstage, desperately trying to think about anything but how many people are currently examining my crotch, when suddenly the volume drops, everything tilts toward the doorway, and I know: Justin Fields has arrived.

Justin. Justin. My hand slips against the microphone grip, suddenly clammy. *Justin. Justin.* My high school crush. *Justin. Justin.* International movie star.

As Justin makes his way through the executives trying to shake his hand and the extras trying to act indifferent, part of me detaches and floats up to the rafters, to a higher perch, a better vantage point from which to view things as I'll later recount them to my friends: *Justin Fields is tall. Justin Fields is wearing a dark suit.*

Justin Fields is coming up the stairs. I turn to look. The actor appears in pieces: sandy brown hair (longish and stylishly unkempt), sapphire blue eyes (large and penetrating, his best feature), an impish grin ("the secret to his success," according to *Premiere* magazine), a lithe, chiseled frame (his abs are covered but I can imagine), until all six feet two inches of Justin Fields is in front of me and smiling.

"Emily?" His hand shoots toward me. "Justin."

"Hi." *Justin Fields is touching me.*

"Wow . . ." He presses his hand to his chest. "You're heart-stopping!"

And I think mine just did.

His head shakes. I get a flash of the impish grin. "I'm sorry. I hope I'm not being too forward."

"Oh no, I'm just . . ." *dying.* "Thanks. Thank you," I stammer. "That's very sweet."

And the penetrating eyes. "I just call it as I see it," he says.

Justin Fields is flirting with me.

Justin gestures to the mike. "You any good?"

I recoil. "Oh no! I'm a terrible singer! I'm lip-synching!"

"Really?" He looks disappointed. "To what?"

"Whitney Houston."

A soft moan escapes his lips. "*Whitney?* But *why?*"

"Dunno. Maybe they thought that most models don't know any jazz songs," I say with a shrug. "Anyway, Whitney's what they told me to practice, so I practiced."

"Justin! Emily! Playtime's over, we need you in position!" Flavio barks. "Later."

As Justin exits the stage, Flavio whizzes rapidly toward it in a manner not unlike the Tasmanian Devil. I step to its edge.

"Okay, Emily, we start now," Flavio says, panting slightly. "This is a very sexy shot we have here today. Very sexy."

"Okay."

"And I change it. I change it a bit from the script."

Change? I swallow nervously. When is this ever for the better? "Changed what?"

His arm sweeps the stage, encompassing the microphone, the instruments behind me. "We've got the best jazz musicians in the city here today. This, as you can imagine, was very expensive."

Flavio pauses to let these facts sink in, and they are impressive. The best jazz musicians in New York City *here*? Like I said, this commercial has a sound track, making them very expensive props. What could possibly be the point of this?

"So I ask myself, why waste such talent?" Flavio continues. "Why not let you talented performers perform?"

You? "Not me," I say nervously. "I'm no talented performer."

"Nonsense. You'll just go along with these cool cats and jive."

Sweat instantly springs though the powder on my upper lip. "I'm sorry, could you repeat that?"

"Jive, Emily, *jive*," Flavio booms.

Is he saying jive or die? My voice, when I finally locate it, is quavering. "What happened to lip-synching Whitney Houston?"

"You can still use Whitney . . ." Flavio does that weighing-the-scales gesture that only foreigners use. "Only you will jive Whitney."

Okay, I'm a skinny, tone-deaf, uncoordinated white girl—what makes this guy think I can jive? "Jive Whitney? Is that even possible?"

In my rapidly rising panic, I've yelled this. Several members of the cabaret "audience" snicker. Flavio's brows float above his glasses. I lean forward and attempt a whisper. "Listen, Flavio—"

"WATCH THE DRESS!" Jamison shouts.

"You've got me confused with some real cabaret singer or something," I say after snapping back to vertical. "Somebody with talent. Somebody else. I can't jive."

Flavio shakes his head disdainfully and locates the cigarettes in his pocket. "Fine, don't jive—or scat, either," he adds as if I'm considering it.

Thank God. I heave such a huge sigh my earrings jangle. "That's good—great, in fact—'cause I've been practic—"

"You will sing Whitney."

The seeping sweat becomes a geyser. "No, no, Flavio, I can't, you see, as I said in the audition, I'm a terrible singer and I don't think—"

One hand hits the stage; the other appears perilously close to torching me with his Cartier lighter. "You listen to me! You are singing *now!*"

I'm not trying to be difficult, I swear, but I can't sing. Really. Just ask Miss Bowzer, my middle-school music teacher. Every year she'd look at me, sigh, and wave in the general direction of the boys' side of the room, not even bothering to place me in a specific location. As a result, I'm an I-don't-know-what-a-tone and when I graduated from Balsam Junior High, I think we both felt the world was a better-sounding place because of it. I don't intend to change that today.

Besides, singing terrifies me.

"I can't sing, Flavio, I *can't*," I whisper. I'm pleading.

Flavio yanks off his glasses. His eyes are like asphalt, flat and hard. "Bullshit! Everyone can sing, Emily, it's like walking! Now, stop wasting everyone's time and DO IT."

I look up. The room is totally silent: eighty pairs of eyes glued on me, including Justin's, who's sitting at a table front, center, and spotlit. My panic must be evident, for he grins his impish grin, blows me a kiss, and starts to chant and clap. "Em-i-ly! Em-i-ly!"

Others, concluding from this turn of events that all I must lack is encouragement, join in.

"Em-i-ly! Em-i-ly!"

Fuccck.

"Okay," I say. "I'll do it."

Flavio heads for the camera. "All right, let's go! Guys, warm up."

"Miss Woods?"

I turn around. It's the bassist. "What number would you like to start with?"

For over two hours, I sing. Fifteen minutes into "Fly Me to the Moon," Flavio barks into the walkie-talkie that I should "forget Frank." Fifteen minutes after that, I've exhausted my jazz repertoire, so I switch to

Aretha and do "Respect" for a while before moving on to "Lola." These are songs from my "Diva Mix" but I don't feel like a diva, I feel terrible. After all, it's hard to be "sexy, sexy, sexy" as Flavio keeps screaming (for some reason always in triplicate, like XXX) when you're screeching like a drowning cat.

"Pretend the microphone's a giant cock!" Flavio shouts. "Have your way with it!"

I should shout back. I should shout, "Flavio, so help me God, if you so much as say the word *cock* one more time, I'll shove this microphone where the sun don't shine—*comprende?*"

But I don't. What I do is sing.

"I never thought I'd miss Whitney," Justin jokes afterward as we walk down the hallway.

I smile wanly. The oddest thing about the whole experience was that no matter how bad I sounded, Justin and the extras beamed and applauded like they were in aural ecstasy. (When the cameras were rolling, that is. Between takes I heard snickering, punctuated by wicked peals of laughter.) "Poor baby," I say to Justin, jutting my lower lip. "You actually had to act."

"No, just . . ." He pulls a sliver flask out of his coat pocket.

I gasp. "You didn't!"

"I most definitely did," Justin says. "I spiked my coffee."

Come to think of it, he really seemed to enjoy my not-so-grand finale. "No wonder; I didn't think you were that good an actor," I quip.

"Coming from such a talented musician, that really hurts," Justin shoots back.

We've arrived at my dressing room. As I reach out to punch Justin's arm, he grabs it and holds on, turning my body until I'm up against the wall. His blue eyes sparkle. The impish grin is back. His hand traces my arm. "Fortunately, you have other assets," he murmurs.

"And *you* must have beer goggles."

"Emily . . ." Steve's voice travels the length of the hall. "Your car service will be here shortly."

I straighten. "Okay, thanks."

He glances from me to Justin. "Need anything else?"

"No thanks! See you tomorrow!"

"See you."

I look at Justin, suddenly self-conscious. "Well, thanks for walking me. Today was fun," I say, though it wasn't, of course; the fun part is now.

Justin frowns. "Was fun? *Was?* Who said it's over? I've had four cups of coffee and most of this—" He shakes his trusty flask, which indeed sounds close to empty—"and I'm raring to go, so hurry up, get changed and I'll take you out. We'll have dinner, hit a few clubs . . ."

Justin Fields is asking me on a date.

His blue eyes get close, then closer. His lips brush my ear. "Or better yet, I have a suite at the Royalton. We just could go there."

Oh. I swoon against the wall until a light switch digging into the small of my back jolts me back to reality. "Tonight? Oh, Justin, I can't."

"Mmm?" He brushes back my hair. "You're not serious."

I press my fingers against his wrists. "Actually I am. It's Byron, my agent? He wants me to hit a few parties with him."

"I'll come with you."

Pause. It's right before show season—a good time to meet editors and designers—"career development," as Byron put it, but if I bring Justin, Byron will be so enthralled, he'll forget all about me. The editors, too. Then again, if I have Justin Fields on my arm . . . "Okay. Sounds good."

But Justin bridles. "Do try to contain your enthusiasm," he says coldly.

Shit. I paused for too long. "No! I mean it! Come with us! It'll be fun!"

He steps away, releasing me. "I don't think so."

Shit. Shit. Shit. "Oh, well, maybe tomorrow then? I'm free tomorrow. See you then? Okay, see you. Okay, bye!"

I leap into the dressing room and close the door. God, I fucked that up . . . and God was he pissed! Weird just now, that final look. Justin seemed so . . . shocked. I can't believe he cared so much. Then again, Justin's a movie star; he doesn't hear the word *no* too often, I guess.

"There you are!" Jamison trots from the wardrobe room. "Great news. I just got off the phone with Sophie. You're getting the 40 percent.

". . . Emily? The dress?"

"Oh . . . right." I shake my hair as if tossing off the last three minutes, and walk rapidly toward the mirror. "Really? That much? "

"Yes, thanks to me. And Emily, in my humble opinion, I think you should take it. At that price, the dress is a steal. And it looks amazing. Killer!"

Once again, I examine the dress from all angles. "You think?"

"Definitely."

I run my hands across the vines, noting the incredible workmanship. Forty percent off $6,000 is a lot, but I'm making a lot, too: $33,000. *Thirty-three thousand dollars*—what's the dress then, like ten percent? Ten percent's nothing! Besides, this is the dress I met Justin Fields in.

"Okay. I'll take it."

Jamison hugs me, then starts unbuttoning. "Good! Now, let me quickly call Sophie back—that way you can take it home. And who knows? You might want to wear it tonight! Do you have a credit card?"

But of course. The dress comes off. As I sort through my Chanel bag and pull out the matching wallet (the latter purchased as a reward for this commercial; guess there's nothing wrong with two rewards), I catch a glimpse of my George Hamilton–level tan, now crackled by streaks of sweat. "Yuck," I grumble. "I cannot wait to get this crap off me."

Jamison shrugs. "Don't, then. Take a shower."

"There's one here?"

He gestures with the thin sliver of plastic I've just handed him. "In there. It's nice. Girls use it all the time. There's shampoo, conditioner, body scrub—everything."

"Cool."

As Jamison runs off to secure my latest designer gown, I step into the shower. The warm water cascades over my body. I feel quenched, refreshed, and . . . terrible. *Justin. Justin.* Why did I hesitate? Am I nuts? I must be nuts. At the very least I should have calmed him down and pushed for tomorrow night. Because I'm free tomorrow night—or if I'm not, I will be. Of course I will be. It's Justin Fields. Shit! I'm an idiot! I'll change and go find him at once.

Justin has to agree to tomorrow night.

But what if he doesn't?

Don't even think about it.

Justin. Justin. I plop a dollop of shampoo into my palm and lather up. If I go on a date with Justin, then I'm dating Justin Fields. Justin Fields, movie star. Justin Fields, my high school crush. *Justin. Justin.* If Justin and I get married . . .

The bathroom door squeaks.

"Hey, Jamison, you get her?

". . . Jamison?"

I stick my head out of the curtain. Hands grab my hips and yank me backward. I'm too startled to scream; I jolt up high, my sudsy body slipping through the hands—escaping—until I crash down on a bar of soap and lose my footing. *Splat!* My forehead careens into the taps. I squeal in pain.

"Shh! Shh!" Strong hands spin me around.

It's Justin.

"Shh!" Justin places his hand over my mouth. "Shh!" He's got his smile on, that impish grin, only his big blue eyes are now lifeless and cold. The eyes of a dead fish. "Shh!" he whispers again. He pushes me against the wall. I feel the taps dig into my back, the shampoo stream down my head and sting my eyes, the water get hotter and hotter. I feel Justin's lips and tongue run rampant across my face, neck, shoulders, breasts—angry kisses that give way to bites. I feel his hand pinch my nipple and insert itself between my legs.

Justin Fields is raping me.

And then I feel the soap dish on the ledge, the wonderfully over-sized ceramic soap dish, in my hand, in the air, on his head.

Clunk.

I'm in the Town Car. Jamison raps on the window. "There you are!" he cries breathlessly. "I got Sophie. You're good to go!" As he opens the door to hand me my dress, he studies my face and frowns. "Something wrong?"

I want to tell Jamison, I really do, but as I open my mouth I realize that if I tell, I don't shoot tomorrow, and if I don't shoot tomorrow, I don't get paid. I don't get $33,000, so I pluck my credit card and new dress from his outstretched hands and muster my biggest smile.

"Nothing, I'm just tired, I guess! Thank you *so* much! See you tomorrow!"

Tomorrow comes: *Day 2 of 2: Justin's Penthouse*. This is the nuzzling scene, the part where Justin seduces his dream girl over Da Vinci coffee. Every time the actor touches me, I jolt, but I pretend it's not happening. So does he. I can't go very far—I'm stuck on the set, inches away from him—I can only ignore. Justin ignores me, too; he says nothing.

The only thing we exchange is the flask.

Flavio's still pissy and I feel like hell, but I get through it. As a matter of fact, it's not too bad, thanks to the whiskey and my little pouch (I've got a dealer now, did I tell you?). I snort the cocaine between takes. Ro shoots daggers at me but I don't care. The cool white powder gives me courage.

Chapter 28

Don't Call, Don't Write

After the Da Vinci commercial wraps, my busy schedule continues. Options pile on my chart from *Glamour*, *Bazaar*, and *Vogue*. I shoot four pages for *Self* ("8 Ways to Show Off Your Healthy Bod!"), and still more Bergdorf's and Saks. I do a print campaign for Carolyn Roehm and book a Pantene commercial. I might not get out of bed for $10,000 a day, but $10,000 a week? No problem.

A couple of weeks of this and I'm summoned to the agency.

"What's up?"

Justine prods some papers with the end of her pen. It's show season and the agency's been crazy. By this hour on a Friday afternoon, my booker's at her peak breathing-through-an-Iron-Lung manner of speech. "Byron . . . and . . . Francesca . . . they want . . . to talk . . . to you," she wheezes.

"Francesca? Who's Francesca?"

The baleful gaze shifts toward Byron's office. "In . . . there."

The head of Chic's got his I'm-with-a-VIP face on—as cool and un-blemished as the butt of Michelangelo's *David*. As the door swings closed, he strokes the chest of his pima cotton shirt and purrs, "*Francesca*. It is my *pleasure* to *introduce* you to *Emily*."

A petite woman with a mass of ebony curls and a sleek beige suit is perched on the edge of the Le Corbusier chair. Her crimson lips part into a warm smile. "Hello, Emily."

"Hello."

"Emily? If you please?" Byron circles his finger.

I do a 360. Francesca looks at Byron and nods.

He smiles. "Don't you think?"

"Definitely."

"I *thought* so."

"You thought what?" I ask.

"Have a seat."

I sit down. Francesca becomes more firmly ensconced in her chair, pulls a black nylon satchel with an unfamiliar triangular logo on her lap and tugs out a magazine. "Here you go," she says. "Fresh from Italy."

No way. It's the latest issue of *Amica*. I'm on the cover wearing a red beaded Versace dress, huge gold earrings, and a megawatt smile. I smile back: cover number two. I did it! "This is great!"

"Isn't it?" Byron says. "It's my new favorite. It's going right on your card."

Francesca nods. "It's beautiful. And Alfredo Robano is so well re-spected in Milan—another reason it's the perfect time."

I look up.

Byron folds his hands. "Emily, Francesca's the scout for Certo, the largest, most successful agency in Milan. They'd like you to come work for them."

"Very much," Francesca emphasizes. She touches my forearm. "Your video, your covers, your campaign with Justin Fields—all of these have led to a tremendous interest in Emily Woods in my country."

"And it's about to be show season, so the timing's perfect," Byron adds.

"So you'd want me to go right away."

Francesca shrugs. "Tonight, tomorrow, Sunday—any of those would be fine."

Italy for the shows. I missed out on the shows here—too busy working to do the castings. Now, I'm getting another opportunity. "And I'd stay . . . ?

"Already taken care of," Francesca says. "We have a standing agreement with a charming *pensione*—of course, given the season, things might be a bit lively there the first few weeks; after that, it should quiet down considerably."

Weeks? "You mean days . . ."

The curls shake from side to side. "No, weeks."

Byron smiles. I don't have a specific thought, just the awareness of a cold chill spreading from my abdomen to my limbs. "How long are you thinking I'd come for?"

"Oh, at least three months," Francesca says. "Though six would be ideal."

I try to laugh this off. "Oh, I'd love to come for six months, but I've been *so* busy here. Plus, I have an apartment, lots of friends. I just don't see how . . ."

I wait for Byron to say, "No way! I can't lose such a good girl for so long!"

"Isn't this *exciting*?" he trills. "Milan will be great for you!"

"What!"

I must really deliver this word with some heat, because Byron turns to Francesca and says. "Will you excuse us for a minute?"

"But, of course."

We enter the hallway. Byron grabs my arm. "Emily! You're embarrassing me!"

"*I'm* embarrassing *you*? *You're* freaking *me* out!" I fume. "What's going on? Why should I go to Milan for six months when I'm so busy here—and that's before I got this second cover. That's cover number two! I did it! I'm one of your girls now, Byron! I'm on the trophy wall again!"

After this last point, I spin around, planning to back it up with a visual demonstration, only my second *Amica* cover isn't there. My first one, either. "Byron, you're behind . . ."

I stop. In the top row is Fonya's Italian *Vogue* cover. From several weeks ago.

The chill returns. "Byron, what's going on?"

"*Amica* is a weekly publication, and we don't put weeklies up on the wall," Byron says evenly. "No bad magazines, bridals, or weeklies—but you knew that."

No. I didn't. "Why not?"

"Because we don't."

"But *why*?"

"Because they're not the right caliber," Byron says in the same dulcet tone. "We don't put *New York* magazine up, either, if that's any consolation."

It isn't. I've never worked for *New York* magazine. I don't have two covers from *New York* magazine. And if my covers aren't on the wall then . . . "I guess this is your way of telling me you're not going to be my booker again, are you?"

Byron strokes my hair. "Today? No. But I bet I will be as soon as you get back."

I'm angry now. Blindingly, stingingly angry. I take my copy of *Amica*, which sometime during the last minute I've managed to roll into a baton, and pound it against my open hand. *Thwack!* "You're sending me away!" *Thwack!*

"Because you need to go."

"But *why,* when I'm doing so well?"

"You're doing fine," Byron says.

Fine? "FINE? Byron, remember the Café Tabac party? All the attention I got from Isaac, Todd, and Grace! Grace Coddington from *Vogue*! *Vogue* keeps optioning me!"

"*VOGUE* KEEPS RELEASING YOU!" Byron blasts.

My eyes sting. The entire room turns. Francesca stares through the glass. "Emily, I'm going to be blunt here," Byron says as if this will be something new. "You have a solid—*very* solid—career, but no one in the top tier is frantic to book you. *No one.* Not Grace, not anyone—you understand? There is no feeding frenzy. And, as I see it, there's only one way to make that happen."

"The shows."

"Correct."

I stare at the trophy wall, too upset to see it. *Vogue* has optioned and released me three times since the agency party—so what? They'll come around one day, I know they will.

Byron's hand skins my shoulder. "Emily, trust me on this, if they're not desperate to book you, they won't; I've seen it dozens of times before."

I'm silent. He continues. "You missed the New York shows because of bookings. Don't miss Milan, too—not when you've already been optioned for several shows already."

My ears prick. "I have?"

"Yup." Byron ticks his fingers. "Ferré, Feretti, Conti . . ."

"Conti is holding time on me?"

Byron smiles. "Yes. And I know I don't have to tell you what a big deal that is . . ."

No, you don't. While there might be several leaders of Italian fashion, there's only one king: Tito Conti. The man's won countless awards for his men's and women's wear. He has eponymous boutiques around the world. But most of all, his name is a powerful brand, synonymous with success. Wearing Conti says you've made it, and if I work for him, it means I've made it, too. All the top models do his show; all the top editors attend it. Booking Tito Conti would be a coup.

Byron turns. His hands clasp my cheeks. "Emily, *darling*: Now is your chance—will you just go ahead and *take* it?"

"So . . . you're going to Milan?"

"Yup."

Jordan slides next to Pixie, I make room for Mohini. My friends canceled last week's standing breakfast date and were going to do the same with this one had I not called them back and informed them of my imminent departure. Now here they are, rolling into Tom's Diner fifteen minutes late, all clad in a motley assortment of sweats, including Jordan, who's as unmade up as I've ever seen her—so bare-faced, in fact, it's looking highly probable she rolled out of bed five minutes ago.

Jordan drums her palms on the tabletop. "How long's the trip?"

"Three months, maybe more."

"Cool!" Mohini says, opening her menu.

"Yeah, lucky you!" Pixie enthuses. "Italy's amazing: the architecture, the art . . ."

"Really?" I say. "Even Milan? I heard it's sort of industrial."

She shrugs her thin shoulders. "Yeah, but it's just a short train ride away from Florence, Venice, Portofino, Tuscany . . ."

"You can travel on weekends!" Mohini adds.

"Yeah. . . ." I start playing with the tines of my fork.

"You'll have a blast," Jordan says.

Perfect. No, really. I didn't want any of my friends to be even a teeny bit sad. I wanted them all to beam at me like a bunch of beauty contestants so that I would beam back until my face hurts. Totally.

Fortunately Nikos, the crabbiest waiter on staff, comes over, giving our cheeks a welcome rest. "Enough about me," I say once the coffee's been poured and he's rumbled off. "How are you guys?"

Mohini rests her cheek in her hand and exhales. "Three weeks into the semester and I'm already swamped."

"But in a good way," Jordan says quickly. "Right, Hini?"

"Yeah, good, definitely," Mohini amends, nodding her head so vigorously her glasses seem in danger of taking a trip of their own.

Hmm. I stare at Jordan, but she's sifting through her book bag.

"Omigod! Em! Our room is fantastic! Remember Kevin and Dave, the guys across the hall? Well, they throw the *sickest* parties!" Pixie proclaims, before launching into a detailed description of several recent examples, all involving hookups, throwups, and breakups disbursed among a random cross section of party-goers.

"Sounds fun." I sip my water, suddenly parched. "And how are your classes this semester? It must be nice to have the requirements out of the way." This is one of the things I was most anticipating about junior year.

Jordan thrusts out her arms. "Yes, once you've built a solid foundation you're free to *soar!*"

All three of them erupt in laughter.

"What?" I say. Obviously, it's an imitation, I just don't know of whom.

"Professor Klyber," Pixie says eventually.

"Klyber's the Intro to Architecture professor," Mohini explains.

"I know who Professor Klyber is—I was the one who suggested we take his class!" I snap; everyone's so nonplussed it's killing me.

"Of course you did. How stupid of me; I forgot. I'm sorry," Mohini says so quickly that I feel dumb for overreacting.

"Klyber's a real piece of work, Emma Lee," Jordan says. "Hysterical!"
Pixie's head bobs. "So funny!"

I grin in anticipation. "He is? How?"

"It's hard to explain," Jordan says.

Oh. The food arrives. Mohini grabs the syrup. "But Klyber's not nearly as strange as Dumai," she says as a moat rises around her pancakes.

"That guy is such an asshole!" Pixie says.

"You're telling me," Jordan snorts between bites of her sausage and egg. "That poor girl in the front row!"

"She was in tears!"

"That was the harshest exchange I've ever witnessed!"

"I *know*!"

"Why? What happened?" I say. I have no idea who Dumai is either but we seem to have flown past that.

"He was really mean," Mohini says.

"But I think you had to be there, " Pixie finishes.

Right. I take a bite of my breakfast, noting that my scrambled egg whites have even less flavor than usual, my toast is as dry as sawdust. For a moment, the only sound is the scraping of utensils interrupted by the faint tinkle of ice against plastic, then Pixie's eyes fly to the wall. "Omigod, is that the time?" She hops to her feet. "I'm late! I'm supposed to meet Timothy!"

"Wait . . . *now*?" I say.

"Unfortunately." Her balled napkin plops onto her waffles.

"Timothy as in Hutton? That's still going on?"

"Not for long! But I'll tell you all about it in December—or next year, I guess, depending on your plans!" Pixie ruffles her hair, grabs her purse, and hands me a ten. "Bye! Have fun! Call us when you're back!"

"Okay . . . Bye."

I turn around just as Jordan's wallet hits the counter. "Not you, too!"

"Sorry!" She juts her lip. "Told Ben I'd meet him in front of Butler."

"Jord, it's a Saturday morning."

"Yeah."

"In September."

Jordan zips the front of her sweatshirt. "Yeah," she says. *And?*

"Since when do you hit the books so hard?"

"Since I decided to get more serious about school." She pulls money from her wallet, her backpack already over one shoulder. "Hey, don't be so surprised, Emma Lee. People change."

Okay, this was a dig. I rise and step toward her, almost grateful. Enough with all this fakery—finally the truth is coming out: My friends are devastated that I'm going, so devastated that all they can do is pretend not to care.

Only I'm engulfed. "Bye darlin', I'll miss you terribly!" Jordan says, squeezing. When she pulls back, I see red-rimmed eyes brimming with tears. "But, honey, I just *know* you'll have *just* the *best* time!"

"Okay, thanks. You have just the best time, too," I mumble.

"I'll try. Send us a postcard, 'kay? B'bye!"

"Bye."

As I sink into the booth, Mohini rises. "Sorry, Em. I've got lab."

The bank clock on Broadway says 11:58. *Eleven fifty-eight.* My three best friends in and out in under an hour. Actually—no, they were late, so it was more like forty minutes. Forty fucking minutes. To say what? *I'll tell you next year? Call us when you get back? Honey? Darlin'? Send us a postcard? A postcard. As in one postcard. One postcard in three months. Bye! Bye! B-bye?* What a bunch of crap!

A guy on a bicycle whizzes past, one arm outstretched in greeting. "Hey Pol-llyyy!"

Polly? Polly! Who the *hell* is Polly?

Wheet! Wheeew! A catcall comes from the next corner, breaking my concentration. *Wheet!*—Oh, please. I smooth down my shirt and toss my hair—*Wheeew!* And then, in violation of my street policy—which is to ignore, always ignore—a violation that's clearly occurring *only* because I'm *totally* stressed—I turn and give the guy a haughty glance. Only he's not whistling at me—he's not even looking at me; his eyes are glued to some girl a few steps behind me who's, like, five feet two inches and not even cute.

Okay, that does it. "Tax-eeee!"

"Bergdorf's," I tell the driver, "and step on it please!" *Oh God.* Tears spring to my eyes. *Five feet two? Five feet two!* I unzip my purse and pull out my makeup kit—clearly, I need it—then continue with my melt-down. *My friends don't even care that I'm leaving. Mohini, Pixie, Jordan: none of them. Not one.* A tear spills down my cheek; I dab it away. *I didn't think modeling would isolate me so quickly but it has, evidently.* Then cover up my red cheeks with a cream concealer followed by a light layer of powder. *I'm on my own. I am my own island, the Isle of Emily. I have no friends. None. ZERO. My taxi could be swallowed up by a giant rat and no one would even blink. Well, they might blink, but it would have to do with the rat, not with me. My friends care more about rats than they do about me. They don't give A RAT'S ASS about—*

"Hello? Hello! Is anybody back there? You said Bergdorf's, Miss, well, this is it!"

Oops. I pay, exit, and touch up my eyes and lips via the display windows before whisking through the revolving door. *Why don't my friends care—why?* I wonder, still upset, though admittedly a tad more composed at the sight of all the bags and baubles. When I disembark on a higher floor, I feel even better. The winter palette, the heavy fabrics, the flattering light—it's all so orderly, so soothing, and soon, I'm calm—calm enough to tune in to a different voice in my head. *Well, Emily,* the voice says, *what is it you wanted them to say?*

What is it I wanted? I reach the end of the hallway and bank left. Salesclerks see me and walk to the edge of their respective turfs, their predatory instincts masked by polite smiles. I've wandered into Donna Karan and am sorting through a rack of gray-toned wool separates, when the answer comes to me. *I wanted them to tell me not to go.*

"Would you like to try that?"

I've moved to evening wear. My hand's clutching a dress. "Sure." *Yes, that's it: I wanted them to tell me not to go, because I'm not sure I want to go.*

I follow the salesperson to my dressing room and close the door. By all accounts, Italy's an amazing country, and living there would be an awesome experience.

. . . And yet for some reason I keep thinking about Jordan's comment, the one she made that time we fought in the kitchen. The one that went: "What's next, Emma Lee?"

The dress is on now. I zip the zipper, button the button, and walk so close to the mirror my nose fogs the glass and I'm staring into the blackest part of my eye. "I'm going to Italy," I say, waiting for my reaction. "Italy. *Italy!*"

"Italy's wonderful!" the salesclerk says, using this as an excuse to enter. "And so is this dress!"

I think, the voice says as I wait to pay—I'm getting the dress plus a pair of $480 loden suede walking shorts that I didn't try on but I'm sure will be fine—*what I wanted was this*: Pixie: "Omigod, you don't even know anyone in Milan!" Jordan: "And you *so* enjoyed your last experience living abroad!" Mohini: "What about your education?"

"That will be $1,440."

Only they didn't. I toss my Bergdorf's charge on to the counter and look around. The Donna Karan mannequin, formerly standing tall in a double-breasted pantsuit, is now on the floor, her legs and arms akimbo as her torso is hoisted into a chocolate brown bodysuit: "a leotard at four times the price," Mom always says.

Well, of course. I want someone to play devil's advocate? Someone to say *don't* to my *do*? *Can't* to my *can*? *No* to my *yes*? There's only one person for the job.

Mom and I haven't spoken in a while, I realize in the cab, not since the day I called home to tell my parents I'd dropped out of Columbia. When I said the words, I expected Mom to start ranting, per usual. Instead, she started crying, which really freaked me out, so I started crying, too. "I'm sorry," I blubbered, as in, sorry I've upset you; sorry I have to do this. As usual, Mom misunderstood. At the sound of my tears, hers dried up. "So," she said, her voice suddenly hopeful, "does this mean you'll reconsider?"

"You're so manipulative!" I hissed and hung up.

Since then our exchanges have been limited to answering-machine messages of the I'm-just-checking-to-make-sure-you're-not-dead variety.

Maybe it's time to say more.

When I get home from Bergdorf's, I try on my new dress to see how it looks with my new Manolos (cream satin with a rhinestone clasp; I picked up a black pair, as well, to go with my new Gaultier). I'm high-stepping around the apartment (our former summer sublet—I extended the lease), trying on accessories as I formulate my words for the call, when the phone rings.

"Emily?"

"Dad! That is so weird! I was just about to call . . ." I trail off. My father just called me Emily. He never calls me Emily, unless . . .

The next words out of his mouth are choked. "Something happened against Michigan. A bad tackle. He went down. Didn't get up."

Tommy. I slide down the wall. Words, sight, breath—everything's suspended. *Dead. My brother's dead.*

"His knee," Dad's saying. "His knee is destroyed."

"B-but he's alive?"

"Yes."

The tears that flood my face are tears of relief. The news broken, Dad starts speaking more normally, but my heart's pounding so loudly I only hear snippets. "Ripped his ACL . . . PCL destroyed . . . Structural damage to his meniscus . . . Benched for the season . . . Rehab."

Once I realize how good the news is, I realize how bad it is. Football is all Tommy ever wanted to do. This year, he finally made it to the position of starting quarterback at the University of Wisconsin. Now he isn't. He's out for the season, maybe even for life. He must be crushed. "Is—is he there?"

"He's still in surgery," Dad says. I hear a muffled noise then, "Emily?" It's Mom. "I'm sitting here and I'm thinking this is so crazy, it's all so crazy, and I've been making a huge mistake. I had thought—well, you know what I thought. But sitting here has made me realize that things happen, things happen that you don't expect and everything can change so fast and it's *so* . . . awful, Emme. It's so awful."

I swallow. My eyes water. I've never heard my mother like this. "Terrible. I know," I whisper.

"No—I'm talking about *you,* Emme. I'm saying you should do what you want. If you want to model, it's okay with me. No, it's more than okay, it's great. You're my daughter and I love you and that is what counts, that's . . . everything. If modeling is what you want to do, then do it and do it well, and do it while you can. I've been wrong to tell you otherwise. There, I said it—how are things?"

My brother's in the hospital, my mother's unglued; there's only one answer. I force air into my lungs and squeeze my eyes shut. "I'm fine, Mom. I mean, upset about this, obviously, but otherwise fine. Don't worry about me."

"Good," she says, sounding the teeniest bit better. "I'm glad. What's going on in your life—anything new?"

"Well, um, Byron wants me to go to Italy but—"

"Italy? Italy's *wonderful*! When?"

Wow, she really *is* unglued. "Tomorrow."

"For how long?"

"A few months. But, Mom, now that this happened, I don't think—"

"You'll go?" she finishes. "No, you should go! Trust me, Emme: Your brother would feel worse if he knew you were forgoing a chance like this because of him; my God, at least *one* of you needs to pursue your dream! He'll see you when you get back. I mean this! Oh, here's the doctor, I've got to go. We'll call you soon with an update. Italy, great! Bye! We love you!" Click.

I need a cigarette.

I crawl to my purse, pull out my Marlboro Lights, and crawl back, leaning against the wall and smoking for I don't know how long as my brain rolls tape of my brother though the ages. In most frames—so many—Tommy's the athlete, his jersey sweaty and stained, his face shiny, the pertinent athletic gear wedged nonchalantly under his arm. He might have won, he might have lost, but you cannot tell from looking at him; his eyes always reflect a total love of the game, glittery and bright, pure confidence.

Brring. Brring.

I practically swallow the mouthpiece. "What'd they say?"

"You're there!—I got her! JUSTINE, I GOT HER!—I've left you a *gazillion* messages; where have you *been*?"

Oh. "Hi, Byron, I—"

"Never mind! Something's happened, Emily, something *terrible*! A model slotted for the Tia Romaro show had an accident—okay, a permanent nosebleed because she's fried her septum with coke but you didn't hear that from me—anyway, they needed another girl *immediately* so I gave them you, but that was *two* hours ago, so *hurry*!"

"Tia who?"

"Christ, Emily, dear, I need you to FOCUS! Tia Romaro, the up-and-coming Cuban designer, has a show tonight and *you're* in it! There'll be some press but not too much, junior editors but no big names—it's the perfect place for you to break in your runway skills."

Break in or break? "Byron, I'm not sure I can do this right now . . ."

"Why not?"

"It's my brother—he's in the hospital."

"Is he dying?"

"No, it's—"

"Is he in New York?"

"No—"

"Emily—Emily dear, listen to me. I'm *crushed* that this happened but what can we *do*? I'll tell you what: I'll send him a fruit basket and *you*—you'll do the show. Of course you'll do this show! I know you can—especially since you're getting *help!* Raphael—you know, the walking tutor? Well, he's agreed to coach you for an emergency session, which you need because you're confirmed for *four* shows in Milan, now—*four!* And optioned for several others. You'll *adore* Raphael. He's taught Iman and Naomi and Nikki—"

"Byron, I can't! I'm too upset now—"

"You're upset, I'm upset"—indeed, Byron sounds upset—"and I'll tell you what will make you even more upset: you making a fool of yourself in front of Anna Wintour, Liz Tilberis, and every other major editor in the cosmos."

"I thought you said the major editors won't be there."

"Well, they'll be in ITALY, won't they?" he yells. "They'll be at CONTI! And you'll be there NEXT WEEK! Emily, your reputation is on the line here, and so is Chic's, so I suggest you GRAB your stilettos RIGHT THIS VERY INSTANT and GET to the lobby of the Puck Building NOW, okay?"

"But, By—"

"NOW! NOW! NOW!"

Chapter 29

Runaway

"*ou* are late."

In the cab on the way downtown, I tried to imagine the look of a professional walking tutor named after an Italian Renaissance painter and came up with an outfit pulled together by a five-year-old run amok in her mother's closet: lots of feathers, flowers, and pink. But Raphael's flawless ebony skin and six feet four inch frame are swaddled in white: white suit, white shirt, white sunglasses, white loafers. Even the cane, which he's rapping in a sharp, impatient staccato against the tiles, is white.

"Sorry," I tell him. "I came as soon as I could."

Not that I'm dressed normally. Raphael steps forward and fingers the lapel of the jean jacket I threw on over my Donna Karan evening dress in a vain attempt to call it daywear. "Denim and diamonds, I love it!" he declares. After his approving nod extends to my stilettos, Raphael grabs my hand, drags me around the corner to Mulberry Street, stops, and says, "Go."

"What, here?"

"Yup."

"On the street?"

"Yup."

"On the cobblestones?"

The cane taps impatiently. "Look, sugar, if you can strut your stuff here, you can strut it anywhere, got it? C'mon now, give it to me."

Gingerly, I lift my hem and start navigating my four-inch heels through the rough terrain. The problem is, I'm not interested in strutting my stuff here, there, or anywhere—how could I be? Sometime during the short ride to SoHo, the tape playing in my head caught up to the present moment. I now see images of Tommy falling on the field and writhing in agony. I picture the stainless steel operating table on which my brother's being cut open—right this very moment. I imagine the steel plates and screws that will pin him back into place. And finally—and mostly this—I see Tommy's face when he wakes in his hospital bed and realizes what he's lost: a season, a career, a lifetime of dreams. Because, sports aren't what Tommy does; they're who he is—who is my brother now?

Ow! The cane jabs my ribs. "Miss Emily, are we walking or are we wading through a creek here?"

Raphael has dropped the Gene Kelly pose and is now barking and galloping alongside me with all the sweetness and light of a drill sergeant. "C'mon, drop that hem! Raise that head! Loosen those hips! What are those hands doing? Eyes up! I said *eyes up*! And—turn!"

I turn and find myself in a face-plant on the sunroof of a four-door sedan, thus triggering the car alarm.

Raphael crouches opposite and raises his sunglasses, his eyes narrowed. "If this was a runway, you'd be in Pat Buckley's lap."

"If this was a runway, it would be smooth," I counter.

The cane hits the pavement. "Miss Emily, get your eyes *off* the road and *on* me. Follow me! Now, first lesson: Walk in my footsteps as we crissss with the right foot . . ."

As the cane, which I'm now keeping a careful eye on, juts right, Raphael's left foot moves across the plane of his body until it lands in the opposite footfall. I watch his large frame seamlessly stretch and contract, suddenly as elastic as rubber, and clumsily try to follow suit, noting how my hip juts out to compensate: *Swish!* "Then we crosssss with the left," he continues. "Crisss—right foot! Crossss—left foot! Criisss—right! Croosss—left." He increases the speed. "Criss—crosss! Crisss—crosss!" And starts clapping a beat. *Clap. Clap.* "And . . . we're walking! We're walking!"

Actually, *I'm* walking; Raphael has now pulled aside to watch. "We're walking and—turn!"

This time, I manage to stay vertical, but that's about all I can say. Raphael has no such reserve.

"Is that a tutu I see before me? Are those toe shoes? I didn't say 'Twirl' I said 'turn'!" he barks. "*Turn!* Why aren't you walking? C'mon, walk this way! C'mon! *Criss. Cross. Criss. Cross* . . . And . . . we're walking! We're walking!"

I criss-cross-turn up and down the cobblestones. Raphael doesn't look pleased. But, he doesn't hit me either.

"Now, lesson two," he shouts. "When you crisscross, I want you to loosen that pelvis—really set it free, okay? C'mon now." *Clap. Clap.* "And . . . we're walking! We're walking!"

". . . C'mon, free it, really free it!"

". . . Free that pelvis!"

". . . C'mon, think black cat! That's it! Slink! Slink! You're a black cat! C'mon!" *Clap. Clap.* "And—we're walking . . ."

For the first time, I'm gliding more than wobbling; I've got a groove going. *Criss cross! Slink slink! I'm a black cat! I'm a black cat! Criss cross! Slink Slink! I'm a black cat! I'm a black cat! Criss cross* . . .

"Better!" Raphael cries. "Slink! Miss Emily, slink!"

A family of tourists, clearly on the wrong block, squeal to a halt, their cameras already firing. I lose my concentration and resume wobbling.

"No! No! No! You're not leading with your *pelvis*! Walking is all about the pelvis! Like this!"

As Raphael thrusts out his pelvis and wiggles it in a manner that could get him arrested in most states, I dutifully criss-cross-slink–stick out my pelvis–and-shine, the perspiration beginning to form as I keep time to the tattoo of his cane.

"And we're out of time."

What? I look at my watch. "It's only been fifteen minutes!"

"Yes, and you were supposed to be upstairs precisely ninety minutes

ago," Raphael says. "The show starts in thirty, and you still don't have
hair and makeup. So I suggest you go inside now, before they have a
total conniption."

"But my turns," I stammer. "I'm not—"

"Just remember: criss cross, turn not twirl, slink slink, plus everything else we've just practiced and you'll be—well, you won't go skittering off the runway, I don't think," Raphael concludes, glancing briefly
at the location of the face-plant, the car still whirring and beeping in
agitation.

"Well, those are great tips and everything but—"

The back door to the Puck Building opens. "Hold it!" Raphael yells.

I take the hint and jog toward it. "Okay . . . thanks." My fingers
flick behind me. "Bye!"

I hear his throat clear. "Ahem, sugar . . ."

Whoops. I race back to double-kiss him. "Bye!"

"That's touching, Miss Emily, really, but . . ." His thumb rubs
against his fingers.

Oh . . . right. "How much?"

"Four hundred."

I nearly collide with another car. "*Four* hundred dollars for *fifteen*
minutes?"

"Plus all the wait time," Raphael says.

"What are you, a limo?"

"Sugar, I'm a Rolls." Raphael extends his hand. "Come on, you're
late and I bite, what's it gonna be?"

I pay my walking tutor off with a stack of travelers' checks intended for
Italy and race inside the Puck Building. Backstage, it's chaos. In a raw,
loftlike space brimming with racks of clothing, dozens of assistants and
nearly nude models—multiplied once and again in the copious banks
of mirrors—scurry every which way, ping-ponging in response to the
shouts of the few who are running the show:

"—Twenty minutes to showtime! Twenty minutes!"

"—People, I'm seeing too much blush on these girls!"

"—This is royal blue! The belt for outfit number seven is sky. Go
and check every accessory bag immediately!"

"—I want ringlets, not corkscrews!"

"Emily Woods, where the *hell* have you been?"

A PA promptly plunks me in front of two addled assistants. As one proceeds to work on my face with such haste I feel as if I'm being scribbled on, the other makes stabbing motions into my locks with a curling iron.

"—Fifteen minutes to showtime! Fifteen minutes!"

"—Dressers, any makeup on the collars and you won't be coming back!"

"—Attention: The shoes are missing for outfit number four!"

"Hey, Em!" Fleur finds a stretch of open mirror and leans in to inspect the Tia Romaro Spring 1991 Face (strong brow, strong lips, framed by the aforementioned ringlets), which causes her to frown and reach for a tissue. "I didn't know you were in this," she murmurs, preparing to redo her lip line. (If a model's going to retouch one thing on her face, her top lip is the top candidate—for some reason it's the hardest for others to get right.) "I didn't see you at the fittings or any of the rehearsals."

Any of the *rehearsals*? Instantly, my throat tightens. "I-I wasn't at them," I finally manage. "I'm filling in for Inez."

At the sound of her name, Fleur's eyes go as round as a Kewpie doll's. "Oh! They just announced that! I can't believe it! What an accident!"

"So tragic," the hairdresser says.

"Yeah, it's too bad," I say. "But it sounds like it might have been a long time coming."

A newly created curl bounces in the air. "What was, the taxi?"

Taxi?

"I don't think she even saw it," Fleur says earnestly. "That was the whole problem. And now, here she is, in a hospital, fighting for her life."

Oh. Her booker lied.

"It's so tragic," the hairdresser says again.

"Tragic," agrees the makeup artist, "especially for Tia. I mean to lose her muse like that."

I can hardly get the word out. *"Muse?"*

The pencil peels from Fleur's lips. "Oh . . . didn't you know? Why, they're as close as sisters—escaped from Cuba on the same dingy and swam over a half a mile in shark-infested waters off the coast of south Florida, or something like that—but that's great for you! It means you'll get all the attention!"

I snort. "I doubt that."

"—Ten minutes to showtime! Ten minutes! This means EVERY MODEL should be in wardrobe THIS INSTANT!"

Fleur purses, blots, and drops her lip liner into her robe pocket. "Well, first is first."

"—FLEUR, this means you! EMILY WOODS, you've got ONE minute!"

"Gotta run! See you onstage!"

First. I'm going first. In my first runway show. If my throat felt tight before, I now have the sensation I'm twisting in a noose. I try to swallow, only I don't have enough to work with, forcing a coughing fit.

The hairdresser pats my back. "You okay?"

Well, actually . . . a thought pops into my head; I sit upright, suddenly hopeful. "Hey, I can switch places with someone? Change the order maybe?"

His head shakes curtly. "Sorry, babe. The programs are printed in order of the outfit. You're going first. It's a done deal."

"—EMILY WOODS, get into wardrobe NOW!"

There are two kinds of models who do the shows in earnest: the kind I'd like to be, a top-tier girl who does them because the designers simply *have to have her;* and the kind I'm glad I'm not, a runway specialist by default, a girl who has the figure for shows but lacks the face for print. For both of these runway regulars, show season can be grueling. New York, Milan, then on to Paris: multiple shows per day for weeks on end. Late-night fittings followed by later-night photo shoots (top-tier girls only, please). No food because you've got to be rail thin, which is fine because there's no time to eat anyway, or sleep; there's barely enough time to run to the venue and walk. To get through it, girls often rely on uppers: coffee, speed, or cocaine, depending on their bent. But I'm jittery enough, thank you very much, and besides, it seems in bad form to consume the drug my predecessor OD'd on, so as I walk toward the changing area, my pounding heart and clenched throat point me in a different direction: the open bottle of Veuve Cliquot on the counter. I swipe it and throw it back.

"—Use the belt from number thirteen then, just be sure to put it back before you change her into number twenty-six!"

"—People, I said ringlets, *not* Orphan *Fucking* Annie!"

"—Hey, down it or drop it: there's no drinking near the clothes!"

I down it, drop it, then walk into the changing area. Every model has a rack of clothing with her name on it and an assigned dresser (FIT undergrads, I'll later learn, no doubt working for next to nothing, for the thrill of it). Nadege, Gail, Michelle, Meghan—there are no super-models, just plenty of top-tier girls, and the bigger the name, the more celebrities and editors seem to surround her, which explains why as I make my way to my spot, I'm nearly squashed by Andre Leon Tally's size-seventeen foot as he barges through hollering "YASMEEN! YOU LOOK HEAVENLY"

"—Jesus Christ! No smoking near the clothes!"

"—I can see that thong: Get that thong off!"

On the ~~Inez~~/Emily rack are four outfits, their corresponding accessories secured in Ziploc bags that have been pierced by hangers and ordered from left to right. Already, my dresser, having heaved a sigh of relief at the sight of me, is pulling outfit number one off the hanger: a fitted floral pants suit.

"—Five minutes to showtime! Five minutes! Girls, get into formation ASAP!"

I step into my pants. My dresser pulls them up—only she can't. The cotton has hit my hips and skidded to a stop.

Shit.

"—Formation! Get into formation!"

Panicked, she eyes me wildly. "Doesn't it fit?" Then raises her hand. "Excu—"

"*Stop!* Don't do that! Wait!" I hiss. With jackrabbit speed, I jump up and down until the pants are as high on my waist as possible, suck in my belly, and pull the zipper up.

"—This is makeup: *Makeup!* On the *sleeve!*"

"—Well, stuff the shoes then!"

"—I said *formation,* not a fucking *gaggle!*"

As for the jacket, I can't even close it. *Shit. Shit. Shit.* Somewhere in the process of blowing out her septum, Inez managed to get insanely skinny.

"—Formation! Final call: Formation!"

My dresser raises her hand again. This time, I can't stop her. "Cyril!" she bleats. "Outfit number one doesn't fit!"

"What?" Cyril, the man currently having a meltdown about line formation, and thus most likely the show's producer, rushes over, his mouth gaping in horror. "I can't believe this! Your agent gave me your measurements. You're supposed to be the exact same size as Inez!"

"I am!"

"I don't think so!" he snaps.

Some girls stare, others avert their gaze. Out of the corner of my eye, I see Tia Romaro pacing. "I mean I was," I stammer; I only worked with Inez once and it was a while ago, but I remember we had a similar build. "I think she might have shrunk."

"Oh, *please,*" Cyril spits. "When does that ever happen?"

House music thrums the airwaves, which is clearly a cue; Cyril jolts into action. "Okay, we'll cheat the leg length by ripping the hem. As for the jacket, Emily, I want you to remove it *right away* and dangle it from your finger—no, over the shoulder, I think—whatever works. Just get it off early, before your turns, okay?"

I nod. My heart's now pounding so hard it whirs in my ears like a helicopter—*whump, whump, whump*—syncopating with the throbbing beat and drowning out the ambient commotion. I feel my hems rip, my face being dusted with powder, my sleeves get yanked. *Whump, whump.* I see the girls laughing and flitting behind me, including Fleur, who looks at me and says something that is about as intelligible as the adults on *Peanuts. Whump, whump* . . . And then the music switches to Sinead O'Connor and someone in a headset presses her hand against the small of my back, shoves me behind a white screen, and says, "You're on!"

When the lights hit me, I'm so blinded that for a second I can't breathe, like I've been plunged in water.

"Go! Go!" she hisses.

I don't move.

"GO!"

You can do this, Emily. It's only walking. I take a step. *Criss* . . . The now extralong pant leg gets lodged under my heel and—*fuck!*—for one terrifying second I feel my foot slide against the smooth platform before it catches and holds. *Cross* . . . The other foot is better. *Criss* . . . Okay, chin up! Shoulders back! Eyes up! *Cross* . . . My eyes, now up, start to adjust. Christ, there are at least two hundred people here. *Criss* . . . Don't look. Just don't look. *Cross* . . . . Shit, I just looked at Downtown Julie Brown and Rob Lowe—ROB LOWE is here? *Criss* . . . And Kirstie Alley? And that guy from *21 Jump Street*? My God, he's cute. *Cross* . . . Oh God. Oh God. Oh, don't look; just go: Go! Go! Go! *Criss cross, criss cross, criss* . . .

And then I've got it—or, at least, I'm going. I seem to get into my groove of earlier. I glide along the smooth, white runway, numbly, effortlessly, my step and breath suddenly working in tandem. *Criss cross. Slink! Slink! Criss cross.* The room, the crowd, the flash of the strobes, the other models—colors and shapes blur and whirl together as if viewed from a spinning top until I'm behind the screen again. *Wow.* I feel flushed and excited. It wasn't that bad. In fact, a few more round trips and I could see liking that, loving it even. I'll become a runway regular, a catwalk star in high demand.

Only Cyril's waiting. "What the *fuck* was *that*?" he spits.

After, it's easy to see that I screwed up. I was used to cobblestones and those damn four-inch stilettos, see. The combination of flat shoes, a smooth surface, and a nervous system in a state of emergency was bound to make me walk "as if I was shot out of a fucking cannon," as Cyril puts it. Plus, in my haste, I forgot to remove the jacket, I didn't turn in places where all the other girls turned, and when I did turn, I twirled so fast that "no one caught the goddamn outfit on film." Yes, it was all just a blur.

Of course, by the time I realize this, it's too late. Already, my remaining three outfits have been distributed to other girls in the show, girls who are no doubt thinner and experienced enough to handle the burden of an additional quick change. All that's left for me to do is go.

Chapter 30

Outfoxed

I go all the way to Milan.

Milan sucks.

"Modelo! Modelo!" the boys cry. They follow me down the sidewalk and through the subway cars. If I'm stationary, they grope me. Grown men, too.

When I get to where I'm going, things aren't much better. Thanks to the four shows I've booked—Byblos, Krizia, Lancetti, Genny—I have plenty of fittings. These aren't too bad—a lot of standing around while a bunch of people measure everything from my forehead to my ankles and talk in a language I can't understand—but when I'm not doing fittings, I'm doing castings, and Milan seems to know only one kind: open castings, cattle calls, where the lines snakes out the door and down the block. I go on a lot of them: for advertising, for editorial, for shows I'm not yet optioned for. A surprising number of them insist on Polaroiding me topless.

Three days of this and I start to rebel.

"Not more castings," I tell Massimo, my agent at Certo (I haven't seen Francesca since I arrived). "They're a complete waste of time."

Massimo strokes his hair. He's tall, tan, bald, and ponytailed—a sneak preview of Lorenzo Lamas fifteen years hence. "That's how we do it here," he says.

"And why are they all topless?"

"Italian advertising is very sexy."

"For a *bank*?"

Massimo takes my elbows in a way that might be kind were it not for the sensation he's trying to clamp me. "Emilia, trust me: After the shows are over, things will settle down. You will have individual appointments with editors, photographers, designers. You will be one of my big stars, I'm certain of this. But for now, when it's so busy, this is how it goes, so just relax and play the game, okay?"

Okay, Massimo, I'll play the game. After all, why shouldn't I? It's only one week until the shows start—until I'm walking the runway for the four shows I've booked, plus Conti, Versace, Prada, and Gucci. True, the latter group hasn't confirmed yet, but it will, I just know it. Massimo and Byron know it, too.

So until then, I'll bide my time.

I spend my evenings at the Darsena, the resident hotel where most visiting models stay. I arrived here expecting a charming inn with terracotta tiles and crackled walls, *not* a loud and no-frills operation with temperamental air conditioners whose tempers flare whenever it gets over ninety degrees, which is often. Yes, the Darsena is a dump. Every night, I trudge upstairs to the fourth floor, shower off the smog (which blankets the city like a dirty rag, making it hard to breathe), then trudge back downstairs to the café across the street where I nurse a glass of wine. And I watch.

This is show season, peak season. Even so, there are more models than there are jobs, which means that many Darsena residents have to find other ways to make ends meet. Not long after the sun cedes to subtler illuminations, the models come out, often alone, sometimes in twos or threes. If they're male, they climb aboard a van that drives them to a nightclub located two hours outside of the city where they get paid to ask women to dance, to flirt a little, to get the party started. They drink for free. At the end of the night they get $100 cash and a ride home. It's called "dancing for dollars."

The female models have more options. If a girl already has a lover, she'll be picked up by one of the many motorbikes or sedans constantly idling outside our entrance. If she's looking for love, she too can take a van ride, only this ride stops at a restaurant. I know because I went.

A model told me about the van at casting. One night I was lonely and curious, that emotional blend that often leads to rash decisions, so I hopped onboard. The van was crowded and buzzing with English as a second language. It drove us to a seafood restaurant on the river with yellow stuccoed walls and white chairs. The men were there already—not many, just four, which meant that each guy got a girl on either side and then some, inspiring them to slide their arms across the chair backs and flash each other shit-eating grins. Anything we wanted was free. Most models limited themselves to wine, maybe a salad, except for the bulimics, who ordered three-course meals. As they ate and ate, the men laughed and clasped their skinny arms in wonderment.

After that, it was on to a nightclub. En route, as the wind thrashed our hair—we were now in expensive sports cars and traveling at quite a clip—we passed a row of prostitutes. Transvestites. The guy in the passenger seat jutted his chin toward them and said, "They give the best blow jobs."

The driver agreed.

The club was open air and had many floors, like a ship. Plastic fruits and flowers intertwined with little white lights swung from the ceilings and railings. "It's nice, no? I'm an owner; the restaurant we ate in belongs to my father," the man from the passenger seat explained. "Every night I go out like this, surrounded by beauty. We Italians have a real appreciation for it."

"So I've heard," I responded, realizing right then and there that this phrase was obviously coined by a man; a woman would have come up with a different phrase, most likely involving the word *pervert*.

At the club, the drinks were free, too, naturally, but, "you'd better watch yours like a hawk," a girl named Suki warned. "Guys put stuff in them so you can't move."

I frowned. We were at a dance club: "What could possibly be the point of that?"

Suki shot me a look.

Oh. Oh God.

That's when I slipped out of the club and hailed a taxi.

Yes, Milan sucks, but everyone wants in. Yesterday, a NO OCCU-
PANCY sign got hooked on to the Darsena placard, and now—right this
moment—Massimo is pulling me aside at Certo. "Emilia, your roommate is here."

I blink. "My *roommate?*"

"Didn't I tell you?"

"No."

Massimo scratches his head. "Is it a problem?"

"Hmm . . . ." I'm irked about the situation, certainly. On the other
hand, I'm also a little bit lonely. "Who is she?"

"Lauren Todd." He smoothes my collar. "You ever heard of her?"

"Nope."

"She's been around forever; a great model," he says. "American and
tough—like you. You'll like her."

On the way back to the Darsena, I add up what I've learned about
Lauren and picture the model equivalent of a redwood: some partially
petrified, heavily madeup creature with a laugh that's rich and gravelly
from too many cigarettes and trips on the Concorde—Suzanne
Pleshette, only taller. But when I open the door, I see that Lauren has
silky blonde hair and hooded brown eyes, the kind that look like they
keep a secret, and I know her face well—not from anything I can recall
immediately, more of a general familiarity: a timeless beauty who's put
in the time.

We introduce ourselves. I look around, embarrassed. This morning, I couldn't decide what to wear, and much of my wardrobe is strewn
around the room. A tank top floats on a lamp shade. A white g-string
lies crumpled where I stepped out of it. Lauren skirts this and other detritus as she continues to unpack her belongings into a succession of
neat piles: lights, darks, lingerie, toiletries. "Do you mind if I take the
right side?" she asks, her hand swirling to encompass the bed, the bureau, the closet: the right of everything. "For some reason I always
prefer it here."

"Of course." I scoop my panties, the tank top, and the rest and deposit them into my duffel. "You've stayed here before?"

Lauren emits something between a laugh and a groan. "My God, yes—two dozen times at least!"

Two dozen? While we reorganize, I try to assess her age: late twenties? early thirties? It's hard to tell.

An hour later, we head out to dinner. Downstairs, Lauren glances at the vans and says "Ick." When we pass what I've come to think of as my little café, she says "Overpriced," and guides me around the corner to a tiny establishment where the husband and wife shower her in kisses. Sipping the cold white wine that's as "divine" as she's promised, I get the facts. Lauren's twenty-eight, she's with Click in New York and so is her husband, Will, a model/actor who's hoping to parlay his big break as a construction worker in a popular blue jean commercial into a more permanent gig.

"Have you seen the ad?" she asks. "He's shirtless, sweaty, and wielding a jackhammer."

I haven't. "It sounds great, though."

Lauren nods. Her fingers twirl a lock of hair. "It got him an audition, a recurring role on *General Hospital*: Luke's long-lost step–foster brother . . ."

Her brows lift to see if this registers. "I don't watch *General Hospital*," I'm forced to admit. "But I'm sure he'll book it and be great."

"Yeah." Lauren's face retreats into her wine. "Yeah," she murmurs. My low TV I.Q. seems to disappoint her more than I would have expected, and sitting here, before her creased brow and tense fingers, I wonder why Massimo described her as tough.

On our way back to our room, Lauren looks up at the façade of the Darsena and mutters, "I hate it here."

"I do, too," I say. I mean it, but I figure Lauren doesn't—why, then, would she keep coming back?

Once in our room, we swap portfolios. You'd think models would do this all the time, like peacocks showing their feathers, and maybe the males do it regularly, I don't know, but we females have to like each other first.

Lauren's book is amazing. For starters it's full, which almost never happens because most agents would rather leave pages blank than fill them with subpar shots, only there aren't any of those, either—just page after page of tear sheets from *Vogue, Bazaar, Moda, Amica, Elle,* and scores of others. The dates are cut off the bottom of most of them, I notice—an agent's not-so-subtle solution to the three month expiration date problem—but it doesn't matter; the shots are good, *Lauren's* good: by turns steely, sexy, and playful. Turning the pages, I feel like I'm looking at a photo album of a round-the-world tour, destination Lauren Todd, the rickshaws, pyramids, and golden Buddhas relegated to the role of lifeless props beside her.

"Great," I murmur, over and over. "Beautiful." When I reach the end, I flip back to one of my favorites, a *Bazaar* shot of Lauren lounging coolly against a doorway in a black tuxedo—shades of another young Lauren—before braving a glance at the model herself. "Why come to Milan when you have all this?" I ask, slightly awed. "Or don't you mind it here as much as you said?"

When Lauren looks up, her fingers resting on the lion tamer, the photograph she's already identified as my best, her features are lifted in surprise. "We're models, Emily; our books are never finished, right?"

"Of course."

"And I work well here so . . ." Lauren's head ticks sideways: *so here I am.*

"Makes sense."

Her spine stiffens. "But this is it. This is the last time," she says in a voice that's suddenly louder and harder. "After this trip, I'm going to stop being twenty-eight and I'm going to have a baby."

My mouth opens. The phone rings. Lauren lifts the receiver. *"Will!"*

I take my journal outside and sit on the stairs, hoping for a breeze. It's 9:00 P.M. Most of the residents are out dining and dancing. Except for a distant radio, the courtyard is quiet, allowing Lauren's exclamations to penetrate. "Aww," I hear. *Aww.* It's only one sound, one long, low moan, but it says so much. That Will didn't get the part. That there'll be another skipped birthday, another trip to Milan. That there won't be a baby. That Lauren Todd is tough. Tough as nails.

Of course, I said; I guess I didn't mean it. The idea of spending years on the road accumulating tear sheets like steamer trunk stickers suddenly makes me feel homesick, so I go down to the lobby and place some calls. But no one I dial is around.

☆

Meanwhile, I continue to go on show castings. But while I'm trying to incorporate Raphael's advice into my walk, I still lack the grace and poise of the more seasoned models, particularly when strutting my stuff in front of a half-dozen scrutinizing show producers and designer employees. "A little stiff," they sniff at Prada. "Not enough experience," they tell me at Gucci. Versace, too. The options come off.

These rejections bring me down; *Milan* brings me down. Each day that I navigate the city streets—those noisy boys and their groping hands—I return to the Darsena a little bit sadder, a little bit more homesick, until I feel that way all the time. It's as if the smog blanket is pressing down on me, suffocating me, graying my vision, so that I no longer see the blue-sky, sunny side of things, only the shadows: like the way the fourteen-year-old in the casting line reaches under her shirt and unhooks her bra, casually, unthinkingly, the way one might adjust a barrette. Or the way Giuseppe, the president of Certo, walks through the agency lobby, parting girls the way one might a curtain, without the slightest bit of acknowledgment. Or the way the BMW slows down outside the Darsena entrance and two faces peer out: the driver's, rubbernecking a leggy brunette, his eyes full of desire, and the child's. He stares out the rearview window, his eyes round, his mouth wide, trying to understand.

"Relax," Massimo says one afternoon when I'm in the agency, lamenting. "Tito Conti, the most important designer in Italy, is still holding an option on you, a strong option."

"An option is not a booking," I point out.

"It will confirm," he says. "Relax."

I've had way too much espresso to be able to relax. Besides, Massimo's been wrong before. I rise and start pacing. "Tell me how to make it confirm."

"Practice your walk. Get Lauren to help you."

I nod. I've already asked her. "What else?"

"Start coming to dinner. A group of us go every night: me, Guiseppe . . . the most powerful figures in fashion."

As I spin to face Massimo, two questions spill from my lips. "When?" and "Where?"

☆

Hours later, my agent's answers have guided me here, to a sleek slip of an establishment off Via Montenapoleone. I adjust the bodice of my black Dolce dress (tight ruched cotton with a deep scoop neckline and cap sleeves, purchased today because I had *nothing* to wear), finger the fringe of my black shawl, and proceed to our table—the largest, the longest, anchored just under the awning, in full view of customers and pedestrians alike.

I slide into the vacant chair next to Massimo. *"Ciao."*

"Emilia! *Buona sera!*" Massimo kisses my cheeks repeatedly and pours red wine into a grapefruit-size goblet before making the introductions. Holly and Cesario, Jenny and Dante, Christy and Aldo . . . all around the table, young kits and silver foxes are paired off like salt and pepper shakers, the girls dressed like me, in show-off mode, the men in tailored suits and starched shirts.

Massimo raises his glass. *"Salute!"*

"Salute!"

Sipping my wine, I continue to study the men. Powerful—this I believe, but leaders in fashion? I can't see it. I tip sideways and whisper. "Who are these guys?"

"The owners of Certo."

"*All* of them?"

"Si." Massimo shifts toward me, his demeanor now didactic. "Emilia, here in Milan, many gentlemen like to own a part of a modeling agency—a little piece," he qualifies, pointing to a bread crumb on the table as if visual aids were required. "Here, it is a hobby."

"I see."

"Yes, my angel, we Italians like to mix business with pleasure."

This is spoken by the man on the other side of me. He's smiling, pleased he's remembered the cliché—or maybe it's because he's dispensed with visual aids in favor of a more hands-on approach: his hands on my thigh.

I startle. Massimo pretends not to see. Perfect, my agent, the pimp.

Suddenly, the silver fox remembers his manners. His hand moves northward. "I'm Primo," he says, extending it.

"Emily."

Our rings clink. "So, Emilia, you're American?"

"Yup," I say Americanly, then point. "And you, Primo? Where are you from?"

This is a joke. Primo doesn't get it. Instead, his smile widens, clearly delighted to have been seated next to a girl whom he's now identified as grade A bimbo. He leans in. Once he's practically wearing me as an accessory, Primo purrs, "My *bambina,* I'm from Milano and you—why, you're breathtaking!"

"Thanks." I reach for my glass.

"I mean it." His toes nudge mine, presumably to initiate a game of footsie, something I didn't think people actually played. "A young Sophia Loren."

Sophia Loren is a busty, exotic sexpot. Unfortunately, I am nothing of the kind. I scoff. "Yeah, right."

Color drains from Primo's face. "Not Sophia," he backpedals. "Claudia Cardinale!"

When celebrity comparisons happen at a photo shoot, it's usually the makeup artist making it clear just how much of his childhood was spent indoors watching old movies with his mother. The more famous the makeup artist, the more obscure the reference. One time Francois Nars told me I looked like a 1950s actress I later saw listed in the credits as "Girl #2 on subway platform." You think I'm kidding.

"Claudia Cardinale?"

"No, no, you're right, not Claudia," Primo says, deciding, despite considerable evidence to the contrary, that now would be a good time to return to my thigh. "Nor Sophia. Just a stunning young Raquel."

When celebrity comparisons happen over dinner, it's because the guy wants to sleep with you.

"Er, excuse me."

I'm in the entranceway, inhaling a much needed cigarette, when Massimo comes over, his friendly expression undermined by eyes etched with concern.

"Emilia, my tough girl, be nice to Primo, won't you?" he says. "Primo, our boss?"

"'Our boss' had his hand on my crotch."

For a second, Massimo actually looks pleased, like a tutor whose star pupil has outperformed even his highest expectations, then, "Okay, well—"

"I'm not having sex with him."

Massimo leaps so far back, he nearly lands in the gutter. "Whoa, whoa, Emilia—*sex*? Who said anything about *sex*? All you need to do is be Primo's friend, that's all!"

"His *friend*."

"Yes, friend. Friends help friends. That's what friends are for, right? Right. Primo can help you."

"Can Primo help me book Tito Conti?"

"Si, si, certainly."

I exhale. Primo's fingers circle my waist. "Come, finish your cigarette at the table."

"In a minute."

When Massimo leaves, I finish my cigarette and light a second. I'm feeling cranky, intensely cranky, only I don't know whether it's because I've been put in this situation, or because I can't follow through with it.

Milan sucks.

I return to my seat. When the meal is over, the table stirs. "We're going for drinks," Massimo informs me.

I remind Massimo about my early appointment with Tito Conti. He gathers my hands. "Emilia, relax! It's one drink! After that, we're off to the clubs, but you can skip that part if you want to and run off to bed."

Pause.

"One drink," he urges. "Right down the street."

I glance at Primo. I'm tough. I took self-defense . . . and if I piss off my booker, I might as well pack up and leave because my career in Milan will be over before it has even begun.

"Okay, one drink."

On the way out, one of the couples departs, eliciting low whistles and wry smiles from the men. The rest of us proceed along Via Montenapoleone, dodging puddles. A twist, a turn, a side street, and we've come to a piazza, the picture-postcard kind with crumbling stonework, a patinaed Virgin Mary, and a gurgling fountain. Establishments ring its perimeter; we secure a table at one of them. "Cesario and I are getting ice cream," Primo says, indicating a striped awning. "You want some?"

"No, thanks."

He clutches at his stomach, as if in pain, "Oh, come on! Massimo!" he cries. "Raquel here can have some, can't she?"

Massimo eyes me sourly: *Emilia the tough girl, the difficult one.* "Of course she can. Come, come, Emilia, have some!"

I order a single scoop. The bulimics order sundaes with extra whipped cream. The men saunter off. Dante heads in the other direction, toward the bar. A few minutes later, a waiter delivers a gleaming tray of bottles: chilled vodka, cranberry and orange juice.

Jenny pouts. "Hey! Where's the champagne?"

"Yeah, champagne!" Holly echoes.

"In a while," Dante says.

When Primo returns with ice cream, I thank him but feign immersion in a conversation about Atlanta. He curls over me; I'm engulfed by cologne. "Drink?" he asks.

"No, thanks."

He fixes me a vodka cranberry.

The ice cream chills a few of the girls, so we migrate inside, to a lounge area with low couches, sheer billowing panels, and many candles. As the drinks are dispersed and refilled, our group gets rowdier and rowdier, particularly Christy, who, after demanding that the volume be cranked, has flung off her sandals and is now jumping on the couch. Someone has coke, I bet. I think fleetingly about having some.

"You're not drinking," Primo says.

"It's a little strong," I tell him. Actually, the cocktail tasted bitter, probably in contrast to the ice cream.

"Let me fix you another."

"That's okay. I should get going, anyhow. I've got a big day tomorrow."

This comment is ignored. Not by me. I look at my watch; it's 1:00 A.M. Okay, enough. I rise, using a "bathroom break" as an excuse to check out the taxi situation. Several are lined up around the corner. I'm about to sneak off when, *shit,* I realize I've forgotten my shawl. It's brand new, a beautiful lightweight merino wool. I have to go back.

Things are different when I return. It's quieter, not because of the music—"Pump Up the Jam" is cranked so loud I feel the bass in my ribs—but because of our group. The girls have stopped dancing. Chirsty's collapsed against a cushion, her mouth slightly ajar.

Her head lolls. "Hey," I say, pointing anxiously. "Is she okay?"

"That girl's had too much to drink and you've had too little," Primo says, handing me a fresh vodka cranberry filled to the brim. "*Salute,*" he cries. "To American beauty!"

"To American beauty!" the men echo.

Holly giggles. "Christy's drooling!"

As Christy's head lolls in the other direction, I shiver. Because something's not right here. "Hey guys, I think Christy needs to go to the doctor."

"She needs to go home," Aldo says, rising.

It takes two men to carry Christy out. I watch—I'm shaking now—then rise to my feet, my fingers clutching the shawl.

Primo eyes me. "Where do you think you're going?"

"Relax," Massimo tells me.

Primo's tugging at my shawl. "Yes, Raquel; listen to your agent—relax and finish your drink."

"I feel dizzy!' Holly announces.

Women: See how they doze. As Holly collapses sleepily against Jenny, my eyes slide to their empty glasses, to Primo, then to my drink and I know: These girls were drugged. So was I.

I'm gonna be sick.

I'm still kneeling in front of the fountain, my stomach's rhythmic clenching now more of a flutter, when Massimo touches my back. "You okay?"

"You *cocksucker!*" I say after wiping and whirling. "You *prick!* You fucking *asshole!* You're my *fucking* agent—how could you? I've got shows to do! I've got *Tito Conti!*"

And then I stop spewing. Because I realize: Massimo couldn't care less. Because booking me for modeling work—that's not his job.

Well, I care.

All night long, I circle the Darsena courtyard, practicing my walk. *Criss cross! Slink slink! I'm a black cat! I'm a black cat! Criss cross! Slink*

slink! I'm a black cat! I'm a black cat! If it's tiring, I don't notice, I'm fueled by my indignation—*Slipping girls drugs? That's sick! Who does that?*—by my rage—*Assholes! Cocksuckers! Pricks!*—and by my own ego—*Well, fuck them! I'll show them! I'm going to make it on my own!* When the place starts to stir, I go to the little café. When I spy Lauren leaving, I go upstairs, I shower and I change. Dabbing on the concealer, I stare into my sunken eyes: *Oh, Tito Conti, King of Italian Designers, I need you more than ever.*

Chapter 31

Showstopper

Tito Conti, Incorporated is a walled and gated complex spanning an entire city block in the heart of downtown Milan. I'm stopped at a security gate. As one guard looks through my belongings (including every page of my portfolio, presumably for a flat, thin weapon) another scans a roster.

"You're seeing Carlotta, *sì?*" he says.

"*Sì.*"

Another minute and the gates part. I swallow nervously. Lauded in many design magazines, the complex, a succession of granite squares, opaque windows, and dark, reflective pools, is more than a tad imposing. My nicotine- and caffeine-charged heart kick-starts into high gear.

This is it. This is Tito Conti.

The guard has pointed out a door. I follow a slate path that cleaves a courtyard of fruit trees, their boxy shapes currently being serviced by two gardeners with long cutting blades, pull a steel handle, and gasp.

I'm in a room that's large, airy . . . and lovely. Sunlight filtered through leaves flickers across a polished cherry floor. Simple furniture done up in a range of grays, from dove to charcoal, is softened by cashmere throws and mink pillows. A broad bookcase displays objets of stone and mineral. Two dachshunds doze in front of a fireplace, their long forms nearly invisible against a chocolate brown area rug. And, dappling every surface, are black-and-white photographs of a silvered, chiseled Tito with Kevin Costner, Glenn Close, and a host of other Hollywood A-listers, their awards glinting in the strobe light.

This is it. This is Tito Conti.

I approach the dogs slowly, my fingers outstretched. "Hi, babies!"

Wheet! Wheet! A shrill blast penetrates the stillness. I turn toward the large window just in time to see four guards hightailing it across the courtyard with such haste that they knock one of the gardeners off his ladder. The dogs start yapping. What? *What?*

Wheet! Wheet!

The door opens. "*Privado* residenci!" one cries. "Out!" cries another.

Before I can utter my own cry, I'm grabbed, hauled outside, and deposited through another door, this one leading to a long hallway lined with models.

Oh . . . of course. My sense of panic evaporates, replaced by irritation. There are thirty models in front of me, thirty at least, for how many open slots: one? two? So much for my "strong option."

Suddenly, I'm spent. But when I slump against the wall and close my eyes, I see a limp, drugged-out Christy being dragged across the room. *No.*

The line shuffles into a dressing area that's low-ceilinged and dingy, with yellowed Formica counters. "Girls: Put this on!" a woman barks, handing out bundles. "Remove everything else, including all makeup and jewelry! Secure your hair behind your head!"

I unravel the bundle. It's a nude body stocking, sheer as a pair of hose. "Wait . . . everything?"

The woman, Carlotta I presume, turns. She's wearing a simple gray shift, no discernible makeup, and a tight bun: the headmistress effect. Her voice matches the look. "You may wear a G-string if you insist," she says crisply. "But Mr. Conti prefers you wear nothing; it makes for a cleaner line."

A quick glance reveals no other model is wearing a G-string; guess

I won't, either. But as I gather up the sheer legs, I notice dark footprints in the feet and my thumb runs over a snag. *No.*

"Ick," I mutter, "this has been worn."

"Only for a minute," Carlotta says.

"And it has a run."

Thin lines spider from Carlotta's lips. *There's one in every bunch,* she seems to be thinking, but she walks over to a closet, pulls out a fresh body stocking, and hands it over.

I thank Carlotta. She eyes my feet. "No model is allowed to audition unless she's wearing plain black pumps two to three inches in height," she crows triumphantly.

Oh right, I was told this; I've been a bit out of it since the drugging, I guess. In fact, all night I've felt strange; untethered.

"Here." A naked blonde brandishes a pair of pumps. "Borrow mine," she says. "Just audition before me."

I smile. "Thanks."

"That is, so long as . . ."

I trade my new body stocking for her used one.

"No jewelry! No makeup!" Carlotta reminds us. But when she leaves the room a minute later, thirty girls pull out compacts and start doing rapid touch-ups to zits, blood vessels, and other imperfections—anything to give a girl an advantage over her neighbor—until efficient footsteps herald her return.

"Okay." She counts off six girls and flicks her fingers. "Come."

Usually, models are quite chatty at castings but something, perhaps it's the nudity, perhaps it's the import of the job, has flattened the levity here, and after the six girls exit, it's silent. A few compacts reemerge. A girl gnaws at her raggedy cuticle. In a reflection of a reflection, I spy twenty-four stockinged models in high heels and tight buns. We look like blow-up dolls, like sex toys, and I can't even find myself. *No.*

Not five minutes later, two of the six return, followed by three, followed by one. Tears flow, cheeks are red, only the final girl is anything approaching composed. Twenty-four girls calculate: *five no's, one maybe.*

This is it. This is Tito Conti.

I'm in the next group. Backstage, Carlotta hands us each a laminated card with a number. "A few rules," she intones. "One: You are not to look at Mr. Conti. Two: You are not to speak to Mr. Conti unless answering a direct question. Three: You are not to smile while you walk. Four: You must spit out your gum. Five: No jewelry." With this, Carlotta pauses. Her eyes dart, pouncing on the hand of the girl next to me. "Off!" she snaps.

The girl recoils. "It . . . it bride ring," she says in halting English. "Not off."

Carlotta reaches forward. *No.* Once the wedding ring is extracted—a painful process, judging from the look of it—she continues. "And six, the final rule: You must keep your eyes open at all times."

I don't get rule number six until approximately ten seconds later, after Carlotta's pointed the way through a heavy curtain and we're standing in a pitch-black auditorium on a runway that's blasting so much light, it feels as if we're navigating the circumference of a lightbulb. Our eyes water and squint.

This is it. This is Tito Conti.

"Stop," a voice booms—Tito's voice? "And spread out."

We spread across the horizontal part of the runway T.

"3, 5, 2—you may leave," says the voice.

Number two scurries off, already sobbing. I twist my laminated card; I've forgotten my number.

"Numero uno, stand still! All of you: Hold your numbers to the side!"

For several minutes, the three of us stand there, naked under the hot lights as people we can't see talk about us, their voices low but animated.

This is it. This is Tito Conti.

"Okay, now walk, please, beginning with numero uno."

Criss, cross! Slink slink! I lead the pack down the runway and back.

"Number six: You may leave. Numbers one and four, spread apart."

I'm still here; I can't believe it. I stare out into the auditorium. By now, my eyes have adjusted enough that I'm able to make out the bodies behind the voices. Three rows away is Mr. Conti, looking as tanned and handsome as ever in a white cotton shirt and blindingly white teeth, circled by several employees in shades of gray: the sun and his solar system.

"Do not look at Mr. Conti!" Carlotta stage-whispers.

Right, rule number one. I shift my gaze to some empty seats, my eyes burning as I try to keep them open. Meanwhile, Mr. Conti and his retinue continue to talk, their voices getting louder and louder, until there is no attempt to keep the volume down, no attempt at all.

"Numero quattro . . . . Numero uno . . . Numero quattro." I can't understand most of it, until, "cellulite . . . cellulite . . . cellulite . . ." a word that, evidently, along with "Coke" and "okay," is part of the universal language.

This is it. This is Tito Conti.

"Numero uno: Turn and face the back wall!"

I can't understand most of it, but Quattro can. Her head starts to sag, her eyes take on the telltale glint of a girl about to lose it.

"Numero quattro! Chin up!" booms the voice.

Quattro snaps to attention.

"Grasso . . . cellulite . . . gamba," *fat . . . cellulite . . . legs* say the voices. That'd be me.

"Smile!"

"Brutto denti . . . brutto . . . multo brutto." *Bad teeth . . . ugly . . . very ugly.* That'd be Quattro. A tear slides down her cheek.

"Numero uno, turn and face front! Numero quattro, face the back!"

This is it. This is Tito Conti.

"Numero quattro, no crying!"

And this is crazy.

"No!"

I have not thought this. I have not mumbled this; I've said it. Loudly.

"Shh!" Carlotta hisses.

I shield my eyes.

"Put your arm down!" Conti booms.

"No!" I say again.

I am no longer untethered; I have snapped. I walk to the edge of the stage, my eyes never leaving the designer. "We are five feet away from you—five fucking feet—and you're talking about my *cellulite*? And this girl's *teeth*? This girl's a *knockout*! What is *wrong* with you?"

Every single face is asking this exact same question, only they're asking it about me.

Exactly. I turn toward numero quattro, my movements suddenly lighter: "And what is wrong with *us*? Are we really so desperate to work for this *asshole* that we'll take being treated like this? We're being treated like *shit*!"

Nobody moves. Nobody blinks. Behind me, I hear Carlotta's rapid steps recede down the hallway.

"Well, not me," I raise the sign. "Not me," I say again. I grip the cardboard with both hands. Now that I'm not shielding my eyes, it's bright, impossibly bright, but I lift my chin anyway, I lift it up high, and I pull. The numero uno splits in two and blasts apart. "Not anymore," I say. "I'm done here."

Oversized sofas with floral slipcovers. Aubusson-inspired rugs. Beaded chandeliers. An old steamer trunk with a wire birdcage perched on top: By the look of things, I'd say Chic's been attacked by a grandmother. I survey the new landscape just a few feet from Byron, who's giving a tour to a girl I don't know. "It's called Shabby Chic—*chic*! *Isn't* that just *perfect*? It's the latest thing! It's from *England*! Though I must say I had *no* idea it was so *expensive* to *peel paint*! Anyway—oh!"

Byron takes one look at me and points to his office. "You! There!"

I make my way to a so-old-it's-new leather club chair. Byron slams the door. "Where've you been?"

"Balsam."

"Emily, you walked out on Tito Conti, the biggest designer in Italy—do you know what a mistake that was? Because it was huge. *Huge!* Something you might not recover from for the rest of your career. You did that and went *home*?"

"I'm done with modeling," I say steadily. "I quit."

For a long time, Byron just stares. Finally, he marches over and lifts a lock of my hair. "Your ends are a little ratty, you could use a trim."

"Er, thanks." I smooth it down.

He grabs my hand. "Have you been biting your nails?"

I make a fist. "Yup."

He clasps my chin. "And are you bloated? Or PMSing? Because your face is a little puffy . . ."

"Byron!" I shove my chair back. "Didn't you hear me? I've quit—

I'm done with modeling, finished. It's over! That's what I came in here to tell you!"

"I see . . ." Byron walks behind his desk, sits down, and starts inspecting his pant cuff. It's a brisk October day and he's dressed accordingly: varying shades of gold, right down to the new highlights now glinting in the setting sun. It's like I'm talking to an Oscar. "So I guess that means you don't want to hear about how no one is pissed at you anymore because I took care of it," he continues, "or how you're now on hold for the biggest job of your life, is that correct?"

For several seconds, we're in a standoff, feigned apathy verses feigned indifference, until *ugh.* "What job?"

I'm handed a one-page mock-up. *Ménage Cologne— pleasure must be shared* it reads next to a drawing of a half-naked man flanked by two long-haired temptresses in silk teddies, only one of whom is facing the lens.

"It's Gaultier's follow-up to Gaultier Le Male," Byron explains. "The company's so excited about it on account of the scientific component. It's supposed to change your pheromones so that they attract his, his pheromones so they attract yours, something like that," he explains. "Anyway, this scent's been seven years in the making—seven! That's a marriage!—and *finally* it's ready for worldwide release. Needless to say, Gaultier wants Ménage to make a huge splash, which means a tremendous ad budget and the right girl. The budget they have. The girl they've been trying to find for months, they told me, and lately they keep circling back to the same name over and over again: Emily Woods."

"Emily Woods." I repeat my name slowly, as if I don't know her.

"Yes, darling, you! They thought you'd be perfect!"

"Let me guess: my bathtub scene."

Byron claps his hands. "Clever girl! Yes, the Thom Brenner video was one of their key sources of inspiration!"

Terrific. That's my legacy: fondling Fonya. I drop the ad. "So Fonya's in it, too."

"No, no! Fonya's locked up contractually for De Sade: torture his senses. Great scent by the way. *This* ad is all about you! You: full frontal! They'll find another number two, somebody cheap!"

I study the ad again.

"Which brings me to the best part: fifty thousand for the shoot, another fifty if they use the film—U.S. rights, that is. Foreign markets should have similar packages. Of course, you'd be doing in-store appearances, as well; they want to copy what Guess? did with Claudia, I heard, so that means plenty of clothes, and of course you'd be in all the shows, ready-to-wear *and* haute couture, which means plenty of trips to Paris."

Briefly, I imagine floating down Parisian boulevards in designer gowns before homing in on the money: so much money! I picture fifty, one hundred, three hundred thousand dollars piled on the ground like so many leaves: That's enough to cover the rest of college . . . and graduate school . . . and a down payment on an apartment. And surely this job would help me get other good jobs—lots of good jobs. "When's it shooting?"

Byron exhales. "Well, let's see . . . they're still working out packaging. Apparently they want the bottle to have three figures, but the first attempt looked like a three-*headed* figure, so it was back to the drawing board. I'd say January."

"And how many other girls are on hold for my slot?"

"No one from here. No one from *any*where that I've heard of. I think this campaign is yours for the taking, Em, I really do. Still, just to be safe, I think you should drop a few pounds."

I nod. I probably gained two or three pounds at home. "I can lose five."

"*Five?* Ten."

"Ten?"

"Ten, twelve."

"*Twelve?*"

"What do you mean, *twelve?*" Byron cries. "You've lost twelve pounds before!"

"Yeah, when I was twelve pounds heavier!" I retort. "Byron, you'd have to chop my arm off to get twelve pounds off!"

"That's what every girl tells me! Listen, Em, the trend is skinny, skinny, skinny and I think it's going to be *huge,* I really do."

"How disappointing I'll miss it."

Byron rises. "Emily Woods, you're on hold for the *largest* booking of your *life*—don't tell me you're walking away! Listen: I'll tell Gaultier your mom's still upset and needs you at home, that should buy us another two weeks, during which time you just lose as much as you possibly can—ten, twelve, fourteen—whatever. No pressure!"

"Why's my mom still upset?"

Byron looks puzzled. "How would I know?"

Jesus. "No, you just said . . ."

"Oh! I told everyone your father died of a drug overdose. Anyway—"

"You told people my father *died* of a *drug overdose?*"

"Yes! Wasn't that original? An unusual twist on a familiar plot, I thought." Byron chuckles. "Plausible, too, given your father."

Pause. I may have mentioned my father's fondness for weed once, but "Byron! My dad smokes pot occasionally, he doesn't *mainline!*"

"So? Most people don't know that! Don't worry, Em, they swallowed the story hook, line, and sinker! In fact, a few bouquets arrived for you, nothing centerpiece-worthy, I wouldn't say—"

"WELL, WHO WOULD LIE ABOUT HER FATHER DYING OF A DRUG OVERDOSE?"

Shabby Chic falls silent. Byron shakes his head. "Emily, my darling, you're missing the point here: You walked out of four shows and basically told Tito Conti to fuck off, but I fixed it! *Nobody's* mad. On the contrary, you're now the *top contender* for one of the *biggest* fragrance campaigns that this *decade* will ever see, so *cut* me some slack here, *okay?*"

I'm breathing hard. My hands are shaking. I study them.

". . . $50,000 minimum, Em. Most likely much, much more."

". . . Plus if you thought the Brenner video gave you exposure, just think of what this will do. We'll get you media coverage on the in-store appearances, interviews . . ."

I'm done with modeling, I said in Balsam; *I'm going back to school.* But as I look out Byron's window, I don't see books or classrooms but me, slinking down the runway in haute couture. My name is in lights. The crowd chants: Emily! **Emily!** Emily!

Epilogue: Paris, 1992

"Oui, oui, comme ça, Amelie, comme ça!"

Click. Click.

"The Eiffel Tower is coming out of her head. She needs to move left."

"Okay, move left, Amelie! Left!"

"That's too far."

"Okay, move right!"

"Okay, there! Now give me your best profile."

"Your other profile!"

"Okay, no, the other!"

"Is that really your best?"

I stick out my tongue.

"Oui!" Click. "That's it! That's the shot!"

Pixie replaces the lens cap. Jordan stretches. "Okay guys, can we hit a patisserie now or what?"

"Noo!" I protest. "Let's sit here for a minute and enjoy the sunset!"

Jordan's hands slide to her hips. "Emma Lee, we've been to three

museums, two ills, or whatever the hell it is they're called, and one
cathedral the size of a football stadium—I'm starving!"

"Omigod, I'm sure the French would love to hear Notre Dame
likened to a football field."

"Does 'airplane hangar' work for you, Pixie Stick?"

"Philistine!"

"What's that mean?"

"Grrrrr—"

"Guys!" Mohini makes a time-out sign. "It's Emily's birthday. If she
wants to look at the sunset, we look at the sunset."

I smile. "At least *some*body loves me."

"Don't count on it," Jordan mutters, but she's smiling, too.

The four of us walk over to the Champ de Mars and take a seat on
the grass. It turns out, my friends were messing with me that day at the
diner. It was all Pixie's idea. "But, omigod, we never meant to make you
feel bad; we never thought it would work!" she explained later. "Though
all's well that ends well, I suppose, right?"

"Is that a baguette that man's carrying or is he happy to see us?"

"Jordd!"

Yes, all's well that ends well. And it has. After graduating Phi Beta
Kappa, Mohini's decided to return to the Hubble base station this fall,
much to her excitement, though it means a long commute to see Miles,
her Rhodes Scholar boyfriend. ("You cannot have babies with him,"
Jordan's already cautioned her. "You won't be able to deliver them on
account of their head size.") Jordan is off to Wall Street, specifically the
Goldman Sachs analyst program. She'll share an apartment with Ben,
who will be working for the NRDC, and Pixie, who'll be interning at
the Metropolitan Museum of Art "and *not* dating Pixels," she avows.
"It's time to be on my own for a while."

And as for me?

First things first—I quit modeling. I wish I could tell you it happened the day Byron and I discussed the Ménage campaign, but it
didn't. Instead, I lost the weight (not all: seven pounds to be precise,
enough that I stopped menstruating) and went on the audition, the
first of several visits to Gaultier that ultimately concluded here, in Paris,
with a meeting with the designer himself, who immediately offered his
condolences and told me that a thousand dollars had been donated to

NarcAnon on my father's behalf. In the end, I almost booked the Ménage campaign, almost. It went to Fallon Holmes instead. Who? you
ask. Exactly. Fallon's not a supermodel. She is, however, a top-tier girl
who'd been recently lured to Chic from Elite. Byron, eager to prove his
superiority over John Casablancas, made sure Fallon nabbed the campaign. "It was so hard to decide," the Gaultier people ultimately con-
fessed. "The two of you look so much alike you could be sisters."

By then it was early January. I started stacking up my job skills
against Mohini's, Jordan's, and Pixie's. What *were* those skills? Good
with jewelry? Knows how to work a pocket? I could just imagine putting those on a résumé. No, like Tommy who healed, then traded his
pads for software, it was time to move on. When Columbia University
started its spring term one week later, I was there: Emily Woods, student. One semester behind, a depleted bank account, but happy.

"Why'd you stay in it for so long?" people ask. "Why'd you finally
quit?"

"She came to her senses," Mom likes to say. I'd say I woke up from
a dream. You see, if I go back—way, way back, to my original goal, the
one conceived lying on the floor of my bedroom—it was to be one of
the beautiful girls in the photos. Not to look like her: to *be* her. To have
that life, a life that was glamorous and fun and happy. I thought that
looking that way was the hard part, but if you could cross that hurdle,
if the genetics were there, then the rest would follow. And it did, to a
certain extent: champagne and celebrities, the Four Seasons and the
Delano, exotic attractions both near and far.

It's just that that wasn't all that happened.

Still, dreams die hard, don't they? So I pressed on. I kept thinking I
was in a dip in the road, stuck in the trees, mired in the third act of a
great romance, and if I pushed forward, rose just a little bit higher, just
a little bit more, that I'd get *there,* to that place, that glamorous, fun,
happy place. What hit me that day on the runway at Tito Conti's was
that I wouldn't. The drugs and the modelfuckers and the bulimia and
all the other elements that I'd ignored for so long because they didn't fit
in the picture *were* the picture. I just didn't like the picture.

After that, I had nothing to aim for so I stopped. The coke, too.

On the street, I run in to models I used to know. Kate Moss is one
of Byron's girls now—no, *the* girl—and her look is starting to spread

across the globe like some chronic wasting disease. To keep up, the other girls are dropping those ten, twelve, fourteen pounds and getting their breast implants taken out. "I told Dr. Ricsom to put them on ice," Genoveva joked when I ran into her at LaGuardia and discovered there was less of her to run in to. "Because you never know what will be beautiful tomorrow."

"Amelie! Amelie!"

A guy on the other side of the Champ de Mars gets off his bike and waves.

I wave back. "Gerard!"

Pixie pokes me. "And *who* is Gerard?"

"Gerard is the birthday present I picked up for myself this morning on the St. Germain de Pres."

"Gerard's a hunk," Mohini concludes after scoping him out with her binoculars.

Jordan arches a brow. "Noo! Let's *enjoy* the *sunset?*"

I laugh—we're all laughing—and jump to my feet. "Come on! It's time to eat cake!"

After much deliberation, I settle on an éclair. It's large, delicious, and I enjoy every bite.

About the Author

Robin Hazelwood was a model in New York, London, and other places from the mid 1980s to the late 1990s. She graduated from Yale University. This is her first book.

Acknowledgments

My agent, Suzanne Gluck, plucked me from obscurity, then pushed me to do my best. Also at William Morris: Anna Deroy, Alicia Gordon, and Erin Malone, who answered a zillion e-mails with headers such as "oh, and . . ." At Crown, I am indebted to Kristin Kiser and my dynamic editing duo, Rachel Kahan (briefly) and the kind and talented Shana Drehs. Betsy Rapoport, you were the light in the thick, dark jungle; I'll swap bad jokes and baby names with you anytime. Tina Constable and the entire Crown Publicity team really went to bat for me, especially Sarah Chance. Grace McQuade and Camille McDuffie pinch hit and truly delivered. Daniel Coppens created a terrific web site. Related Media got my slide show up and running. Laurie McGee taught me how to spell X-Acto knife. Linda Tresham sold me great eighties mags. Victoria Aitken and Annie Gow provided London color, James Park and Jay Kirkorsky illuminated Columbia, and Gina Cambre and Rachel Feinstein reminisced. (Girls, if I had to go back, I'd share a skanky model apartment with you anytime.)

My earliest reader, Peetie Basson, fostered a love of creative writing: Thank you for being such an excellent teacher. My early readers, Laura Bradford, Alex Heminway, and Alex Tolk, provided shots of encouragement—or simply shots—at a critical moment. David Kirkpatrick dared me to shoot the moon. And Anne, Andrew, Ingrid, Matt, Danielle, David, Michelle, Rob, Katie, Adam, Jody, Betsey, Charlotte, Claire, Soly, Gail, Jennifer, and Willy cheered, counseled, and distracted me, as did my sisters, Katie and Sara Hazelwood, along with their families. But most of all, I'd like to thank my parents, Anne and John Hazelwood, who heard the words "I'm quitting my job to write a novel," and didn't hang up the phone.